The man shut the door and nudged her over toward the bed.

"How old are you?" he said. "Seventeen or eighteen or what?"

Clara shook her head.

"Or thirteen?"

She felt sleepy, and so she lowered her head and moved toward this man. She caught sight of his face in the shadow and saw that it was sleepy like her own, slow and hungry. Something ached in her to see him like that. He pulled her over to the bed and they fell down together. She clutched against him wildly. "Don't stop," she said. "Don't stop."

But he did stop. She heard him breathing and in that moment her body just waited, suspended and frozen in a daze of sweat and disbelief. He said, "How the hell old are you?"

"I don't know—eighteen."

"No, you're just a child."

"I'm not a child, I never was."

Another Fawcett Crest Book
by Joyce Carol Oates:

EXPENSIVE PEOPLE

A Garden of Earthly Delights

Joyce Carol Oates

A FAWCETT CREST BOOK
Fawcett Publications, Inc., Greenwich, Conn.
Member of American Book Publishers Council, Inc.

For my husband, Raymond

A Fawcett Crest Book reprinted by arrangement with Vanguard
Press, Inc.

Library of Congress Catalog Card Number: 67-19288

Second Fawcett Crest printing, July 1970

Published by Fawcett World Library
67 West 44th Street, New York, N.Y. 10036
Printed in the United States of America

ONE

Carleton

1

Arkansas. On that day, many years ago, a truck carrying a number of migratory workers collided with a car on a country highway. It was May 19, the side of the road was soft with red clay, and in the light rain the people milled about with an air of festivity.

Carleton Walpole was a man who looked as if he had forgotten his age. At times he looked young, at other times the dirt-ridged creases in his forehead grew sharper until he looked like an aging man or one weakened by sickness. Seen alone in one of the small towns they passed through, staggering drunkenly back to the labor camp or sitting by the side of the road and tossing pebbles at cars, he seemed an ordinary young man of his type: from Kentucky, maybe, driven out of his home by complex facts he had never understood, maybe under thirty but getting too old for this anonymous shiftless role. But seen with his family—he had two children already and another on the way—there was something that must have ached in his backbone, forcing it up straight, and the sides of his eyes, too, ached with some forlorn, inexpressible anger he could not get into focus and so could not exorcise. He had a long, narrow face, handsome at times but rather ugly at other times when his aching, creasing doubt overtook him, light hair that had been almost white when he'd been a child, and empty blue eyes in which the sky was reflected endlessly. When he moved quickly and jerkily his face seemed almost too narrow, sharp as a knifeblade, and one's muscles stiffened involuntarily against the violence this man hinted at, without knowing. But he could move slowly too; he had inherited someone's grace—though in him it was simply an opaque resistance, like someone moving with effort through water.

The truck had had thirty people in it that day, of all ages. Carleton had been standing with some other men at the back, watching the road move out from beneath them, when the accident had happened. It wasn't the first accident this

9

driver had had. But they never got used to the sudden lurching, the squeal of brakes, and that hushed instant when everyone's heart paused—then the crash itself, this time not bad. The truck tilted sharply, but no one moved. They did not move for a few seconds. Then the children began to cry, the women shouted for help, and everyone woke up—another crash.

Carleton was one of the first to jump out onto the road. It was raining, but the rain was warm. His heart still thudded violently, his temples throbbed, because his wife Pearl was pregnant and the baby was due soon.... These thoughts flicked in and out of his mind all the time, in the middle of laughing with someone or picking along the rows of dusty strawberries, but because he was so accustomed to them he had become hardened. He yelled, "Pearl? Pearl?" but the noise was too much; she was at the front of the truck. In groups the kids jumped down onto the highway, vastly excited. Carleton saw his own kids push out and down and he glanced at them as if checking to see if they were hurt, then he forgot about them. The youngest, Mike, who was three, was shouting in rage at another child—Carleton could see his son's furious wet tongue. Men, women, all people Carleton knew, so accustomed to one another that they were like members of one great indifferent family, brothers and sisters who had nothing to hide from one another any longer—they jumped down into the gray rain and pushed their way around to the front of the truck, where the driver was arguing with a stranger whose nose was bleeding. Carleton checked to see if anyone was dead up front—the driver's kid brother was riding with him but wasn't hurt. The kid was about eighteen and drank Cokes all day long; Carleton had had the small hope that he might have been lifting a bottle to his mouth just as the crash occurred and that his face had been all slashed up: but nothing. The kid yelled at Carleton, "That bastard over there don't know how to drive! He come around the turn in the middle of the road, ask Franklin, go on and ask him—it ain't our fault!" Carleton pushed the kid away. In the car—nothing. The stranger had been alone. Only his nose was bleeding and he hadn't anything to wipe it on, so it kept bleeding. He sat inside his car as if hiding there, while Franklin, the driver and foreman for this run, screamed at him. The man in the car had a wild, exotic look, his face smeared with blood and his eyes darting everywhere; he was either hiding in the car or couldn't get the door open. It was smashed in about a foot and the window was shattered.

They examined the truck's fender. Not bad, but it would have to be fixed. The last time they'd had trouble it had been raining too; the brakes on the truck were bad or something. At the time of the accidents—there had been four since Carleton and his family had joined up—everyone was excited and angry, but in a few hours they forgot about it. If Franklin promised to buy a new truck everyone believed him, and he believed himself, but if nothing ever came of it no one thought that very surprising or important. They supposed the chances had it that there wouldn't be another accident too soon; the more accidents you had the less there were in store for you.

"Nobody's hurt," a kid said. Carleton had seen for himself that nobody had been hurt. The rain fell gently, as if trying to calm everyone's throbbing hearts, to quiet their loud voices and their jerky eyes, but it had no effect on Carleton. He felt cheated. Pushing up to the front of the crowd, he looked at the smashed car door and touched the shattered window—but that wasn't much. In his imagination there was a blunt vivid image of Franklin or the kid brother or the driver or someone, anyone, lying dead right in the middle of the road, and he felt cheated because everyone was still moving, no one was dead, nothing ever happened.

He went around to the back of the truck and climbed in. A few of the women and some small children were still there though the truck was tilted clumsily. "What the hell are you still doing in here?" Carleton said to his wife. She was standing. She had a round, pale, sullen face; he often remembered, when he wasn't with her, how pretty she had been. She was much younger than he, though he too was young. She had been fifteen when they had married and while he had never noticed any change in her, except her pregnancies, somehow this other woman with the soft, almost formless body and the formless mouth had taken her place.

"Well, you all right?" Carleton said. He did not want to show much concern for her in front of the other women.

"Hell of a lot you care," she said.

His mouth grinned at her voice, because it must have meant she was all right. A few years ago he could believe what she said but lately he wasn't too sure—she had a way of slurring facts that he hated because there was already so much he could not get hold of. Simple, clear things, like what she'd done with a dollar bill or where the youngest kid had gone or what had happened to someone's shoes: there were times when she couldn't remember what was going on.

11

Pearl pushed by him and he caught her by the arm. "Hey, I want to go down and look," she said.

"Nobody got hurt, it's nothing. Some guy's nose is bleeding."

She went to the drop-off and was going to jump, but Carleton helped her down. His face was flushed now with something more than disappointment.

"Goddam dirty bastards that run into us," Pearl muttered. "They ought to kill them, they ought to do something—you men ought to do something, what the hell's wrong with you?"

She was a head shorter than he but he had to walk fast to keep up with her. That big, swollen body and that white face—she was strange, there was something frightening about her. She could flare into a rage and strike out at anyone around her, Carleton or the kids, and know exactly what she was doing even if it didn't make sense to anyone else. She wore a cotton blouse that should have been buttoned up higher, and a cotton skirt of red and white squares that would have been pretty except for her huge stomach.

"You men should take care of sons of bitches like that," she shrieked, pushing her way through the crowd. She grabbed Franklin's arm. "Why the hell don't you look where you're going? Who gave you a license? You let my husband drive and pay him, he's better than you— What about my baby? What about my baby?" Then her attention was taken up by the man in the car, who was now wiping his face on his shirt. Pearl thumped on the car hood with her little fists, screaming at him. "You want to get killed? You want your whole car smashed in? You want your face smashed in? Go back home and learn how to drive, what the hell are you doing out here on the road? What about my kids? Look here, you bastard," she said, pressing her hand against her stomach, "what the hell about this? Huh? You think you got a right to crash into anybody you want to?"

Anger always excited and pleased them; it was sacred. Carleton thought at first that she was a little crazy, getting so mad over nothing, but the longer she yelled, the better she sounded. Other women joined in. The woman who was going to help Pearl with the baby when her time came yelled along with Pearl. She put her arm around Pearl's shoulders. In the rain everything was slow and dreamy, except for the voices. Carleton put his hands in his pockets and stood with his legs apart, listening. They would squabble for a while and then someone would drive to a gas station and later a tow truck would come. Someone always took care of these things. Then

12

they would get back in the truck and drive all night, because they had a big job to do the next day and they were losing time. . . . Right now they were on holiday. This was something that didn't count, this accident, it was a nice surprise. Carleton's five-year-old, a girl, showed him a bump the size of a fat strawberry on the side of her head. She kept feeling it and asking everyone else to feel it. "How'd you get that?" Carleton said. "Knocked against the side," she said. She passed on to show it to someone else. She looked like Pearl, Carleton thought, but then when she was apart from him she might have been anyone else's kid. There were too many kids on the road with them, that was a problem. Too much noise and they were always sick, throwing up or coughing, and a few of them always died—that was the way children were. Something in him recoiled from the thought of children—his own or anyone's—because of the way they were made, how they came together in tiny parts inside the mother's body, and how dark and wet it must be there—that was ugly to think about.

Carleton spat. He was getting bored.

He talked with another man, whose last name he couldn't remember. This man called himself "Red." He had dark hair that might have been red in the right light. He was alone, he had a family left somewhere—like Carleton, he was from Kentucky and he was trying to pay off debts. Of such matters they talked in low voices and their lips stiffened. Had they talked to other people about this money they owed, their shame would have sickened them, but with each other now it was all right. It had taken them weeks of groping around before they found out the "facts" about each other. The way they handled their *a*'s and *i*'s, the way words slurred out into an extra syllable or two, let them both know they were almost kin, but it took them a while to realize this. They did not ordinarily think about such things. Red owed two thousand dollars yet while Carleton had worked his debt down to sixteen hundred, owed to his wife's brother. At one time he had owed a sickening three thousand, more money than Carleton had ever imagined, and it had all been lost—two wet springs in a row and that was that. Everything had been washed away. But now it was down to sixteen hundred. "This is our last season," Carleton said. He watched to see how Red would take this, but the other man showed no emotion. He was about Carleton's age. Carleton never thought to see himself in other people, but the two men shared the same expression—a moody, doughy look of dissatisfaction that

13

hadn't quite attached itself to anything permanent yet. They stood back against the truck on its tilted side, to get out of the rain. Carleton pushed a kid aside. The truck had high rusted sides and a canvas top that had washed out to no color at all. The truck stank. Rain did not wash the smell away but stirred it up. Sometimes Carleton noticed the smell and sometimes he didn't. "This is our last season on the road, these goddam crappy trucks," Carleton said, striking his fist lightly against it. "We're going to pay her brother off and we're going back. Her brother's a real nice guy."

They talked for a while about "going back." Neither could have said in which direction Kentucky was, nor did they have any vision of "Kentucky"; what was that, exactly? Each remembered his own farm and a few other farms and that was it. Though they had been traveling for a long time, back and forth, from south to north and back again, they did not remember anything they had seen. They were driven into camps in the early morning or late at night and these camps were all alike: some had tents, some barracks. But the smell was always the same and the garbage was always the same. There was no point in looking at anything because there was nothing to be seen. They liked to stare out at the road and watch it move under them because this meant they were getting somewhere, but as for really seeing anything—no. They needed eyes only for getting around and picking fruit and taking care of themselves. They did not need to see anything or to be conscious of anything.

"Going back" to Kentucky was expressed in an ambiguous sweeping gesture of Carleton's arm, flicking out in the same direction as Red had flicked his; they knew enough to agree with each other. There was something about the warm, wet day and the over-hung sky that oppressed them, and the festive air of the breakdown had already passed over into something else in the men—a restless boredom. The children liked being stalled, and the women had no opinion; opinions belonged to men. Red said that he too might get off the road at the end of the season and find another kind of work, maybe with a construction crew. Carleton was silent, jealous of Red not because he thought this hope would work out but because Red seemed to think it would. Carleton himself had been hired for construction work once but the deal had been withdrawn for some reason. But with that kind of work, he thought, he would be the only person in the family who could work and they needed more money than that—in the fields his wife could work and so could the kids. This was against

14

the law in some states or areas but nobody was clear about it and the "law" did not mean anything real. Very rarely did they come across the "law" and then it turned out to be someone who looked just like Carleton, with the same lean severe face and the same look of being cheated. They went out looking for kids in the fields, but the kids could hide, and even if they didn't get out of sight fast enough nobody cared.

Carleton wiped his face, listening to Red talk. He had a strange sensation that everything had happened before. Hadn't he heard Red say this? Or someone else say it? Up and down on the season the same things happened, over and over again, and Carleton had been riding with it for a long time. He coasted along with it. He was lucky enough to be able to turn his mind off and not see or hear or think when he wanted. They were paid at some farms for the basket, and at some farms for the day; the second way was best, but in any case Carleton always saved out three or four dollars that he put in his pocket safe from Pearl or anybody else, no matter how much money they needed, and with this he was able to spend one night drinking whenever it happened that he could not turn his mind off. . . .

". . . those old bastards riding with us, taking up room," Red was saying. He had worked himself up into a kind of anger.

"Yeah, those old bastards," Carleton said. There were several old men on their crew. They were slow pickers and got in your way and smelled like old dogs. They were just bums and hadn't come from real farms the way he and Red had. Seeing them kneeling in the fields would give you a surprise if you weren't ready for their faces, which were burned and creased and worn out from the sun. Carleton resented them without knowing why. His own father was dead now, but he had loved him very much, and he loved his mother too and was overcome with humiliation when he thought of her living with one of his brothers because he, Carleton, wasn't able to take her in. Uneasily, his mind would jerk away from such thoughts and attach itself to something else.

"They don't pay their way on the truck here. They don't pay as much for the run as we do," Red said.

"They don't make as much money."

"They should go off and croak somewhere in a ditch."

Carleton spat angrily. Everyone was milling around, children were whimpering. Up front the yelling had stopped.

15

Pearl and the women with her had shut up. Carleton thought it strange that Pearl should get so loud and angry. Back home she had never been like that; her voice had been different. But in a way he was excited by her now, with her white arrogant face and her white, huge belly, and the anger that could come out of nowhere and give her a ferocity she had never had back home.

"Now what? Camp out in the rain?" someone said. If anyone jostled Carleton he shoved him out of the way. There were too many people on this run and like any big family they got on one another's nerves. When a child died and everyone had to stop in one of the towns, they felt nothing but impatience and boredom; why couldn't people take care of themselves? It was important to keep going because what if there was a big rain, what if the crops rotted? And you could get pneumonia if the weather got bad enough, and sometimes the farmers wouldn't let children out in the field— that way everyone lost money. But there was no point in worrying about it, just as there was no point in trying to figure out from the sky what the next day's weather would be. You could predict nothing. If a rainstorm came, it came, and tornadoes could sweep down out of nowhere.

A tow truck appeared. Everyone watched. It was a big clumsy truck with a blue-black coating of paint that had a strange sheen; many people had scratched their initials into it. A red-faced man was driving and Carleton caught something in his face—some tension—that he knew was a familiar look but not one that made sense. The women dispersed. There were too many people milling around. Some kids were playing in the ditch water. Pearl ran up to Carleton and pressed her palms against his chest. Carleton didn't like her to do that while Red was looking, but her urgency kept him quiet. She had a queer, pinched look. "Franklin told me to go to hell," she said. "He told me if I didn't like it I knew what I could do, and that's you too—"

Carleton shoved her away, embarrassed.

"Well? Well?" she shouted.

"You're crazy, go somewhere and sit down. Keep your mouth shut."

"What are you going to do about it? What he said?"

She had not noticed Red. Carleton wondered about this. There were times when Pearl screamed at him without really noticing him either, and at those times he felt a sensation of iciness on the back of his neck, as if somebody dead were breathing on him.

16

"I don't feel right," she said suddenly.

"Go somewhere and sit down. Where's Esmelda? Go by her—"

"I don't feel right," she said shrilly.

Carleton stared at her. Why was she pressing against him now, not in an embrace but in a peculiar kind of skirmish, striking at him with her fists and then tugging at him? It occurred to him that she did not know what she was doing.

"Walpole," someone was shouting, "can you come up here?" It was the driver's voice. "We need some help up here."

"Don't you go by him!" Pearl said. "I don't feel right but it ain't spost to be time—I—"

"Hey, Walpole! Red!"

Carleton felt his body break out into sweat. He stared at his wife's face and could not understand at first what was happening. There was this strange tie between them: they lived together, they slept together. In the fields they worked together. They had lived together back home too but that was a long time ago, did it have anything to do with now? It was strange how they were always together, as if a force like the wind or the tide always drove them back together onto the same beach.

She began to shriek, clawing at him.

"Jesus Christ," Red said, jumping aside as if he thought he might be in danger.

Someone yelled: "Pearl's sick! Pearl's sick!"

Carleton looked past her to get help—he needed a woman's eyes to catch his. Who was going to help her with the baby? Esmelda, where was she? He tried to keep his face from breaking into pieces but everything was so quiet except for Pearl's screams, he felt paralyzed, she clawed at him but he hardly felt the pain. Then there were women around them. He felt them take over, claim Pearl.

"Now what? Now what?" Franklin yelled. He was a big, heavy man, as tall as Carleton. He must have been fifty. "Dirty white trash, scum lower'n niggers!" he yelled into Carleton's face. Carleton shrank away, against the truck. His knees were trembling. He had forgotten Pearl and was conscious only of Franklin's ugly breath. "She did it on purpose, got herself worked up!" Franklin yelled. "Don't tell me! Don't tell me!" There were tears in his eyes. He had lips like pieces of meat, uncooked and slippery.

"You let Carleton alone," someone said.

"She did it on purpose to make me mad! To keep us

here!" Franklin cried into someone else's face. "Don't try to tell me! I don't want no more women having babies, they ain't coming along! Why the hell did she go crazy like she did and get so mad? If she dies it ain't my fault!"

"You watch out, he'll get mad," Red said, indicating Carleton.

Carleton felt a flicker of interest at this remark, but he could not keep it up. His mind kept falling off Franklin and Red and the people around him, trying to attach itself to something else. There was a commotion at the back of the truck. He understood vaguely that Pearl was there, that the women were around her and helping her, and that it had nothing to do with him. He heard a thick, choked animal's scream. He muttered: "It ain't my fault, I didn't do it. It ain't my fault." If the sheriff came up speeding and splattering mud he would say right out that it wasn't his fault, he didn't know anything about it—

He began running but someone caught him. "They won't let you go there," someone said. Carleton clutched the man's shirt. He remembered that Pearl had had other children—he forgot how many—and each time it had almost killed him. The first time had been the worst, when he had lain down and cried, hating the trap that had resulted at last in his doing what no man should do—when had he cried before in his life? Men did not cry. He tried to remember other women having babies on the road. In the truck. They could get infection and die, and the babies often died. But he did not care about the baby. It did not exist, it wasn't real. Pearl's screams were the only real thing. In his mind were mixed pictures of several Pearls, the young girl he had married and the woman who had just been screaming into his face and the woman who squatted alongside him in the fields.

"They'll take care of her," a woman said. She had a big, broad, motherly face. Carleton felt his strength ebbing gratefully out into her. Her tanned skin was coarse and thick; there were fine, filmy, almost invisible light hairs on her cheeks. In the rain she looked as if she were centuries old, a statue submitting itself to any weather. She and the man smiled at Carleton. Their smile mixed up with the rapid, high shrieks from the back of the truck. "They took some canvas down," the woman said, "so she's all safe and dry. You know it don't make no difference—a hospital or anywhere. You know that."

Carleton tried to say yes.

"Jesus, them hospitals are bad," the man said. "Sometimes

18

they cut open the wrong people. They put you to sleep and you don't never wake up. You ever been in a hospital?"

"I never was and never will be," the woman said, answering for Carleton. "I ain't one of those people comes down with the least little thing—nor my kids neither. Colds and stomach trouble, that's just the way kids are, so what?"

Carleton heard his wife shrieking again. Around him people were talking with the woman as if they were trying to keep Carleton back with their talk, make a wall of it around him. He jerked his head to one side, then to the other, like a horse trying to get free. He stumbled to one side. Franklin was handing him a bottle. "Jesus Christ, you take this," he said.

Carleton drank from it. When he stopped drinking he heard the screaming again, so he drank more. "You better save some of it," a woman said. With her kind, cautious fingers she took the bottle away. Carleton pushed past them and saw some kids giggling together. They scattered when he came.

Someone pulled him back. "It's nice and dry under the canvas for her," Carleton was told. "Her time just come, that's all."

"When it comes it comes."

"She oughtn't to of got so mad——" Franklin said, but stopped as if someone had cut him off.

Carleton found himself standing out by the tow truck, where a few men stood around. One of them was the man who had driven the truck out—he stared at Carleton with a hard, set face. Carleton looked away. He was afraid of throwing up in front of everyone. If that happened to him everyone would remember it and laugh at him. So he pressed his burning face against the big hook that was suspended from a thick chain, and he groped his way to the back of the truck where another chain had been thrown and a length of rope lay coiled up. He hid his face in his hands. Behind him was silence, then the screaming began again.

He wished she would die. If she died and stopped that noise, then he wouldn't have this awful force pressing on him, wearing him down. He felt as if the air had turned hard and heavy above him, pushing him down. She screamed again. He could remember no love for her because such pain had nothing to do with love. Love was something you needed time for, your mind had to be at rest for it. . . . Why had he come so far? What was he going to do? He had already killed Pearl, she had died somewhere on one of these highways or in some heat-drenched field and he hadn't noticed it at the time, and now her body existed in nothing but agony and he vowed that if she got through this he would leave this life and take his family back home, in two months, before the long summer began; he would work every minute of the day, he would do anything, he would get them all back home again before it was too late and they forgot where they really belonged—

The baby born that day was a girl: they called her Clara, after one of Carleton's sisters.

2

Somewhere there was a photograph of Carleton and Pearl before their wedding: Carleton tall and awkward and Pearl fragile beside him, not touching, their hands curiously close and yet distant hanging down at their sides. It had been a bright, brilliant day, and both of them were shot into vicious clarity as if examined by a sinister light. They'd been standing by the side of the good barn, and the roughened wood was also illuminated in strange, meticulous detail. Beside Carleton, the girl he was going to marry stood so firmly as to unbalance his height, and her shy, toothed child's smile took away from Carleton's expression the seriousness it should have had.

Pearl's collar buttoned up high around her neck; it must have been too tight. Her face was pretty but fragile. It had the misty, airy appearance of a face that is about to disintegrate into features—small smiling eyes, small nose, small lips. A pretty blur not made human even by the bright sunlight. But Carleton's eyes were clear and direct and the line of his nose was firmly outlined against his cheek. His mouth was a mature, hard line, though he'd been no more than a boy when the picture had been taken. He might have been staring into the future and looking down one of those black-top highways into the endless distance, squinting against the sun, so grim was that look. But Pearl beside him stood with her feet apart in a strangely flat-footed child's pose, with the sun blinding her so that she could see nowhere into the future, see nothing.

When Carleton looked at that photograph, years later, something tugged at his eye muscles. But he never cried. What was sad was not the fact that the two young people in the picture had gone away, but the fact that he could not stand against that particular barn wall any more and look off into the barnyard and the old house that faced it. That house and that barnyard were hundreds of miles away, a thousand miles away. He could not get to them no matter how urgently he desired them. At night before sleep the monotonous images of rows of beans or strawberries would give way suddenly and he would be surrounded by a circle of smiling, warm, familiar faces, the faces of his family and relatives, and his dream might open up suddenly (the walls falling away by magic) to show him the back garden, the side orchard, the barnyard with its rotting, rich-smelling haystack, the barn itself—everything! And his eyes would ache at the knowledge that he could not push his way through the density of sleep to get to those things, not really.

His mother had been a strong quiet woman whose hands had smelled of something sweet—soap, sugar, syrup. She had aged quickly and then grew no older for years. Since the age of sixteen she had worn her hair pulled back into a crude knot and never had she cut her hair—never. Women who played with their hair or smeared lipstick onto their faces or squashed their feet into tiny high-heeled shoes belonged to a special dark, limited, fenced-off world; Carleton's mother despised it. Carleton remembered her in connection with food. He remembered her hands setting dishes on the table, dishes so hot she needed potholders to carry them; and he remembered her spooning food out for the various babies; and he remembered her squatting with a grunt to scrape food into the cats' tins outside, after supper. The cats would mew and rub against her thick-stockinged ankles, like clever children. And he remembered her hunting out the special eggs chickens try to hide from people, back in the thickets and under the barn walls.

His father had been a blacksmith, and Carleton and his other brothers had gone around with him to farms, riding in the wagon. They had all felt important. Later on, when their father got old and had pains running up his side, none of the boys had wanted to take over the blacksmithing because the old man would have been jealous. . . . He could remember his father's long, slow dying, back in the dark bedroom with its air thick with months of exhaled breath, and how the old man had seemed to grab at them with his eyes, hating something in them that let them run outside and away from him, away from his pain. He had had nothing to say to his sons. Carleton had brought his first baby in for the old man to see, but that hadn't worked out right. His father hadn't cared. Carleton had then felt the baby to be an embarrassment, a failure, because he loved his father and wanted to give him a gift, give him something, but he had no idea what his father wanted. Later that day, in the parlor, he sat quietly and watched his mother fondling the baby, transformed with love the way Pearl was transformed in that baby's presence, and it came to Carleton that there was nothing you could give to a man who was dying. There was hardly anything you could say. He was going one way and you were going another and that was that.

After his father's death everything had come along quickly. His own little farm and Pearl, and the next year another baby, then the weather turning on them as it had and trouble with the market and his falling into debt. In the world of his childhood women did not swear or use vulgar language, ever, and men did not use this special language before them, and just as rigid as this was the fact that men did not borrow money and shame their families. But those things happened. Everything changed. It was like the earth turning to sand and falling away beneath your feet, something dazzling and clamorous. You could get your balance back but you could never get used to it because nothing was the way it should be, nothing came along right, everything was changed. Carleton and Pearl had moved into a city and lived in a dilapidated old hotel for a while, children and all, until the "picking" truck came in and they were signed up along with everyone else. It was a way to get quick money, they were told. Everyone had relatives who went on the season and traveled from camp to camp, and the more children they had big enough to work, the more money they made: that made sense.

The first summer they had put the baby down at the end of each row and Pearl checked him as she worked along. It had been dusty and hot and the baby had cried, but in a high, rasping voice, as if it hadn't enough strength. One day Pearl had gone in their cabin to get the baby—it was sleeping in a cardboard box on the floor—and she came right up to a large rat that was sniffing at the baby's face. The rat's tail had been stiff and curved. Pearl had stood there looking down at it for a while. When Carleton came in the rat ran away and later on Pearl could only remember it occasionally; she remembered the tail and spoke sometimes of a rat's tail. Carleton would try to remember it for her, to fit the memories together into something that made sense, because he had a terror of things getting lost. Even ugly things. If anything got lost it would be that much harder to get home again.

He was still a young man. In taverns the men wrestled and he won most of the time, except if he was too drunk. He had muscular arms and legs and shoulders and even his stomach looked like a mound of muscle covered with blond hairs. Men always liked him and a certain kind of woman never stopped looking over his way; it had always been like that. He was a young man still, and if he sometimes felt old it was because of the mess of facts he had to sort out and get straight in his mind, things that had happened to his parents and to him and to other people, things that added up and defined life, like facts in a great book. He had so much to think about that he could not bother looking at mountains or rivers or woods or even other people. There was no time.

3

Florida. One day, five years later, Carleton and his family were finishing supper. Sweat ran down his face as he bent over his plate. He could feel beads of sweat on his back, on his chest. He stared at a droplet that fell onto his food, and it struck him with the slow certainty that truths had for him now that he was sorry the workday was over. Out in the field picking was one thing because he could turn his mind off. He could feel his consciousness drain out into the worm-colored plants and the clods of dirt, losing itself in nothing. Dirt did not have to think and Carleton's mind eased out into it, to peace.

But with other people he had to keep his mind on. Sometimes it slipped off and lost itself in the sky over someone's shoulder, or in a gesture someone might make—scratching his head, picking his teeth. When he forgot himself and blacked out like this Carleton was frightened. With Pearl he had to fight to keep his mind clear, because he could sense her fuzziness, her sleepiness, and there was something in it he desired. Everybody talked about her now. Kids laughed at her. Carleton was used to seeing people like Pearl, but at a distance. His trouble was that he was too close to her. They had five children now, one of them a new baby, and with each child Pearl had become sleepier, slower to recover. The kids did not bother Carleton; they were afraid to make noise when he was around. Only Clara was bold with him: she was his favorite, with her white-blond hair and her blue eyes just like Carleton's, a child so pretty he could almost lose himself just looking at her. But even she could annoy him if it was hot like this and his supper didn't taste right.

"Here, pass that," Carleton grunted. Sharleen, his ten-year-old, passed him a saucepan. Something in his stomach recoiled at the sight of the mashed potatoes inside, but he spooned some on his plate automatically. They were his favorite potatoes. He ate, leaning over the table, waiting for the food to taste right. Mike finished eating and ran outside. Pearl was sitting with her plate up on the window sill, just beneath her chin as if she was afraid of dropping food. Her pale blond hair was stiff with grease. Carleton, eating, watched her bring forkfuls of food to her lips, taste them timidly, and finally eat. Her shoulders were rounded, sitting as she was. Her head was bowed over her plate as if in contemplation of something profound and complex. Carleton watched her meek, childish profile and did not let himself worry about what he was going to do. He had found out in the many years they'd been traveling this way that it was best not to think or worry, because unexpected things happened all the time. There was no point in preparing for trouble because it might not come, or another kind of trouble might come instead. People like Pearl got along best in this life because they did not have to think at all. Once in a while she would get furious at something and fight with him, but he could take care of her. She never bothered anyone else. The kids could kick and scream, running around her, and she sometimes did not even notice. Most of the time she sat still and quiet, waiting, looking as if she were peering along the ground for something to pick, some pod or piece of fruit to snatch up and put in her hamper. There was that slightly greedy, conspiratorial squint about her eyes that Carleton had seen in the older fruit bums who tagged along with their working crew.

Next door a radio was blaring: loud music that Carleton liked.

"Next month we're taking off and going to Jersey by ourselves," Carleton said. He might have been talking to Sharleen, who was the only one old enough to listen, or to Pearl, or to no one. When he was with his family his voice was slow and cautious. His words were sometimes slurred, as if he were pretending to be drunk. At night when work was through and he was liberated from them, spending his time in

24

a tavern or with a woman, his voice was just like anyone else's: it could climb higher and higher, get more and more excited and pleased with itself, it was a young, hard, harsh voice that strained to get free. Here, cramped in this little cabin, his voice was cramped and sweaty like his body and he seemed to hear each word more clearly.

"Up there there's no wetback bastards," he said.

There was food on Clara's face. Carleton wiped it off.

"We going in a bus?" she said.

"Ah, hell, we ain't going nowhere," said Sharleen.

Carleton looked at her.

She was a thin, nervous, sallow child with scabs on her arms and legs. Carleton thought they were from bugs, he didn't know. The scabs looked like ordinary scabs except they were hard and thick, and when she picked them off, the wounds bled again and formed new scabs. She had a rat-quick face, narrow little eyes that were always suspicious.

"Shut your face," Carleton said.

Clara was feeding the two-year-old, Rodwell. The boy snapped at the spoon and it fell onto the floor.

"Dirty messy pig," Sharleen said.

"He can't help it," said Clara.

"Both of you shut up," said Carleton.

Clara puffed out her cheeks and stared mockingly at Sharleen. Carleton watched them with a strange remote interest, as if he'd seen these two children many times before, locked together in a hot inertia of hatred as they were now. He wanted to hurry and get out and get to town but he ate slowly, he could not taste the food, he kept waiting for that tiny little pain—almost a pain—in his stomach.

Sharleen slapped Clara and Clara shrieked.

"I said shut up!" Carleton said. He brought his arm around and struck Sharleen's chest. She fell off the edge of the bed she was on, but jerked around to face him. Clara laughed. Sharleen's plate was on the floor.

"She's a little crappy bitch!" Sharleen said.

Clara laughed happily. She caught Carleton's eye and he was struck, oppressed by her gaiety. There were five years between the girls, but Clara did not seem much younger. Outside, the difference was obvious, but here in the cabin where they all lived pressed up against one another, she seemed much older than she was.

Rodwell began to cry.

"You, get out," Carleton told Sharleen. "You started him in. Clara, take care of him, will you?" Sharleen ran out. He

would have to get out himself, fast, before the other baby
started in crying. Clara brought her face close to Rodwell's
and talked to him. At the window Pearl sat, eating slowly,
holding her red plastic fork in her fist. It was "her fork";
nobody else could have it.

Clara said, "Why are they so fat, them nigger ladies?"

"They just are."

"Mommy ain't fat."

"Some people are fat."

"You ain't fat and I ain't either. Sharleen is skinny and
ugly."

She had one arm crooked around Rodwell's neck. The boy
cried with great effort, sucking in air desperately, his little
chest pumping. Carleton thought sometimes that the boy
would suddenly stop—the little machine would break down—
but he kept going, kept going. Rodwell and now another
baby. There were so many kids around—Mike was always
running somewhere, he bruised the fruit and talked back, got
slapped around by everyone, and Sharleen was sour and
nervous. Only Clara pleased Carleton, because she had her
mother's old look, her mother's slowness and peacefulness,
but there was no film between her and the outside world as
there was with Pearl.

Carleton touched Clara's warm forehead. He could feel
her skull. She stared at him, smiling. The other children
would have flinched away, expecting to be hit, but not Clara.
She seemed to him like a pretty little animal, a pet like the
dog he'd had so many years ago, back home. . . . He had
caused her to be born, he thought. He was her father. The
other kids did not matter, did not count, because they were
like anyone else's kids. The camp was crawling with them.
Kids, babies. A dead baby had just been found down in the
filthy stream behind the outhouses, and the sheriff's men had
been on the foreman's back. Too many babies. Carleton had
his own idea whose the baby was, like everyone else, but he
wouldn't talk. What difference did it make? But at the
thought of death, of babies dying, he felt a rush of fear for
Clara. She was not sick. She was all right. He would take
special care of her.

"Gonna bring you a candy bar, if you're good. You take
care of those two," he said.

"Where you going?"

He made himself finish the cold potatoes. You had to eat,
that was a rule. Everyone knew it. If you stopped eating and
only drank, you were on your way out. Pearl was now

pushing bits of food around on her plate. "You can wash this stuff out, Clara," Carleton said.

"That's Sharleen's job."

"You want a candy bar or not?"

"They'll take it away from me."

"They will not."

"They will too. They always do."

"Like hell they will," Carleton said. He stood. The air near the ceiling was heavy and hot. Flies buzzed languidly, too lazy to bother with the food. He stretched his arms and yawned. A tiny flicker of excitement began. He was going out, he'd saved money all week for this, the vicious sunlight slanting off the packing sheds and piercing his eyes, the pounding sun on the back of his head, the gabble of those Mexicans—he would get past all these things. He would get past them like a runner sailing along a road, racing along the way you could run sometimes in a dream.

He nudged Pearl. "Goin' out for a while," he said apologetically. She turned to look at him. There were shadowy smudges beneath her eyes and lines edged with dirt fanning outward. Carleton had seen people stare at her, disquieted by those eyes—a child's eyes, yet outlined with wrinkles. Her skin burned deeper and deeper on the top but stayed bloodless underneath. Far inside her face, secret inside that network of dried wrinkles and groping, expressionless calm, was the same child who had smiled out into the photograph.

"Goin' out, be back pretty soon," he said. He wanted to avoid her eyes but was fascinated by them, as people are fascinated by the eyes of store dummies. "Clara's gonna wash up."

"I'll wash up," Clara said.

Pearl prodded at a back tooth with her tongue, found something, and reached with three fingers to dislodge it.

"Be good, baby," Carleton said, squeezing past Clara.

It was almost twilight. The look of the sun setting excited him. He could feel muscles in his legs tingling with excitement.

He walked through the camp. This camp was better than the last one, where they'd lived in tents. When it rained the tents bunched up with water and fell in. Everything had turned to mud there. Here, there were tar-paper roofs to the shanties and that was as much as anyone wanted—it got hot but not wet. Heat did not really bother them any more. The other day Carleton had been questioned by a man in a white shirt who was sweating and nervous, about how long he'd been working on the season, how much money he made, how many children he had, where he'd come from "originally," how he could work in such heat—a nosy bastard, everyone had laughed at him. But it had struck Carleton that he no longer minded the heat. He even liked sunny days better than cloudy days, because if it rained they lost money; best of all were days with a little high filmy cloud, but you couldn't trust clouds at all. Carleton had explained all this contemptuously to the man, who was taking notes in a notebook with a black and white swirled cover. His mind had been snapped on by this bastard and later he could not turn it off. The questions the man asked him made him think suddenly that there were people who didn't know the answers to them, people who were not doing what he did. There were thousands, millions of people who were not on the season and who did not kneel in the dirt and pick beans and strawberries and tomatoes and lettuce. . . .

Someone was yelling out on the lane. But it was just kids, nothing interesting, and Carleton walked right through them. He noticed how they watched him—even the biggest kid watched him cautiously, like a dog. This made Carleton want to reach out and poke him in the chest, he didn't know why. But he just walked through them and they waited until he was past before they began fighting again. Carleton had been in a real fight a few days ago and had almost killed the son of a bitch who was making trouble. It happened back by the unloading sheds, away from the fields, and the foremen didn't know about it until it was too late. But nothing much happened. The other guy, a bastard from the east, had two loose teeth and that was about all. Carleton could have killed him, though. He had had to hold himself back. A terrible thirst had welled up in him, something dry and choking all the way down to his stomach and up into his mouth, and he had had to switch on his mind and turn it up high, like a radio blaring an alarm, to make himself stop kicking the man's face.

He had a good friend once, Red, who'd killed someone. But it was a mistake—he had killed someone from town, and they came out and arrested him and kept him and the workers packed up and left in the truck and Red didn't leave with them. Carleton learned from someone he met in South Carolina two years later that Red had had his neck broken and that was no joke. So Carleton had stopped kicking and the kid had two bloody loose teeth, but so what?

He looked in at his friend Rafe's cabin, and there was

Rafe's big fat wife nursing a baby. She made a gesture to close her dress, then the gesture turned into a slight outward-turning of the palm, and she smiled.

"Can I come along tonight?" she said.

"Oh, is that Walpole?"

Rafe leaned over to look out the door. He had a queer angular head, his dark brown hair was thin and damp, and it was always a surprise to Carleton to think that Rafe was only twenty-eight.

"Can I come along tonight?" his wife said.

"Yeah, well, we got our plans," Carleton said, grinning. He put one foot familiarly into their doorway. Rafe's wife Helen was fat and pretended to be afraid, but like all women she could be wild; he had fooled around with her once and he knew. "Maybe could be you got business of your own, huh? Waitin' till Rafe is gone."

She shrieked at him. Carleton ducked, pretending, and he felt his lungs expand with good will. This was how it should always be—this kind of talk, fooling around. He had been crazy to feel sorry when work was out. It was crazy to think that way. This was the good time right now, work over and done with for the day, the stinking cabin with his nut of a wife left behind. All that wasn't really him. When he was out with real people like Rafe and his wife, Carleton couldn't understand why he never remembered how happy he was with them when he was back at work the next day. Instead, his thoughts kept wandering back to "home," years ago.

"How's Pearl, any better or same?" Helen said, stretching her mouth downward. Carleton shrugged his shoulders. "She's a real pretty thing, real pretty," Helen said sadly. "Rafe wouldn't mind no blond-haired girl, but he got me instead—haha. Ain't that right?"

"Haha is right," Rafe said. He stepped out and looked around as if sizing up everything. There was about half a foot between the cabin and the ground; the shack was propped up on concrete blocks. Under the cabin and scattered around in front were pieces of garbage and old rags.

"Rafe likes to have a good time and I don't say no," Helen said loudly. She leaned out the doorway and called after them. "I know how it is, men like you an' him. I don't blame nobody. Rafe an' me—"

"That's enough," Rafe said over his shoulder.

They walked out toward the road. Carleton turned and happened to see Clara behind him—she was just running behind a tree. "You, Clara!" he yelled. "Get the hell back home, you want me to give it to you? Huh? Want me to burn your ass off?"

"Is that Clara?" Rafe said.

Carleton waited. After a moment the little girl looked out. "You get on back home," he said, more kindly. She ducked back behind the tree, waited an instant, and then ran back toward the cabin.

"Real cute girl," Rafe said.

"Some nigger kid was bothering her," Carleton said. "The other day."

Rafe began to swear, evenly and hissingly, in a polite way as if he owed this to Carleton.

"If anybody gets killed it ain't my fault. Two nigger families in here and them Mexes stink as bad," Carleton said. His voice was getting younger. He felt a surge of dark enthusiasm, a force like a balmy, stormy wind, so strong that it would be enough for him and Rafe both. After a day out in the fields they needed this. "I don't give a damn if their cabins are down by the crick or not, down the hill or not, the fact is they're in the camp and startin' to get fresh with our kids and what're we goin' to do about it?"

"I know by Jesus what I'm going to do," Rafe said.

"Look here," said Carleton. He took a jackknife out of his pocket and opened it. Rafe had seen it many times before but pretended to be interested. "You see this-here little thing?"

"Better not let anybody see it."

"The hell with that."

"Well—"

"I know how to use this thing. Just let anybody try me." Carleton closed the knife, wanting it to make a hard clicking sound. It closed silently. There were rust marks on it. He recalled finding it one morning on a bus floor. He had bent down to fix his shoe and seen it there, lying in the dust, and the way his eye sprang to it made him know it was meant for him: it was a gift.

"I wouldn't go nowhere without it," Carleton said. His jaw felt stiff. He held the knife in the palm of his hand and looked at it, as if all his strength were compressed there, secret and sly, the sharp blade waiting inside the mother-of-pearl handle.

Rafe made a noise to agree with him. Back at the camp, with so many children milling around them, they had looked like one kind of young man. Now, walking in the middle of the dirt road, their hands in their pockets as if this were an important part of their appearance, they looked different—the jagged slant of Carleton's glance, his pursed expectant lips, the aggressively aimless jutting of his elbows, the soft urgent pliancy of Rafe's big body brought them out from their surroundings as if they were about to be illuminated in the headlights of an oncoming car. They walked forward with rapid, long strides. Everything was still; the usual insects, a few birds, dogs off in the distance. Carleton did not listen to the silence because it made him restless. Sometimes when he could not sleep, late at night when the camp was finally quiet, he would whisper names to himself: names of his family first, then distant relatives, then neighbors, then distant neighbors, stretching back for years, hundreds of miles, to astonish him with the number of years he had been alive on this earth. Only when he felt that he had named everyone, and that he knew where he was among them, could he fall asleep.

This town was nothing much, but better than the camp. It began around a bend in the road, where suddenly there was a creek that forked, and a little topless bridge over it, and a sawmill on the creek, and a few scattered houses with chickens running loose around them. Then came the town—a few long buildings with false fronts. Across the way a coal yard. When Carleton had first seen the town, on the bus going through to the camp, the place had been empty with noon heat; now there were cars and people everywhere. Carleton and Rafe began to walk faster. Someone was ahead of them, a few kids. They stopped to throw stones down from the bridge. From somewhere ahead music came; hearing it made saliva rush into Carleton's mouth and he realized that he was hungry, starving, for the sound of music like this and for kids throwing pebbles down into a creek.

There were a few other men from the camp inside the tavern, but most of the men were strangers. It was a big, open, hot place; in the back half the floorboards gave way to packed ground. Flies and mosquitoes buzzed. A large shaggy dog lay asleep beneath a table. Carleton felt his eyes ache with pleasure of such fine heavy odors—men's bodies, beer, food, smoke. He and Rafe were suddenly shy and stood with men they knew. They shouted above the noise into one another's faces. This town was worse than the last place. It was better than the last place. Two of the men were foreign-born and spoke English contemptuously; they kept sliding back into another language that was so hissing and coarse that Carleton's heart leaped with hatred for it. Rafe reached

31

around Carleton to pay the bartender, whose eyes did not quite raise themselves to Carleton's. Carleton drank beer and thought of the money he had put aside and how it would be enough for tonight: he could forget everything. He could turn off his mind from everything. A mosquito bit his cheek. He and the other men fell silent when a group of other men brushed against them, without looking around. Sweat ran down their faces and backs; their forearms were grimy with dirt. But they thought they were better than Carleton and the men with him. You could tell that. One of them wore a Western hat that seemed to Carleton comically stupid; he wanted to point at it and laugh. The hat was cream-colored and perched on top of the man's head as if it were about to be knocked off by someone.

"Lookit that bastard," Carleton whispered to Rafe. Rafe made an agreeable noise. Carleton scratched at his cheek; something itched there. He had another glass of beer and some of it ran over onto his fingers. He wanted to ask the two men—who were arguing now in their queer language—where they came from, why they didn't go back there, why they didn't shut up. Other people were looking at them. A woman with long black hair was leaning around, listening. Her lips stretched into a grin at the sound of their ugly words.

"If they can't speak English they should shut up. Go back where they came from," Carleton said. He pretended someone pushed him and bumped into one of the men. This man was short, with shoulders that had bent gradually forward until they remained that way; he had a look of perpetual blinking alertness, as if he might at any moment squat down and snatch something up from the ground. Carleton didn't know where he had come from—somewhere in Europe probably—but he suspected that everyone in that country spoke this shameful language in the same rushing, eager, ugly way, and that their hair was thin and oily like this, and their eyes squinting as if in perpetual confusion over their surroundings.

Carleton kept bumping into him, so the man moved aside. He was about forty. The other man was a little taller and he kept shouting at someone. Carleton could not decide if he was happy or angry. He shouted in that language—Carleton's muscles twitched to hear it—and a young boy in a dirty undershirt answered him. Carleton saw people smiling at them, at the way the boy's ribs moved inside his undershirt.

"Outside. Out," someone yelled. It was a woman behind the bar. Small damp strands of hair kept falling onto her forehead and she kept pushing them back, angrily. "No kids in here. Get him out."

Someone tapped the boy's shoulder. The father leaned forward with a look of fear and cunning. "What? What you say?"

"Get him out of here."

"What?"

"The law. It's the law."

"Law?" The man had a dark, worried face, but there was something suspicious about him; Carleton could tell that. He'd seen the women these men had—big slow women with dark eyes and thick waists, skin like lard. Like the Mexican women he saw occasionally, they could smile and the smile could turn into anything, in a second. You could not trust them.

"Hey, you understand English? You?" someone said to Carleton.

It was one of the young men who had just come in. Carleton stared at him, frightened. "You understand, hey? Explain it to your friends."

Carleton said furiously, "They're not my friends!"

"You come from the same place—"

"They're not my friends."

This man was younger than Carleton, little more than a boy. Carleton stared at his thin, blemished cheeks and thought that this might be it—what he was waiting for. He was waiting to fight. He wanted to kill somebody.

"That guy is an American," someone said.

"There—there is kid," the father said. He pointed at a boy of about four who was playing at the end of the bar.

"That's somebody's kid who works here," the woman said.

"Another one there—"

"Her? She ain't no kid!"

People were looking at them. The boy's eyes were razor-sharp, like those of an animal surprised in the brush. His father shrugged his shoulders and laughed, pretending it was a joke. "They making fun," he said.

"It's the law, goddam you!" Carleton hissed.

"What you say?"

Carleton nudged the man with his elbow, hard. Shame made him reckless.

"What's wrong, what's doing?" the man cried.

"Stupid goddam bastard!" Carleton said.

The shorter man moved toward Carleton, but something happened: a second went by in silence, both men hesitated, then it was over. Sweat had broken out all new on Carleton's body.

The two foreigners with the boy left.

"They stink. They eat slop and they stink," Carleton said loudly.

"They eat snails or worms or something," Rafe said, speaking to Carleton but really to the other men. "They do that back where they come from."

"Bad as wetbacks," said Carleton.

The men on his left eased back a little. They turned away. Their attention, which had so humiliated him, had excited him also and he missed it. He took out a piece of rag and unfolded it: two dollars saved.

He and Rafe drank whisky. They talked louder and louder, sometimes slapping each other's arms. It might have been that they had something urgent to say but did not know how to say it. Two young girls in bright, fussy dresses tried to talk to them, but Carleton knew better; he'd been fooled enough times by girls from towns. Their perfume and high-pitched voices excited Carleton but he did not look at them.

"He's afraid—he's married. I bet he's married."

"I bet he has eight children."

"They all have eight children!"

"I wouldn't want to be married to one of them, then."

The girls giggled together. Carleton, who had been brought up to admire people with eight children, felt his lips spread in a grimace of hatred: not for the girls, but for anyone with eight children. Some of the foreigners had eight children.

"I think the fat one's cute."

"I like the skinny one."

"The skinny one has eight children and the other one—"

"The other one's gonna have his own baby!"

Carleton roared with laughter, punching Rafe's arm. He rocked from side to side in the luxury of this laughter, which had exploded out of him from nowhere. Rafe tried to grin, he nodded in time with the laughter. Carleton felt a thrill of excitement as he realized that other people were laughing too, that he was laughing with them and that Rafe stood for a moment by himself.

In a while the girls' attention drifted to someone else. Carleton looked around to see them talking with a man in overalls, with a foxy, soiled face.

He and Rafe had another drink. There was something about this place that made him happy. On Saturday nights when he could get drunk he was always happy. The week

34

dissolved, was sucked away as if drawn out one of the windows of the endless buses they rode, or out the back of one of the junky trucks. Whatever was thrown out there— garbage or papers or a kid's toy snatched away by another kid—just disappeared into the distance. Carleton, who looked out windows or out the back of a truck not in order to see anything but in order to watch distance being overcome, had sometimes thought that he might throw his own kids out there, one by one, and then Pearl, and last of all himself— then he'd be done with it. It was because of such thoughts that he was sometimes afraid to think.

But the taverns were different. Even though they were the same tavern, or looked the same, there was nothing frightening about them. In the noise and the pushing he felt himself accepted; he was one of those who made noise and pushed. The foreigners and even Rafe were not accepted, but he knew he would be, and he would be liked by everyone if only he could stay in one place long enough. There was always something about the rhythm of the men's voices, the smiles of the women, that made him know they would accept him if only they didn't know he was from the camp and couldn't guess that he had a wife like Pearl and five kids. He never doubted that they were better than he was. He could tell that by their faces. Next month he would go up to New Jersey and get another job—someone had said they needed men there. There were no jobs down here, that was for sure, just nigger work and picking, which was nigger work too but nobody admitted it. . . .

"Hey, how about it?" Carleton said suddenly. He put his elbow down hard on the bar and waved his fist at Rafe. This meant he wanted to see who could force the other's arm down. "Think you can beat me?"

He always beat Rafe at this and he knew he could tonight. He wondered if the girls were watching him.

Rafe's eyes moved oddly in their sockets, as if they were greased. "Hell with it," he grunted.

"You afraid?"

"Jesus—"

"Buy you a drink if you win!"

"Walpole, for Christ's sake—"

"Come on!"

"Your big mouth—"

"You coming or not?"

Carleton's face went hard. Beneath all his smiling there was this other face, hard as burnt ground. Rafe stared at him, then after a moment he smiled too. They clapped their hands together as if both had waited a long time for this moment, Rafe moved about until he was the way he wanted to be, then they began to push. Rafe's hand was plump and damp. Carleton could feel how hot his own hand was, he could feel the very bones inside his flesh aching with strength he had never been able to use up.

"Come on, skinny! I'm for that real cute skinny boy!"

"Ain't he cute?"

The girls came back. Another girl joined them. Carleton felt one of them touch him accidentally, and a haze passed before his eyes. Pressed back inside his body, like blood thickened and teased by the heat, was a column of strength yearning for freedom.

He lunged forward and pressed Rafe's arm down.

They applauded and laughed, relieved. He could hear relief in their laughter but could not understand it. Generous with victory, Carleton clapped Rafe's wet back— "Good try! Real good try!" Rafe shrugged his shoulders and forced his mouth into a smile. "You're gettin' stronger all the time," Carleton went on, flushed; "you maybe've been practicin' with your wife, huh?"

Rafe said nothing.

"Lots of practice with your big old wife, huh?" Carleton said breathlessly. He did not want the moment to end. He brushed his damp hair out of his face and this gave him an excuse to glance around; he saw people looking toward him.

"You mean you don't practice none with your wife?" one of the girls said to Carleton. Her cheeks were bright with boldness. "Don't you have no wife?"

"I bet he does!" another girl said.

"Don't you have no wife, you? Hey?"

Carleton ignored her. He knew he could draw her attention to him by looking past her. She laughed and pushed forward, smelling of perfume and beer. He had no idea how old she might have been—maybe twenty, or younger—and she had long black hair and a small sun-tanned bright face. Carleton waved one arm in a meaningless gesture that might have meant dismissal, then turned back to Rafe as if Rafe were more important.

"Guess I owe you a drink, then," Rafe said.

"Forget it. I saved lots of money this week."

Carleton took out his money. He was so excited his fingers trembled. Here it was, his own secret money: nobody knew about it but him!

"I'll buy it," Rafe said.

"Look— We're friends, right?"

"You need your money more than me."

"What, what's that?"

"Your five kids—"

Carleton squeezed Rafe's wrist; his fingers wanted to keep going and break the other man's soft bones. He knew the girls had heard this and that Rafe had said it so they would hear. "You bastard," he said, choking, "look here, I got lots of money saved—we bring in more money than you and your fat wife any day— You got that?"

"You take care, now."

"We're gettin out of this crummy place anyway, whatdaya think of that? You'll never get out of it—you're just white trash and you ain't from anywhere, you could be a nigger or—"

Rafe pushed him away. Carleton felt his face about to break into a thousand jagged pieces. The air around him, so delirious and happy a moment ago, was changing. It seemed that he could see things more clearly now—the wet top of the bar, its rough splintery wood, someone's soiled sleeve moving against it, the gritty front window that should have looked out onto the main street. The air was singing with anger.

"You want to try it again? Even up with the drink?" Rafe said.

He closed his big hand into a fist and set his elbow down hard on the bar. "Hey, you guys," said the woman behind the bar, "you want to fight, you can do it somewhere else." They ignored her. Carleton, excited, grasped Rafe's hand. But before he could get in a good position Rafe began to force him down. "Wait!" said Carleton, but Rafe paid no attention. Carleton felt his elbow slip and then Rafe's hot heavy arm lay on top of his. Both men were sweating and smiling hard. Carleton smiled to get past the taste in his mouth, which seemed to be oozing up from his guts.

"Try it again!" he said.

They grasped hands again. People crowded around to watch. Carleton felt someone brush against him and wondered if it was that girl again with the black hair— He jerked forward and his hand slipped in Rafe's. Both their hands were wet. Rafe grunted and tried to defend himself; he was strong, but his strength was lost in his stomach and fat thighs. Carleton slowly forced him back, down, and Rafe had to twist his body to ease the pain. When Carleton forced his

37

arm down flat, something happened—Rafe lost his balance and almost fell. He knocked some glasses over.

"Damn you, get out! Big pigs! Cows!" the woman behind the bar screamed.

"Go outside—"

Carleton and Rafe ignored them. They finished their drinks and then turned back to each other. Both laughed. Giddiness swirled around Carleton, who hadn't had so much attention since his last fight—and there had been no women there to make it so exciting. "Here's a dollar I can beat you again," Carleton said.

"Like hell you can," said Rafe.

Still grinning, they took hold of each other again. They were panting now. Carleton had the dizzy feeling that he'd been here before, done all this many times before. He grimaced at Rafe's tight grip. As they struggled he saw Rafe's sweaty oiled face through his own trembling lashes—Rafe looked like someone he had been struggling with for years, a cunning, dangerous stranger—

"Come on, you fat bastard! Fat cow!" Carleton hissed. His legs were rigid with exertion. He could feel Rafe's breath on his face. It seemed someone was whispering right behind him, a woman, and he would have given anything to know what she was saying—was it about him? He and Rafe were grinning and their eyes bulging, like creatures caught on the bottom of the sea, sinking beneath tons of pressure. Carleton felt as his enemy not just Rafe's bulk but the amused skeptical eyes of the other men, who did not accept him because he did not live here, though it was clear to anyone—to the women, of course to the women—that he was exactly like them and should have been taken in, he was like the best among them, his body and his hard strong arms and his narrow face with those knifing eyes—

The girls cheered and clapped. Carleton had won again.

"Gonna give up now?" he crowed.

He paused to give his pumping heart time to recover. When he shook his head he saw droplets of sweat fly out, and this made him laugh. He looked around and caught the girls' eyes and laughed with them.

"This is just puling stuff," Rafe said contemptuously.

"What?"

Rafe kept smiling and this reminded Carleton to smile. "Maybe could try something else," Rafe said.

"Better give up or your big old wife will get mad," said Carleton.

38

Rafe pushed him. Carleton blinked, squinted at him. Rafe raised his hand, his fingers outstretched in a gesture of good will, and made a feint at Carleton. Both men were still smiling. Carleton, laughing, did the same back. "You think my pa never taught me none of this back home?" he said. He could not remember if his father had taught him anything. But just saying the word "pa" sent more strength into his body. "Hey you!" Carleton gasped. Rafe had slapped his face, hard, with the flat of his hand. It was the way you might slap a bad child. Carleton's face stung, it burned. He heard someone giggle and the burn vibrated. For a moment Carleton could not see, then his vision cleared and grew sharper than before and he saw Rafe's yellowed teeth revealed in a hard, rigid grin, like the grin on a man who has become a statue. Rafe lunged to slap him again but this time Carleton had closed his hand into a fist and struck him hard, in the chest. He struck him again in the jaw.

"How'd you like that?" he said, panting. "Ready to go home?"

"You hillbilly bastard," Rafe said. His big broad face was pale, the blood had deserted him. He circled Carleton clumsily, trying to move inward, and Carleton was conscious of being young and strong and handsome, and he could not quite keep distinct the image of himself as he must be in the eyes of the spectators and the image of himself as he was to Rafe, who knew him. He kept wanting to do something fancy, to get someone to giggle at Rafe. So he made a clownish dancing step and rolled his eyes. But Rafe kept bearing in, not smiling. He hit Carleton hard in the chest and Carleton staggered backwards. Someone screamed behind him.

"Sons of bitches gonna break something," the woman behind the bar yelled.

Carleton paused, trying to get his breath but pretending to be waiting for that woman to shut up. He stood with his head bowed and his mouth open, gasping for air. He was sucking at it but it wouldn't come—an ugly greenish taste was spreading in his mouth and if he threw up everyone would laugh—

"S'pose you had enough, huh?" Rafe said.

Rafe's grin was watery and strange.

"He's cuter than you, mister," one of the girls said shrilly. "He ain't no fat ass like you!"

"Gonna give me that dollar?" Rafe said.

Carleton stood waiting, waiting to get strong again.

"Poor hillbilly bastard—"

Carleton spat toward him. They circled each other again. Now and then they laughed airily, breathlessly, but Carleton felt the laughter jerk up out of his bowels like something foul. His head was pounding. His chest hurt. His knuckles were scraped. He noticed a smear of bright blood on Rafe's forehead and wondered if it was his own.

He was suddenly afraid of Rafe, but he could not stop himself from snapping his fingers in the man's face. He made a noise as if he were calling pigs. Rafe rushed at him, they collided, and Rafe jerked Carleton's arm around so hard Carleton cried aloud. He struck Rafe on the back of the neck, a quick desperate blow such as a child might make. Both men jumped away from each other.

They panted, staring.

"He's just jealous, blue-eyes," a girl said.

"I don't like no fat man myself," said another.

Pricks of excitement darted at Carleton's skin. These words made him suddenly happy, drunk. He snapped his fingers again in Rafe's face.

"You better lay off," said Rafe. He tried to let his shoulders go limp, to show Carleton he was quitting. "Don't want to get hurt, huh. We both got to work tomorrow."

"You said somethin' about a hillbilly," Carleton said, smiling. His words were light as air, floating up. He kept wanting to laugh.

"If your arm gets broke who's gonna pick that crap?" Rafe said. "You better lay off."

Carleton snapped his fingers in Rafe's face just once more.

He saw the blow coming before it struck. Rafe swung his arm around and hit Carleton on the side of the face. Everything exploded in his brain and he felt something hit him—the floor, maybe the edge of the bar. The girls were screaming. Someone cried, "Watch out!" Carleton stumbled to his feet and lunged forward, anywhere, to get out of Rafe's way. But Rafe overtook him and struck him again on the back. He pounded Carleton's back with his fists, almost sobbing. Carleton managed to squirm away. He pushed someone aside. When he could see again it was Rafe he was looking at—he was coming toward Carleton with something long and thin in his fist, maybe a rod, a short pole, something Carleton could not recognize.

Nobody moved except Carleton and Rafe. Carleton felt the flatness of his image in the eyes of these strange people, who might have been watching from a great distance. He

40

wanted to break through that flat image: he wanted to come alive to them. The girls, who were making all the noise, were not really the ones who counted. They were just women. It was always men who had to be conquered. Rafe did not seem to understand that anyone was watching but was lumbering drunkenly forward, falling forward, his familiar face smeared with dirt and blood like the face of a man about to die, and his arms thrashing about like crazy—

"Hillbilly bastard—stinking—bastard—" he grunted. Carleton swerved backward and fell against a table. Something overturned. He was terrified by the silence he and Rafe were caught in and by the fact that Rafe did not seem to understand how they were in this silence together. Rafe had something in his hand and was trying to hurt Carleton. Carleton had his knife out, had it open, and as Rafe moved in at him he ducked under his arm and sank the knife into his chest.

Carleton had jumped past Rafe. The blade had gone in, he knew that, but Rafe did not yet know it. Everyone watched them closely and the silence was sharper than before. Rafe swung at him and the rod hit Carleton's shoulder and numbed him; Carleton could not believe that he had been hit so hard. He switched the knife to his other hand and brought it up from his knee, catching Rafe in the thigh. This time Rafe yelled with pain. The poker clattered to the floor. Rafe rushed right at Carleton, headlong, and seized him in his arms. He screamed into Carleton's ear as if trying to explain something to him. Carleton tried to get free but Rafe tightened his embrace, they grappled together, back against the wall where no one stood. Carleton kept slashing at him with his knife. He felt the narrow little blade cutting in, catching in the cloth and breaking free, rising and dipping, and still Rafe did not fall away. Rafe clutched at him as if to get away from that knife, to hide in Carleton's arms. Carleton began to sob, trying to get loose, and he slashed the blade now across the back of Rafe's neck. Like a razor, it brought blood at once, in a thin watery line. Rafe grabbed Carleton's head. His voice was climbing with pain and terror. He squeezed Carleton's head, squeezed it between his big hands, his thumb falling accidentally against Carleton's eye and squeezing that too, and Carleton's lungs were about to burst with all the pressure. "Let go, let go!" he sobbed. He felt as if his skull were being slowly squeezed out of shape. Rafe's hands grappled with his head as if caressing it, a stroking of love gone mad, and just by accident Carleton's knifeblade

41

took hold of something and plunged and plunged into it, sinking in softly so that Carleton was striking him with only his hand, a gentle, slowed-down blow, and then Rafe suddenly released him and fell away.

Carleton jumped craftily to one side. All his muscles were alive, as if electric current were flowing through him. He saw Rafe bending over, hugging his bleeding stomach, and then he fell. "Call me a hillbilly!" Carleton shrieked. He punched Rafe on the top of his head, the way you might pound a table, and Rafe fell heavily to the floor.

"Nobody better call me a hillbilly, Walpoles ain't no hillbillies!" Carleton screamed at all the faces. There was a remote roaring in his ears like the wind blowing up into a storm and he wondered if he would ever get to where it was quiet again.

4

South Carolina: spring. A woman in a dark dress stood in the entranceway and waited until everyone passed by and settled inside. It was hot. The schoolroom smelled of something nice—wood and chalk and something Clara did not recognize. The woman had broad shoulders and a heavy, solid body that reminded Clara of a tree trunk: the way she stood there waiting, her face hard as the children hurried by, sometimes slowing one down by grabbing the back of his neck, you'd never think she could come to life and walk to the front of the room. Her hands were big and veined and her neck was veined too, but she had a winter kind of paleness that set her off from the people Clara was used to seeing. There was no telling how old she was. Clara's last teacher, a few weeks ago in another state, had been like that too—different from the women at camp. She used her words more cautiously. Clara had never heard anybody talk as much as schoolteachers talked and she thought this was wonderful.

But people on the outside always talked more. When you met someone from camp outside, in town, you could tell they were from camp; there was just something about them, people as far apart as Clara's father and Nancy and Clara's best friend Rosalie and Rosalie's whole family.

"Stop that! I said stop that!"

The teacher was after someone. Clara and Rosalie giggled,

pressing their hands against their mouths. They heard a scuffle, and choked sounds of laughter. Their spines tingled but they didn't turn around to look even though everyone else did—they were new here and kept themselves tamed.

"He hit me first, goddamit," a boy said.

"Get over here—sit down!"

After a moment the teacher came to the front of the room. Clara saw her eyes flick over her and Rosalie and the other new kids from the camp; they were all together, sitting up near the front with the little kids. Rosalie was a year older than Clara; she was eleven; but both she and Clara and the boy with the splotches on his neck were with the little kids. They giggled and hid their faces in their books when the teacher was with the other grades. Clara's knees were hard against the bottom of the desk. She was getting big. She could feel herself growing. She was as tall as Rosalie and would be taller, and as tall as some of the girls from the farms. Being with the six and seven-year olds made her want to baby them, the way she babied her two little brothers. But they didn't like her. She wondered why the teacher had put her and Rosalie and that boy up front with such little kids.

On the first day, the teacher had held a book up too close to Clara's face and said, "Read this." Clara had blinked at the type nervously. Rosalie had her own book and held it hard against her stomach, her head bowed, but she did no better than Clara. "You're both slow. Far behind," the teacher said, not looking at them. And then Rosalie had started to giggle and Clara joined in, and the teacher had gotten mad at them both. Rosalie's mother, who had brought them over, had hollered at them and said it was a fine beginning for them, what the hell was the matter. . . ? Rosalie's mother had worn shoes with black bows on them that day, just to take them over to the school.

Now the teacher was approaching the first-grade group. It was only nine o'clock and already hot. Clara liked the heat, she could feel it get inside her and make her sleepy; she liked to close her eyes in the sunlight and fall asleep like one of those happy clean cats you saw sometimes around farms. She'd looked out the bus or out the back of the truck many times to catch sight of those cats—sometimes they'd be sleeping on a stone wall right out by the road, their fur ruffling in the wind. A patch of sunlight fell through the window and onto the teacher's arm. Clara watched it. The teacher's arm was lard-pale but had dark hairs on it like men's arms. The teacher had a solid, thick waist. Her belt was thin and had begun to turn over on one side, showing a cardboard lining. Clara watched her dreamily through her lashes. Everyone hated the teacher but Clara didn't; she liked that kind of skin and she liked the big round pin on the woman's collar, a round gold pin that looked like the sun. She would buy a pin like that someday, she thought, with her own money, and maybe she would be teaching school too—

"Hello. I am a boy. My name is . . . Jack," one of the six-year-olds read. He was from a farm. He sat across from Clara and up one, and Rosalie sat right behind him. Rosalie had long stringy red hair and surprised eyes. If she was caught doing something bad she turned those eyes on you and you had to laugh—once at recess, in the last school they'd been at, Clara had seen her opening up a handkerchief and when she snatched it away a little tin whistle fell to the ground. The whistle had been someone else's, a girl's, but Clara would never tell; she thought it was funny. Things came into Rosalie's hands as if they were just lying there waiting for her. She never stole things but only "found" them.

"I live in a white house. This is my house. . . . This is my dog. My dog is black."

The boy read slowly, emphasizing each word the same way. He was the best reader and Clara kept hoping he would make a mistake. She followed the words with her eyes, memorizing them. She knew where the sound "house" was because there was the picture of a house over it. The house was white with three big trees in the front lawn. Clara loved the pictures in the book and had stared at them many times. Her favorite was the one of the mother and the baby sitting in the kitchen. It was toward the end of the book, so probably they wouldn't get to it; they'd be moved to another state by then. This picture showed a woman with nice short yellow hair holding a baby on her lap. The black dog was sitting and looking up at them and it looked as if it were smiling. Behind the woman was a big window with white curtains with red polka dots on them, and plants in flowerpots on the window sills, and a clock. But the clock was fake; if you looked close there was no time on it. To make Rosalie jealous, Clara told her that she had been in a real house once, up in Kentucky.

"Next, Bobbie," said the teacher.

Behind them something was going on. Clara heard a book fall but she didn't dare look around. One day the teacher had shaken her and she hadn't even done anything—someone else had been laughing. So she sat with her mouth frozen into a polite little smile while the teacher's face reddened with that look all adults had that showed they wanted to kill. Behind Clara there was quiet.

"Pick up that book," said the teacher.

A desk squeaked as someone bent to pick it up.

The teacher stood staring for a while. The red backed out of her face unevenly. Then she woke up again and said, in a sharp, vicious voice: "I saw that! You—get out in the entry! Get out, you little pig!"

She began to yell. She threw down her book and rushed up the aisle. Clara and Rosalie looked around, their fists pressed against their mouths to keep from laughing. They laughed at everything here in school—what else could they do? Everything was so strange here! Kids as big as they were sat at desks and read haltingly out of books instead of working out in the fields to make money—why was that? If the people from town hadn't come out to the camp in cars and talked with someone, she and the other kids would not be here. It was all so different, so strange. She laughed at everything. People who picked fruit laughed to give themselves time to think. Clara was maybe doing the same thing. She looked around and saw the teacher shake one of the boys—he was big, about twelve. A farm boy. His name was Jimmy and he had done something nasty in the girls' outhouse once, on the floor. The teacher shook him and knocked him back against his seat. The desks were attached at the bottom and so the whole row rocked.

"Stand out in the entry—you filthy little pig!"

He went out, his shoulders hunched with laughing. The teacher wiped her face. Clara saw her eyes move over the room jerkily, and something twitched in her cheek. It was a little twitch like a blink. Clara thought that when she was a teacher she wouldn't yell so much. She would smile more. But she would shake up the bad boys and scare them. She would be nice to the girls because the girls were afraid; even the big girl with the braids wound around her head, who was thirteen or fourteen, was quiet and afraid. Clara would be nice to all the girls but hard on the boys, the way her father was. He whipped Rodwell all the time but never Clara. . . .

"Read. Start reading!"

She was pointing at Clara. Clara's face tried to ward this off by smiling the way Rosalie's mother had smiled, but it did no good.

She bent over the book. Silence. She could feel something

45

itching up high on her legs but she could not scratch it. The words danced.

"I live in a white house. . . ."

"He just read that! We're on the next page."

The teacher walked heavily toward them. Rosalie was hunched over her book, not looking at Clara. Everything was quiet except the flies.

Clara stared over at the next page. Her breath was coming fast. There was a picture of a strange man on that page, dressed in a strange way. He had a white shirt on but it was half covered up by a kind of coat, a short coat, that didn't come closed all the way up in front but left part of his chest to get cold. A red thing was tied around his neck. The strange coat was blue and the man's trousers were blue too. Clara wondered what kind of man this was supposed to be. He was smiling but she had no idea what he was smiling at; it looked as if he was just smiling, by itself.

"Go on and read. We're waiting."

Clara gripped the book harder.

"You can't be that stupid!" the teacher cried. "Go on and read!"

"My . . . My . . ."

The teacher leaned over Clara. With one long impatient finger she tapped at Clara's book. The baby had spilled something on this page and Clara's face burned with shame.

"Begin with this word. This word!"

She was tapping at a word. Clara knew it was a word, it was letters put together, it was like the letters up at the top of the blackboard that went all the way across the front of the room. . . .

"Say it, come on! Say it!"

"My . . ."

Clara felt waves of heat rise about her. She and the teacher were both breathing hard.

"*Father*. Say it—say *father*."

"Oh, Father. Father. Father," Clara whispered. "My father . . . My father . . ."

There was silence when Clara's voice ran out. Someone giggled. The teacher's finger did not move. Clara could feel heat from the teacher and she could hear her breathing—she wanted to get away from here, get far away and sleep for a long time. That way no one would be mad at her.

"How am I supposed to teach you anything? What do they expect? My God!" the teacher said bitterly. Clara remained sitting as straight as possible, the way Rosalie's mother had

46

sat. It was the way to be. After a hot, ugly moment, the teacher said: "How long are you people going to be here?"

She leaned around so that she could look at Rosalie too. But Rosalie sat the way Clara was sitting, with her own finger on the page, pretending not to notice. "How long are your parents going to be living here?" the teacher said. "Do you have any idea?"

This frightened Clara more than anger, because she did not know what to do with it. She could hear something nice in the teacher's voice. She smiled, then stopped smiling, then looked over at Rosalie in panic. Rosalie turned and caught Clara's eye and both girls giggled suddenly. Their giggles were like something nasty.

The teacher made an angry noise and straightened up.

"All right, next. Bobbie. You read," she said. Clara could tell that the teacher's voice was now going high over her head and that it could not hurt her.

At recess they ran outside together. The teacher stood in the entry and made them pass one by one. If a boy pushed anybody she grabbed him and he had to wait until everyone else was out.

Clara and Rosalie approached the other girls. The girls did not pay any attention to them. There was a high concrete step in front of the school, cracked and crumbling, and a walk that led out to the road. Clara and Rosalie sat on the edge of the big step, by themselves but close enough to the other girls to hear what they said.

The boys played games, running hard. Cinders were tossed up when they skidded. They threw cinders and bits of mud at one another and at the girls. The girl with the braids cried when she couldn't get flaky pieces of mud out of her hair; the pieces were caught. The boys ran by Rosalie and Clara and said, "Let's see your nits! You got nits in your hair!" One of them grabbed Rosalie's long hair and jerked her off the concrete step. Rosalie screamed and kicked at him. "You fucking little bastard!" Rosalie screamed. The boys giggled and ran around the schoolhouse.

Clara shrank back. She heard the teacher's footsteps in the entry. The teacher ran out and grabbed Rosalie's arm and shook her. "What are you saying!" she cried. Rosalie tried to get away. "What did I hear you say?"

"They pulled her hair," said Clara.

"Don't you ever talk like that again around here!" the teacher said. She was very angry. Her face was red in splotches. Clara, crouched back against the wall, stared up at the teacher's face and couldn't figure out what she saw: the big, hard, bulging eyes, the stiffening skin, the mouth that looked as if it had just tasted something ugly.

Rosalie jerked away and ran out to the road. "You come back!" the teacher cried. Rosalie kept running. She was running back toward the camp; it was about a mile down one road and a little ways down another. Clara pressed her damp back against the wall and wanted to take hold of the teacher's hand, to make it stop trembling like that. Her mother's hands had been nervous too. If you touched them and were nice, sometimes they stopped, but sometimes not; sometimes they were like little animals all by themselves. When her mother was dead and in that box, her hands had been quiet up on her chest and Clara had kept peeking and watching for them to shake.

The teacher turned around. "She's a filthy little pig," she said. "She shouldn't be in school with— You tell her mother that she can't come back if she behaves that way. You tell her!"

Ned, the boy from camp, was squatting nearby. He began to giggle slyly.

"What's wrong with you?" said the teacher.

He stopped. He was maybe thirteen but runty for his age; his nose was always running; he was "strange." His parents let him come to school because he was too stupid to pick beans right. He bruised them or pulled the plants out or overturned his hamper.

"Tell her mother that— I don't know—" The teacher's face was heavy and sad. She was talking only to Clara. Clara wanted to cringe back from those sharp demanding eyes, she wanted to protect herself by making a face or swearing or giggling—anything to stop the tension, the seriousness. The teacher said, "What are going to do with yourself?"

"What?" said Clara brightly.

"What are you going to do? You?"

It was like a question in arithmetic: how much is this and that put together? If the things were called beans Clara could add them together fast, but if they were squirrels or bottles of milk she could do nothing with them.

"You mean me?" Clara whispered.

"Oh, you're all—white trash," the teacher said, her mouth hard and bitter. She hurried by Clara and into the entry. Her footsteps were loud.

"White trash," said the girl with the braids.

48

"White trash," said Ned, smirking at Clara.

"You shut up—you're the same thing!" Clara snarled in his face. She hated him because they were together and there was nothing she could do about it. When the other kids laughed at them they made no difference between Clara and Ned—and Rosalie—and the twenty or so bigger kids from the camp who had come to school on the first day, then never showed up again.

Inside, the teacher was ringing the bell. It was a loose, rusty bell the teacher shook angrily by hand.

They ran back in. Clara's head had begun to ache. She sat at her desk and picked up her book and looked again at the white house and the man who was a father but who did not look like her own father or any father she knew, and kept looking at it as if trying to figure it out, until the teacher told her to put it away and do her writing. Penmanship. Clara felt heavy and hot and sad, imagining already school over in the afternoon and the way she would have to run to get away from the stones and mudballs. She and Ned would both have to run, cutting across muddy fields, with the boys laughing behind them. . . . "White trash!" They were white trash, everybody knew that, and what it meant was that people were going to throw stones: you had to get hit sooner or later.

5

New Jersey: tomato season. They came up together in a rickety old school bus. Carleton sat with Nancy, and across the aisle Clara sat with Rodwell and the baby, Roosevelt, on her lap. The bus was noisy and every one was eating or smoking; Carleton took a bottle out of a canvas bag on the floor now and then, and he and Nancy drank from it.

"I never been this far north before," Nancy said.

"Well, I been here before," said Carleton.

His voice was flatter than it used to be; sometimes it surprised him. When Nancy acted like a young girl and made her eyes get big, he wanted to grab the back of her neck and shake her. He knew she was pretending and he hated people who pretended anything.

"You been everywhere, the whole world over. I never knew anybody like you," she said.

In the other seat Clara was holding Rodwell and Roosevelt apart. Rodwell must have been teasing the baby. "She's a

49

real cute kid," Nancy always said of Clara. "I never seen any kid nice like her, her age." Clara was nice because she made supper if Nancy didn't feel up to it: she could make macaroni with cheese, and hot dogs, and rice with cheese. She could sweep out the single room they'd be living in, place after place, and if she didn't like Nancy she gave no sign of it. "She's done real well without no mother and everything," Nancy said vaguely.

"Her mother taught her a lot," Carleton would say.

He stared out the window. It was cloudy with a light film of grease from where he'd leaned his head before. Outside there was nothing—countryside. He did not bother looking at anything, but populated the empty land with running and leaping figures, horses of a kind he thought he remembered from back home, beautiful long-haired collies, and visions of himself running effortlessly alongside the bus. Nancy had a certain close, sweet, stale odor about her that he liked, but he did not like to listen to her chatter. She was good in a group of people, especially when everyone had been drinking; she could make them all laugh and the men all liked her. But when they were alone her little exclamations and her slow pretended awe over Clara made him tired.

Carleton imagined a horse thundering along outside, keeping perfect time with the bus but having nothing to do with it. He could feel the horse's muscles plunge and jerk, could feel the soft earth give way beneath its hoofs. . . . He did not like to listen to Nancy because behind her talk he could sometimes hear Pearl, the way she had been years ago. Many years ago. In the end, Pearl had been just like a baby. She had had no mind at all. The doctor had been angry at Carleton but wouldn't quite look at him, because of Pearl's being pregnant—this was in one of the little towns. The doctor had been younger than Carleton but still he had thought he could talk like that to Carleton, his words coming out fast and harsh enough for anyone from the South, and Carleton had stood there taking it, frightened and helpless. He remembered the young man's glasses, which were taped together with white adhesive tape right in the middle, and the way they kept sliding down his nose while he talked angrily at Carleton without ever looking at him. Carleton had been respectful and had tried to understand what the man said, but it came fast and angry; he wasn't used to anyone talking that fast. Pearl was lying on one of the mattresses in the cabin moaning. "This should never have happened," the doctor had said. "What wrong with you? Don't you people ever—" Carleton had no interest in the vague undefined world of what should not have been; there was enough to bother with in this world. So he tried to understand what was happening. Pearl had died because of some bleeding, and the baby had died too. Carleton remembered blood everywhere, and flies. Clara and the other kids were in the foreman's cabin, where there were two rooms. He remembered all that but it was not exactly clear why she had died, it "just happened," as people in the camp said.

Nancy was about eighteen. She was the daughter of a man Carleton knew and she wanted to leave Florida, so she just ran away with Carleton and his kids. She had dark hair cut very short and jagged about her face, exposing the tips of her soft ears, and when she laughed she squinted with hilarity— everything was so funny, she made you want to laugh along with her. That was one thing about the bus and the camps, Carleton thought; everyone was quick to laugh. They were good people. Right now they were laughing on the bus, carrying on. Just behind him was a family from Texas, Bert something and his wife, both of their faces tanned and round, and across the way were two of their children, Rosalie and Sylvia Anne, and behind them two more children—two boys. Carleton didn't like so many kids but he liked Bert and his wife because nothing got them down. Rosalie was Clara's best friend, but Carleton didn't like her quick clever eyes. They all liked to laugh. Carleton didn't mind hearing them, but he was different and thought of himself as different: he was better than these people, whose parents had traveled on the season too, because his family owned land and were farmers and he was about ready to go back there himself. The problem was that in 1933 everyone had it bad.

"I sure do like New Jersey. We're in it now," Nancy said. She was talking with Bert and his wife. "I s'pose you been up here too?"

"Look, I been all over," Bert said.

They laughed at this or at some comical twitching of his face. Bert always made everyone laugh, especially women. Carleton stared out the window at his leaping figures and saw that they jumped and twisted with a freedom that was almost desperate—there he was himself, free, able to glide along inches above the ground, easily outdistancing this old bus. A young Carleton, running along, letting his arms swing— The Texas couple started talking about something that had happened back home, a hurricane, and Carleton tried to shut his mind off since he'd heard this four or five times already.

He concentrated on his running figures but Bert's voice kept coming through.

Bert was a thin, earnest man of about forty, with a meek bald head shining through his hair. But his earnestness and his meekness kept giving way to big mocking good-natured grins; he couldn't stop grinning. His wife had no face that Carleton could remember. It was just a woman's face.

"Somebody with no head?" Nancy shrieked.

"It was a nigger. We all seen it ourselves," Bert said.

Nancy giggled. "You're kiddin' me!"

"Honey, I ain't kiddin' you. Why for would I kid you?"

"Seen worse things than that," his wife said, pushing forward. "Don't you believe me? That was one real hard storm in Galveston."

"What's Galveston?" said Nancy.

"Yeah, we seen some sights," said the woman enthusiastically. Her voice slowed as she raked through debris and peeked into darkened ruins of houses. "A funnel come right down out of the sky—"

Carleton squirmed in his seat. The harder he stared at the figures the less clear they became, as if they were afraid of a funnel sweeping down out of the sky and destroying them. It was like a dream: when you tried to keep it going, it faded away. He heard the Texas couple's friendly drawling voices beating against him and felt a sudden violent hatred for them, even for Nancy: they were stupid, they didn't understand! They belonged in this life because their families hadn't been any better. They could see that Carleton was different and when they talked to him they were serious; they didn't fool around with him. But he didn't care about what they thought. It was other people he wanted to take him seriously, men who hired day labor on the roads or for digging trenches and pole holes. Those men had different, shrewd faces. They talked faster and didn't bother to joke and laugh apologetically during every pause. They always said to Carleton, "There's men of our own that ain't got work. . . . Nobody's building right now. . . . My brother wants a job too, but. . . . You're from the camp outside town, huh . . .?"

Carleton always stood straight and was conscious of his muscular arms and shoulders and legs, but it was hard work to keep his shoulders back the right way when he was used to stooping over all the time. And his face, too—he had to practice to make it like the faces of men outside. Outside the labor camps. In the camps, people grinned and let their faces go, their muscles sagged, their mouths were opened because

52

it was easier that way to take the heat; but in town Carleton had to make everything tight and taut and hard as if he were about to be in a fight. He was convinced that this would work if it was some other year than it was. In a year or two he would be all right.

The bus had turned off the highway and was heading down a dirt road. Everyone was hot and hungry; the babies were crying. Carleton felt a ball of something hard in his stomach that must have been hunger, so he sucked at the bottle of whisky again. It hurt as it went down, then it stopped hurting.

"His hair bleaches out light as some man in the movies," Nancy said proudly. She stroked Carleton's upper arm. She was talking to the couple from Texas and both of them were probably looking at him, wondering why he didn't turn around and be friendly. . . . Well, let them wonder; let them go to hell. He hated them and everyone on the bus except Nancy and Clara and his kids, and if they all died it wouldn't mean anything to him, they were just trash. . . . He imagined the bus crashing and them dying in the flames, except his own family getting free and safe. Little thrills of excitement rose in him when he thought this way. He could imagine himself jumping out of the wreckage, jumping clear. And his kids in his arms. Clara, Rodwell, Roosevelt. . . . Then they could walk away and go somewhere else to live. That was what it would be like to be free.

The camp was just off the dirt road, but hidden by a little scrubby orchard. When they got off the school bus everyone felt the ground wobble. Carleton looked anxiously about to see what it was like. Nancy helped Roosevelt down. "He shouldn't ought to do that in his pants, old as he is," she scolded. "You got to teach him better, honey. You're his sister."

"I thought he was better," said Clara.

The open ground before them was cluttered with junk. In the very center was a burnt spot and pieces of junk that couldn't burn were still lying there, blackened. On both sides were shacks, whitewashed some time ago. Out at the other end was a field that was probably a tomato field. Carleton shielded his eyes and looked over that way—heat waves glimmered there like water. "They painted the places up nice, that was nice of them," Nancy said. She was carrying her clothes and other things rolled up in a quilt. "What do you think, honey?"

"Looks all right," said Carleton.

They were assigned to their houses. Carleton never looked at the crew recruiter, who talked just as loud to everyone—Carleton as well as those old deaf bastards who could hardly walk—and who pretended that Carleton wasn't as good as he was himself. This crew recruiter also drove the bus to make a little more money.

"This'll suit us fine. Ain't this fine?" Nancy said.

"Somebody left some clothes for us," Clara said, picking something up off the floor.

They were always happy on the first day. Carleton stood with his hands on his hips and looked around the shack. It was just one room but it was bigger than the last one. There were some cobwebs and dead insects and some junk on the floor, but Clara and Nancy would take care of that. Carleton said nothing and let them unpack. He tested the light bulb and it worked. That was good. He plugged in the hot plate and that worked too. With his knee he prodded the mattresses; they were all right. When he was finished he jumped down from the doorstep and stood in front of the shack with his hands still on his hips.

Each of the shacks was numbered. Theirs was ∂. Carleton stared at this figure in disgust, to think that he would have to live in a shanty with a six painted backwards on it, as if he himself had been stupid enough to do that! Children were already out playing around the shacks. The shacks were propped up off the ground on concrete blocks and some of them did not look very stable. Carleton walked slowly along, his hands on his hips as if he owned everything. Back between the shacks were old cardboard boxes and washtubs. Some were turned over, others were right side up and filled with rain water. He knew that if he went over to look he'd see long thin worms swimming gracefully in the tubs. Out in front of some of the shacks were big packing crates filled with trash. Some kids were already picking through them.

"Roosevelt, get the hell out of that crap!" Carleton said.

He cuffed the boy on the face. Roosevelt had a narrow head and light brown hair that grew out too thin, so that he looked like a little old man at times. There were hard circular things on his head, crusty rings that had come from nowhere, and two of his teeth had been kicked out in a fight with some other kids. He shrank away from Carleton and ran off. "You stay out of other people's goddam garbage," Carleton said. The other children waited for him to get past. They were afraid of him.

The rest of the men were outside now, waiting. They spent their time working or drinking; when they had nothing to do, their arms were idle and uneasy. Two of them squatted down in the shade of a scrawny tree and took out a deck of cards. "Want to try it, Walpole?" one said.

"You don't have no money," Carleton said sullenly.

"Do you?"

"I don't play for fun. You don't have no money, it's a waste of my time."

"You got lots of money yourself?"

The Texas man, Bert, appeared in the doorway of a shanty, stretching his arms. He had taken off his shirt. His chest was sunken and bluish-white, but he looked happy, as if he'd just come home.

"C'mon play with us, Walpole," he said.

Carleton made a contemptuous gesture. He had some money saved and maybe he could double it if he played with them, but he had come to despise their odors and stained teeth and constant, repetitious talk; they were just trash.

"I got no heart for it," he said.

He walked by. He could hear them shuffling cards. "We don't go out till the mornin'," someone said. Carleton did not glance around. His eyes were taken up by other things, drawn back and forth along the rows of cabins as if looking for something familiar. Some sign, some indication of promise. There were a number of sparrows and blackbirds picking at something on the ground; Carleton tried not to look at it, but saw it anyway—a small animal, rotted. It made him angry to think that the farmer who owned this camp didn't bother to bury something like that. It was dirty, it was filthy. The whole camp ought to be burned down. . . . And the junk from last year, last year's garbage still lying around. Carleton spat in disgust.

He had left the packed-down area between the shacks and was looking now out over a field. The tomato plants were pale green, dusty, healthy. Carleton could see in his mind's eye the dull red tomatoes, rising and falling as if in a dream, and his own hands reaching out to snatch them. Out and down and around and back, in a mechanical, graceful, endless movement. Out and down, tugging at the stem, and then around and back, putting the tomato gently in the container—then inching ahead on his heels to get the next plant. And on

55

and on. He would squat for a while and then kneel; the women and kids and old men knelt right away.

It used to be that he would dream about picking after he had worked all day, but now he dreamed about it even before he worked. And the dreams were not just night-dreams either, but ghostly visions that could come to him in the brightest sunlight.

"Son of a bitch," Carleton muttered.

He turned and shaded his eyes to look back over the camp. He saw now that it was the same camp they'd been coming to for years. Even the smells were the same. Off to the right, down an incline, were two outhouses as always; it would smell violently down there, but the smell would be no surprise. That was the safe thing about these camps: there were no surprises. Carleton took a deep breath and looked out over the camp site, where the sun poured brilliantly down on the clutter: rain-rotted posts with drooping gray clotheslines, abandoned shoes, bottles of glinting red and green, tin cans all washed clean by the rain of many months, boards, rags, broken glass, wire, parts of barrels, and, at either side of the camp, rusted iron pipes rising up out of the ground and topped by faucets. A slow constant drip fell from the faucets and had eaten holes into the ground. Alongside one of the shanties was an old stove; maybe it was for everyone's use.

It was another bad year, Carleton thought, but it would get better. Things had been bad for a long time for everyone—they talked about rich men killing themselves, even. The kind of work Carleton did was sure, steady work. Up on high levels you can open a newspaper or get a telephone call and find out you're finished, and then you have to kill yourself; with people like Carleton it was possible just to laugh. It was the times themselves that were bad, Carleton thought. It was keeping him down, sitting on him. But he would never give up. When things began to get better—it would start up in New York City—then men who were smarter than others could work themselves up again, swimming upward through all the mobs of stupid, stinking people like the ones Carleton had to work with. They were just trash, the men squatting there and tossing cards around, and the fat women hanging in doorways and grinning out at one another: Well, we come a long way! Ain't we come a long way? Some of these people had been doing field work now for twenty, thirty, even forty years, and none of them had any more to show for it than the clothes they were wearing and the junk they'd brought rolled up in quilts. . . . This was true of Carleton but he had a family to keep going; if he didn't have that family he would have saved lots of money by now.

He did have about ten dollars, wadded up carefully in his pocket. Nancy knew nothing about it and what she didn't know wouldn't hurt her. It struck Carleton sometimes that he should spend this money on Clara—get her a little plastic purse or a necklace. He did not feel that way about his other children. Mike had run off a while ago and nobody missed him; he'd been trouble at the end. Carleton had had to give it to him so hard that the kid's mouth had welled with blood, he'd almost choked on his own blood, and that taught him who was boss. Sharleen was back in Florida, married. She had married a boy who worked at a garage; she liked to brag he had a steady job and he could work indoors. But she never brought the boy home for Carleton to see. So he had said to her: "You're a whore, just like your mother." He hadn't meant anything by that. He hadn't thought about what it meant. But after that he had never seen Sharleen again. He was glad to get rid of her and her darting nervous eyes.

The fear he saw in his children's faces did not make him like them. Even Clara showed it at times. That wincing, cautious look only provoked him and made him careless with his blows; Nancy had enough sense to know that. What Carleton liked was peace, quiet, calm, the way Clara would crawl up on his knee and tell him about school or her girl friends or things she thought were funny, or the way Nancy embraced him and stroked his back.

Carleton was hungry. He headed back toward the cabin. The square now was filled with children and women airing out quilts and blankets on the clotheslines. Bert's wife was flapping something out the doorway. She had a beet-red face and surprised, tufted hair. "Nice day!" she said. Carleton nodded. Two boys ran shrieking in front of him. He saw Clara and Rosalie by the men who were playing cards. Clara ran out to him and took his hand. He thought how strange that was: a girl runs out and takes his hand, he is her father, she is his daughter. He felt warm. "Rosalie's pa won somethin' an's goin' to give it to her!" Clara cried. Carleton let himself be led over reluctantly to the card players. Bert was making whooping noises as he tossed down his cards. He chortled, he hooted, he tapped another man's chest with the back of his fingers, daintily. Carleton's shadow fell on his head and shoulders and he grinned up at Carleton. Behind Bert were the rest of his kids. The girl's hair was a frantic red-brown, like her father's, and she had her father's friendly, amazed, mocking eyes. "Here y'are, honey," he said. He dropped some things in her opened hands. Everyone laughed at her excitement.

"What's this here?" Rosalie said. She held up a small metallic object. Clara ran over and stared at it.

"That's a charm," said Bert.

One of the men said: "Don't you know nothin'? That ain't a charm!"

"What is it, then?"

"A medal," the man said. He was a little defensive. "A holy medal, you put it somewheres and it helps you."

"Helps you with what?"

Rosalie and Clara were examining it. Carleton bent to see that it was a cheap religious medal, in the shape of a coin, with the raised figure of some saint or Christ or God Himself. Carleton didn't know much about these things; they made him feel a little embarrassed.

"It's nice, I like it," Rosalie said. The other things her father had given her were a pencil with a broken point and a broken key chain.

"How does it work?" said Clara.

"You put it in your pocket or somethin', I don't know. It don't always work," the man said.

"Are you Cathlic or somethin'?" Bert said, raising his eyebrows.

"Shit—"

"Isn't that a Cathlic thing?"

"It's just some medal I found laying around."

Carleton cut through their bickering by saying something that surprised all of them, even him. "You got any more of them?"

"No."

"What're they for?"

"Jesus, I don't know. . . . S'post to help a little," the man said, looking away.

Carleton went back to the shanty, where Nancy was sitting in the doorway. She wore tight faded slacks and a shirt carelessly buttoned, and Carleton always liked the way she smoked cigarettes. That was something Pearl hadn't done. "Y'all moved in?" Carleton said. He rubbed the back of her neck and she smiled, closing her eyes. The sunlight made her hair glint in thousands of places so that it looked as if it were a secret place, a secret forest you might enter and get lost in.

Carleton stared at her without really seeing her. He saw the gleaming points of light and her smooth pinkish ear.

Finally he said, "Don't think you made no mistake, huh, comin' up here with me? All this ways?"

She laughed to show how wrong he was. "Like hell," she said.

"You think New Jersey looks good, huh?"

"Better than any place I ever was before."

"Don't never count on nothing," Carleton said wisely.

Which turned out to be good advice: that evening the crew leader, a puffy-faced, lumpy man Carleton had always hated, came to the camp to tell them it was all off.

"Come all the way here an' the fuckin' bastard changed his mind, says he's gonna let them rot out there," the man shouted. Flecks of saliva flew from his angry mouth. "Gonna let them rot! Don't want them picked! He says the price ain't high enough an's gonna let them rot an' the hell with us!"

Carleton had heard announcements like this before and just stood back, resting on his heels to absorb the surprise. Around him people were making angry wailing noises.

"What the hell is it?" Nancy said faintly.

"It's his tomatoes, he can let them rot if he wants," Carleton said, his face stiff as if he wanted to let everyone know he was miles away from this, miles and years away. It did not touch him.

It turned out finally that they got a contract to pick at another farm the next morning, so they had to ride there in the school bus, an hour each way, and could still stay at the camp site—it was the only one around—if they paid that farmer rent (a dollar a day for a cabin); and out at the second farm they had to pay that farmer for a lunch of rice and spaghetti out of the can and beans out of the can and bread (fifty cents for each lunch, thirty cents for kids); and they had to pay the crew leader who was also the recruiter and the bus driver for the ride (ten cents each way, including kids), and then had to pay the recruiter twenty cents on each basket for finding them this other job, because he was their recruiter, and, when that job ended, they had to pitch in to give him fifty cents apiece so that he could ride around the country looking for another farm, which he did locate in a day or two, some fifty miles away, a ride that would cost them fifteen cents each way. At the end of the first day, when they were paid, Carleton won five dollars in a poker game and felt his heart pound with a fierce, certain joy. The

59

rest of these people were like mud on the bottom of a crick, that soft heavy mud where snakes and turtles slept. But he, Carleton, could rise up out of that mud and leave them far behind.

6

One day Clara and Rosalie went to town. The town was about seven miles from camp and the workers often passed through it on their way to and from the farms they were day-hauled to. Whenever they rode through, Clara and her friend stared hungrily out the window, trying to catch someone's eye. Clara thought that towns were elaborate, with their crisscrossings of streets and their stores built so close together, one right on top of another. She wondered if you could get lost in a town.

Nancy had said bitterly that it wasn't right for Clara to take an afternoon off, she was a big hungry girl who always ate more than her share, but Carleton said she was to shut up. Clara could go. It was Rosalie's birthday that day; she was thirteen. Rosalie's father gave her fifty cents to spend, for a present, and Carleton gave Clara a dime. Waiting out by the road for someone to come along and give them a ride, the girls were excited and uneasy. When their eyes met they laughed together breathlessly.

"Guess you showed that bitch Nancy," Rosalie snickered.

"The hell with her," said Clara.

"Thinks she's so smart, comin' along with you guys," said Rosalie. "I wouldn't let no old bitch like that in my house if my ma died."

"She don't bother me much."

They fell silent. A car was approaching.

"What if it's some bastard that tries to get smart?" Rosalie said.

"Nobody's gonna do that with us," Clara said. But she felt her throat muscles tighten as the car came closer. She hoped it would go past.

The car went past.

"Some goddam selfish son of a bitch," Rosalie said, rubbing her nose.

A few more cars went by. A truck went by, but it slowed before it passed them. The girls waited patiently. When a car approached they were serious and polite, their lips closed. Rosalie's hair had been washed and brushed so that it did not look so stringy. Clara's hair hung down past her shoulders and was a gleaming ash-blond, like her father's. But the girls' faces, lost inside their long hair, were thin and nervous. People said Rosalie looked like a rat, the way her eyes darted. She had the look of someone about to be hit. Clara had her father's eyes—a frank, puzzled blue—and her cheekbones were high like her father's, giving her a suspicious, hungry look. But when she smiled her face was transformed and she was almost pretty. Both girls had on their best dresses and both dresses were a little too small for them, uncomfortable under the arms.

They got a ride finally with a man who did not look like a farmer. "Room for both of you up front," he said kindly. They slid in. The man drove along slowly as if not wanting to jar them. The girls stared out at the familiar road; it looked different, seen from a car window instead of from the bus. From time to time the man glanced over at them. He was about forty, with slow eyes. "You girls from the camp back there?" he said. Clara, who was in the middle, nodded without bothering to look at him. She was inhaling carefully the odors of an automobile. It was the first time she had ever been in one; she sat with her scraped legs stuck out, her feet flat on the floor. Rosalie was investigating a dirty ashtray attached to the door, poking around with her fingers.

"Where are you girls from?" the man said.

"Not from nowhere," Clara said politely. She spoke the way she spoke to schoolteachers, who only asked questions for a few minutes and then moved on to someone else.

"Not from nowhere?" the man laughed. "What about you, Red? Where you from?"

"Texas," said Rosalie in the same voice Clara had used.

"Texas? You're real far from home then. But ain't you sisters?"

"Yeah, we're sisters," Clara said quickly. "I'm from Texas too."

"You people travel all over, huh. Must be lots of fun."

When the girls did not reply he went on, "You must work hard, huh? Your pa makes you work hard for him, don't he?" He tapped on Clara's leg. "You got yourself some scratches on your nice little legs. That's from out in the fields, huh?"

Clara glanced at her legs in surprise.

"Them cuts don't hurt, do they?" said the man.

"No."

"Ought to have some bandages or somethin' on them. Iodine. You know what that is?"

Clara was staring out at the houses they passed. Small frame farmhouses, set back from the road at the end of long narrow lanes. She squinted to see if there were any cats or dogs around. In a field there were several horses, their heads drooping to the grass and their bodies gaunt and fragile.

"Pa had a horse once," she said to Rosalie.

"What was that?" said the man.

Clara said nothing. The man said, "Did you say they hurt?"

Clara looked at him. He had skin like skin on a potato pulled out of the ground. His smile looked as if it had been stretched on his mouth by someone else.

"I mean the scratches on your legs. Do they hurt?"

"No," said Clara. She paused. "I got a dime, I'm gonna buy somethin' in town."

"Is that so?" said the man. He squirmed with pleasure at being told this. "What are you gonna buy?"

"Some nice things."

"Can't get much with a dime, little girl."

Clara frowned.

"Your pa only gave you a dime?"

Clara said nothing. The man leaned over and waved a finger in front of Rosalie. "Your pa ought to be nicer to two nice little girls like you." They were approaching a gas station. The road had turned from dirt to blacktop, getting ready for town. "Could be there's some soda pop at this garage," the man said. "Anybody like some?"

Clara and Rosalie both said yes at once.

The man stopped and an old man came out to wait on him, wearing a cowboy hat made of straw. Clara watched every part of the ceremony; she was fascinated by the moving dials on the gas pump. The driver, standing outside with his foot on the running board to show he owned the car, bent down once in a while to smile in at the girls. "Wouldn't mind some pop myself," he said. They said nothing. His foot disappeared after a moment and he went into the gas station. It was a small wooden building, once painted white. As soon as the screen door flopped closed behind him, Rosalie opened the glove compartment and looked through the things in there—some rags, a flashlight, keys. "Goddam junk," Rosalie said. She put the keys in her pocket. "Never can tell what keys might open," she said vaguely. Clara was looking in the back seat. One brown glove lay on the floor, stiff with dirt.

She lunged over and got it, then sat on it because there was nowhere to hide it.

The man came back carrying three bottles of pop, all orange. As he drove he drank his, making loud satisfied noises. The girls drank theirs down as fast as they could.

"Ain't this good for a hot day?" he said, sighing.

They were nearing the town now. To Clara and Rosalie this town was very big. It was ringed with houses that were not farmhouses and buildings that did not seem to have anything for sale in them. There were areas of wild land, then more houses, a gas station, a railroad crossing, and then before them on an incline was the main street—lined with old red-brown brick buildings that reared up to face each other.

"You girls never said where you were goin'. I bet you're goin' to the show."

"Yeah," said Rosalie.

"You like them shows?"

He had slowed the car. It came to a stop. Clara was surprised to see nothing much about them. They had just crossed the railroad tracks and now there was a great field with old automobiles parked in it.

"The show don't begin till five o'clock, so you got lots of time till then. Two cute little girls like you. You want to come visit at my house?"

They sat in silence. Finally Rosalie said cautiously, "We got to be home again fast."

"How fast is fast?" the man said loudly, trying to make a joke. He was pressing against Clara while he talked. "Only this minute got into town; you ain't already goin' back, are you?"

"I need to get somethin' for my leg, my leg hurts," Clara said. She was leaning over against Rosalie to get away from him.

"Does your leg hurt?" the man said in surprise.

"Stings real bad," said Clara. She could sense Rosalie listening to her, puzzled. Clara did not know what she was saying but her voice seemed to know. It was not nervous and it went on by itself. "It hurt when I fell down yesterday and made me cry."

"Did it make you cry?" the man said. He put his hand on her knee, cupping it gently. She stared at his hand. It had small black hairs on its back, and fingernails that were ragged and edged with dirt; but it was a hand she felt sorry for. "A little girl like you oughtn't to be workin' in the fields. There's

63

a law against it, you know. They can put your pa in jail for it."

"Nobody's gonna put my pa in jail," Clara said fiercely. "He'd kill them. He killed a man anyway, one time." She looked at the man to see how he would take this. "He killed him with a knife but I'm not s'post to tell."

The man smiled to show he did not quite believe this.

"I ain't s'post to tell," Clara said. "They let him go 'cause the other man started it an' my pa was only doin' right."

She looked at the man. A strange dizzy sensation overcame her, a sense of daring and excitement. She met his gaze with her own and smiled slowly, feeling her lips part slowly to show her teeth. She and the man looked at each other for a moment. He took his hand away from her knee. Something strange seemed to be happening but Clara did not know what it was. She seemed to be doing something, keeping something going. The sun was warm and dazzling. Then she forgot what she was doing, lost control, and her smile went away. She was a child again. She leaned against Rosalie to get away from the man's smell.

"We got to get out now," she said.

Rosalie tried the door handle.

"That door opens hard. It's tricky," the man said. His face was damp and he kept looking at Clara. "You got to be smart to open it. . . ."

"It don't come open," Rosalie muttered.

"It's a little tricky. . . ."

Clara held her breath because she didn't want to smell him. He leaned over to tug at the door handle, pretending to have trouble with it.

"Open it up!" Rosalie said. Clara's heart was pounding so hard she could not say anything. The man grinned apologetically at her, his face right up against hers, and finally he got the door open. Rosalie jumped out. Clara started to slide out but he took hold of her arm.

"Listen, little girl," he said, "how old are you?"

Clara slashed at his hand with her nails. He winced and released her. "Goddam old asshole!" Clara cried, jumping out. "Go fuck yourself! Take this—it ain't no good!" She threw the glove at his face and ran away. She and Rosalie jumped the ditch and ran into the field, laughing. She could hear Rosalie laughing ahead of her.

They hid behind one of the junked cars. The man was still parked by the road. Clara peered through a yellowed, cracked old windshield and watched him. He leaned around,

64

looking outside like a lost dog. Clara pressed her knuckles against her mouth to keep from laughing.

"Think he's gonna tell the police?" said Rosalie.

"My pa will kill him if he does."

Finally he closed the door and drove away.

It was a warm, bright afternoon. Both girls forgot about the man in the car and looked around, ready to be surprised and pleased. The junked automobiles all around them looked as if they had crawled here and died; their grills were like teeth lowered into the earth. The girls walked along, bending to look inside at the tattered seats and the torn upholstery. Once Clara slid into an old car and turned the steering wheel, making a noise with her mouth that was supposed to be the sound of an engine. She tapped at the horn but it did not work.

"I'm gonna have a car like this, only a real one," she said.

They kept smiling, they didn't know why. Nothing smelled bad here. There was only a faint metallic odor, and the odor from occasional pools of oil. No smell of garbage or sewage. A few dragonflies flew about, but no flies. And every car was something new to look at. There were old convertibles with the tops half ripped off, as if someone had attacked them with knives. There were old trucks that looked saddest of all, like tough strong men who couldn't keep going. There were red cars, yellow cars, black cars, the paint peeling and rusty or overlaid with another color so that the two colors together made a third strange color that was like a wound. Clara could not examine anything close enough. They had come to town and already they were seeing things they'd never seen before. Windows everywhere were cracked as if jerking back from something in astonishment; the cracks were like spider webs, like frozen ripples in water. Clara stared and stared, and what she saw got transformed into new, strange things. A piece of rubber was a snake, sleeping in the sun. A scraped mark on a car was a flower, ready to fall into pieces. In a yellowed car window was a face that might have been under water, so blocked out by the sun behind it that she could not make it out—it was her own face. Clara and Rosalie stared at everything. They kept smoothing their dresses down, wiping their hands on them, as if they'd been invited to visit and were ashamed of the way they looked.

"This one here—lookit. What's wrong with this?" Clara said sadly. The car was a dull, dark blue and looked new to her. She tried to imagine her father sitting in the driver's seat, one arm hanging loosely out the window. They looked under the hood and saw some weeds: no engine. "My father used to have a car like this, in Florida," Clara said.

They climbed up on the hood of one old truck, then up on the roof of the cab. The metal surface was hot and smelled hot. On the roof of the truck was an old tire. Clara sat on it and hugged her knees.

"Why'd you act so funny with that bastard back there?" Rosalie said. Her freckles gave her a sandy, quizzical look. "You acted real funny."

"I didn't either."

"Yes you did."

"Like hell I did."

"You talked different—like Nancy or somebody."

"I never talked like Nancy!"

"I was scared, I thought you an' him were gonna leave me," Rosalie sneered. "Thought you were gonna run off with him."

Clara laughed contemptuously, but she felt nervous. She knew what Rosalie meant but was just as puzzled over it as Rosalie was.

After a while they jumped down. Rosalie lost her balance and had to push herself up off the ground with one hand. She made a face as if she'd hurt herself. "You all right?" Clara said. But Rosalie straightened up and was all right in the next instant. The religious medal her father had given her had come out and caught the sunlight.

They made their way through the cars and came out to the road.

"Clara, you afraid?"

"No."

They came into town on the main street, heading right in. Both felt their knees tremble a little. Their eyes grabbed at people's faces as if looking for someone they knew. Once in a while people stared back at them. A boy of about sixteen, leaning against a car, watched them go by and grinned at them.

"Thinks he's so smart," Rosalie muttered.

They lingered in front of store windows, pressing their hands and noses against the glass. When they moved on there were spots where they'd touched the glass. They stared at the bottles and boxes and pictures of handsome people smiling out at them in the drug store window, and at the old dead flies at the bottom, and at the strange green thing made of glass with water in it that hung down from a gold chain. The smell of food made their mouths water violently. They

moved on slowly, fascinated by the great confused display in
the five-and-ten window. Clara tried to look at everything,
every mysterious object, by itself. There were skirts and dresses
laid out, and socks, and lamps, and spools of thread, and
purses, toys with wheels, pencils, book bags like the kind they
had noticed other children bringing to school in the past.
Pearl necklaces, silver bracelets, jars of perfume, lipstick in
gleaming gold tubes. And bags of candy, cellophane bags so
that you could see the chocolate candies inside. Clara's eyes
ached.

"C'mon, let's go in," Rosalie said. She pulled at Clara and
Clara hung back. "What's wrong, you afraid?"

"I don't want to go in."

"What? Why not?"

She stared at Clara contemptuously, then turned to go in.
Clara watched her push the door open and walk right inside
as if she had been doing things like this all her life. After a
second she hurried in behind Rosalie. Rosalie said, "I been in
stores like this lots of times."

There were a few other people browsing through the store,
all women. Clara and Rosalie followed one young woman
who carried a baby, anxious to imitate her. She paused to
examine a pair of scissors. Clara came up to the counter
after the woman left and looked at the scissors, wishing she
could buy them. Nancy would like her better if she brought
her back a present like that.

She felt the dime in her pocket again. Her fingers were
beginning to smell from it. Rosalie had her mother's black
change purse out. She counted the coins inside. "I guess I'm
gonna buy somethin'," she said. Clara looked around shyly. A
salesgirl was leaning across a counter to talk to another
salesgirl. Both wore cotton dresses and looked quite young.
Clara stared at them, trying to make out their conversation;
she could not imagine what it would be like to be one of
those girls.

"I'm gonna work in one of these places someday," she said
to Rosalie.

"Yeah, lots of luck."

Rosalie was examining tubes of lipstick. She handled them
carefully and with respect. The salesgirl, a woman of about
twenty-five, watched them without much interest. She had
glamorous red lips and arched eyebrows. Clara stared at her
until the girl's expression changed to let her know that she
should look at something else. "These are all nice," Rosalie
said, loud enough for the salesgirl to hear. Clara stood behind

her, a few feet from the counter. She was fascinated by the way everything gleamed. The lipstick tubes were made of gold. There were some small plastic combs for sale, all colors; they cost only 10¢. Clara wanted one of the combs suddenly, but she had intended to buy Roosevelt a present with part of her dime.

"I wish I could get one of them," she muttered in Rosalie's ear.

"Go on, buy one."

"I can't. . . ."

"I'm gonna buy this one," Rosalie said. She handed the tube of lipstick and the fifty-cent piece to the girl. Clara watched each part of the procedure, so that when she was a salesgirl she would know what to do. She thought she could do it as well as this salesgirl, who was a little slow.

"Thanks an' y'all come back," the girl said tonelessly.

Rosalie walked over to another aisle and Clara followed her. Rosalie took the lipstick out of the bag and dabbed some on her mouth, then she rubbed her lips together. "You want some?" she said to Clara. Clara liked the way the lipstick smelled. It was a smell she could not place, something new and glamorous. "I better not, Pa might get mad," she said sadly.

"Hey, why didn't you buy one of them combs?"

"I only got a dime."

"What're you gonna buy, then?"

"Some toy for Roosevelt. . . ."

"Hell, get something for yourself."

They came to the toy counter. A fat blond woman with cheerful pink cheeks was in charge. "Can I help you little ladies?" she said. Clara and Rosalie did not look at her. Their faces were warm.

"How much is that there?" Clara said. It was the first time she had talked to a salesgirl and her words came all in a rush.

"That airplane? Honey, that's twelve cents."

Clara stared at the airplane. Then she realized she could not afford it. "I can give you the two cents," Rosalie said, nudging her.

"No, never mind."

"Oh, Christ . . ."

Clara could feel the salesgirl and Rosalie watching her. She pointed to a bag of marbles. "How much is this?"

"Honey, that's a quarter. That's expensive."

"Go on and buy the airplane, what the hell," Rosalie said.

She was leaning against the counter in a way that surprised Clara; she looked as if she'd been shopping in stores like this all her life.

"How much is this?" Clara said, pointing at something blindly.

"Honey, that's got real rubber tires, you see them? That's expensive."

Clara swallowed. Her face was hot. She would remember this moment all her life, she thought—the colorful toys, her sweaty fingers closed about the dime, the saleswoman's pity, Rosalie's contempt. "This one," she said, "what about this?"

"That's just a dime, honey."

It was an ugly little doll without clothes. Clara did not want it but had to buy it. "Here," she said, thrusting the dime at the woman. "I'll buy this."

She stared at the saleswoman's pudgy hands, waiting. The saleswoman did everything quickly and dropped the doll in a bag. "Here y'are, sweetie," she said, stooping so that her smile would be in Clara's range of vision. "You come back again real soon, huh?"

Clara took the bag from her and hurried away.

Outside, she discovered she was trembling. Rosalie ran out behind her. "You act crazy or somethin'," she said. "What's wrong with you?"

"Nothin'."

"Why the hell'd you buy that crappy old thing?"

"Shut up."

"Shut up yourself—"

"You shut up first!"

Clara walked stiffly ahead of Rosalie. Her lips shaped the words she would have liked to say to Rosalie, except she and Rosalie had fought already and she knew Rosalie could beat her.

"Act like goddam stupid white trash," Rosalie hissed.

"You know what you can do."

"I got fifteen cents left, all for myself."

"You know what you can do with it, too."

"Go to hell."

Clara stopped at a curb. There were no cars on the street. She held the paper bag up near her chest so that if anyone looked, they would know she had bought something. Rosalie waited behind her for a few seconds, then Clara turned. The girls looked shyly at each other.

"Let's go up this way," Rosalie said.

She was pointing up a side street. They walked along

together as if they hadn't argued. The street was bounded on both sides by a dirt walk and by buildings that looked empty. One of them was an old church; its windows were boarded up and weeds grew everywhere. "I want to go to church sometime," Clara said.

"We went once, it was lousy. Pa was snorin'."

"Did he fall asleep?"

"He can fall asleep anywhere—out in the field if he wanted to."

"My pa—" Clara thought of what to say, wanting to say something, but she knew she hadn't better say it: that her father sometimes did not even sleep at night, but stumbled outside to walk around and smoke, all by himself. He was like a stranger then, when he woke her up at night, stumbling over her and her brothers on his way out. He would never say anything.

They were passing old frame houses. On a porch two withered little women watched them. Clara and Rosalie lowered their eyes as if in shame at being so young. They walked faster. It was hot in the sunlight but they did not mind. Clara saw that there was a smear of lipstick on Rosalie's lower lip and she felt a tinge of jealousy.

"Okay, kid," Rosalie said, "want to see something?"

She took a comb out of her pocket—a red plastic comb like the ones Clara had seen. "What's that?" Clara said.

"It's for you, stupid."

She held out the comb for Clara.

"Where'd you get that from?"

"From the bean field, stupid."

Clara took it wonderingly. But Rosalie had more to show: another tube of lipstick, this one with flashy pink jewels on it, and a spool of gold thread, and the celluloid airplane, and some tiny limp colored things that Clara could not identify.

"What's that?" she asked breathlessly.

Rosalie pulled them apart. They were made of rubber, blue and red and green. She put the end of one to her mouth and blew. It was a balloon.

Clara clapped her hands over her mouth to stop her laughter. "How'd you get all them things?"

Rosalie held out the airplane to her. "I told you—from the bean field. Ain't you seen things like this out in the bean field?"

"You givin' this to me?"

"For your little brat brother. Go on, take it."

"It's awful nice. . . ."

70

Rosalie shrugged her shoulders. Clara looked at the things, biting her lip. They were such a surprise, such gifts. She tried to run the comb through her hair but it caught right away on some snarls.

She and Rosalie walked along with their arms linked. "You're awful nice, Rosalie," Clara said. Rosalie laughed like a boy. "I shouldn't of been mean, back there," Clara said. "Hey, what if you get caught?"

"So what?"

"What if they put you in jail?"

"I'm gonna get in trouble anyway, so what's the difference?" Rosalie said. Her mouth was twisted down.

"Huh? What kind of trouble?"

"You'll find out."

Their arms fell loose of each other, as if by accident. Rosalie said in a sneering voice, "Bet you'd be afraid to take things." Her face was slightly flushed, as if she had just said something she regretted. "You're a little baby sometimes."

"I don't want no police after me."

"Hell, they don't get you. People holler at you, that's all."

"Did they ever catch you?"

"Sure, three times. So what? Nobody put me in jail."

"Were you scared?"

"The first time."

"Did they tell your pa?"

"So what if they told him?" Rosalie said sharply.

Clara saw some kids coming and wanted to cross the street, but Rosalie wouldn't. The kids—three boys and a gawky, scrawny girl—let them get past, then they began whooping and throwing stones at them. Clara and Rosalie started to run. "Dirty bastards!" Rosalie yelled over her shoulder. The kids behind them yelled too, laughing. A stone hit Clara's back but didn't really hurt, it just made her angry. She and Rosalie ran wildly down an alley, across another dirt lane, and through someone's junk heap. A battered old kettle struck her leg, knocked down from higher up on the pile, and she cried out with pain.

Then they were in a back yard, behind a fence. They stared at each other, panting. Their eyes were big.

"Where are they? Ain't they comin'?"

"I don't hear them——"

They waited. Clara whispered, "I'd like to have a knife like my pa does, to kill them. I'd kill them."

"I would too."

After a while Rosalie looked over the fence. "We might

71

could run out the front way—I don't see nobody back here—"

They caught their breaths and ran, Rosalie first. Down a nice brick walk and out onto the street. Clara kept waiting for someone to yell out the window at them.

"Look at the grass they got here," Rosalie said.

It was like a rug on the ground, green and fine.

"Jesus Christ," Rosalie said. They walked along the street, bumping into each other. They had never seen such nice white houses. "The people that live here got money. They're rich," she said.

"We better get out of here," said Clara.

"Yeah. . . ."

"We better go back. . . ."

Clara was staring at a house some distance from the street. It was a bright clean white like the house in that schoolbook, with trees in the front yard. There were two stained-glass windows in the entryway. For some reason Clara started to cry.

"What the hell?" said Rosalie. "You sick?"

Clara's face felt as if it were breaking up into pieces. The stained-glass windows were blue and dark green with small splotches of yellow. "I could break that window if I wanted to," Clara said bitterly.

"What, them windows?"

"I could break it."

"Well, you ain't goin' to!"

Rosalie pulled her along. She acted nervous. "We better be goin' back, I'm hungry. Ain't you hungry?"

"Or I could take that," Clara said. She was pointing at a flag that hung down from the front porch. The porch had been screened off with dark, green-gray shades.

"Yeah, sure."

"I could take that easy as anything," Clara said. She rubbed her eyes with her hands, as if to make the red and white striped flag smaller, to get it into clear focus so it wouldn't mean anything. "I ain't afraid—"

"You are too."

"Like hell I am."

"You're so smart, go on and take it!"

Clara stepped on the grass. Her thudding heart urged her on, and the next thing she knew she was running and was up on the porch steps, then she was tugging the stick out of its slot. It was a thin little pole that weighed hardly anything. Rosalie stood back on the sidewalk, gawking.

72

"Hey—Clara! Clara!"

But Clara did not listen. She tugged at the stick until it came loose. Then she ran back to Rosalie with her prize, and both girls ran down the street as fast as they could. They began to giggle hysterically. Laughter began deep inside them, rushing up to the surface like bubbles in the soda pop that forgotten man had given them.

7

A month later, about six o'clock in the evening, Nancy was sitting in the doorway, smoking, her legs outstretched in front of her. Both her arms rested comfortably on her stomach, which was beginning now to get big. Clara was scraping food from the supper dishes into a pail. She sang part of a song she heard out in the field:

> *Whispering hope of his coming . . .*
> *Whispering hope . . .*

She had a thin, tuneless, earnest voice. Everyone in the camps sang, even the men. Clara's father did not sing, though. People sang about someone coming to them, someone saving them, about crossing the bar into another world, or about Texas and California, which were like other worlds anyway. Clara asked Rosalie about Texas, was it so special, and Rosalie said she couldn't remember anything. But Rosalie always laughed at everything; she didn't take anything seriously. She was like her father and that whole family. Clara liked to laugh at things too but she was like her father and knew when to stop laughing. In a group of men Carleton would be the first to smile and the first to stop, because he was smartest. Then he would sit back on his heels or turn his face slightly away and wait until the rest of the men finished laughing.

"Clara, get me a beer," Nancy said.

Clara got a bottle of beer out of the cupboard. When Nancy turned to take it from her Clara saw that her face was creased with tiny wrinkles. She was always frowning these days. Clara waited while Nancy opened the bottle and stopped to pick up the bottle cap. Those little caps could cut somebody's feet; Clara went around picking them up in the cabin and around the cabin, outside, where Nancy and Carleton let them roll.

"Is Rosie better now?" Clara said.

"No, she ain't better, and you ain't goin' to go an' find out," Nancy said.

Clara hadn't been able to see Rosalie for four days. Rosalie didn't go out to work in the morning, and when Clara got back on the bus with her family they wouldn't let her go down to see Rosalie. Rosalie's father, Bert, was out working today and Clara had noticed how cheerful and nervous he was—he mixed with work crews from other camps and was always in the center of the loudest group, where people were laughing and talking and maybe passing bottles around. This was against the law. You weren't supposed to mix with the people from a certain camp because they always caused trouble, there were lots of fights, but Bert did whatever he wanted to. He liked everyone.

"Somebody said there was a doctor out," Clara said.

Nancy did not bother to turn. "What's it to you?" She sat with her shoulders slumped inside a soiled shirt of Carleton's. Her hair was stiff with oil and dust from the fields; everything she said or did was slowed down. Clara, who remembered how happy Nancy had been a while ago and how, at night, she used to laugh and whisper from the mattress where she and Carleton lay, felt sorry for her—she had never been jealous of Nancy's happiness, because she thought that anyone's happiness would turn out to be her own someday. Now, Nancy's slurred words and irritated face frightened Clara because there was no reason for them. She could not understand what was wrong.

Rodwell and some other kids ran past the shanty, yelling. Nancy did not bother to look at them. "He better watch out, that big kid's gonna beat him up," Clara said. The kids were gone. They ran between two of the shanties, pounding against them with their fists as they passed, as if they wanted to break the shanties down. Roosevelt was out somewhere, Clara didn't know where. Their father was out talking the way he was every day after supper. When Clara was through with the dishes she'd go out to find him, squatting on the ground with some other men, and when she came up to them she would hear important, serious words that made her proud: "prices," "Roosevelt," "Russia." She did not know what these words meant but liked to hear them because they seemed to make Carleton happy, and when he came back home later in the evening he would often talk softly to

74

Nancy about their plans for next year. He would tell Nancy and Clara and whoever else wanted to listen that the country was going to change everything, that there would be a new way to live, and that when they went through a town the next time he was going to buy a newspaper to read up on it. Nancy was not much interested, but Clara always asked him about it. She thought that "Russia" was a lovely word, with its soft, hissing sound; it might be a special kind of material for a dress, something expensive, or a creamy, rich, expensive food.

It began to rain outside again, a warm, misty drizzle. "Christ sake," Nancy said sourly. "More mud tomorrow."

Clara couldn't see much out the window, because it faced the back of another shanty, so she went over to Nancy and looked out; she had to be careful because Nancy didn't like anyone standing behind her. A few people across the way were standing in their doorway too. They were a funny family no one liked because they couldn't talk right. Clara and Rosalie didn't like the girl, who was their age, because she talked funny and had thick black hair with nasty things in it. Nancy told Clara that if she came home with lice she could sleep under the shanty. She could sleep out in the outhouse, Nancy said. So Clara and Rosalie and all the other kids pretended to be afraid of the kids in that family, circling around them and teasing. The people in that shanty threw their garbage out in the walk, too, and that was against the rules.

"Lookit them pigs over there," Nancy said. "They ought to be run out of this-here camp; this is for white people."

"Are they niggers?"

"There's a lot more niggers than just ones with black skin, for Christ sake," Nancy said, shifting as if she were uncomfortable. "Where's your father? We're s'post to go down the road, what the hell is he doin' with it rainin' out?" Her voice went on listlessly, with a kind of dogged anger. It was as if she had to stir herself up when she began to forget about being angry. She scratched her shoulder. Clara watched how the worn green material of the shirt was gathered up and then released by Nancy's fingernails. It was hard to believe that Nancy was going to have a baby: Nancy was not much different from Clara.

"I'm gonna see Rosie," Clara said.

"Like hell you are."

"How come I can't?"

"Ask your father," Nancy said. "What about them dishes, anyway?"

Clara splashed cold water from the pan onto the dishes. Each day when they came back on the bus she went out to get water from the faucets, then kept this water around until the next day. She washed the plates by putting them in a big pan and pouring water on them and swishing her fingers around. Then she took the plates out and put them face down on the table to dry, so the flies couldn't get at them. There was old, faded oilcloth tacked on the little table, and Clara liked the smell of it. She liked to clean the oilcloth and the dishes because they were things she could get clean while other things were always dirty—there was no use in scrubbing the walls or the floor because the dirt was sunk deep into them, and if she tried to clear away the junk around the cabin it would just come back again.

"I'm goin' out now," Clara said.

"It's rainin'."

"Everybody else is out."

"So the hell with Rodwell and Roosevelt," Nancy said, drawling. "If they want to get worse colds, let them."

Roosevelt was bad: he ran out any time he wanted, and he never got over being sick. He was sick all the time now and wouldn't lie still. He wanted to come along to the fields with everyone else, then when he got there he wanted to play with the little kids and not work; if Carleton slapped him he would mind the way an animal minds, not wanting to but doing it out of terror. "Roosevelt's poison, that kid, an' Rodwell ain't much better," Nancy said. "I told him I wasn't goin' to bring up no baby of mine around them. I told him that."

Clara's face got warm.

"I could leave here any time I wanted," Nancy said. She drank from the bottle and then swished what was left around, holding it up so she could squint at it. "He don't give a damn, that's his trouble. He's always talkin' about some goddam half-ass job with buildin' a road or somethin'—when was he ever on a road, huh? That's another question. There's all kinds of bastards that want to do that, and chop down son-of-a-bitch trees, and any kind of crap you can think of. But this crap here, crawlin' around in the mud, this is so lousy nobody else wants it except niggers. You tell him that huh? You tell him I said so."

"Pa said we were goin' to leave real soon," Clara said. She felt older than Nancy. It would come on her all of a sudden, a sense of expansion, a sense of dizzying growth, as if she had been given a special kind of eyesight so that things looked different to her than they did to other people. Other people stared down or their eyes hopped around; Clara's were different. She wanted to see how everything was.

"Yeah, I heard that before."

"Pa says—"

"Pa says, Pa says. There's a lot of crap that Pa says an' he ain't gonna fool me with it any more." Nancy finished the bottle and tossed it out onto the ground. It struck something hard and made a noise but it didn't break.

A woman ran up from the cabin next door. She had a paper over her head to keep off the rain. "Hey, Nancy, they're comin'!" she said. She was barefoot. Clara saw how her toes curled in the mud. "They're here right now—they just come in!"

"Is Carleton down there?" Nancy said, scared.

"All the men are there, they're gonna protect him." The woman was breathing hard; she was excited about something.

"Who's comin'?" Clara said. "What's wrong?"

The woman and Nancy exchanged a quick, secret look. They were both frightened but suddenly they both laughed. It was a thin, nervous laugh; it ended almost as soon as it began.

"Who is it? What's wrong?" said Clara. Nancy knocked her back when she tried to step past her.

"It's none of your goddam business, you stay here!"

"Where's Pa?"

"Just where you'd think, a stupid son of a bitch like him," Nancy said shrilly.

"My husband's there too, who you callin' stupid? They ain't stupid!" the woman said sharply.

"You goin' down to watch?"

The woman was almost dancing from side to side, her feet were so excited. Nancy grunted and slid off the doorstep. She said to Clara, "Not you, stupid. You stay here. Stay right here."

"What's wrong?"

"Your pa told you to stay inside—"

"Where's Pa?"

"Shut up, it's none of a goddam kid's business," Nancy said.

She and the woman hurried away in the rain. The woman let the piece of newspaper fall. Clara jumped down and ran after them, staying behind. There were lots of kids milling around. At the other end of the camp there was a crowd. Clara's mouth went dry with fear. She did not bother to brush rain off her face. In the doorways of cabins along the row people stood staring out quietly. Women stood half-dressed, watching. Clara slowed down, not wanting to get there. She saw that the crowd was out in front of Rosalie's house.

She wanted to think it was some sickness, like they'd had in one camp. A bad sickness. That time some men had come in a car and gave everyone shots from a needle; it hadn't hurt much. And clothes and things had been burned in a big fire, and everyone had watched. But she did not think it was this because of the way everyone was acting.

Carleton was up there, near the front, with a few of the other men from camp. By pushing her way through, squirming under people's arms, Clara was able to get close to her father but she could not hear what he was saying. Then she saw some strange men—they were men from town. There was something about their clothes and their faces that meant they were from town, not just from another camp. Clara heard people yelling. The sound of men yelling was terrible, not like the sound of women or kids yelling.

Someone appeared in the doorway of Bert's cabin. It was a man, backing up. He was pulling someone out. Carleton and the men around him started forward, but were stopped. The men from town yelled at them. Clara began to shiver violently. When her father was yelled at like that his back seemed to give way, just a little. She had seen that. The rain got in her eyes and made her vision confused but still she had seen that. She called out, "Pa! Pa, over here!" People from camp milled around her but paid no attention. The rain made them strange and nervous with one another. There was a space between them and the men from town, and now Clara saw that some of those men had guns, shotguns, and one of them had a uniform and boots on; he was a sheriff or some kind of under-sheriff. She saw how Carleton kept pushing forward and how strange his face was, and how the men from town looked at him, waiting. She saw all that without wanting to and it made her heart pound so violently there was a roaring in her ears.

They were dragging Bert out of his shanty. One man jumped down, another was behind Bert, and with a shove they got him out. He lost his balance and fell in the mud. Then some of the men from town rushed over and began

78

kicking him. Clara saw a spurt of red. She saw his face lifted by someone's boot, his head snapped back, and then he was lost in a rush of legs. The only shouting came from that group. Everyone else waited. People around Clara were inching back. "You let him alone, I'll kill you!" Clara screamed. A woman knocked against her, in a hurry to get back. Someone kicked her leg. She began screaming: "Pa! Pa! Rosie!" Other people pushed against her, going backward, and she wanted to get forward, up front. She caught a glimpse of Nancy, off to one side between two shanties, holding her skirt bunched up in front of her stomach, standing on tiptoes, her face the face of a woman forty years old and not twenty. Her face was white, hard and wild.

Then she saw Rosalie's mother in her doorway. She was screaming at the men who were beating her husband. The rain came in a wall and got her dress wet, darkening it, but still she kept on screaming. Clara could not make anything out except two words—"His property!" A rush of more words, then "property—his property!" She began to swear at them, screaming, and a woman from camp tried to get up on the doorstep with her to make her stop.

Clara stood there staring until someone grabbed her arm. It was Nancy. "Let's get the hell out of here," Nancy said. Clara whimpered, like a child. Nancy put her arm around her shoulders. They ran back to the shanty. The lane was almost empty in the middle, and on both sides people stood waiting, silent, watching the beating that was going on. Roosevelt crossed the dirt square ahead, crying. "Roosevelt, honey," Nancy said, "you come on home an' I'll give you a pop. Your daddy's goin' to be right home himself."

They climbed into the shanty. Roosevelt lay down on the mattress he shared with Clara and Rodwell and hid his face. He was sobbing and choking. "Now we're just goin' to shut this door," Nancy said shakily. "Where's Rodwell?"

"Better shut the door," said Clara.

They closed it and stood there, looking at one another. Clara's teeth were chattering. Nancy said, "Roosevelt, honey, don't lay there with that dirty thing by your mouth." He had his face pressed right into the mattress. His hands were on the back of his neck in a strange way, as if he were trying to push his face hard into the mattress to hide there. His body shook as he sobbed. "They ain't comin' down here," Nancy said shrilly. "You know how it is, it's like this: you do somethin' wrong and they come to arrest you. An' if you don't come right out of your house they can hit you, that's the law, but nobody's goin' to get us—we ain't done nothin' wrong. Your pa—"

"They're gonna kill Pa!" Clara said.

"You're crazy, they are not."

"What if they shoot him?"

"Nobody's gonna shoot him—"

Clara sat by Roosevelt, her back against the wall. She drew her legs up to her chest and hugged them. They waited. Nancy stood by the door, opening it now and then, cautiously at first and then more frequently. Finally she stood with it open a few inches. "It's almost over now," she said. "They'll be back in a minute."

Clara thought of her father, and Rosalie, and Rosalie's father. She kept seeing the man's face kicked up, the eyes open, and that spurt of blood . . . she kept seeing it over and over. She began to cry.

"No gun went off yet," Nancy said.

They listened. Roosevelt kept sobbing. After a while they did hear a gun go off, but it sounded far away, maybe out by the road. Then there was another shot. "What's that there?" Nancy said. She stood with her face and stomach pushed out through the opening in the door, and Clara knew she wasn't afraid any longer.

Carleton came back a few minutes later. Nancy let out a cry and jumped down to him, and Clara wanted to get up but couldn't; her muscles went rigid. Even her face muscles went rigid. Roosevelt turned over on the mattress. When Carleton came inside they saw blood on his shirt and on his face. Clara wanted to think it was from someone else, but she could see that he was still bleeding. Nancy, chattering away like a crazy person, put a rag in the water pan and touched it to Carleton's head, but he knocked it away. The door was pushed slowly inward, but it was just Rodwell. He was soaking wet.

"We couldn't do nothin'," Carleton said.

"You tried real hard, everybody saw it," Nancy said shrilly. "Everybody in the whole camp saw it—didn't they? Clara? Didn't they?"

"Some bastard hit me with his gun—he kept on— I— I couldn't do nothin'—"

Carleton had a wild, harrassed look. He was panting. His eyes looked strange, as if he couldn't see right. "We couldn't do nothin," he said again tasting his words. He seemed to be explaining something to them that he did not understand himself. His face had never looked so narrow, so thin, as if drawn in by anguish and terror, not the terror of seeing a man beaten but the terror of having to stand and watch. His blond hair was wet. His forehead was a network of dirty ridges, and these lines kept shifting and changing as if he were trying to adjust something inside his head, get something in focus. "We tried but we couldn't. They smashed in his nose—his face was all kicked in— They kept kickin' him— He didn't even yell out, he was drunk, they snuck up on him and got a drunk man like that, an' dragged him out by the road—that guy had boots on— Then they—"

"They killed him," Rodwell said.

"That's a lie!" Nancy said. "Nobody killed nobody, now shut up! Get the hell out of here!"

Rodwell shrugged his shoulders. He slipped back out the door.

"Nobody killed nobody, this is the United States," Nancy muttered. "Here. Put this on your face." When she pressed the rag back on Carleton's forehead this time he did not push it away. "Bastards that drink too much an' can't take it— makin' a mess—I knew this camp wasn't any good—"

Carleton put his hand over hers, where she held the rag. Clara watched them. Nancy said in a rush, "Out in the field today Bert bought some of that junk, that moonshine slop, why didn't his wife make him stop it? She thinks she's so smart—"

"It wouldn't of done no good," Carleton said. He closed his eyes. "Anyway, it's better he's dead. The way they were goin' to leave him, he wouldn't of been no good to himself or anybody else. They kicked his eyes an' everything—his chest—"

"You stop talkin' about that!" Nancy screamed.

She turned around wildly, to show that this meant Clara too. "I don't want to hear no more about it, we're gonna stay right in here tonight an' go to sleep an' that's that, an' go out workin' tomorrow an' the hell with it! You, you little bitch," she screamed at Clara, "stop lookin' like that! Sick cow! Take care of your brother and shut up."

Clara heard them whispering that night, and she heard lots of people talking quietly in the days that followed. Someone said that Bert's family was on their way to Texas, but someone else said they hadn't any money so how the hell could they go there?—and someone else said that the crew leader kicked them out, on account of they couldn't make enough money without Bert; and someone else said no one had a right to do that to Bert, that the girl was his property if it was his daughter, it wasn't his fault, whose fault was it? Clara found out that Rosalie had had a baby before it was ready to be born, and that the baby was born dead, and that people from town had found out about it and came out. That was all.

The shanty where they lived was empty for a while, then a new family moved in. It was a family from West Virginia. Clara never saw Rosalie again and never said anything about her, but she thought about her all the time: Rosalie leaning against the dimestore counter like that, like a grown woman, smiling and confident, and Rosalie picking tomatoes alongside her in the sunshine, and that baby born dead that Clara had never seen but knew very well, as if it had been her own baby instead of Rosalie's, and that quick, lightning-flash of Bert's face rearing up white and smeared with blood before they closed in on him.

8

Florida, a Sunday afternoon sometime later. Clara was alone, watching Nancy's baby, when she heard voices outside and then a hesitant knocking at the door. They were living now in a camp made up of a number of long low buildings with fifteen sections in each and concrete floors that could be washed easily; each section had just two rooms and two windows, one in front and one in back. In this camp the buildings had brown siding that was rough when you touched it and roofs that did not always leak. The outhouses, down at one end of the camp, had concrete floors also. Clara had never seen anything like it.

The only trouble was that here an odor of harsh antiseptic was everywhere, floating everywhere. Clara had hated the smells of the other camps, but this was worse because it seemed to be eating its way into your lungs to get you clean even if it killed you. When they had first moved in they'd been amazed at the way the garbage and trash were carted off, to be burned in a big dump pile some distance away, and at the way women could wash their laundry in a big roofed area; then the antiseptic smell had begun to bother Carleton. Things bothered him first, before they got to the others. But it was certainly a new world: a doctor and a nurse even came around to examine them, and there was a grocery store they could go to with special tickets so that they didn't pay out money by hand, and there weren't many insects. But the antiseptic smell was so strong it stayed with them everywhere, even out in the orange groves where the sweet pungent smell of oranges should have dominated.

That day Nancy was out visiting a few doors down and Carleton was gone for the weekend, off on a job that had to do with the highway. This was outside a small town named Florence. They'd been living here for a month now and the walls of the room had been decorated by Clara, who cut things out of magazines and newspapers and tacked them up to make the place pretty. When she heard the knocking she wasn't surprised, because there were some older boys—seventeen and eighteen—who hung around and bothered her. So she put the baby down on the cot and glanced at herself in Nancy's mirror, propped up on the window sill.

When she opened the door, two ladies were standing on the boards that had been placed in the muddy walks.

"Yeah?" Clara said brightly.

The ladies were from town, you could tell that at once—they wore hats and their faces were soft and powdered and made gentle with so much time to think, and they wore boxy shapeless suits that must have been expensive because there was no other reason to wear them. One of the ladies wore glasses and Clara looked at her, supposing she was the one to talk to; she looked like a schoolteacher.

"I'm Mrs. Foster," she said, "and this is Mrs. Wylie, we're from the First Methodist Church in Florence. We came out for a little visit—"

Clara nodded happily. But she could not think of anything to say. Mrs. Foster went on carefully, pronouncing her words so that any child might be able to understand: "We've been visiting some of your neighbors today. We thought—perhaps — It's so lovely of you to have this displayed, to take such an interest—" She indicated Clara's faded American flag that was propped out the window. Clara always put it out, good weather or bad. This flag was not like the flags she saw flying at the tops of big buildings or in miniature on cars, whipping furiously in the air. Those flags stood for something abstract and hard to understand. Clara's flag stood for something simple.

"Yes, that's wonderful," the other woman said. "It shows such an . . . an interest—"

"It brought us right over here," Mrs. Foster said. "There's nothing so wonderful as people taking a patriotic interest in their country." Clara stepped outside. She was glowing with

83

pleasure but she couldn't help being nervous, and she kept waiting for the baby to howl behind her. "I'm real glad you like it," she said a little vaguely. She smiled a weak, hesitant smile at the ladies and waited for them to take the burden of talk from her. Through her lashes she saw the woman's glasses glitter in the sunshine and hide her eyes, and the other woman's powdery nose was a little shiny—still, they must smell of perfume, Clara thought, and underneath their white gloves there were probably expensive rings. They both carried dark purses. Clara felt a surge of joy just to think that she was talking with them, women who lived in real houses and went to church and didn't even need to carry money around with them.

"We—"

"We thought—"

Their words tripped over one another. Clara leaned forward as if anxious to help. She saw that some kids were watching a short distance away.

"Tell us your name, dear," Mrs. Foster said.

"Clara."

"And where is your family, Clara? There is no work today, is there?"

"Not today, no," Clara said earnestly. She was glad to be able to answer these questions right, to say something that made sense; she clasped her hands together childishly and pressed them between her knees. "Nancy's around nearby—that's my stepmother—and my pa's gone away for a few days but he's comin' back tonight, and the baby's inside, and the boys are somewhere—one of my brothers is right over there, he's there," Clara said pointing.

The women turned. Roosevelt was with the group of kids who were watching, and when the women looked at them they yelled with laughter. Clara shook her fist. "What the hell's wrong with you, you crazy?" she yelled back. Then it occurred to her that she shouldn't have yelled. She saw how the ladies exchanged looks. "They don't mean nothin'," she said weakly.

The old man next door had wandered out and Clara saw that his pants weren't fixed right. She hoped the ladies wouldn't notice but they seemed to be looking everywhere. She said, "Would you maybe like to come inside?" The ladies' faces showed that they had not thought of this and wanted only to get away, but their voices and quick nods said yes.

"We like this place real well," Clara said. The ladies

84

followed her inside. Their faces were strained. Clara saw some strange discrepancy between their mouths, which were smiling, and their eyes, which looked frightened and a little like her father's eyes when he was thinking fast. "This here is Esther Jean," Clara said, picking up the baby. "Ain't she a cute baby? Her eyes were blue but now they ain't."

"Is it your baby?" Mrs. Wylie asked.

Clara laughed happily. "It's my stepmother's. I ain't married—I don't have any baby. It's none of my baby," she said, as if this were a funny joke the lady had made up and she had to appreciate it. "No, it isn't my baby," she said, smiling.

She sat on the cot and rocked the baby just a little to keep it quiet. The ladies bent over Esther Jean and made noises like anybody else did around babies, so Clara thought they must be nice. If their black, heavy, thick-soled shoes were taken from them, and those hats and those suits, and they just had cotton dresses to wear they might look like anyone else in the camp, maybe worse.

"The purpose of our little visit is to inquire about whether . . . to see if . . . anyone here would be interested in coming to our church," Mrs. Foster said. The way she said this made Clara know that she'd said it before. "We've been visiting with a family up that way—a very nice family—and an old couple, and the young woman a few doors down with all the children—"

"One of them's my brother," Clara said.

The woman stared at her blankly. Then she said, "Yes, your brother. Which one is he again?"

"Mary, is that important?" Mrs. Wylie said nervously.

Clara smiled just to be so close to them and to hear them talk. It never occurred to her that they might say anything important. She and her family had been "interviewed" many times by different people—she forgot their reasons—and those people had always asked questions that were stupid but you had to pretend they weren't just to be polite. When you lived in a camp you were polite to people outside, because that was how you got along.

"But that boy—that one boy—" Mrs. Foster hissed.

"He didn't do nothin' wrong, did he?" Clara said.

"Yes, he did something quite bad," Mrs. Foster said. She looked fragile behind her glasses. Clara wondered what people who wore glasses did when someone knocked them off. She saw that Mrs. Foster was not really like a schoolteacher. Her words kept breaking down and getting soft, and a schoolteacher's words got harder the longer she talked. Clara decided she wouldn't be a schoolteacher after all but would be a lady like Mrs. Foster, because she was so gentle and delicate and you could see she never worked at all. The other woman was nice too but she reminded Clara of a bird; maybe her nose was too sharp.

"Well, they ain't gonna do nothin' bad when I'm around," Clara said. "I think it's real nice you came to visit, it's real nice, I wish my pa was here. He's real interested in things, in newspapers and things."

"Oh, does he read the Bible to you?"

"What?"

"Does he read the Bible? Do you have a Bible here?"

"I guess not," Clara said. She tried to smile, but it was clear that she had disappointed them. "But I'm real interested in it myself. I just don't have much time."

"Clara, have you ever been to church?"

"I guess not," Clara said, pretending to think. "I seen some, though. I always wanted to go inside."

This was the right answer: she saw them both smile at the same time.

"We're having a prayer meeting tonight," Mrs. Foster said. "We are hoping—Mrs. Wylie and I are hoping—the Reverend, his name is Reverend Bargman, the Reverend is so very interested in you people—he wants to bring you into our community—"

"It's tonight at seven," Mrs. Wylie said quickly.

"If you'd like to come we'll arrange to pick you up—my son is driving us tonight. The family down the way just might come too, they promised us they'd think hard on it! Isn't that nice? And—and— A lovely child like yourself, this would be such a fine opportunity for you—"

They all smiled at one another. The ladies looked around at the walls, decorated with pictures of mountains and castles and movie stars.

"I'd sure like to come," Clara said shyly. "I sure appreciate it—"

The door jerked open and Nancy came in. "What the hell's this?" she said. She was drunk but she looked a little frightened.

Clara jumped up. "Some ladies from town, from the church," she said. "They're askin' people to a thing tonight, to the church tonight—"

Nancy nodded as if she'd been through this before. "Well, count me out. Is she wet again?"

"I guess so."

86

"Why didn't you change her, then? She's been wet all day. Goddam dirty kid, it's a dirty kid," Nancy whined to the ladies. "What can you do with a dirty kid that craps all over the place? It ain't my fault," she said, beginning to cry.

The ladies moved out, already saying good-by nervously, and Clara went with them. "My stepmother ain't feelin' well but she's real nice," she said. She was talking quickly to the ladies' backs. "She's real nice most of the time."

"We'll come to pick you up at seven," Mrs. Foster said, distracted.

"A few minutes before seven," Mrs. Wylie said.

Clara hurried along beside them, walking in the mud while they walked on the planks. "There's some real nice people down in that house, maybe they'd be interested," she said helpfully.

"I'm afraid we must be getting home—"

"A nice old lady that sits around readin' the Bible or somethin'," Clara said.

"Yes, next week we must—"

The ladies were afraid of those kids, Clara saw that. They were watching them out of the corners of their eyes. Roosevelt was there, crouching on one of the steps. He looked skinny and sick compared to the other kids, who were nudging him out. "Hey, look! Lady, look!" the kids yelled happily. Clara wanted to run over and punch them, make them shut up, but she couldn't even shout anything because she knew the ladies would be upset. "Hey, look! Here!" Roosevelt was holding something and shaking it. He had a pale, queer face, that Roosevelt, and his skull showed through his hair. Everyone was laughing. Two women stood nearby laughing along with the kids.

Roosevelt did his usual trick while the town ladies gagged and hid their faces—he bit off the head of a bird and spat it out.

"You little—Little—" Clara choked.

The ladies were hurrying away, out the lane. Clara followed, trying to apologize but not knowing what to say. "My brother was the one in back, the one that didn't laugh," she said miserably. "My brother— He ain't just right in the head or somethin'—but he didn't laugh— He—"

"Will your mother allow you to come tonight?" Mrs. Foster said. She barely turned to Clara. Her face was gray. She seemed to be waiting for nothing in particular, no particular answer—yes or no, anything to be liberated.

"Sure," Clara said. "I want to go to church real bad."

The lane led out to the road; Clara was ashamed of how rutted it was. On the shoulder of the road a car was parked and a young man with a blank, bored face sat inside, smoking. Clara noticed that the ladies were getting their polished shoes dirty but they themselves noticed nothing. Their legs worked fast inside their long skirts.

"Should I wait out here after supper, then?" Clara said.

Mrs. Wylie glanced at her as if she did not remember her. This lady's face, too, was a queer gray-green; the powder looked like ashes. Clara knew that what Roosevelt had done was bad, but she always thought you should try not to notice things that are embarrassing; that was why she was smiling so hard. "After supper?" she said, bending to peer into the car. Something about the word "supper" might have made the ladies shiver. The young man behind the wheel, a heavy, beefy boy of about twenty, was staring at Clara. He did not smile.

"That will be fine," Mrs. Foster said. She had taken a handkerchief out of her purse and was dabbing her forehead and upper lip with it.

At six-thirty Clara was out on the road, waiting. She had combed her hair and was sorry she didn't have time to wash it; it needed washing. She wore a blue dress and some blue flat shoes that were called "ballerina" shoes and were only a little scuffed. She carried a purse made of yellow felt that she had made herself from scraps. It was still very light; the sun wouldn't go down for hours. Clara waited for the other family to come out, but they didn't, and she talked with some kids playing out by the road, and then Nancy and another woman who were going to walk to town just for something to do, both carrying their babies. When she was alone she felt shivers of excitement running up and down her. "I'm going in to church tonight," she said to herself.

After a while the car did arrive. The same stocky boy was driving.

"Okay, jump in," he said. "Are you all that's comin'?"

He was smoking a cigar as he drove and it smelled bad. Clara tried to make herself like it, as if it were the sign of church, of a new world. She kept glancing at him nervously and when he looked at her she smiled. He said nothing. Clara thought he drove sort of fast.

"Is it hard to drive a car?" she said.

He shifted the cigar around in his mouth and took a while to answer. "Depends on how smart you are."

"How old do you need to be?"

"You ain't old enough."

He said no more. Clara was staring out at the houses they passed, at people who had nothing else to do but sit on their front porches and watch traffic go by. She felt something ache in her that was mixed up with the heavy sweet smell of lilacs from the big bushes by everyone's front porch.

At the church—not as big as Clara had hoped, but clean and white—the boy said to Clara, "When you get sick of that crap in there, come out. I'm gonna be over there." He pointed down the street to a gas station.

Mrs. Foster was waiting inside for her. She held a book pressed up against her chest, and when Clara came in she seemed almost ready to embrace her. "Ah, yes, yes," she said, smiling sadly, "so wonderful that you could—such an opportunity for you—"

Clara looked around, smiling in her confusion. The church reminded her of a schoolhouse. There were maybe eight people there, sitting in pews right up at the front.

Mrs. Foster kept talking about the "opportunity" Clara had. She walked with her up the aisle, whispering and nodding sadly. Mrs. Wylie was sitting by herself in one of the pews, her head bowed, whispering to herself. Clara noticed that the other people—three men and four women and a crippled boy with a crutch propped up near him—were also whispering to themselves. The men's voices occasionally turned into murmurs.

Mrs. Foster had her sit on the side. She felt cold and shaky. At the front of the church was a raised platform, and on that was a podium for the minister. Off to one side was an organ. She waited, glancing over now and then at the praying people, who seemed very serious and unaware of anything except their prayers. After a while there was a bustle in the back and Clara saw an enormously fat woman in a dark silk dress come in. She smiled at Mrs. Foster, who was back at the door waiting for people to come in, and her eyes were fast and bouncy like a girl's. Clara saw that her dress was stuck to her legs and looked funny. Then another man came in, tall and thin and stoop-shouldered. He whispered to Mrs. Foster and they both looked over toward Clara. She began to smile at them, but they did not quite see her—not exactly her. Then the man came over to her and put out his hand for her to shake. Clara saw that there was a dull red rash on it, as if he'd been scratching himself there hard.

"My dear, I am Reverend Bargman. Mrs. Foster has told

me about you. Let me say we are all so happy you came tonight."

Clara smiled. He was a tall, earnest, gawky man, with a smile that cut the lower part of his face in two. "You may be entering the threshold of a new life. A new life," he whispered. Clara nodded eagerly. He went on for a minute or two, using the words "threshold" and "opportunity." Then he excused himself, stood for a while near the wall with his hands behind him, staring at the floor, and finally shook his head as if to wake himself. He strode to the front of the church, scratching the back of his hand.

He began:

"My dear brothers and sisters in Christ, let us give thanks for our being here this evening—for our church, our wonderful new building— And let us begin by singing together hymn 114. All together—let us rise and sing all together—"

They moved slowly. He seemed to be pulling and nudging them with his hands and little prodding movements of his body; everyone stood. Clara stood. She had found a hymn book on the pew beside her and leafed through it. They had already begun singing, without any music behind them, before she found the hymn in the book. They made a thin, discordant mixture of voices that kept trying to waver apart. Clara stared hard at the music in the book. She had never seen music before. And the words were big words. She felt perspiration break out on her and she wondered if everyone was waiting for her to sing her part— Just ahead of her the fat woman sang, raising and lowering her head with a deliberate meekness. She was a warm, energetic partridge of a woman, with damp spots on her dress that looked like wings folded back.

Clara had thought the song was ending but it began again. The back of her neck was damp. She raised the book closer to her face and tried to read the words. Then she noticed that the minister was crying! He sang words that Clara could not even make out and these words were so sad that he was crying. He shook his head sadly. Clara waited tensely, wondering what there could be in words to make a person cry. She only cried when something real came along. But she never did find out what the words meant. After the song ended a few people cleared their throats, as if self-conscious at the silence. The minister closed his hymn book and everyone else did the same. They sat.

"I see," he said, with a special little smile, "that I have not

90

worked hard enough this week. I have not worked hard enough."

There was an intake of a breath or two. Clara did not understand. "Only this child is new to us," the minister said, looking kindly at her. "I have not worked hard enough this week. I have not brought people to our worship of Christ."

Mrs. Foster sighed.

"No, I have not worked hard enough. Just this child. . . . And it is through the efforts of Mrs. Foster and Mrs. Wylie that. . . . No, I have not worked hard enough." He did not wipe his eyes or even his nose, Clara saw. He let the tears run down as if he were proud of them, and when he smiled she could see tears glistening around his mouth. He bowed his head and clasped his hands before him, out before him as if he were going to help pull someone up there with him, and prayed aloud. Clara stared at the top of his head. It was thick with dark hair in some places but thin in others; she wanted to laugh at it. Everything made her so nervous that she wanted to laugh. He prayed in a loud, demanding voice that got more and more angry as it went on, about Christ and blood and redemption and little children and sin and the world and money and city-life and the federal government and the Sunday collection and Pontius Pilate . . . and his voice was angry and hard as any man's, not about to cry at all, and he began to pace tightly around on the little platform as his voice rose higher in a sudden upward swerve, as if something had caught hold of it and jerked it right up toward heaven. "God is watching! God is listening! You people in sin, how can you think God isn't with you all the time? Right now, tomorrow, yesterday, next year—always—God is always with you—"

Just when his voice was hardest, though, it collapsed down into a sob. He could not get his breath for a moment. Clara pressed her hand against her mouth to keep from smiling. In the center section women were crying freely, their heads bowed; the men stared down at the minister's shoes. Only the crippled boy was looking around the way Clara was. Their eyes met and he seemed not to see her; he had lines on his forehead and around his mouth like a man getting old.

Someone had once told Clara that God was watching her, or maybe Christ, someone was with her all the time and watching her. She hadn't bothered with it because it didn't make sense. It might or might not have been true, like many complicated things, but since it didn't make sense she forgot about it. But tonight when the minister said the same thing, it

91

struck Clara that if God was watching anyone, it was not the people here. He was probably watching other people who were more interesting. Clara knew that God would never bother with her and she thought this was a good idea.

The minister was clearing his throat and Clara cleared her throat involuntarily, in sympathy with him. She felt the way she felt when her father or Nancy were acting silly, wanting to help but a little impatient. Then something extraordinary happened: the fat lady with the damp dress lumbered out of the pew and headed for the platform. Clara wondered if she was going to hit the minister or do something violent—maybe she was his wife. She could see the woman's thick, pale, doughlike arms, the flesh swinging free just beneath the sleeves, and her legs in brown stockings round and thick as tree limbs, working her up to the front. There she knelt, heavily, and buried her face in her hands. She was sobbing too and the minister bent over her and let his eyes streak across the pews as if drawing everyone else up. "To Jesus! To Jesus!" he whispered loudly.

A man in a yellow sports shirt crawled over another man's legs to get out into the aisle. He was panting and his skin was yellow, like his shirt. Clara began to tremble, thinking everyone was crazy. This man went up to the minister too and knelt, bowing his head sharply. Clara waited to see who would be next. She began to shiver. It was all so strange. Something was happening all around her. In the air around her things seemed to be moving, invisibly bumping against her; was that why everyone was sobbing, out of terror? Why else would you sob if you weren't hurt, except out of terror at being hurt in the future? Her smile jerked into a look of anguish, as if she wanted to sob along with them but could not. Her eyes were dry. Her throat hurt. Those sobs filled the air in a way that the singing had not—the air was crowded and breathless with these sobs of guilty people, and the melody they made was one Clara understood better than she had understood the words of that song.

She understood something then: that these people had done something bad, something wrong, and that they would never get over it.

She slid sideways to the aisle. She saw the minister's pouchy eyes fall upon her as if he'd been trying not to look her way and had suddenly let himself go—but Clara had already turned and was running out. Her ballerina shoes made a flat, flopping sound. There had been one second when she might have gone up to the minister, but she hadn't; so she ran back down the aisle and to the door and outside. She was still trembling. She discovered the hymn book still in her fingers, and let it lay on the top step where they would be sure to find it.

9

First they went to a little restaurant near some railroad tracks. There were several trucks parked outside, and inside were men who shouted and laughed in one another's faces. Their fists and elbows struck the tables accidentally and made them wobble. Clara, who had never been in a restaurant before, said right out to the young waitress: "I'm hungry. I want some hamburgers. I want a Coke."

The boy was older than Clara had thought. He had a blotched, heavy face with eyes sunk back into his skull. He kept joking and interrupting himself and laughing nervously; he played with his car keys for a while. In his shirt pocket were five cigars wrapped in cellophane. Clara smiled at him and showed her teeth and kept pushing her hair back out of her eyes. With the table between them and other people around, what did she care? "You got out of there faster'n I did," he said. His name was LeRoy. He was Mrs. Foster's only son and he was going to join the Navy and get out of Florence forever, as soon as he had some operation he had to have before they'd let him in. "My old bastard of a father that's dead now, he had me carry anvils and junk all around the barn. That's what done it," he said sourly, smiling and twisting the cap on the ketchup bottle. He got ketchup on his fingers and wiped them underneath the table.

A song began on the jukebox. It was a country song with a twangy, forlorn, sleepy voice. Clara tried to imagine what that man would look like and she knew he wouldn't look like LeRoy. But LeRoy hummed along with the music, grinning and squinting at her and turning the cap on the ketchup bottle nervously. He seemed so excited he couldn't sit still.

"Don't you want nothin' to eat?" Clara said.

"I'm just gonna sit and watch you."

He shook his car keys once more and dropped them in his shirt pocket. He laughed and snickered at something he thought of, then put his elbow down on the table and his chin in his palm and watched her. Clara ate her hamburger fast, licking her lips and then licking her fingers. She drank the

Coke so fast it hurt her throat. This made LeRoy laugh. "You're such a cute little girl," he said. "I bet you know that."

He wanted to drive out to the country, but Clara said she knew a place she wanted to go—it was a tavern she'd heard about. People from the camp went there. She wondered if she had made a mistake, going with him, when he did not quite turn into the tavern drive but idled out on the road, saying something vaguely about a better place a few miles on. He hadn't looked at her. "Like hell," Clara said. So he turned into the drive. Clara got her door open fast and was outside before he had even turned off the ignition. He jumped out and ran around the car, his feet making heavy crunching noises in the gravel. He started breezy little sentences that went nowhere, like "If my Ma— What a night— That's the way things are—" He opened the screen door for her and Clara went inside as if she'd never seen him before. "My sweet Jesus," the boy said, wiping his forehead.

Clara felt a little dizzy with excitement. The man behind the bar, who looked like LeRoy, said: "How old are you, sweetheart?"

"How old do you need to be?" she said.

The man and LeRoy both roared, this made them so happy. Clara took the bottle of beer someone handed her and sipped at it, looking around. Her eyes darted from face to face, not as if she were looking for someone she knew but as if she supposed there was someone here who might know her. Her hair was hot and heavy about her head. One time in the evening LeRoy took a bunch of it in his hand and Clara jerked away like a cat.

"Okay, no scratchin', no bitin'!" LeRoy laughed. He put out his hands to defend himself. Now that he had been drinking a while, his laughter was wheezing.

People kept coming in. Clara noticed a man with blond hair at one of the back tables; her heart gave a lurch, she thought it might be her father. But when he turned she saw it wasn't, thank God. He was maybe twenty, maybe twenty-five, she didn't know. She forgot about him and then saw him again and had the same tripping sensation around her heart. He sat leaning back in his chair with his legs crossed off to the side, listening to what his friends were saying but not really with them. Other people moved a great deal, shuffling their feet and gesturing with their hands, but this man sat still.

Someone at the man's table nudged him and swung his

head around to indicate that Clara was watching. The blond man turned, frowning. Clara was clicking the top of a beer bottle between her teeth, and her eyes narrowed almost shut when he saw her. LeRoy slid his heavy arm around her shoulders and seemed to be coming in at her from far away. Clara stared at the other man and only after a moment did she shake herself free of LeRoy. "You're just like a cat, a pretty cat," LeRoy said. "I got a cat at home. Her name is Lucy." He stroked her hair and Clara reached around and hit him with the back of her hand, negligently, on the chest; some men around them laughed.

"Old lard-ass, get your hands off," Clara said.

When she looked over there again the blond man was just turning away. Something rushed to her head, hot and heavy through her throat. She could feel her veins swelling. LeRoy jabbered and laughed about something and Clara walked away. She pressed the sweating bottle against her cheek, then against her other cheek. Someone collided with her and she stepped aside without looking at him. A wild, shrill sensation rose in her, a sense that she was going to lose her balance and trip, something was going to happen: just as at the church she might have run up to the front like the others and fallen to her knees. This wildness had sent her running out instead and then got cooled by the outside air and by LeRoy but now it was coming back again and she felt she could have done something with her hands, her nails, even her teeth—she could tear at someone's face with her teeth. She was still watching the man with the blond hair. From where she stood now she could see the side of his face, and it seemed to her that the God the minister had talked of was present. He was this hot pressure that hung over her, this force lowering Himself into her body, squirming into her. That God was still hungry, the hamburgers hadn't done Him any good, and He made her think of all those nights she'd lain and listened to Carleton and Nancy—not hating them, not hating Nancy, but just listening and listening to know how it would be with her someday, since when it happened to her she wouldn't be able to know any more than Nancy knew.

There was one woman at the table and three men. Clara looked at her once and then forgot her. The blond man's head seemed to become vivid in the dim light, just as she watched. Waves of heat seemed to tremble about it, the hair pale like her father's, but the man's shoulders stronger than his, younger and straighter, a different person—he was a different person. Clara's lips were dry. She stared at that man

95

and stood lost in a trance, a little drunk, sweaty and tired, her eyes aching from all the smoke. She might have stood there all night if he hadn't turned around. He did not smile. After a moment he got to his feet.

"You looking for someone, little girl?"

He came right up to her and bent to look in her face. Clara stared at him. He was a little different than she had imagined—his eyebrows were strange, hard and straight so that they almost ran across his forehead in a single line. His chin was square. Clara wanted to cry out in terror that she had wanted someone else—someone else! But she said nothing. Her eyes felt glassy.

"You here with anyone?" he said. He looked around. "What are you doing here alone?"

Clara brushed her hair back out of her eyes. She could not think of anything to say.

"I'll drive you back to where you're going," the man said.

"I don't want to go anywhere."

"I'll drive you there."

He took hold of her arm and pulled her along. Clara hurried to keep up with him. They stepped out into a cloud of moths and mosquitoes. The man said, "Are you from around here?"

"From Texas," Clara said.

"What are you doing here, then?"

He looked at her in the blast of light from the neon sign. At his car he opened the door for her and pushed her inside, the way children are pushed here and there, as if it were easier to just push them than to explain what they should do. He got in beside her. He said, "You're not from Texas or anywhere near. You don't talk it." He backed the car around. "Now, which way do you want to go?"

"Out that way," Clara said, pointing down the road.

"Nobody lives out there."

He paused, not looking at her. Then he drove out onto the road and turned back toward town. He had not looked at her since they'd left the tavern. "You're not thumbing your way through here, are you? Because you better be careful doing that."

"I can do anything I want to," Clara said.

Before he came to the town he turned into a drive. The house there was a big, three-story building with a wide veranda; lights were on in some rooms and off in others. "I'm in and out of this place myself," he said. "Tomorrow I'm leaving." He turned off the ignition. Clara waited. Something

96

hot and swollen was inside her head so that she could not think right. "You're on your way to Miami, probably, but I'm not," he said.

"Ain't goin' to Miami," Clara said.

He turned off the headlights and turned to her. Clara smelled whiskey around him; it reminded her of Carleton. He took hold of her and would have hurt her shoulder if she hadn't twisted free. She was breathing hard and her head ached. But the dizziness inside her made her want to press forward against him, hide herself against him and fall into sleep. It wanted to stop her seeing anything and thinking anything. The man reached over and opened the door on her side and pushed her out, and slid out with her. Standing out in the driveway, where everything was dark and quiet, he put his arms around her and kissed her and then let her go, his breath nervous. "My place is around back," he said, pulling her along. Clara stumbled on boards propped up around the corner, against the house. The man opened a door in the dark and they went in together. There was another door right inside.

The room must have been an addition on the back of the house; it was made of boards that were just boards, rough and unfinished, and the floor was the same way. A cool draft came up through cracks in the floor even though the night was warm. There was a bed and a stand with a basin on it that had a rusty bottom; there was just a little water in it. On the floor there was a hot plate with just one burner.

The man shut the door and nudged her over toward the bed. He was as tall as Carleton. He took off his shirt and his chest was covered with dark blond hair. Clara stared at his chest as if hypnotized. She felt the cool air rising between the floor boards.

"How old are you?" he said. "Seventeen or eighteen or what?"

Clara shook her head.

"Or thirteen?"

He screwed his mouth up into a look that meant he was judging her. She had seen people from town, or farmers who owned land, looking at her and her family that way. They looked at everyone that way who lived in the places she lived and did the work she did. It did not occur to Clara that they might have looked at her another way. She felt sleepy, and so she lowered her head and moved toward this man. She closed her eyes against his hot, damp skin. When his mouth pressed against her throat she drew in her breath sharply, thinking

97

that she would not have to do anything at all; she would just press herself against him. But she must have stumbled backward because she knocked the basin over. The man kicked it against the wall, laughing. He pulled her over to the bed and they fell down together. The bed had been made up, just sheets and a pillow but still someone had made it. It felt cold. The ceiling and the wall wavered over Clara, seen through her hair or through his hair and then blotted out by his face. He was lying on top of her just as Clara had imagined someone lying on her, years before she had ever seen this man. And she held her arms right around his neck just as she had imagined she would.

She caught sight of his face in the shadow and saw that it was sleepy like her own, slow and hungry. Something ached in her to see him like that. She clutched against him wildly. "Do it to me, don't stop," she said. "Don't stop."

But he did stop. He fell back beside her. She heard him breathing and in that moment her body just waited, suspended and frozen in a daze of sweat and disbelief. He said, "How the hell old are you?"

"I don't know—eighteen."

"No, you're just a child."

That word was one that had nothing to do with her—she exhaled her waiting breath in a sound of contempt. "I'm not a—child," she said angrily. "I'm not a child, I never was."

He swung his legs around and sat on the edge of the bed. "Christ," he muttered. Clara watched him. Far away there was the sound of a car horn fading. Clara felt how alone they were and how dark it was outside, how easy it would be for them to be lost from each other. A pool of darkness seemed to open at her feet, chilled by the night, and this man could fade away into it and be lost.

"I love you," Clara said bitterly. "I never was any child."

He looked around back at her. There were little lines around his eyes, as if he was used to squinting too often. She could see fine light stubble on his chin, she wanted to touch it, to move her hand over it. But she did not dare. His skin was damp, his hair damp. Looking at him, she seemed to be seeing more than he wanted her to; he made a face and turned away.

"No, please, I love you. I want you," Clara said. She spoke violently. A pulse in the man's neck jumped and she could have slashed at it with her teeth. Her body ached for him and he was keeping himself from her, it wasn't right, everyone always said how any man could be ready for a woman any time. "I want you, I want somethin'!" Clara said. "I want somethin'!"

"Look, where are you from?"

"I don't know what I want but I want it! I don't know what it is," she sobbed.

"I sure as hell don't know either."

After a moment he got up. He went out. Clara heard him in the corridor, heard a door open. She lay still, panting, her jaw gone rigid with anger. She could not remember how he had looked now that he was gone. When she thought of men, of love, she had always thought of an impersonal heavy force, a man that was no particular man but just a pressure, coming against her and letting her fall asleep within it and taking care of her—arms that were just arms to take care of her, a body that was heavier and stronger than hers but would not hurt her—and she would pause no matter what she was doing, dreamy and entranced, a kind of sleep easing over her brain until she had to jerk herself out of it and wake up— Now she felt that langorous sleep move over her, weighing down her eyelids, and the man who had just been with her was no more real than the ghostly men who had come and slipped away when she bent to pick beans or strained up to pick oranges, either way tempting that flood of warm dizziness into her brain that marked the point at which she stopped being Clara and became someone else with no name.

She could ease into that darkness and become a girl without any name: someone who wanted, wanted, who reached out in the dark for someone to embrace her in turn.

The man came back. He was carrying a bucket of water. He closed the door behind him with his foot and went to the hot plate and set the bucket down. He plugged the hot plate in. Clara watched him in silence, wanting to laugh because it was all so strange, so nervous. He squatted by the hot plate and watched the water, his bare shoulders twitching as if uneasy with her staring. But he himself was not uneasy.

He said to her, "Take off your dress."

"What?"

"You're dirty, take it off."

Clara's face went hot. "I'm not dirty!"

"Take it off."

"I'm not dirty—I'm—"

He had blue eyes, a cold blue-green. They were not like her own eyes. His eyebrows made one shadowy ridge over his face. He was squatting a few feet from the bed, one hand

99

lazily on his knee. "I'm dirty too. Everyone's dirty. You want to take that off or should I do it for you?" he said.

Clara sat up. She had kicked off her shoes. "You take it off," she said spitefully. He did not move at once. Then he grinned at her, a grin that flashed on and off, and got up. She let her head droop forward as he reached under her hair to undo the buttons at the top of her dress. He unbuttoned them and Clara stood so that he could pull the dress off. She snatched it from him and threw it down onto the floor. "What are you going to wear out of here except that?" he said, and picked it up. She was standing in a short cotton slip on which she had sewed pink ribbons. She tore one of the ribbons off before he could stop her. "You said I was dirty!" she cried. "I hate you!"

"You are dirty. Look at this." He rubbed her wrist and tiny rolls of dirt appeared. Clara stared. His fingers made red marks on her skin. "Your hair too," he said. "You should wash your hair."

"My hair's nice!"

"It's nice but it's dirty. You're from that fruit pickers' place, aren't you?"

"People always say my hair's nice," Clara sobbed. She looked up at him as if waiting for him to say something different, something that would show he had only been joking. "Other people think I'm pretty—"

He parted her hair with his fingers and bent near. He thinks I have lice, Clara thought. She felt sick. "Son of a bitch, you son of a bitch," she whispered. "I'll get my father to kill you—he'll kill you—"

He laughed. "Why would anyone want to kill me?"

She tried to push away but he caught her. He pulled off her slip and made her stand still so that he could wash her. Clara shut her eyes tight. She felt the angry pressure of tears behind her eyes, but another pressure, a sweet feeling, that did not let her cry. She thought that no one had washed her for years. Her mother had washed her years ago but she almost couldn't remember that. Maybe she couldn't remember it at all. Now this man rubbed soap between his hands and washed her, and she shut her eyes tight with the feel of his warm, slow, gentle hands. She knew that the ache in her loins for him would never go away but that she would carry it with her all her life.

He washed her and dried her with a thin white towel. It wasn't big enough and got wet right away, so he finished drying her with his shirt. Clara stood with her hair fallen

100

down one side of her head. She felt the man's breath against her face, against her shoulders. When she opened her eyes he was handing her clothes to her.

"You're going back home," he said.

She nodded meekly and took her things.

"I don't want them to hurt you back there." Clara turned slightly, shyly, as he spoke. "Do they knock you around much back there?"

"You mean my pa? No."

He helped her button up the dress. Clara stood obediently. "I'm tired," she said. "I don't feel right." He said nothing. When he was finished, Clara turned sharply. "I lost my purse," she said.

"What?"

"I lost my purse—"

"What purse?"

She looked around. She saw nothing.

"I don't remember any purse," he said.

They went outside and he drove back to the camp. It was late; Clara could smell that it was late. She wondered if Carleton was back. The dull, sullen ache in her body for this man did not go away but grew heavier at the thought of what might happen to her if Carleton was home.

She opened the door. Insects were swirling around his headlights.

"You want money to buy another purse?" he said.

"No."

"I thought that's maybe what you wanted."

Clara had never thought of that. She felt hot and ashamed. After a moment the man said slowly, "Look, if you want to see me before I leave—come early tomorrow. But you better stay away."

She nodded and ran down the lane.

Her brain was pounding with terror. She had never done anything like this, had never gone so far. She felt driven by the same God that had possessed the minister, making his voice shrill and furious at once, making his legs jerk him about on that platform. God had torn out of that man's mouth sobs and groans of desperation; Clara understood what he must have felt.

She ran along the big low building until she came to their place. Then she stopped. The door was open and the lights were on. "Is she out there?" her father's voice said. Clara paused, outside the circle of light, then came forward. Carleton was sitting inside, on the end of his cot. Clara saw

Nancy's face. Roosevelt and Rodwell were hiding behind her. Carleton got to his feet and came to the doorway. He walked so carefully that she knew he was drunk.

"Somebody seen you where you shouldn't of been," he said. His face was ugly. Clara did not move. She saw his arm draw back even before he knew what he was going to do.

"Bitch just like your mother!" he said.

He began to beat her. Inside, Nancy shrieked for help. Clara tried to break away but could not because he was holding her. Lights came on. Someone yelled out. Carleton was swearing at her, words she had heard all her life but had never understood, and now she understood them all—they were to show hate, to show that someone wanted to kill you. Then Carleton let her go. He stumbled backwards and she saw that two men were holding onto him. "They want to get up an' leave, they don't stay home, they run off—the bitches— just like their mother," Carleton shouted. "They don't stay home but run off! Bitches don't love nobody— Clara don't give a damn, my Clara—" He began to sob. Someone shook his shoulders to quiet him down.

"You let that girl alone tonight, you hear?" a man said.

"She run off an'— Dirty filthy bitch like all of them—"

"Walpole, are you goin' to let her alone?"

They got him inside and on the cot. He fell asleep almost at once, as soon as his head was down. Clara rubbed her face and saw that it was bleeding. She looked at Nancy just once and then quit looking. She knew that Nancy had been in the tavern somewhere, that Nancy was the one who'd seen her, but she did not care. The blood that ran into her mouth was the only real thing: she could taste that. Roosevelt and Rodwell, her brothers, were nothing to her. Let them look. Let them snicker. Nancy was nothing. Her father, snoring damply on the bed, his face flushed and his shirt unbuttoned to show his sunken chest and his soft, spreading stomach, was real to her now but not for long.

The neighbors went back to bed. Nancy turned off the light. They lay in the dark and listened to Carleton snore, and then everyone went to sleep except Clara. She lay still and thought. It was as if a great cooling breeze had been blowing toward her for years and now it had overtaken her and was going to carry her with it. That was all.

10

Carleton woke up. Someone was shouting in his face. "What's wrong with you? Get up!"

He opened his eyes to see a strange woman shouting down at him. She had a round leathery face with exaggerated eyes that could have been anyone's—a man's or a woman's.

"How long are you goin' to lay there? Goddam you! Your darling little daughter is run off and we got to get to work— it's goin' on six, what the hell's wrong with you?"

He pushed Nancy away and sat up. His eyes darted around the room.

"We got to get out there before the bus leaves," Nancy said viciously. "I fed the kids while you laid there snorin'—what's wrong with you these days? Can't take a little drinkin' no more? It ain't like you worked those two days—what a big joke! Get all the way out there an' the man tells you poor bastards it's all off—"

Carleton got to his feet. He was wearing his clothes from yesterday; his shoes were still on. Inside his stomach a hard knot was forming. He stood with his shoulders hunched and his head bowed, listening and not listening to Nancy, paying close attention to the knot in his stomach. It was familiar but might get out of hand yet. He was getting ready to think about Clara.

"You all right?" Nancy said.

She put one arm around him. He did not move. "You look kinda sick," she said. Carleton pushed her gently away. He did not want to move fast for fear he would get something into motion he could not stop. "Yeah—like I said about Clara—she ran off," Nancy said. She had a whining, defensive voice. "You shouldn't of hit her like that, she ain't a bad kid. You know it. I don't blame her for runnin' off, I run off myself, I wasn't goin' to take none of that crap from nobody—"

Carleton bent over the basin and splashed cold water onto his face. It was strange, but he could feel the water running down the outside of his skin as if it were far away from him, while he himself contemplated it from somewhere deep inside.

"We better get out there. It's goin' to be hot today," Nancy said. His silence made her nervous; she was speaking almost quietly now. "Honey, are you all right?"

The ball in his stomach threatened him for an instant but he fought it down. He didn't want to throw up and have that taste in his mouth. The water on his face made his skin itch and he watched his hand come up to rub it. He watched his fingers scratch at his skin, then he forgot about scratching and stood with one hand up to his face in a pose of abstract thinking. His brain was just now waking up. It told him harshly that he had a lot of thinking to do—he had to get things sorted out. For weeks, months, years he had been letting things accumulate. If he did not get them straight and understand them he would never be able to get free of them and begin a new life.

"Is the baby all right?" he said.

"Sure." Nancy sounded touched by this.

"How much money do you have?"

"What?"

"How much money?"

"You mean—right now?"

"I gave you three dollars Friday."

"I—I had to buy food—"

"Here. Take this." He reached deep in his pocket and took out a soiled ball of material that might have been silk. He unwrapped it and gave her a few dollars from it; he did not notice how she was staring at him. She might have been waiting for him to hit her, so white and strained was her face. "That should help, then you'll make somethin' today. Twelve or fifteen today, you an' the kids."

"Where are you goin'?"

He put the rest of the money back in his pocket. At the mirror he crouched so that he could see his face. The knot in his stomach grew tighter: that did not seem to be his face staring helplessly back out at him. "Christ," he said. He rubbed his eyes, his mouth. Everything was stale from his drunken sleep. An image came to him of Clara cringing back from his hands—but he shook it away. He knew that he would have a lot to shake out of his mind before he could stop thinking.

"Honey, are you goin' after her? Carleton?"

He left the room and stepped into the bright, innocent sunlight, making a face. He might have been walking past a stranger who was pleading with him, pulling at his arm. Nancy said, frightened, "Where the hell will you look? Carle-

104

ton? I mean—where are you goin'? She'll be back! You don't want to make no trouble with people from town—"

Carleton tucked his shirt into his trousers, raising his aching shoulders as high as he could. His two boys were waiting patiently outside. They looked at him. He glanced at them as he might have glanced at two strange boys, one with a lowered, pinkish head and the other with a careful blank face that was poised upon a body about to break into a run at any second. They both had Carleton's look—a long, narrow, thin face—and he had the idea that they would never get much bigger than they were. "You mind Nancy," he said to them.

She followed him along the lane, tugging at his arm. "Look, she'll be back. Clara likes you real well—she'll be back—she only took a few things, an' no money—"

She followed him out to the road. Carleton pushed her back, still without looking at her. He walked in a precarious falling motion forward, as if he were listening to something ahead of him. Nancy began to cry. She cried loudly. As he walked toward town he heard her swearing at him, shrieks of words that flew right by his head and did not hurt him. "I'll kill that baby! That goddam dirty baby!" she screamed.

He listened to her screaming, then he stopped hearing her. He seemed to pass beyond her screaming and beyond her life with no more effort than he might have walked past a crazy woman on the road.

When he reached town he was soaked with sweat. A dusty clock in a gas station said four-thirty but he knew from the sun that it was around six. The town had not yet gotten out of bed, only a few places were open. He walked along the road until there were some dirt paths and he walked on them, up the incline to the railroad tracks and then down on the other side. There were lots of weeds growing by the tracks and many junked and rusting cars and parts. On the other side of the tracks he saw a restaurant that was open. He went inside and asked about Clara. A few truck drivers were sitting at the counter. They watched him closely, as if there were something in his voice that he himself did not know about. "I did see a girl like that last night," the waitress said. She had high-piled brown hair and a very young face; as she spoke to Carleton the freckles around her nose seemed to get darker, showing how young she was. She was almost as young as Clara. Carleton waited, listening to her with his shoulders back and straight even though they ached. He did not seem surprised that the first person he should ask would have seen Clara. The girl talked earnestly, about that lost girl she'd seen, about her long blond hair and blue dress and even a yellow purse—she was excited to think she could remember so much and looked up at Carleton as if awaiting praise for so much information. "Who was she with? Who was he?" Carleton asked, cutting her off. The girl gave a name Carleton had never heard before, but he knew he would not forget it. "Where does he live?" he said patiently, again cutting her off. She told him. It was necessary for her to come out from behind the counter, pretending to be a little frightened, glancing at the truck drivers as she spoke to Carleton. She went to the door and even outside with him, pointing down the street.

He walked off, not hurrying. He did not even want to hurry; it wasn't to maintain his pride that he walked slowly. It was just that he knew he had to go a certain distance before he allowed that hard ball in his stomach to take over.

The house was a nice little house on a side street. In the front yard were beds of flowers that confused him—he had not expected flowers. But when the door opened and a middle-aged woman stared up at him, her face drawn and pale and her hair untidy, he was not surprised. "Is your son home?" he said politely. She clutched a robe of some kind around her. It smelled like moth balls. He could sense her thinking of something to say and then forgetting it because she was so upset. He waited while she went to get her son. Standing on the porch, inside the veranda that was so nicely shaded with big round leaves, he did not even bother to glance in the house, through the door she'd left ajar. He had no interest in anything but groping his way to Clara through a number of people, and those people could interest him only faintly. He might have felt excitement at meeting the boy, but he seemed to know that this was too fast, too easy; it would take more time than this.

The woman was gone quite a while. It might have been ten minutes. Then Carleton began to hear footsteps. They were on a stairway, heavy and reluctant. Someone was whispering, then there was silence. A young man emerged out of the dimness of the house and blinked at Carleton. "You know anything about my daughter?" Carleton said. The boy wore baggy yellow pajamas. At first he stammered and swallowed, he knew nothing. Then Carleton asked him again. He made a hissing sound that was a laugh, raised his eyebrows, scratched his head. "There was someone, I guess," he said slowly. "She was with this guy who comes here once in a while—he don't live here—mixed up with whisky or somethin'—that's what somebody said—I—"

"Where's he stayin'?"

"He goes to this one place when he comes in town," the boy said. He had the waitress' sincere look. He stared right into Carleton's eyes as if the two of them were friends involved in a mutual problem. "Yeah. Yes. Over on the other side of town, a big dirty house where the woman has ten kids—she rents rooms—there's one like her in every town—"

Carleton made a gesture that he hadn't meant to be threatening, but the boy stammered and was silent. "Thanks," Carleton said.

When he got to the house he could feel sweat running off him. On the big veranda with its peeling paint and broken boards he talked to a youthful woman with a ruined, blemished face. She kept staring off over his shoulder as if every word he said pained her. "We need money here," she said, whining, "we don't have nothin' to do with anybody who—"

"Where did he go?"

"He had that room two other times he was in town," she said. "He never made no trouble, I liked him. His business was his own business."

"Where did he go?"

She fumbled with the neck of her dress. Her lower lip protruded in thought, then relaxed. "You can look in his room," she said. "I ain't fixed it up yet. I heard him drive out last night, real late—I was in bed—"

Behind her a man was shouting something. The woman stared over Carleton's shoulder as if the voice were coming from a great distance. Then she turned sharply and yelled back through the screen door: "You shut your mouth an' keep it shut!" When she turned back to Carleton her face was already composed and she was moving. They went down the rickety steps and around to the back of the house. In the soft morning light of this land everything was softened by moisture, even the rotting wood of the house. There was a pile of lumber around the corner, some of it propped up against the house as if children had been playing with it. Carleton and the woman walked in the driveway, which was rutted and wet. Two cars were parked in it, at angles. One of the cars looked as if it had been there for quite a while. Carleton thought he could get it going, maybe, if it was his own car. The only trouble would be getting it out of that mud.

She showed him the room. A flood of sunlight fell onto

the bare floor and partly onto the bed. Carleton looked around. The very bareness of the room satisfied him. He knew it was still too soon to find her. "Where does he go after he leaves here?" he said.

"Why, he drives to Savannah. I think. To Savannah maybe," she said pleasantly, as if offering Carleton a gift. "I don't know why I know that. . . ."

"What does he look like?" Carleton said. His eyes moved slowly around the room. He saw a film of dirt on the window. The room was so empty he might get lost in it, somehow fall in its secret silence and be unable to get out. He kept looking around as the woman described that man, again pleasantly, like the young man and the waitress leaning a little toward him as if about to offer him some of their energy as well as their truthfulness. When she stopped, he felt his mind jerk like a muscle. He jumped forward and began tearing the bedclothes off.

"Here," the woman said nervously, "you don't want to get hot this early in the day—"

When he was outside again he felt better. At first the woman did not want to sell him that car because the kids played in it, and because the man who owned it might be coming back someday; her forehead creased with honesty. Carleton had the eerie, unreal feeling that this morning everyone was sympathetic with him as they had never been before in his life; it might have been that they believed his life was over. But he took out his money and counted it patiently. "Well, maybe you got a hand with cars," the woman said, looking at his money. "It'll maybe start an' maybe won't." Carleton said nothing. She laughed breathlessly and went with him over to the car, tiptoeing and hopping in the mud. "The keys are inside there," she said. Carleton got the door open and slid inside.

It took a while to get out of the driveway, then he was all right. He drove the sputtering car to a gas station and the attendant stared at the car as if he were trying to place it. The boy moved slowly with the hose. "Which way to Savannah?" Carleton said. The boy wrenched his gaze from the car and looked at Carleton for the first time. "Give you a map," he mumbled shyly. He went inside the little building—it was supposed to be a castle, with forlorn whitewashed turrets and peaks that looked like cardboard juttings—and came out again with a road map. "That'll help y'all out," he said in a soft, polite drawl. Carleton opened the map and his heart lurched at the challenge it was—all those lines and colors and tiny numbers! He had never seen anything like it in his life.

This was at six-thirty. At nine o'clock he was on the road, far away. He had not eaten yet and looked at the infrequent restaurants along the road—most of them closed—as if they were additional challenges he had to overcome. And the little towns with their signs that promised so much: they were challenges too. In any one of them he could have stopped the car and just sat there, waiting, or he could abandon the car and lose himself and forget everything. There was so much to think about. And in the country there was the same temptation: the lush green vegetation, the streaked, bloody clay on the side of the road, the low-lying blue sky with its look of moisture about to condense into rain, the random unsurprising farms and houses where people whose names and faces he did not know lived and had lived quietly for years. . . . He shook his head to get rid of these thoughts. And when he did so it seemed to him that he was waking up, again and again, and that each time he woke the air was keener with light and the hood of the old car had more spots free of rust to reflect the sun and that the pain in his stomach had also come awake, slowly and lazily getting ready for the long day.

He had to stop finally, in a town whose name he did not know. He bought gas. He asked the man for sun glasses—there was something shameful about this, and his face reflected it. The man noticed nothing and came back with some white framed plastic glasses; they were all he had. Carleton took them. He put them on and felt panic at the strange look everything had—as if he were staring out at the town with another man's eyes. His vision was narrowed also by the dark green lenses, and the white area at the corners of his eyes was lost to him. He swallowed in terror.

"Nice hot day," the man said, flicking his fingers on and off the hood of the car to show how hot it was. Carleton felt envy for him—sitting back in that little garage without having to do anything or having to think. But he got over the envy by feeling contempt. He hated this man the way he hated everyone who was not himself.

At ten o'clock he was still driving, and at ten-thirty, though he didn't bother to guess the time any longer. He could guess it easily enough—it was something you learned when you picked vegetables or fruit and the sun was always with you but at importantly different places in the sky. Now it did not really seem to be the same sun that was following him. That sun belonged out in the fields, but this sun was white and pure and burning hot, pounding down on him in the old car as if it had something to do with the pounding in his stomach. The two pains were trying to get together, to be one.

It was strange, to be driving like this and to feel his own hands at the wheel. Usually he sat back on the buses and looked out sightlessly at nothing, but now he was driving, himself. He had to watch the road and he found himself staring at odd things in the distance, puzzling them out until they got closer—an old windmill, a bridge, a horse-drawn wagon with two children on it. Something flicked at him as he passed those boys—he wanted to stop and talk with them, he didn't know why. He wanted to say something to them, to ask where they lived. And there was a woman out by a mailbox some miles farther; he wanted to talk with her too. She turned to watch him come and she turned slowly to watch him drive by, as if she rarely saw anyone on the road. Carleton felt a peculiar jumpy excitement at seeing her—he wanted to stop and get out and talk to someone, not to explain what he was doing but to face a person who would know nothing about it, so that he could rest. His eyes had begun to water behind the glasses.

He had no idea what time it was when he stopped at a diner in one of the little towns. His head was pounding. When he got out he was amazed that the air was no different —it was just as it was in the car. Suffocating, baking. It seemed to follow close to him in a kind of halo. He went inside the diner. A few flies buzzed lazily. There was no one sitting at the counter and no one behind it. He sat and waited. There were sounds from the back room, someone laughing, a hammer pounding. After a moment he got up and went around and leaned through the door, stretching his arms out on either side and catching the door frame. The kitchen was cluttered and messy, but with a look of being settled. At a table sat a fat man without a shirt; he was doing something with a hammer. A nerve in Carleton's eye twitched when the fat man struck the table. "Got it!" the man said. A girl in a soiled white outfit was leaning back against a stove, giggling. The man struck again at the table and she giggled louder. Carleton saw that the man had squashed quite a few flies on the table and that there were dozens of dents in the soft wood.

After he had a bottle of pop there and tried to eat a sandwich, he went out to his car. This time it did not start. In the doorway of the diner the fat man watched; he was a kind

110

man; he had left the hammer back in the kitchen. "Might could use some water," he said. Carleton nodded. He tried the car again, then gave up. The man brought him some water in a red plastic sprinkling can. Carleton smiled and said thanks. There was a spreading hot ache in his stomach that he wanted to deceive.

He did not know when he was entering the outskirts of Savannah until he saw a sign telling him this. The sun had moved across the sky by then and was assaulting him from another angle. But when he saw the sign he said aloud, "Now what?" He kept on driving. The steering wheel was slippery with his sweat. "Now what?" But he fought down his panic. There were so many cars here that he had to be slow, cautious. He had to pay attention. He couldn't go off dreaming. . . . It seemed to him that those other cars held enemies who could tell that he was out of place here, a stranger, a man carrying rage inside him the way one might hide a weasel inside his shirt; it would not stay hidden for long.

So he drove on. His eyes began to throb. Black threads appeared and when he tried to focus on them they wavered away. The soft drink and what he had eaten of the sandwich threatened to force themselves up on him; all his energy had to be used to keep them down. And he hated his smell, the stale harsh odor of sweat and fear. He let the car slow until he was hardly moving. This was on the side of the highway. When he felt better he speeded up again, as if he knew where he was going and did not want to be late.

He saw a clock in a window somewhere: it said two-fifteen. This registered in his brain without his bothering to translate it into any meaning. His jaw ached with its rigidity. He wanted to talk, even to himself. He wanted to talk about Clara and to talk to her, plan what he would say to her. But he did not dare open his lips for fear something crazy would come out. The ache in his stomach wanted to turn him into an animal and he had to keep it down.

He drove for some time. He pretended to be looking at people on the street, as if one of them might be Clara. He turned off onto side streets and then onto other side streets. He drove through Negro sections and even here stared at people he could see were black, looking for his daughter. Of the man who'd taken her away he did not think at all. He could not believe he would find her with a man. She would not dare to be out walking with him, out in the sunlight. . . . Then he found himself thinking of Pearl as she had been at Clara's age. Was it Clara he was looking for or Pearl? That

111

blond hair, that childish face, that light, loving laughter . . . it was those things he was looking for. It seemed to him unfair that he should not find them when he was Carleton, Carleton Walpole, who should have had everything he wanted. He was a young man yet. He had strong muscular arms and shoulders and legs; he could fight; he was handsome, women glanced at him in that certain exciting way; his people were waiting for him to move back home. They were waiting for him. The black threads wavered in his vision and gave way to a group of ghostly, watery people who did not even beckon to him but were waiting patiently for him, sure he would return. Who were these people? They were frail, blurred, like people in old photographs, and Pearl was one of them. . . . Carleton let the car drift to a stop. This was on a side street. There was a warehouse nearby, a church, a gas station. A few old houses built right next to one another with hardly room for a kid to run between them, rearing up high and skinny. He picked up the map and with his shaking fingers tried to smooth it out, looking for Kentucky. He looked everywhere for the word "Kentucky." He wanted to know how far away from home he still was. But then a sharp pain distracted him and he stared out the windshield and waited for it to pass.

He got out of the car. The ground quivered beneath him. He thought of going to the gas station and asking if they'd seen Clara, but when he came close enough to see that the clock said only twenty after two, he was terrified. He knew that more time had passed than twenty minutes. At least an hour had passed since he'd seen the other clock. So he began to breathe quickly and shallowly. He walked. The neighborhood was hot and crowded with children; people were happy here. They were white children. Carleton walked along and paused when they ran past, or when a woman pushing a buggy approached him. He wanted to touch these people for some reason. They did not notice him. Sitting on a trashbox at a corner was an old man in rags, and Carleton forced his shoulders back in a gesture of contempt for this old bastard— he would never be like that. He was exhausted and hadn't eaten the right kind of food, that was his trouble.

He walked for some time. His tongue felt swollen in his mouth. He was no longer looking for Clara, since he could not seem to keep her image in his mind distinguished from those of other people he had known. He thought of the word "Clara" but felt only a vague muscular response. It seemed to him that he had been looking for something or someone for a long time and that the final joke on him would be that if he

112

found it he would not recognize it: that was what they had done to him, those bastards who ran things and arranged jobs and took commissions and those bastards who owned farms and hired people to work like niggers, sweating themselves out and hunching their backs forever. But even his hatred for these people was hardly more than a token muscular response, a gesture of clenching his fists that stopped at once because he was too weak.

The sun was hot in the city. It glared down at him as if singling him out for something, some special fate. The sun glasses made his eyes feel strange but he didn't want to take them off; this way he was disguised and protected. With a semblance of alertness, an attitude memorized rather than spontaneous, he glanced about at strangers on the sidewalks as if he wanted to stop one of them to talk or as if he believed one of them might stop him. There was that pain in his stomach that had been bothering him off and on for months, for a longer time than he wanted to remember, and the bloody bowel movements he'd stopped looking at right away. The danger was that if this pain forced its way through his closed lips it might get control of him and he would forget everything. He had to keep silent. If he stopped someone to ask about Clara—about anything—this pain might shriek out instead and he would be lost. So he kept walking, amazed at the heat and at the energy of people who passed him without interest, his knees now and then buckling and his shoulders aching with this unaccustomed rigidity. He was rigid as if holding himself back even at the same time he was forcing his legs to work. He was holding back some exclamation of pain, some admitted discovery he could not yet own up to—

In a store window, surrounded by greenish-tinted glass, a clock said two-thirty. Carleton's head began to pound in panic. He came up to the window and stared at that clock. Two thirty-one. He stared at the clock.

When he turned he crossed the street at once. Cars were slowing for a traffic light and he worked his way through them, not looking at them but extending his limp fingers as if he were trying to exercise a spell so that he could pass through. On the other side he paused to get his breath and his head swam, the black threads crisscrossing in his eyes, so he knew better than to stop. He could not stop until he came to a safe place. Because it seemed to him that something terrible was happening. Time was slowing down for him. Never in his life had time slowed down, but it was slowing

113

down now, stretching out, and this meant that the rest of his life would gape out before him like that long hot road up to this city whose name he had already forgotten in a state he had worked in and traveled through for years but whose name he had also forgotten; he had even forgotten the fact that it might have a name, that this vague field of sights and sounds that glimmered about him for so many square miles might have been named for some reason. So he kept walking in spite of the pain and did not look up at anything that might tell the time. He would never look at another clock again.

He came to a church. It might have taken him five minutes or two hours. He saw out of the corner of his eye steps leading somewhere and so he looked over and saw a church. Vaguely he recalled that Clara had gone to a church—and back home he himself had gone to a church. So he went up the steps and pulled the door open and went inside.

It was a strange place, with a high ceiling that dissolved away in shadow. Figures stood motionless in the half-light; then he saw that they were statues. The sweat on his body turned cold. He groped his way along past the first several pews, then sat down heavily. But he did not feel any relief, any relaxation. He looked around and saw that the walls were made of stone; his church back home hadn't been like this. These stones looked like something frozen but at the same time they looked about to move. There was a peculiar force pulling everything upward, gravitating everything upward toward the shadowy ceiling. The stained-glass windows, seemingly so permanent, moved a little too. Carleton rubbed his aching eyes. It struck him with a slow, cold horror that nothing in the church was still; it had only looked still when he had first come in. Everything was moving. He was the only thing that remained still. In the windows the brilliant reds and blues and yellows glowed and faded, sinking back into themselves and then rearing out as if behind them a heart was beating, and everywhere—he saw this now—there were vertical lines and juttings, arches high up on the walls, that vibrated as if about to come to life. The shadowy ceiling might not even be a ceiling, but the entrance to another sphere, ghostly and quivering with life like the invisible wings of birds. Carleton closed his eyes, and he saw a picture of barren highway, empty highway stretching off into the distance, and on either side of this highway vegetation he had never bothered to look at, an entanglement of bushes and trees and weeds writhing in their own silence, tensing steadily against whatever held them back or whatever kept them from rushing upon the road and overwhelming it. He felt something forcing its way up into his mouth and out through his lips—a groan.

Once he began he could not stop. He forgot everything. He pressed his hand against his stomach and felt the pain come alive there, jerking alive like something that had only stirred in its sleep before but was now rousing itself to fight. He groaned again, his eyes shutting tight, sweat breaking out on his face. Before the pain took over he wanted to think—clearly—he wanted to understand that he was looking for his daughter, the only person he had ever loved, and that he had not found her yet but was in the right city—he had driven hundreds of miles after her!—and that he would find her and bring her back—and he wanted to remember his name, that he was a Walpole and that the name Walpole was important, it pointed to a certain kind of man, that he was this man—he was young and strong and had no debts and never said no to a fight—

But he felt these things slipping off, away. He felt thoughts leaving him, memories he should have sorted out years ago so that when the time came he could put them all together. He was terrified at the thought of dying because it meant that all these things would be lost—who else was there to bring them together, to make sense of them, except him? Everything—everyone—the whole world—was joined in him, only in him. Only in Carleton Walpole. He was the center of the world, the universe, and without him everything would fall into pieces. He felt that. It terrified him that people and places and dates should fly off into nothing, as if into the shadowy church ceiling, belonging to no one and making no sense—who else could know what that photograph meant, of himself and Pearl, and who else could remember his father's face, who else could remember the mistake he'd made with Rafe that time, ending up with Rafe dead and for what reason?—and who else could remember the bastards who had cheated his family, and the good times they'd had, and the weather, all the rain and mud and sunshine, and his children, Sharleen who was off somewhere and Mike who was on his own, and Clara run away with a man he'd never seen, and his new baby back at that camp? There was no one else to remember these things. When he died they would be lost forever; they had no life except in him. If he was allowed to live, Carleton thought, he would change everything. He would think things out and sort them out and untangle the forty-odd years of his life that he had let go wild.

115

He was to live for two months yet, in a strange bed, and there would be whole hours when he would feel almost no pain. But during those hours his mind would be empty and baked clean and he would have nothing to think about anyway.

TWO

Lowry

1

They had been driving for so long that Clara did not think about getting anywhere at all. At first she had watched the sun rise and thought nervously, fiercely, "Nobody's going to get me now. He isn't going to get me." She had stared at the road ahead of them that Lowry overtook always at the same speed, not nervous or worried about anything, and tried to imagine it running back under them and becoming part of the past—all that distance and time her father would have to conquer if he were to get her. She thought of the way he had hit her. She kept seeing his arm drawn back, then jerking out, then drawing back again. . . .

"He made my face bleed," she told Lowry in her thin, outraged child's voice. Sometimes she cried and sometimes she forgot to cry, her anger running out into a sudden sense of being helpless, being lost. "He never hit me like that before, he hit the other kids but not me; I could taste the blood and some people were watching—some bastards were watching—and Nancy was the one who told him—" She would lean forward slightly, staring at the road. Then she would turn to see it still moving back steadily behind them, misty in the morning light, and something about the way it disappeared so swiftly frightened her. She was afraid to think that her father might find her and she was afraid to think that he might never find her.

She slept. In sleep she could hear herself sobbing and she woke up, terrified, not knowing where she was. The rhythm and vibration of travel did not alarm her, it was the smallness of the vehicle she was in that made her realize that something was unusual. Then she jerked awake, seeing Lowry there and remembering who he was and what she was doing with him. This happened several times. Though she could see clearly enough the sun rise and move across the sky and prepare to sink again, it was hard for her to understand that time was really going by. The days of the week had always been very important to them because you had to know how far away Sunday was. That was important. But now, on the road with this strange man, moving so fast, she could not remember what time meant and how it was measured.

They stopped at small restaurants and taverns, in the country or near towns. Clara was used to traveling and did not bother to look at anything in particular; she had too much to think about. And Lowry drove as if he already knew everything, as if he'd taken this route many times before and was not worried. Clara had learned to recognize a certain kind of man. There was one kind who never did anything, and the other kind who took over and got you where you needed to go and made no fuss over it. As long as he was around you did not have to worry. Her father had been like that sometimes, Clara thought, and Lowry was like that too.

When they entered one of the diners Clara's eyes would ache with concentration, because she never knew whom she might meet. There was an air about Lowry of his knowing secrets but not telling them. So she was anxious each time they stopped somewhere, wondering who might be inside, whether it could be someone who knew her and would let Carleton know where she was . . . but of course they were all strangers and after a while strangers began to look alike.

In these small half-deserted places Lowry always took over. He brought in from the outside the vigorous exhaustion of someone who has been driving for many hours and has hours yet to go, but who is satisfied with what he has done. Clara thought, catching his reflection in a mirror somewhere or watching him out of the corner of her eye, that he was a man who had somewhere to get to, while most of the men around him were already as far as they were going to go. And she herself had nowhere to go. She could think of nothing except what she was leaving behind. She tried to fix in her mind that camp back in Florida so that she would always know where she was in relationship to it. The many turns and changes of direction Lowry had taken since Florida were evened out in her imagination, so that wherever she happened to be, her family was exactly behind her though many hundreds of miles away. Lowry was always by her and he was proof that she was no longer home.

Time passed and they kept traveling. Clara liked it when they stopped to eat because the way Lowry ate, so quickly, was a kind of gift to her; it meant he was like other people after all. She had no appetite herself. She was always tired, exhausted, though all she did was sit in the car and watch the road. She would bring food to her mouth slowly and sit there

120

as if she'd forgotten it, not looking at the food or the table or anything. Lowry would say, "Finish it, I paid for it."

One of the places they stopped at was a country tavern set back in a cinder-strewn lot. Clara liked the way it looked from the outside because it had once been a house, there was a place to live in the back and upstairs. She felt a little shy about going inside with Lowry. But everything was familiar; it was the sort of place they'd stopped at before. There was a smell of tobacco and beer and something damp.

Clara said, while Lowry ate silently, "I don't want to die. I'm afraid to die." Lowry was soaked with sweat from driving and this gave him a sleepy, easy look. Clara brought her elbows up onto the table and pressed her fingers against her eyes. Over at the bar, two men were talking in a way that annoyed her. One spoke, and the other waited several seconds before replying. This kept on. Clara stared through her fingertips at Lowry and thought of how much she loved him and how helpless she was because of that.

"What did you say?" said Lowry.

He kept on eating. Clara felt satisfied that he ate, as if the food were something she was giving him. "I said, where are we going," said Clara.

"Who, you or me?"

"Both."

"You have to make up your mind what to do," he said. "I'm getting to where I'm going tomorrow."

Clara pushed her plate away. "I'll pay you for all this—"

"Forget it."

"I'll get a job and pay it back."

"Who the hell's going to hire you? What can you do?"

She wondered if he was joking. She made herself laugh. What she felt for him kept passing over into something else, into rage. She loved him for his face and his strong arms and the way he'd taken her along with him, saving her, but she hated him for the way his eyes could drift anywhere and forget she was sitting across from him. She saw how he forgot her. There might have been a gap in the air where she sat, staring at him secretly, and he did not need to avoid looking at her because he was not even aware she was still with him. When Lowry finished eating he pushed his plate away too and sat back, resting. His eyes moved around. They never found anything worth staying on.

"What kind of a job do you have, where you're goin'?" Clara said.

Lowry shrugged his shoulders.

121

"Can't you tell me?"

"Say that again."

"What?"

"What you just said."

"I— What did I say?— Can't you tell me?"

Lowry smiled. "I like to hear you talk."

Clara flushed and looked away. "Is there somethin' wrong with me, I mean, how I talk—? I never went to school an' learnt anything else. I don't know . . ."

"You're all right."

But she hated the way he said it, she hated his smile. It occurred to her that words were not just things to be spoken but that they had strange meanings you didn't know about, secret sounds to them that told people what they needn't always know. . . . She would wait to hear how Lowry talked and she would talk like him.

In the car, when he was getting sleepy, he talked to keep awake: "I like to drive, I always liked to drive. I like the way the roads are, even the bumpy roads, even the muddy roads. . . . There's all this energy stored up that I got to use up. Every place is the same but you've got to keep going."

Clara mouthed to herself: "Every place is the same but you've got to keep going."

"I never look for anything. What is there to look for? I'm glad I can stay awake for so long. . . . I'm sleepy, my head aches. . . . Driving is part of my job, I'm glad I can go so long without sleeping. But I wouldn't mind if you could take over."

"You want to teach me how?"

He wouldn't answer, as if he were already asleep and driving just out of habit. Clara waited for him to start in talking again. She never knew what he would say; he might say anything. She hoped that would not turn out to be crazy, because then he would get arrested and taken away. She had seen a man dragged out of a camp once, screaming and sobbing, and his wife running alongside him yelling at him. That man had been "crazy." His wife had called the police. He was crazy because he was loud, but there were other people who were crazy and secret about it and these people were never dragged away. They knew enough to keep quiet. Clara thought that when she got old and strange herself, she'd keep quiet; that way no one could get you.

Lowry kept driving. He whistled to himself. Clara felt shy and locked in silence on her side of the seat. She felt so tired, so old; she wanted to ask him, Why am I so old? Why am I

122

always older than anyone else? But she only said, in a voice that broke out a little louder than she wanted, "If you need somebody to help you in anything you do, I can help you. I don't care what it is. You wouldn't need to pay me, but only . . . some food or somethin'. . . . Once I stole somethin' but I don't want to do it no more. But if you wanted me to steal for you I would."

Lowry just laughed.

Clara felt a stab of love for him, a feeling of desperate helplessness. At the base of her spine was a cold numb place into which all her blood ran, draining away to leave her helpless, like a rag doll. She looked at the side of his face as if she thought he could not see her. She stared at his nose, his eyes. His mouth. She remembered his face being so close to her, back in that room, and her mind rocked a little with the enormity of it; she could not really believe it any longer.

"You are just a child," Lowry pointed out.

"You are just a child," Clara mouthed after him.

"I can't be dragging you around with me."

Clara studied those words carefully. Then she said, "Don't you like me?"

"Oh, Christ—"

"I could do things for you—"

"Look, I can't be dragging you around. You're just a child, I don't think of you any other way."

"Don't you think I'm pretty?"

Lowry let that pass. Then he said, "I can't talk to you. It's better to say nothing."

Clara pressed her hands against her mouth, frightened. But she shaped his words, secretly: "It's better to say nothing—" She waited. She wondered whether he would ever turn to look at her the way other men had looked at her, and the way he had once looked at her back in that tavern. After she'd left LeRoy. Why had that gone by, what was wrong? A feeling of rage rose in her at being so strangely rejected.

"I want somethin' more," Clara muttered. She wanted to seize his arm and make him look at her. She wanted to sink her nails into his arm. "You better listen to me, mister."

"What?"

"You better listen. Oh, damn it. Damn it," she said. Lowry must have been startled but he did not let on. Clara felt her face getting warm. "I want lots of things an' I'm goin' to get them—don't you think I'm like my ma or Nancy or anybody. I'm not," she said weakly, her words slowing down, "you ain't goin' to just kick me out—I want more things than just babies like my ma and Nancy and everybody else! Who took care of Nancy's baby anyway? I like babies but I want more than that, I'll show you."

Lowry glanced at her. "What do you want, then?"

"I don't know what it is yet."

"Why are you so mad?"

"I don't know what it is but I want it," Clara said. "I'm goin' to get it, too."

"You don't even have a last name any more, kid."

"I'll get one, then."

"Going to steal it?"

"Going to steal it?" Clara repeated. "Just listen, mister—if nobody gives me what I want, I'll steal it. I want somethin'—I'm goin' to get it—I—"

"You better calm down."

Her heart was pounding furiously and out of her rage came something like joy. She knew that she would find out what she wanted and that she would get it. She knew this would happen.

"First I got to learn how things are," she said.

That night Lowry turned the car off the road and parked it down an old cow lane. He slept in the back seat with his arms hugging his chest. Clara watched him after he fell asleep, leaning over the seat and letting her fingers drift a few inches above him; he slept like a child. His face relaxed and you could tell that his eyes were blind. Clara huddled in the front seat and buried her face in her arms. But she never knew if she slept or not. Everything was mixed up.

Some noise startled her. She lifted her head and it was much later. The air was dark and damp. In the back seat Lowry was still sleeping, breathing in a quiet, harsh way. The sound reminded Clara of dry weeds being rustled by the wind. She turned to watch him, helpless again as that dry draining numbing sensation rose in her. Outside the car everything was dark and formless, and she knew how easily she could fall into it and get lost. He could kick her out, he could forget her. He didn't love her. He couldn't even talk to her, or wouldn't, as if it was better for him just to think things to himself than to say them aloud to her. . . .

All he had given her of himself was his name: Lowry. And what kind of a name was that?

She thought of how Carleton was somewhere behind her. She thought of the long dark distance between her father and her, and how Lowry was taking her away, saving her. But the more she thought of how Carleton would never catch her, the more she wanted her father to appear outside and run up to the car and pound viciously at the windows. . . . And he would kill Lowry, too. He would kill him the way he'd killed a man one time, years ago. And he would take her back home and that would be all.

Lowry slept. He did not need to stay awake and think. Clara felt years older just because of how she had been thinking, worrying herself and thinking until her brain ached. All her life she had loved and hated people but she had never thought about it. Now, at the beginning of her new life, she was going to think about everything and get it clear. Lowry was a man who did not just fall into things, he knew what he was doing. In the camps people just fell into things and that was that. The vast hot fields shimmering with light had been places like those misty spots in dreams where you might stumble and fall and fall forever; and so everyone had been lost right out in the daylight but had never known it. Her father had been lost too.

She knew then that he would never find her. He would never get out of that sleep that spread so hot and heavy over the fields, dragging them all down. She would never see him again.

Lowry woke about two hours later. It was still dark. One moment Clara had been leaning against the seat, thinking hard, and the next moment she herself was waking up. Her mouth was stale and sore. In that first instant of waking her heart pounded as if it were a brain thinking fast, in terror, trying to figure out what was wrong. Lowry yawned and sat up. There was a stale, rumpled intimacy between them that made the darkness limited.

"Did you sleep too?" he said.

She was surprised he should ask this; she stammered in reply. Lowry got out of the car. She heard him walking around in the dark, kicking his way through things. After a while he came back. He turned on the headlights and yawned again. Immediately the darkness fled back and the bushes and trees illuminated by the light turned rigid, as if petrified by Lowry's daring. She was like those trees and bushes out there, petrified by him and helpless. He was one of those men who had come in to get Rosalie's father and punish him, one of those men glimpsed on city streets—with their turned-away secret indifferent eyes. They knew. They could see. They did not live in a world made up by someone else, controlled by someone else, herded around on buses. She felt that he could

125

do anything with her that he wanted and that he knew this but did not care.

He got back on the road and in a short while dawn came. When she began to see things, she wanted to see them the way Lowry saw them. They were in hilly country, but when it got lighter she saw that the hills right around them fell back in waves to mountains, and that the boundary between these mountains and the mountainous clouds in the sky was feathery and unclear. Far away as a mountain was, it looked close up—or close up as it looked, it was really far away. She wanted to cry at how beautiful everything was.

"You must be from around here," Clara said.

"How'd you know that?"

When they descended one of the long hills, the road and the land were spread out before them so vast that Clara thought they might get lost in it, the two of them, and not even the sunlight could help them get out. This land kept her breath inside her. She was fascinated by it but its immensity was terrible—or was everything like this and had she never noticed? Everywhere she looked, her sight fell back for miles. It was as if there were holes and further holes, letting you fall back forever; there was nothing to catch hold to. In this land, the eye lost itself in contour after contour, each imitating the next, slow unravelings of streams downhill or identical trees or mountains at the horizon, making the horizon. There was so much space that lines and shapes repeated themselves over and over.

As they descended the long hill a wind blew steadily up toward them. Clara began to shiver.

"Are you goin' to stop somewhere around here?"

"Yes."

The town was hardly a town at all, just a main street that broadened the road they had come in on. Clara noticed a railroad depot and old-fashioned sleepy buildings with false fronts and a rusted water tower and perhaps a dozen stores, one of them a five and dime that caught her eye at once. "This highway keeps going all the way down to Hamilton," Lowry said. "But we're stopping here." Clara's teeth were chattering. "Now. I was born around here, myself. There's a place for you here maybe if you keep quiet about yourself and don't make any trouble. If you do they'll put you in an orphanage or something. You understand?"

Clara nodded.

"I can maybe get you started around here, find you a place. But that's all."

Clara said, "Do you live right around here?"

"I don't live anywhere."

"Does your father—"

"My father's dead."

Clara stared out at the ugly little town. Lowry had stopped the car. There was a side street that fell back rapidly from the main street, and facing it were a few buildings that had no identity at all. On one side was a granary. This town was like another dream but, unlike the fields, it had no color or heat.

"How come you bothered with me?" Clara said.

"I always wanted a little sister, maybe. No special reason."

She did not look at him. She said quietly, "I could do things for you. I could take care of things, I could cook and keep a house—"

"No. I don't need it."

"I could do anything you wanted—"

"There's nothing you could do I need," he said. "I don't stay in one place long, and nobody comes along with me. I don't need any woman waiting. I don't marry any of them either. Don't think about me because you're just not the one, kid. You're pretty, sure, you're going to be prettier, but I don't care. I see a lot of pretty faces. I don't bother with faces any more. What I want is a voice—when I find her I'll know it, and you're not the one. You're just a brat from the fruit-picking camp and you keep that in mind. Your fingernails are dirty and your clothes are too tight and your hair has never been combed all the way through." He did not speak harshly, but as one speaks in pointing out certain facts. "You understand?"

It happened that he knew people in town and after places opened up that morning he got her a room and a job. The room was up above a hardware store and had a window that looked out over a back alley; Clara could see the backs of houses across the way. A radio was playing somewhere. It was as if she and everyone she knew had been lifted up and shaken violently and set down again in a new place. The job was in the five and dime. Clara shared a long counter with another girl who looked as young as she, a slow frail child with eyes that bulged slightly. They were to sell thread and scissors and ready-made curtains and cloth of all colors and prints. The air of the cramped little store smelled of disuse.

That afternoon Clara had to have something to do, so she unwound a few yards of orange cloth in order to rewind it and straighten it. She saw that there were faint lines, faded

127

lines, on the cloth where the material had been folded around the cardboard center. She knew then that the store was sleazy and that the things that had caught her eye so many foolish times, arrayed in various windows in various towns, had been tricks.

"The name of this town is Tintern," Lowry told her.

"The name of this town is Tintern," Clara repeated.

2

There were times during the next year when she was not able to recall having come from anywhere. The town flowed upon her in fragments, warm and gritty and burdensome, and behind them was Lowry. She was always waiting for him. When she was with him she was nervously waiting for him to leave, waiting for him to get restless. There was nothing she could do. She sank down in Tintern as if sinking into a shallow and familiar area of the sea. Because she had never stayed anywhere for long and had never been able to think of any landscape as permanent, Tintern rolled upon her in monotonous hypnotic pieces that wore away her memory of other Tinterns—the anonymous small towns they'd always passed through on buses or trucks, just backgrounds for the way they lived. But Tintern was permanent. It had always been there, it was settled deep into the ground and so it would remain. This permanence was easy for her to see in the dime store, because there merchandise stayed on counters for months in exactly the same positions; you could get used to anything that way.

There was a movie house and its pictures changed every weekend; that was good. Clara loved the movies. But, sitting in the darkness every week, waiting for surprises, she began to notice that in the movies too there was an eerie sort of sameness—not quite the same faces, but the same people doing the same things.

Lowry appeared out of nowhere to say hello and talk. There was something vaguely possessive about him, but the possession had nothing to do with Clara herself, exactly. She did not know why he kept coming back. There was nothing she could say or do that was able to interest him—she could not get through to where his brain was, secret and private. Other men were different, but Lowry stayed the same. He took her places, showed her around. He listened to her words

128

critically, but not to what she said. Once he took hold of her chin and shook her head gently. "You never used to talk that way," he said. "Where'd you get that word?"

The word was Lowry's favorite word, pronounced the way he pronounced it with the slightest sounding of a final 'g': "Nothing."

From a distance, in the towns he occasionally drove her to, Clara looked older than fifteen—she had the ageless, calm, patient look of girls of her kind who are glimpsed in doorways opening right onto streets, or who wait for their men with arms folded in a casualness that means nothing, leaning against car doors or fenders. Early on Saturday evening she might be glanced at by people with homes to get to just coming out of the doorway to the stairs that led up to her room, with Lowry beside her. There would be the fast, confused blur of her face, and the gaudy blur of her clothing—dime-store sweaters and skirts. She had the kind of face that always astonishes because no one expects it to be that young. Wrapped around her wrist would be the straps of a purse, carried like a playful weapon. The man with her, Lowry, was always in a hurry and walked with his face turned a little away, as if he were already thinking about something else. He had the hard, brittle look of a young man with no youth. Even in the crowded taverns and restaurants, with other men and girls, he had that slightly distracted look. He appeared with Clara to be an older and remote relative, a cousin or uncle entrusted with her for the evening. Clara could feel part of him pulling away from her but going nowhere she could follow. If she took his hand and stroked his fingers, playing at being in love, he did not really notice. She liked to imagine that he did belong to her and that she was like the other girls they saw with men, maternal and flirtatious and possessive, though many of them were displaced from week to week.

One Saturday night they were in a town about twenty miles away, on the same side of the river as Tintern. The place was dark and crowded, and people were dancing; Clara sat by herself in a corner. She had learned to smoke in order to have something o do with her hands. She waited for Lowry to come back, and waited—he had been talking with a woman who had come up to them, some old friend with razor-bright eyes that slashed on and off Clara and forgot her. When Lowry was gone and she had to wait, she needed to be able to do something with her hands that did not show what she was feeling. She did not want anyone to understand, least of all Lowry. She did not want to have to see it herself. That sudden unmistakable knowledge that he was with someone else, hidden away somewhere in the dark with someone else: it was as if a spotlight had been turned suddenly onto her, showing up all the blemishes of the love she felt for a man who did not love her.

When he came back, Clara stood. "I guess you're going to take me home," she said.

There was a faint smear of lipstick on his face. He pulled her along. Clara was wearing high-heeled shoes and she felt suddenly too young for them; she probably looked foolish. "It's time you went home anyway," Lowry said.

He was vague with her. Clara recognized that vagueness, since he had gone off like this in the past with old friends who came up to him and exclaimed over him—two or three times—so she sat quietly enough beside him and smoked another cigarette on the long ride home. She stared out at the road and Lowry said nothing. After a while his silence was like something prodding and teasing her. "You can go to hell, mister," she said.

"It's pretty late. You should go home."

"Then you're going back to her. Don't tell me," she said sharply. "You're going back to that bitch. I hope she gets you sick."

He began to whistle thinly through his teeth. Nothing she said to him meant anything. She supposed he did hear her, but her words were like those of a younger sister; they just did not mean anything. Clara said, "That man I was telling you about last week, he was bothering me again. He said I could pick out any perfume in the store and he'd buy it for me."

"What does that mean?"

"The next time he comes in I'll say yes. That's what I'll say."

"You want to get pregnant?"

"I don't give a damn."

"How many times did your mother get pregnant?"

"None of your business."

Clara threw her cigarette spitefully out of the window.

"Another man, too, who drives a truck—he was talking with me. He makes a lot of money. He said he'd like to take me out sometime."

"Do anything you want."

"Don't you care?"

Clara began to pick the red polish off her nails. The ugliness of the chipped polish satisfied her. "You don't care,

130

you don't give a damn. You're worse than those bastards would be," she said. "Anyway, they don't have a lot of secrets about themselves like you do."

"I won't be friends with any slut."

"I didn't know we were friends."

"Do anything you want. Truck driver, railroad man, any-one—Go lying around in cars or ditches or barns."

"One of them would marry me."

"All right."

"I don't give a damn."

"I thought you wanted so many things."

For some reason Clara thought of her mother. At first, after her mother's death, she hadn't had time to think of her at all. It was something better kept back; it was too awful. Then when Nancy came along it was strange, because to somebody from the outside, the emptiness where Pearl had been wasn't real—Nancy had never known Pearl. So when you were with Nancy the whole idea of Pearl did not make sense. Nancy couldn't remember Pearl so you couldn't talk with her about Pearl, and anyway there was always so much work to do. Fixing meals, taking care of the kids—it eroded everything away—and the memory of Pearl was just a small nagging ache. But now she thought of her mother.

Whenever Lowry spoke of her family she felt something rise up in her to resist him. She did not want to think about them. Lowry mentioned them as if he'd known everything, as if the word "mother" and the word "father" applied to many people, and Clara's parents were just two of them. Lowry seemed to know everything. That was why, when she rubbed his arm and chattered on about what she'd done since he had last seen her, she knew what he was thinking: that this little girl needed him and so he would be kind and patient, but that was all. He was thinking how he had helped get her away from one life and now that she was in another, supposed to be on her own, she still needed help and clung to him like a child. If she imitated older girls it was because she was trying desperately to be someone else whom he might like— so she brushed her hair to stick out and had bangs that fell down frothily onto her forehead, and she had a red mouth that looked like something pasted on her, like plastic lips for Hallowe'en, and there were reddened spots on her cheeks that were either obvious or faint depending on the light. A charm bracelet jangled coquettishly on her arm. But it all meant nothing, it was just nothing. "Nothing." She closed her eyes and found that she was already thinking of her mother,

131

who had also waited for a man. Clara had not known it at the time but she knew it now. Her mother had waited for Carleton to come home and sometimes he didn't come home. And when he did, a day or two later, the front of his shirt might be stained with dirt or blood or vomit, and his eyes would be bloodshot and wild, as if they'd scraped along over every foot of ground he had walked. But her mother had waited for him. What else could she do? She was usually pregnant. One by one the babies had turned her back into a child so that she didn't need to wait, because she might not even have known who Carleton was, exactly. The babies had kept coming and Pearl's mind had buckled under them, giving way, and the last baby had killed her.

Clara felt warm and oppressed. If she could have thought of something else she would have been grateful, but there was no getting around what she had to face up to. This was the way life would be, then. But did all women have to go through it? She glanced at Lowry, wishing he would say something. All he said was not to "make any mistakes." It was clear what not to do, but it was not clear what she should do. What was so terrible for Clara—and for Sonya, who also worked in the dime store and was Clara's best friend, and even for her married girl friend Ginny, and her other friend Caroline—was that there was nothing else for them. There had been nothing else for Rosalie. Or Clara's sister Sharleen, or her mother. There had been nothing else in the world for them, nothing, except to give themselves to men, some man, and to hope afterwards that it had not been a mistake. But how could it be a mistake? There was no other choice.

"I could get married," Clara said shakily. "I'm pretty, men like me. Then I wouldn't be a bother to you."

"You aren't a bother to me."

"There's nothing else for me to do with my life except get married," Clara said. She leaned forward and stared out at the road as if it might tell her something. There were times when an idea brushed against her mind, but she could not seize it. Perhaps if she could read better—if she could write— if she didn't have to struggle so with words, things would come easier for her. She could kid around with men and flirt because that did not take words or thinking. But when she wanted to explain something to Lowry words betrayed her and showed only how stupid she was. She could never fool him, never carry him along on the wave of her emotions.

"There's nothing else to do," she said. "Nothing."

132

She heard Lowry suck in his breath and something white darted in front of the car, illuminated on the headlights, then there was a thud. Clara cried out. "Lowry, stop—Please stop—"

"For Christ's sake—"

"Please stop!"

He put on the brakes. Clara opened the door and ran back. A cat had run in front of the car and been hit, a white cat, and as Clara approached she saw its body twitching as if it were trying to come alive again. Clara knelt by the cat. Its mouth was opened in a snarl, but now its small teeth gleamed sharply and uselessly; it was bleeding from its stomach. She knelt there, staring. The cat hissed. Clara's shoulders hunched slowly and she hugged herself, as if trying to keep herself in, keep the blood from pouring out. It was all so fragile, this flesh and blood; look how her mother had died. One night a man had climbed on top of her and months later, months later she had died because of it. That was how it was. She could see the dying cat through a film of her own, a mist of tears.

The cat went stiff. Even the blood welling around it looked stiff and unreal.

Lowry came back and pulled her to her feet. "It's just a cat," he said.

Clara could not stop crying.

"Come on, kid. I'm in a hurry."

Clara wanted to explain to him that the cat had been alive a few minutes ago, everything in its body had been pulsating and working right, its muscles and fine little bones and its eyes; but now it was all stopped, it was dead. Those two facts were so simple that Clara felt as if she were drowning in them.

"Jesus, kid, you're just like me. You take everything too hard."

He walked her back to her side of the car and helped her in. Clara saw her reflection in the window; she looked astonished and lost. That dark mouth in that white face was laughable. She had an image of bleeding, bleeding not from any particular person or wound but just bleeding, the flow of dark rich blood moving along and getting lost in the dirt. She pressed her hands against her stomach.

"I don't like blood," she said.

"Better get used to it."

As they drove on she noticed that his mood had changed. He seemed inert and heavy. When he began to talk in a

133

minute it was a voice that was sad and angry, forcing its way out of that inertia. He might have been talking to her. "Everything's bleeding to death. I can see it. To be safe from violence you have to be violent yourself—take the first step. That way you control it. You get inside it. Even if you take chances and your luck runs out and you get it in the end— still, it isn't the same thing as just getting run over by a car one day. Or dying of cancer or rotting in jail. You have to get inside it, get right in it."

"That poor cat . . ."

"If you didn't open your mouth I'd forget what you were like," he said. This stung her. "I always think you might be better than you are. Then you open your mouth and that's that."

"That bitch back there, is she—"

"Forget it. I think of us like . . . brother and sister in a way. I always wanted to take care of someone. Someone that needed me." He passed his hand over his eyes wearily, as if he had said too much. "Those girls I go around with, why the hell should you care about them? Nobody gives a damn about them. They don't give a damn about themselves. Forget it."

Clara made a sound like laughing.

"In dreams bodies come to me," said Lowry, "bodies without faces, with no names, nothing, they might be the bodies of dead women; what do I care? But when you wake up you want to get out of a dream like that. You're the only one of them who ever needed me. You didn't have anyone else, you were alone. That makes you different. You were caught."

Clara thought of the dime store and of her room, and of the long road between Tintern and the workers' camp back in Florida. "I'm always going to be caught, somewhere," she said.

He seemed not to have heard her. "You were just a kid. You didn't know anything. I never did one thing in my life before that that I was proud of or liked to think about. But I was glad I could help you. So shut up about the rest of my life, it has nothing to do with you."

"Nothing to do with me," Clara echoed.

"Why are you always doing that. . . ? Look, you've been in Tintern for a year now. Do you miss your family?"

"Yes."

"You want to go back?"

134

She thought of the cat dying on the road. "No. I don't know where they are, anyway."

"You don't have anyone else but me, right?"

"I'm good friends with Sonya and Caroline and Ginny, that's Ginny Brewster, she's married, and there's a real nice old lady—"

"But no other man, right?"

"Mr. Peltier that runs the dime store," Clara said sullenly.

"Oh, him. He doesn't bother you, does he?"

"No."

"You tell me if anyone bothers you."

"Sometimes men go by in cars, they say things—"

"Just as long as they don't stop."

"What would you do if I went with some man?"

"Nothing."

"What if it was you?"

Lowry laughed. "Honey, that won't happen."

"I'm just as pretty as the girl you're going back to tonight," Clara said. She felt drained and exhausted.

"If you'd wipe off all that lipstick," Lowry said. "Frankly, you look like hell. It's a laugh. You wear your skirts too tight. Your legs are skinny. Your arms are skinny too. Whatever the hell you did with your hair so that it's hanging down in your eyes—that's a laugh too. And it looks like you got some cross-eyed girl friend to draw eyebrows on you. They don't match."

Clara laughed angrily.

"Sonya helped me with my hair," she said. "I like how it is."

"Sure."

"I feel so old, so tired," Clara said. "It's hard to know what kind of a face to have."

Back in Tintern he stopped before the building she lived in. "Are you coming in for a minute or going back to that bitch?" Clara said.

"She isn't a bitch, she's just stupid."

"You want some coffee or something?"

"You don't know how to make coffee."

"You could fix it yourself, then."

They went up the dark creaking steps. There were four other rooms in the building, rented out to people who lived alone. "There's a real nice old lady next to me. She has lots of plants. She talks too much, though. Where do you think she gets her money from?"

"Where do you get yours from?"

"Some of it from you and some of it from work. But I'm going to pay back what I owe you."

"You don't owe me anything."

"Yes, I do. I'm going to pay it back."

She switched on the overhead light. The room was crowded with her bed and card table and improvised bureau and the waterfall and sunset scenes she had tacked on the walls. Whenever Lowry stepped into the room she waited for him to compliment her on it, but he never said anything. "This here is new," she said, indicating a small lamp with a fat rounded bottom and a shade decorated with bows. The bottom showed a meadow scene in bright green and yellow and the shade was bright yellow. "I got it on discount at the store. It was three dollars."

Lowry exhaled a breath that might have meant amusement or sympathy.

He sat on the edge of her bed. She had no bedspread yet—she was saving for that—but the bed had been neatly made, the pink blanket primly drawn up over the pillow. On the floor at his feet was a small oval rug of a fuzzy material, deep pink. Lowry looked at it for a second too long.

"That's for when I'm barefoot and it's cold," Clara said.

She colored pleasantly. It was embarrassing and exciting to have him in here; usually he did not have time to stay. She stood to one side, leaning against the counter in the kitchen end of the room. Here there was a small sink with a rusty faucet and a small counter with a hot plate on it. Above the counter was a large calendar showing a baby and two white kittens. Lowry's gaze moved to take in her curtains—fluffy white curtains with red polka dots—and around to her "drapes," dark green with blue stripes, in the front of the room. The floor tilted a little. Clara had covered it with a few small rugs. But most of the floor was hidden by furniture— Clara's cot, her nightstand (a crate painted blue), her dressing table (more crates, with a board between them and a fluffy pink skirt covering them), her card table, her single chair. Lowry stared at everything and after a moment he smiled.

"I love it here, it's real nice," Clara said. "I never had a room by myself before. When are you going to take me where you live?"

"Why?"

Clara laughed. "I'd like to see it."

"Better off not seeing it."

"Why?"

"You might not be so happy then."

136

"I'm happy most of the time," Clara protested. "In the car I wasn't—I felt bad. But sometimes Sonya stays overnight with me and we talk about things—we read things—"

"What do you read?"

"Oh—like this." She showed him a comic book. "And some love stories she reads out loud from magazines. I can't read them too well myself."

"Why can't you?"

"It's too hard."

"Are you going to learn how to read or not?"

"If you teach me—"

"When I try to teach you, you act silly. You can't concentrate."

"I wouldn't act silly now. That was last year, when you got so mad. I'm a year older now."

"Go to school instead."

"I'm too big for it."

"Do they know how old you are?"

"Did you tell them I was seventeen or something? Because you have to be sixteen to quit school but nobody bothers me here. . . . Why can't I see where you live?"

"Your parents couldn't read, could they?"

"Sure," Clara said sullenly.

"What about your brothers and sisters?"

Clara lifted one shoulder in an imitation of Lowry.

"If you want to be different from your family you'd better learn to read. I'll bring something over the next time I come."

"When are you coming again?"

"I don't know."

"Don't you know, really? Because I—"

"I said I don't know."

Clara turned meekly away and took out the coffee things. Lowry got to his feet and pushed her aside. "I'll make it," he said. She stood behind him and linked her arms around his waist. She pressed her cheek against his back but her expression was serious; she was listening to his heart.

"Why can't I come see where you live?" she said. "You know, my pa killed a man once."

"You told me."

"Lowry, am I really skinny?"

"Just your arms and legs."

"Don't you like me, then?"

"Sure I like you."

"In magazines women are thin. . . ."

"Is that perfume?"

"Oh, just some . . . perfume."

"It's too strong."

"It's nice, it's from the store where I work."

Lowry said nothing. Clara stood beside him now. She said, "I like working there real well. I appreciate all you done for me. Sonya doesn't like it, though. She complains about everything. Sonya lends me some jewelry and I lend her things too. We're real good friends."

"Is this the one with the funny mother?"

"Oh, I guess so. She's sort of funny."

"Isn't she crazy?"

"Well, I don't know. . . . She never pays any attention to what Sonya does. Sonya can do anything. She goes out with some men from the gypsum plant. And Caroline, you know, Caroline's going to get married, we think—he works on that real big farm up the valley."

"The Revere farm?"

"Yes. He works there and can make a lot of money. He takes her out to the stock car races. We think they're going to get married."

"That perfume stinks, it's too strong. Is it on you?"

"A little behind my ears."

"It smells like it could kill bugs."

Clara's face went rigid. "I don't have bugs," she said.

"All right, I know you don't."

"I don't and I never did. I never did," she said; and the memory of the lice she'd had years ago made her voice thick with bitterness.

"Honey, I can see this room is nice and clean. It's real clean," he said, rubbing her shoulder. "Every time I been here it's real clean."

She smiled faintly. "Well—yes—I always liked things clean. I always did the floors and dishes for Ma and Nancy—"

"You're a very clean girl."

"Under the sink here is a nice big pan I have. I can take a bath in it if I'm careful. See it?"

"It's a wonderful pan."

Clara frowned up at him. "Are you kidding me?"

"No."

"It's just a pan, it isn't wonderful. You're making fun of me."

"It's a wonderful pan, honey."

Clara turned away, pretending to be angry. She sat on the

edge of her bed and then lay back. The ceiling was high above her and specked with water stains. She thought she saw a faint cobweb thread and her gaze shot to it; she had just dusted the room that day. "I'm happy most of the time but I get lonely," she said. "Back with them, back home, I had to work all the time. Real hard, not like in the store. But they were always with me and I took care of them. Pa didn't drink too much. Here—well—I get lonely and don't have anybody to talk to."

"What about Sonya?"

"She can't stay here overnight too much. She's got to watch her mother and the kids. . . . Her father's supposed to be back, somebody said so. He made a lot of trouble. Sonya doesn't know where he is. Sonya is nice but she's a little wild. She keeps wanting me to go out with some friends of hers but I say no. She thinks you're my boy friend. . . . And Caroline, she's with Davey all the time—that's her boy friend. And Ginny's married. She has me over for supper sometimes."

"Why are you lonely, then?"

"I don't know. I live alone and that's funny. When you're my age you don't live alone."

"It's better than living in a hole with five other people," Lowry said.

"Oh, that way you get used to all sorts of things. You see everything and it doesn't surprise you. Everybody is together. What was your family like?"

Lowry shrugged his shoulders.

"You know the Revere farm?" he said. "Those people own the gypsum land too. I'm from something like that, that farm. But farther away."

"Do you live there now?"

"They lost it in the Depression."

Clara nodded wisely, to show that she had heard that word before. She had a vague idea of what it meant: the color it made her think of was a dark, rain-washed gray.

"My family wanted to own things, then they lost them all. I'm not like them. I don't want to own anything."

"I want to own lots of things," said Clara. "I love these things here, my rugs and pictures." Lowry pulled a chair over by her and sat. "The next thing I'm going to get is a bedspread, then a goldfish."

"What the hell do you want with a goldfish?"

Clara felt a little hurt. "I like them."

"Why don't you get some plants or something? Plants are

139

nice." He was speaking kindly now. He sipped at his coffee but Clara could not drink hers, it was too strong.

"Well," she said, smiling, "are you sorry you didn't go back to her?"

"You're really jealous, aren't you?"

Her smile deepened. "You're here with me and not with her. She must have waited for you."

"I'll see her some other time."

"But right now you're here with me."

"I was already with her once tonight," he said. "Except for that I wouldn't be here."

Clara handed him her cup. "Put it on the table, I don't want it."

"What are you mad at?"

She stood and brushed past him and went to her dressing table. There was a small rectangular mirror propped against the wall. Clara bent to examine herself in it. Over her shoulder she could see that Lowry was not even watching her. He drank coffee and muscles in his jaw and throat moved. Clara laughed softly. In the mirror his reflection turned toward her; he looked amused.

"Why are you so jealous?" he said.

"Did you take her out in your car?"

"Yes, the car."

"Did you like it?"

"Sure."

"Does she do that with lots of men?"

"I suppose so."

"Does she like it too? Do women like it?"

"Sometimes."

"Somebody told me it would hurt," Clara said. She was brushing her hair. "She said it would hurt real bad. But I wouldn't care if I loved the person. . . ."

"I bet you wouldn't."

Clara turned to him. "Last month you left me too and went away with some bitch. You're not going to do it again."

"I knew you'd be waiting."

She threw the hairbrush down. "Christ, you know how I love you, I think about you all the time! I wait all week to see you and sometimes you don't even come—all right, I know you're busy doing something—you have lots of girls—But— then when you leave me like that, leave me sitting—I'll get back at you for that—"

"What are you going to do?"

140

"You make me want to go crazy or something. I could find that girl and kill her, I could cut her throat and have it bleed all over!"

"Okay, calm down."

"I hope they all have babies and die! I hope they die!"

Lowry finished his coffee. He put both cups in the sink and his silence made Clara's face burn.

"Are you coming here next week or not?" Clara demanded.

"I don't think so."

"Why not?"

"One thing or another."

"What about teaching me to read?"

"Some other time."

"Are you mad at me?"

He was lighting another cigarette. "You're just a kid, you don't know what you're talking about. I can't take you seriously."

"You give me some money, then. I need money," Clara said angrily.

"I'll give you some."

"Well, I need it. I need it."

"Will you calm down?"

Clara turned away. Her face was burning. "I get all mixed up with you," she said bitterly. "I think about you all the time, then when you come I'm all mixed up—if we didn't talk I could love you and not think about it, I'd like to hold you, I'd do anything for you, but you say things and make me hate you, I can't help it, and I'll always remember it all my life—how I hate you—"

"What are you going to do about it?"

"Nothing. There's nothing I can do," Clara said flatly. She wiped some of her lipstick off on a tissue. "Damn you, you never said anything about my new dress. It's all wrinkled and wet now."

"The skirt is too short."

"The skirt's too short! Every goddam bitch you ever screwed in your life wears dresses like this—but not me—"

"Clara, shut up about that."

"I can't shut up. All week long I talk to myself in the mirror, practicing to argue with you."

Lowry laughed.

"I'm going to take this off," Clara said. "It's all wrinkled."

She threw the dress onto her bed. Standing in her slip she said, "Someday you might want to love me and then I'll tell

141

you to go to hell. That's what I'll do. I'll be married then and I'll tell you to go to hell."

"How much does a goldfish cost?"

"Oh—not much. You have to buy the bowl too. And some seaweed junk to put in it, and some fish food."

"In the dime store?"

"Where else?"

"If you're lonely you can get a goldfish. I didn't mean to laugh at them."

She touched his leg with the edge of her bare foot. She looked at him and smiled slowly, shyly. "I washed my hair yesterday, just for you," she said. "I know I look pretty. I can see it in people's faces." She sat across from him on the bed and arched her back, leaned forward so that she could kiss him. For her everything was slow and sweet; she had to concentrate on the way it felt because it would have to last her until he came again. She slid her arms around his neck and pressed her cheek against his. "Won't you come next week? Please?"

"I don't know."

"And teach me how to read?"

She felt his hands on her back, on her bare skin. The tension that had been between them so long made her sleepy; she hid her face against the front of his shirt.

"If I come next week are you going to bitch again?" he said.

"What?" she said sleepily.

"If we go out somewhere and I leave you for a few minutes, are you going to bitch about it?"

"No."

"You're not?"

"No."

"Are you going to remember I'm your friend?"

"Yes."

"And nobody else?—fool around with nobody else?"

"Yes, Lowry."

"You're not going to complain about anything?"

"No, Lowry."

After he left she played this conversation back to herself, sitting by her mirror. She felt drugged and exhausted, as if she had spent hours arguing with Lowry. Her body ached dully. She closed her eyes and remembered kissing him. She remembered the way he had leaned around to put the cups in the sink. She remembered him leading her back to the car,

142

when she'd been crying over the cat—had he put his arm around her? She thought so. She remembered him tapping his fingers on the steering wheel.

"But someday I'll get back at him," she said aloud.

3

Waves of excitement ran up and down Clara's body. Sonya was standing in front of a narrow yellow-streaked mirror inside the closet door, and Clara could see herself in it behind Sonya's head and shoulders. "What if he comes and leaves because I'm not there?" she said. "What if I don't get back in time?" Sonya was brushing her hair. She was a large, firm girl with dark hair and olive skin; her shoulders and arms had a look of strength that communicated itself to the hairbrush she was using impatiently. Clara's blond hair glowed out of the mirror in those moments when Sonya moved aside. She watched herself even when Sonya was in the way. She was breathing lightly through her parted lips and stood very still, very straight. They were going to Caroline's wedding and they were both dressed up. There was an odor of something sharp and oversweet in the air—their perfume—and their high-heeled shoes and bright clothing gave the attic room a frantic disorderly look.

"The hell with him if he doesn't wait. He thinks he's so important," Sonya said. She spoke with that emphatic, vague air women use when they are looking at themselves in a mirror. It was late spring now; the air was quite warm. Clara's gaze fastened firmly upon itself in the mirror. The glass made a slight distortion but she did not notice it. She kept thinking about Lowry coming that day, Lowry promising to come that day, and how she had waked with the conviction that he would come, yes—he would not break another promise to her. The look of her own reflection in the mirror made Clara's blood tingle.

"He'd wonder why I was out, maybe," she said.

"Look, you left a note on the door. All right."

"But he'd wonder why I wasn't there. . . ."

"The hell with him." Sonya leaned up against the mirror and turned her head critically from side to side. She was seventeen, but the pouting dissatisfied slant of her eyebrows and mouth made her look older. When she smiled it was

143

always a surprise; her lips were bright red. "Caroline's real lucky, ain't she?"

"Yes," Clara said dreamily. She touched her hair. She was wearing gloves, white gloves. These caught her eye in the mirror and were startling, as if they were things she might have stolen. Except for her shoes, everything she wore—the dress that was too bright a blue, the jewelry with fake gold coating, the fake pearls around her neck—was from the store she had worked in now for two years. "But I keep thinking about Lowry—"

"You think about him too much," Sonya said. She stared at herself sullenly. "Goddam my hair. Son of a bitch."

"It looks okay."

"It does like hell. But what the hell do you care?"

"No, it looks okay," Clara said. She took the hairbrush and brushed at the girl's hair. Sonya submitted in a surly begrudging way. They had been friends now for some time and it was no longer necessary for either one of them to pretend to be nice. From the side, Sonya had a thick, impatient face. Whenever she spoke gently or lowered her eyes in a certain embarrassed way, it was a surprise. Most of the time she imitated the older men she hung around with—not her brothers, who were lethargic and quiet, but the men she went out with to roadhouses in the country and sometimes all the way down to Hamilton on weekends. Their brusque, jostling explosions of humor were reflected in the way Sonya laughed, the laughter bursting out of her as if she could no longer keep it back, and in the way she sometimes reached out and jabbed Clara's arm, like a boy.

An automobile horn sounded out front. "Where the hell is my purse?" Sonya said. "If that kid took it—"

"She hasn't been in here since I came," Clara said.

She put the hairbrush down on top of a cluttered bureau. There were long dark hairs in the brush.

Downstairs someone was yelling, "Sonya! Sonya!"

"Shut up," Sonya said, without raising her voice. She and Clara descended the stairs. The stairs were very steep, so that they had to go down sideways in their high heels. Clara was conscious of her smooth silken legs and of the way her dress clung to her body. She was infatuated with everything about herself and about this day, a Saturday in mid-May, 1936. Downstairs, Sonya yelled out to one of her sisters in the kitchen, "If it starts to rain or anything get that goddam stuff in from the back yard—you hear me?" There was silence. "You hear me?"

144

"Yeah, loudmouth."

"I'll loudmouth you, you little bitch. She's a little bitch," Sonya said. She pushed Clara along to the front door. It was a door they rarely used and both felt strange. "How do I look?" Sonya said, rolling her eyes.

She was almost pretty, a hard-faced, grim, joking girl. The firm athletic swing of her arms and legs showed that she could take care of herself—she wasn't afraid.

Outside, a man was waiting on the porch. He sat on the old davenport that had been pulled out front and covered with a blanket. This man was maybe forty, with serious, eager, suspicious eyes and a face that looked raw because he had just shaved. "Hiya, honey," he said. "Hiya, Clara. Guess who's waitin' out there."

Another man was sitting in the car. Clara made a face and laughed.

"Look, she said she didn't want him along. You deaf or something?"

"Well, Davey invited him to the wedding too. He's got a right to come."

"I don't care," Clara said.

They went out to the car, walking carefully on the boards that led through puddles and patches of mud. The road was muddy too on the edges. The man in the car was a man Clara had met before and hadn't liked; she had the idea he was married or had just left his wife. But she laughed at him and waved him away when he said, "You look real nice, Clara." He opened the back door for her and moved aside. She got in next to him, smoothing down her dress. On the floor of the car were crumpled tissues and cigarette butts. When Sonya got in the front seat her perfume moved in with her, like a cloud. Clara looked out at the damp, misty road and the fields beyond, and then back around to Sonya's house—an ugly little frame house that was little more than a shanty, its wood rotted black. The davenport on the porch looked festive in its yellow blanket. In the doorway, pushing out the screen door, stood Sonya's mother, a short squat heavy woman. Clara waved to her.

"The hell with her," Sonya said sharply.

"I'm just waving good-by," Clara said.

"What's wrong with your mother?" The man in the back seat said.

"You trying to be funny?" Sonya said.

"She ain't any worse, is she?"

Sonya did not bother answering. She leaned over toward

her boy friend and whispered something in his ear. He laughed and started the car.

"I'm not going to the thing afterwards, the reception," Clara said. The man next to her was younger than Sonya's boy friend; he was about thirty. He had rounded shoulders and red, coarse hands. He worked at a planing mill in another town. "I'm going to walk back by myself."

"How come?"

"Somebody's maybe coming to visit me."

"Who's that, that what's-his-name? The one that never shows up?"

"Oh, go to hell!" Clara said. But she was not angry. She was intoxicated with something—she didn't know what. The man beside her, smelling of tobacco and of the peculiar indefinable odor of failure, did not matter. There were many men like him in the country, drifting and suspicious and not to be trusted, puzzled at themselves and what had happened to them; they were everywhere. He had had a good job once, he told Clara. When he was twenty, that young, he'd had a good job—but she was not interested. What did she care about the past, that long ago, when she had been only a child? "Me and my brothers, we done real well. We had real good jobs. My cousins too," he had said. "Then it all folded. Everybody lost out."

"Did you have a car?" Clara had asked.

"No, but—"

She never wanted to listen. If it wasn't this man who tried to talk to her, to explain something meticulously and carefully, it was others; they all felt they must explain themselves and why they were so poor, so shabby. There had been a good time once but now it was finished. Their fathers had lost their land. Farms, money, cattle, crops lost. Now they worked for other people, the sons of these old, lost fathers, in granaries or planing mills or on big successful farms that hadn't been washed away in the Depression. Clara had the idea of a struggle somewhere in the past but because it was over with she could not think about it. It was like her father's long struggle—hopeless because he could not control anything. Lowry was different. She thought of him as different totally from these sad, angry men and from her own father, who would never find her now and who must be off in the East somewhere, traveling endlessly up and down the coast. Clara wanted to harden her heart against him.

"A woman from some school thing came and bothered me," Clara chattered. She began one of her "talks," just

146

taking up time to entertain the men. "She asked me lots of questions, mostly how old I was and where my parents were. I should tell her to go to hell—why is she bothering me? She comes in the store and pretends to be buying something, then she says, how old are you? I said I was seventeen. She said somebody told her about me, that I was living in Tintern all by myself and didn't have no work permit and didn't go to school. I said I was seventeen and didn't need any permit and didn't need to go to school. I was getting mad. That was a week ago, then yesterday she came back again. She's a goddam nosy bitch if I ever saw one, just wants to make trouble. She says, do I have a birth certificate? I said nobody ever gave me one. She says I don't look like I'm seventeen."

"Sure you do, honey," Sonya said.

"She looks just fine."

"Yeah, well. I was working in that goddam dump when I was fourteen and places around here always let me in when Lowry took me, and they sold him drinks for me too, and now when I really am sixteen what the hell but some bastards get after me." She spoke airly and petulantly; she was rehearsing this for Lowry. "Now, yesterday she asked me when I was to a doctor last!"

They all laughed. "Clara, maybe you got some secret you ain't told us?" Sonya said slyly.

Clara blushed. "There ain't nothing wrong with me. I never get sick."

"Could be I don't mean that," Sonya said.

"Why don't they let me alone?" Clara went on. "I really am sixteen so I don't need to go to school. I need to work. That bitch wanted to know how much money I made and what I did with it—what business is it of hers? I said, nobody ever bothered me before in Tintern, and she said she was new on this job and would cover the whole county. I told her she should maybe mind her own business for a change. I said, are you the goddam cops or something?" Clara laughed. But she said, a little anxiously, "You think she could turn me over to them?"

"Hell, no!" the man beside her said.

"You ain't done anything wrong," Sonya said. "It's just the sheriff's men around here, not cops like in comic books and things. I mean, the sheriff's men are just guys we know. They don't hardly arrest nobody."

The man beside her rested his big hand on Clara's gloved hand. "Maybe I better have a talk with that bitch myself," he said. "She shouldn't go around scaring little girls like you."

"I never was a little girl," Clara said vaguely, withdrawing her hand. She looked out the window. A new sense of depression alternated with her feeling of excitement. The wedding they were going to dangled out before her on the damp road, something out of sight, and it had a meaning for her she could not quite assess. Sonya and her boy friend began to talk teasingly to each other, the kind of talk that Clara did not like to hear. The man beside her touched her arm and encircled her wrist with his fingers playfully. She was staring away at the road, as if waiting for something to come into sight that would change everything. They were almost at the edge of Tintern now. There was an old cider mill with a great, stilled wheel, and doors that had long been nailed shut, and old trucks parked in high grass that would never be moved again. The church had been painted white just a few months ago. There were a number of cars and two pickup trucks in the driveway, and people Clara recognized were standing around awkwardly. Two people stood posing for pictures on the front stoop of the church.

"Hey, there they are! Don't she look nice?" Sonya cried.

Sonya's boy friend turned off the road and had to drive up on the grass, up a bumpy incline. There was a lively, almost hysterical air in the way people turned to see who was just arriving, their faces already changing to say hello. Sonya was leaning way out her window and yelling at someone.

"Davey looks scared. I bet he's scared," the man beside Clara said. He squeezed Clara's arm in a pretense of excitement and Clara drew away from him. She opened the door and when she got out she was standing in ankle-high grass. She smoothed down her dress, self-consciously smiling, and walked awkwardly along in her high heels. The air was misty and gentle, getting quite warm. Overhead the blue sky had been shrouded in mist—the sun was obscured by high thin clouds and glowed through them, a glaring diffuse white. Clara's eyes kept jumping around to everyone and waiting for them to say hello.

Some of them did say hello but most of them didn't.

She went with Sonya and the two men right up to Caroline, who was still on the concrete step, posed in a breathless, stiff way with her arms unnaturally straight at her sides. Davey, a red-faced young man in his twenties who gave a superficial impression of being gentle, stood with his arm around her shoulders and tried to ignore the jokes of his friends; his arm looked like a wooden arm resting on the girl. People were shouting and laughing. Sonya teased Caroline

148

about something, then she teased Davey. Davey flushed. The minister and his thirteen-year-old daughter came out behind them on the stoop and everyone laughed—someone had taken their picture along with the bride and groom, by accident. Clara stared up at Caroline. The girl had a thin, eager face, flushed with excitement, and her hair had been pulled up onto her head in a fancy way. Clara stood off to the side and waited for everything to get over with so that they could go into the church. Her eyes had fastened themselves on Caroline: what did it feel like to be about to get married?

She had forgotten about the man who was with her, and was surprised when he nudged her to sit in one of the pews. She obeyed at once. The church was small but its high ceiling and high, old-fashioned windows made it look larger. It was a nice church, everyone said. People crowded together in the center aisle but talked less loudly than they had outside; there was something self-conscious and guarded about their laughter. Up at the front were flowers! Clara stared at those flowers. She had never seen anything so beautiful. And up front, over to the side, sat a woman at the organ, leafing through a book. The book slipped down and she caught it and set it back up. Clara saw her feet begin pumping and then she heard the first notes of the music—it was harsh and strong, very strong. It seemed to come from everywhere at once. The man beside her leaned over with his tobaccoey smell and said, in what should have been a whisper, "There's Davey's boss, see him? That's Curt Revere." Clara looked but did not see anyone.

The organ pumped and sucked at air. A child began to cry. People milled in and took their seats, smiling. Time passed. The bride in her white dress and with her high-piled hair topped with a veil came down the aisle with her father; Clara stared at her in envy. She was so jealous it was almost painful. And back at her room, what if Lowry was there? What if he came and saw her note but decided not to wait? But maybe he wasn't even coming. He hadn't bothered with her for weeks. Beside Clara, the man rested his hands on his knees and nudged her; Clara didn't know why. She felt her heart sinking just at the touch of him. Her mind kept slipping off the wedding ceremony and onto Lowry, imagining him getting out of his car and going to the doorway, climbing the stairs, and not finding her home. . . . A kind of wildness gripped her. She had to get back.

"Lookit that baby there," the man said, pointing.

149

On the open slanted windows flies crawled and buzzed in the warm air. They seemed to be drowsy with the fresh melancholy of spring; they crawled lazily and then jerked into flight and disappeared. Clara saw a fly alight on a woman's hat. She watched it crawl around for a while. As she watched the fly and heard the minister's voice, she thought sadly that this would never happen to her, all this. Her and Lowry. It would never happen. Caroline, who was four months pregnant, was up at the front of this church and surrounded by a community of relatives and neighbors who were pushing her and Davey into a new life—what was supposed to be a new life—but this would never happen to Clara. She did not have what Caroline and Sonya and everyone else had but never thought about: parents, grandparents, aunts, uncles, people who had known them since birth without ever thinking much about it. It was this fact, their being known by a community of people, that Clara would never have; and because she did not have it she supposed she would never be married either.

Her friend Ginny glanced around and smiled at Clara. Ginny and her husband sat with their two-year-old beside them; Ginny held the new baby in her arms. Its head had tilted back and it was drooling colorlessly onto the sleeve of Ginny's new taffeta dress. Clara thought that she should be holding a baby too. Her body ached with the thought. So she made herself look away. The sun must have come out from behind its screen of mist because light broke suddenly and flooded through the windows, falling in a mysterious pattern on certain heads and shoulders but not on others. Clara saw dust motes swirling in the air and realized that they were always there, always, though no one could see them. She would have liked to lean forward violently to see everything that was somehow hidden from her—to seek it out with her sharp eyes, to smell it out, prod it out into the open. She wanted to know everything.

The ceremony was over, and Caroline and Davey were married.

They hurried out of the church and everyone followed behind. People were saying how beautiful it was; how young she was. Caroline's mother, a chunky woman in a flowered Easter hat, was pushing grimly through the crowd to get to Caroline. "Wasn't it beautiful!" someone said behind Clara. Clara wanted to turn and answer, but she did not. She had never felt so much alone before. All these people—they drifted into the dime store and bought things from her, some

150

of them, but they did not really "see" her. They did not care about her. "But where did you live before this?" the woman from the county had asked her. "Where are your parents, are they alive? Can you contact them? Are you all alone here?"

The man with the raw, reddened hands wanted her to stay for the reception, but she said she had to leave. She waved him off. The reception was being held in the minister's house next door. The minister's wife was mannish and loud; she stood on the front porch and waved people inside. "You, where are you going? You in the blue dress!" she yelled.

In a few minutes Clara was free. She hurried along the road, walking in the middle so her shoes wouldn't get dirty. They were already flecked a little with mud. Around her, sunlight shone with that peculiar wet intensity it has in spring, and if she were to lift her eyes from the road she would see the range of mountains to the north glimmering and dazzling in the light—the boundary to another, savage, unpopulated world. The Eden River had carved for them this deep, long valley out of the foothills, and to the south and east hills rolled for miles, endlessly. Clara had always had the strange idea, in this part of the country, that the very sweep of the land did not let people stay small and allow them to hide, but somehow magnified them. Here one's eye was naturally driven to the horizon, to the farthest distance, run up against that uncertain boundary where the misty sky and the damp mountains ran together like the blending of heaven and earth in one of Clara's cheap little prints.

She heard an automobile coming up behind her. She supposed she had to stand aside, to let it pass. So she made a waving gesture and turned to the side of the road, walking cautiously, both arms outstretched as if to help her keep her balance. The road was muddiest at the side. In the car was a man with dark hair that had turned partly gray. He had a severe, critical look that made Clara want to turn away in shame.

"Would you like a ride?" he said.

Clara smiled feebly. "I don't mind walking, I'm used to it," she said.

His car slowed to a stop. She did not know whether he was afraid to splash her with mud or if he was really stopping. She saw that he had a large, heavy head, that his eyes were framed with tiny creases that gave his face a depth she had never noticed in anyone else. Then the car struck her eye: it was new, big. It must have been expensive. She narrowed her eyes at the sight of it and wondered who this man was.

151

"I couldn't stay for the reception either," he said. "I'll drive you back to town."

She did not answer at once. His voice was an ordinary voice, but behind it something was pushing, prodding. "Get in," he said. Clara felt the warm sunlight on her face and the image of herself she had been reserving for Lowry released itself: she felt strong and her body coursed with strength. She smiled at the man and said, "All right."

When she went around the front of the car she reached out with her white glove to almost touch the hood, in a half-magical gesture. She opened the door herself and stepped up into the car. It smelled rich and dark and cool inside. The man wore a dark gray suit and a necktie with tiny silver stripes in it. Clara thought at once that no woman had picked that out for him. He had picked it out for himself.

"Are you a friend of Davey's?" she said shyly.

"Yes."

He drove on. Clara looked around and saw that the countryside was changed a little by the windows of this car: the cider mill and the empty fields and the houses set back from the road looked clearer, sharper. Clara thought that sunshine revealed everything cruelly—the drab little town had looked better in winter, hidden by dirt-streaked slivers of melting snow.

"You can let me out anywhere," Clara said. She saw that Lowry's car was not parked out front. But she could not control her excitement. In the future lay everything— everything. Lowry in the doorway of her room, Lowry in her arms, his face, his voice, his calm stubborn will that was a wall she kept hurtling herself against—"Thanks very much," she said, polite as any child. She was about to get out, but her excitement prompted her to talk. She chatted the way she'd chatted for other men: "It was nice that you stopped because now my new shoes didn't get all muddy. . . . Wasn't it a nice day today? I'm glad Caroline and Davey are married and happy and everything. . . . Thanks very much for the ride."

"Do you live in town here? Where?"

She glanced at him, still smiling. "Upstairs there," she said, pointing. It somehow pleased her that the man bent a little to look.

"Your whole family lives there?"

Clara hesitated. "I live alone," she said, looking down. Then she said shyly, "I work at the five and ten there and got the whole day off today, so did Sonya, just for the wedding.

And somebody's coming to visit me today, a friend of mine. . . . It's all so nice, the day is so nice. It smells nice when the sun comes out. . . ."

She laughed in embarrassment at her own joy.

When she ran upstairs she saw there on her door the note she'd left: "Dear Lowry, I am at a wedding and will be back soon please wait for me Love Clara." Sonya had helped her write it. She had hoped Lowry might come and discover it and be pleased to think that she had written it all herself, that she had learned so much from his teaching.

She waited in her room.

Hours passed, the afternoon passed. She thought of her friends out at the reception. But she had things to do: sewing, mending. There were two stuffed dolls on her bed now, made of old scraps. Clara did not take off her dress and shoes but stayed the way she was, ceremonial and uncomfortable, waiting for him. She sang to herself, breaking off now and then as her heart tripped violently over some small obscure sound that was never explained and never led to anything else. Her bed had a pink bedspread on it now. On her dressing table were bottles and tubes and glittering, gleaming things she was proud of. Sonya's boy friend had driven her and Sonya to a larger town about twenty miles away where they went to a store that had clothing just for women and children—nothing else—and Clara bought a sweater there; it was folded neatly in one of the bureau drawers and she had the drawer pulled out so that she could look at it.

Her card table was now covered with a scalloped cloth. On it lay Clara's white gloves and her pale blue purse, waiting. They continued to lie there in that alert, expectant way even after Clara herself had given up.

4

It was as if Clara were living in two worlds and two times: the one bounded by her room and her job and the drug store and the now-familiar limits of Tintern, and the other spread out aimlessly across the country, dragged back and forth with Lowry in an invisible, insatiable striving. She did not understand him, but she sensed something familiar about the hardness with which he lived. It was her father's hardness brought into sharper focus.

153

"But what the hell do you care about him?" Sonya and Ginny complained. Her friends kept up long monotonous arguments against him, annoyed by the clammy infatuation Clara did not try to hide. Over at Ginny's house, playing with the baby, Clara would have the sudden catastrophic vision of this baby as her own and Lowry as its father, but a father who never stayed in one place and who wouldn't know his own baby—no father at all. She felt icy with apprehension, as if she were inching out too far on something precarious. It was not that she was afraid of losing control of herself or of her knowledge of how things were; like everyone she knew, there was no speculation in her about what was real and what wasn't. It was only the secondary, underlying conviction that she was being betrayed so coarsely by her wishes that frightened her. She hated this backlashing tendency in herself that cut away at the simplicity of her life. "My mother worked all her life and had kids," she told people. "Anything better than that is all right with me." But she did not quite believe this herself.

She loved Ginny's children and her love spread out to include Ginny herself and her husband Bob, a man of about twenty-two who was temporarily out of work. He had pumped gas at a gas station but the station had burned down. Ginny was one of those women who expressed themselves in bursts of generosity, with food or affection or anger; she had a round high-colored face that put Clara in mind of country girls she'd seen walking on back roads all her life. Her husband was thin and gave the impression of lunging when he walked or reached for things. His silence and the passivity with which he watched his own children gave no indication of his impatience. "Gonna get a car from a guy," he'd brag to Clara, and grabbed her by the back of the neck to make it more emphatic. When he kissed her she thought in a panic that Lowry would find out. She pushed him away. "What the hell are you doing?" she said, making a face as if she had tasted something bad. They all must have liked her because she could take nothing seriously—Ginny's husband and other men who bothered her, married or unmarried—as if, in having committed herself to a hopeless infatuation, she was therefore kinder and fuzzier with them.

The less she saw of Lowry, the more she thought of him. When he did come, his face and voice were less real than what she imagined. She felt as if she had loved and married him and endured an entire lifetime, while Lowry himself was still young and indifferent. "I already have a boy friend," she

154

explained to men who did not believe her, but she did not think to extend this perfunctory defense to the man who had driven her back to town from the wedding—and it happened that he showed up again in a few days, in the five and ten. It would never have occurred to her to turn away from him, because she understood that this man was not like anyone else she knew. He did not want the same thing from her.

"How long have you been here, living alone?" he said. She told him, toying with a shining pair of scissors on the counter. Before this kind of man—one who "owned" things—she was shy and a little stubborn; she sensed that what gave her power with simpler men would have no effect on him. "Do you really live alone?"

"I'm of age," Clara said. She flicked her hair back out of her eyes and met the man's steady, gray, impenetrable stare. "I take care of myself."

"Do you go to church?"

She lifted one shoulder in a gesture of indifference and then stopped before the gesture was completed—it was better to say nothing bad about religion because it might do her harm one of these days. "Well, my folks never went to church."

"That's too bad." His hands rested on the edge of the counter and were perfectly still. Clara noticed things like hands: her own were always doing something, Lowry's fingers were always tapping impatiently, Sonya was always fooling with her hair. "At your age you need guidance. You need a religious foundation for your life."

"Yes, sir," Clara said.

Two tiny lines appeared between her eyebrows. She said, feeling a little embarrassed, "But I can take care of myself." This came out more aggressively than she had wanted, so she softened the effect of her words by brushing her heavy hair off one shoulder and letting it fall loose on her back. "Where I come from," she said softly, "you learn to take care of yourself when you're a little kid."

He leaned forward as if he could not quite hear her. "Where do you come from?"

She bit her lip. She almost smiled. "Oh, from anywhere. From all over." It was not flirtation, though it had the style of flirtation; she stared at him seriously to make him understand this. "We didn't have no particular home, we traveled on the season."

His silence indicated that he knew what she meant. Then

155

he said, in a harsh, paternal tone, "People should have done more for you than they have. Society has failed you."

"Society—"

"There are probably hundreds of girls like you—" He reddened slightly. "Have you gone to school?"

"Oh, there was some woman in asking about me, from the school board here or something, I don't know. She asked me did I go to the doctor this year or to the dentist, things like that. Somebody said they could take me out of here and put me in some home or reformatory or something—but they can't because I'm of age. Can they do that?"

"I don't know."

She felt a little disappointed at this answer. "Well, look, I don't want no home with other girls, I want everything I have right now the way it is and I want to be free and the hell with charity. My folks never took no charity, nothing. My pa—"

"I don't know the county board," he said quickly.

"Yes, well, that's all right. I was just saying." Clara lowered her gaze. The man inhaled deeply. Clara was conscious of other people in the store either watching them or very carefully not watching them, but they were not forced into any kind of unity because of this. They stood alone, awkward and a little resentful, as if each had somehow failed the other.

Clara said, "Did you want to buy something?"

"My wife wanted some thread," he told her, and already his eye was running along the rows of thread. "Gold thread—"

Clara looked through the spools of yellow thread. It was smooth, smooth, packed down to an incredibly satiny smoothness; it was delightful to touch. "What about this one?" she said dubiously. He nodded and she saw the dark yellow transformed to "gold." "Is this all, mister?"

"Yes."

He made no move to leave but leaned on the counter, rubbing his hands against the lower part of his face. She saw that he wore a wedding band. "What kind of a man would wear a ring?" she thought at once. His hands were like any man's except for the ring, and the edges of his white shirt by his wrists and the dark sleeves of his suit coat. He was wearing a suit and tie in Tintern on a Wednesday. Clara believed she had seen him somewhere before having come to Tintern, or perhaps a picture of him: why did she think that? He summoned up in her blood a vague trembling response, inarticulate. She did not resent the way he looked but she resented a little the way he made everything around him look cheap and inadequate. Lowry, beside this man, would not stand straight enough; Clara would want to be poking him to make him stand straight. This man's shoulders and back were straight and firm, and nothing could tease him into looking any other way. She had no idea how old he was.

"My name is Curt Revere," he said.

"My name is Clara."

"Clara what?"

She rubbed the damp palm of her hand along the spools of thread, turning them slowly. "Oh, just Clara," she said. One of the spools jerked out of place and rolled down to the edge of the counter. It would have fallen to the floor but the man caught it.

"Did you run away from home?" he said.

"There wasn't any home, how could I run away from it," Clara said sullenly.

He waited for her to continue. She stared at the spool of thread he was holding. "What the hell business is it of yours!" she said suddenly. Her face felt as if it had cracked. She began to cry. He fitted the spool back into place, taking some time. Clara wept bitterly without bothering to turn aside or hide her face. She was used to crying. "You leave off askin' me those things," she said in a child's voice, and as she looked up at him the memory flashed through her mind of where she'd heard his name before: Lowry had mentioned it and that man had mentioned it. Caroline's husband worked for him. The corners of her eyes ached as she tried to get him into focus. There was something wrong, something terrible about him, she was on the brink of a precipice, her whole life could be ruined: he had money, power, a name. The very air about him seemed to tremble. He had a name that people knew.

"Well," he said gently, "if you don't have any last name then you don't have any. Maybe you lost it somewhere."

He tried to smile but was not too good at it. After a moment he moved uncomfortably, a little abruptly. Clara felt paralyzed by her recollection of who he was, as if he were an enemy she had been hiding from all her life. She tried to remember where she had seen him before, or what she had seen that he reminded her of. . . .

"I could suggest that they stop bothering you, the people from the county board," he said. Clara, hearing this, drew her hands together in a meek, prayerful gesture. "You are

157

obviously able to take care of yourself, no matter what your age—"

"I'm over sixteen."

"Yes." He paused. Clara waited stiffly for him to continue. "In my car the other day you said something about—about— You said you were happy. You seem to be happy. You're obviously able to take care of yourself—"

"I'm happy," Clara said rigidly. "I can take care of myself."

"You said you like the weather. . . . You were happy." He smiled a little. His smile was the kind directed to dogs and babies; it did not anticipate any response. Now he noticed the thread in his fingers and said, "How much is this?"

"Five cents."

He took out a coin and handed it to her. "You want a bag or something?" Clara said. He said no, he'd put it in his pocket. As soon as it dropped in something touched Clara, some near-recognition. She felt different at once. "Your wife is sewing something made out of gold," she said, with one of these mysterious spurts of daring she was to have several times in her life. She smiled. "Somebody told me you lived on a big farm," she said, talkative now that he was ready to leave, "they said how nice it was—lots of hills and trees and horses—Nobody has big farms around here, but if they do they're land-poor; you're different. I don't know why," she said, moving along the counter in the direction of the door, urging him along by running her hand on the edge of the counter with a playful meticulous precision. "I don't know much about it because my folks never had a farm or any place that you could settle down on, but anyway the ones that did lost them—the banks took them or something. I don't understand any of that. But you, you didn't lose yours, I'm glad for that." She reached the end of the counter and leaned a little forward; for the first time she was conscious of her bare arms and the pale gold hairs on them. In the sunlight she would be sleek and golden. She looked at her arms and then slowly up at Revere.

Revere stared at her. He seemed not to have heard any of her words, but only the musing, singsong tone of her voice. Clara came around from inside the counter and walked with him to the door, as if she were seeing him out of a place that belonged to her. Outside, his car was parked by the walk. Two children were in it. One of the back doors was swinging idly open and a boy of about eight sat with his legs out; another boy was struggling with him, trying to slide his arm

158

around his neck. They argued in low, hissing voices, as if they had been forbidden to make any noise. Clara said, "Do you have any other children besides them?" "Another boy, two," Revere said. She shaded her eyes. She and Revere stood in the doorway. Clara had the door open, holding it there with her body. She was wearing a pale yellow dress whose skirt now fluttered about her knees in the wind. "That's real nice," she said. But she said it sadly. Revere said nothing and she did not look at him. Silence fell upon them as it had in the store, but she felt somehow linked to him by it—they were both looking out of this silence at his children, who were fighting with each other and had not noticed them.

When she went back inside, Mr. Peltier was waiting for her. He sat most of the day in the back room, drinking, and came out into the alley to watch the Negro boys unload things from trucks that stopped a few times a month. He wore a white shirt and a tie and showed by his dress that he was different from other Tintern people; he had a malleable reddened face. "How much did he spend?" he said. Clara smelled about him the odor of the store itself—something sour and unused. "Five cents," Clara said, smirking. "Five cents," he repeated. He almost smiled. "That goddam cheap bastard. That dirty son of a bitch of a cheap bastard. Five cents." "Maybe he never came in to buy anything," Clara said. He seemed to catch her words as if they were a trifling little blow directed at him, and he jerked back his head in a gesture of mock surprise and mock humor. "Then what did he come in here for?" he said.

5

"I'm thinking of how quiet it is."

"That isn't anything to think about."

"I can hear it, all this quiet. I think about it a lot."

They were standing on a bridge, looking down at the river. It was July now and the river had begun to sink. Clara leaned against the rust-flecked railing and stretched out her arms as if appealing to something—the river disappointed her with its slow-moving water, its film of sleek opaque filth. Its banks were far apart but the river itself had dwindled to a low, flat channel in the center of rocks that looked made of some white, startling substance that would flake off at the touch, like chalk.

159

"It's real quiet here," Clara said. "It's like this all over but you don't hear it."

Lowry kicked some pebbles off the bridge. Not much of a splash: the pebbles just disappeared into the water. Clara waited for him to speak. But it was like waiting for that splash—the more you listened for it, the less you heard.

On both sides of the river the banks lifted to a twisted jumble of trees and bushes. These banks eased in to obscure the river's path, twisting and writhing out of sight. "Rivers go like this," Lowry explained, making a line in the dust with a stick. "First they go straight like this; they run fast. Then they get slow and go like a snake. They pick up dirt and junk on the corners then and slow down. So they meander more. They meander bigger and fatter until this happens." And he surprised her by running a straight line through the very center of the curves, jabbing the stick in the dust hard to show the first river back again—the straight line.

"Is that the truth, honest?" Clara said lazily.

Lowry tossed the stick over the side of the bridge. It seemed to fall slowly and hit the surface of the water without a sound. They watched it float under the bridge and away.

"This river is dirty," Clara said. "By the other side, there, it's awful dirty. People let all kinds of junk drain into it, sewer junk, Sonya told me. That makes me sick."

The heat seemed to flatten out against them. Clara shook her hair out of her eyes. This silence of Lowry's was just like the silence she always listened to and so it did not surprise her. She pressed her fingers against her eyes and made the sunlight do tricks for her; she'd done that on the buses and trucks they had taken, years ago. If a person wanted something bad enough, Clara thought, he should get it. If he wished for something hard enough, he should get it. She took away her hands and the placid river returned, unchanged. She looked up at Lowry, who was leaning back against the railing; he smiled. His hair had bleached even lighter in the summer sun. His face was tanned and his eyes were a mild thoughtful blue; he looked as if he had two parts to him, the outside part and the inside part that wanted to get out. She supposed that when he was anywhere his eyes showed he was thinking of another place, and when he was with anyone he would be thinking of someone else. His trouble was never to be where he wanted to be.

"You don't have much to say, do you?" she said.

"Might be I don't."

160

"What did you do with yourself since you came out here last?"

"Oh, one thing or another."

"You're awful secret."

"You're awful nosy, little girl," he said. His smile showed that he was using only the top part of himself with her. Clara would have liked to seize him and stare into his eyes, deep into his eyes, to locate the kernel at the very center that was Lowry—why was he such a mystery? Or was he an ordinary man, the way all men would be if they were free and weren't held down? She could half-close her eyes and imagine herself moving toward him invisibly, trying to embrace him in an invisible embrace, and Lowry dancing forever out of her grasp. It did not seem fair to Clara that she should ache to the very depths of herself for this man who could not take her seriously—it was not normal that he should resist what other men accepted so indifferently, marriage and children, family, domestic history. Wilder men than Lowry had surrendered to it; for instance, her father. But they had surrendered without knowing they might have escaped it. It was Lowry's trouble that he knew too much without knowing enough of anything. He watched his feet carefully. He watched what his hands blundered into. He was not like the other men in Clara's life, her father and others like him, who stared wildly about on all sides, trying to figure out what was coming at them. They had never understood it was themselves they had to watch.

"Do me a favor?" Clara said.

"What?"

"Look at me serious. Say my name serious."

He was lighting a cigarette. He stopped sucking at it and said, "Okay. Clara."

"Is that serious as you can get?"

"Clara. Clara," he said, the end of his breath making the word droop suddenly into a seriousness that was dismal. It struck Clara that her name, which was the sound for her in people's minds, had nothing to do with her at all and was really a stupid name.

"I wish I was someone else. I mean, had another name," Clara said. "Like Marguerite."

"Why that?"

"I heard that name somewhere."

Out of everything she saw before her, only Lowry was like a dream. He was like a dream person who shows you only his outer self and that is why dreams are so frightening: there is

161

another dimension you cannot see. Behind him was the railing, as real as anything and behind that the tangled bank of the creek piled high with weeds climbing on top of weeds and turning brown at their tips in this heat—the sweet, faintly glimmering heat of midsummer that was all Clara could remember having felt. And beneath and out from them was the river, which had a name—the Eden River—which, like Clara's name, did not really name it. Birds flew in small scattered bunches out of the bushes by the shore, crying out to one another. Now and then a wind started up and blew Clara's hair out from her face and cooled her warm skin, proving itself real, blowing out of the hot depthless space of the summer sky, which was blue but flecked with cloud like scrawls. Only Lowry was not quite real. If Clara were to touch him his flesh might come off in her fingers just to taunt her; or her fingers might sink way down to show her that there was no end to him, no way to figure him out. If he knew how I think about him, Clara thought, he would change. He just doesn't know. Then she thought: Nobody loves anybody else the way I love him.

Each time he came to visit she had to worry about his leaving too soon. It was a tugging thing, the way he would get restless and be ready to leave even before he had thought of it. Clara always thought of it, dreading it, and ideas came to her of ways to put off that time as long as possible. She might have been in a contest only with herself. "Let's go walk down there," she said. He was agreeable. His car was parked off the bridge and up on the side of the road, a new car. They passed it without comment and climbed down the embankment. A few feet from the bottom, Clara jumped. A shock went through her when she landed flat on her feet. It did not hurt: the shock was that she had so solid, so responsive a body and that the earth had pressed back so hard against it, yielding up nothing. Lowry came slipping and sliding down, holding the burning cigarette in his hand as if he were a city person awkward in this business but not giving in to it.

They headed for the riverbank. In July there were many kinds of insects, so Clara stepped carefully through the weeds. "It's real pretty here," she said shyly. "Nicer than up on the bridge." She looked over to where they had been standing and could not imagine herself and Lowry up there together. "Don't you like how peaceful the river is, Lowry?"

"It's nice."

As if to ruin its peacefulness, he picked up a flat stone and

162

threw it sideways. The stone skipped three, four times, then sank.

"Did you do that when you were a little boy?"

"Sure."

She smiled to think of it, even though she could not quite believe he had ever been a little boy. She picked up a flat stone and tried to throw it as he did, slanting her wrist sideways, but it sank with a gulping splash. "Girls can't do that," Lowry said. He walked on and she followed him. Down by the riverbank there was a path fishermen used. They followed it along and walked away from the bridge. Clara heard, past the noises of the insects, the silence that covered this whole countryside. She felt as if she were walking through it and disturbing it.

"Don't you ever get lonely, Lowry?"

"Nope."

"Do you do a lot of thinking?"

"Nope."

She laughed and slid her arm through his. "Can't you say anything but nope?"

"I don't think much," Lowry said seriously, "but there are pieces of things in my mind. Broken pieces. They buzz around like wasps and bother me."

Clara glanced up at him as if he'd admitted something too intimate.

"But I don't worry."

"I don't either," said Clara.

He laughed and she pressed herself against him. "Look," she said, "can I ask you something?"

"What?"

"How come you're here with me right now?"

He shrugged his shoulders.

Clara ran from him. She jumped down into the creek bed, where it was dry. "Look at this, Lowry," she said. It was part of an old barbed-wire fence, lying frigid and coated over with bleached grass. Lowry's look said clearly, So what? Clara said, "You would wonder how things get where they are. This thing here—think where it used to be. Over there's a bicycle tire somebody owned. Wouldn't you like to know how things end up where they do?"

"Maybe."

"They get in the water, then drift down here. . . . I'm so happy," Clara said exuberantly, hugging herself, "but I don't know why. I love everything the way it is. I love how things look." She actually felt her eyes sting with tears. Up on the

163

bank Lowry sat down heavily and smoked his cigarette. He wore the faded brown trousers he had been wearing all summer and a tan shirt with rolled-up sleeves; he brought his knees up to lean on them and his ankles collapsed themselves in the grass, so that the outsides of his feet were pressed flat against the ground. He looked as if he would never get up again and never care to. "You don't listen to me!" Clara said angrily. "Goddam you anyway!"

His gaze was mildly blue. She saw his teeth flash in a brief smile.

"You think I'm just something you picked up on the road, and when you can't find some bitch to lay around with you come around here and visit!— Oh, Christ," Clara said, heaving a large stone out into the water. She laughed and her shoulders rose in a long lazy shrug. "What do you think about when you're with them, then?"

"Clara, I don't think about anything."

"When you're with them?"

"Sometimes I don't remember who they are."

She liked that, but she did not let on. Instead she picked up another stone and threw it out into the water. It sank at once. "But I'm happy anyway," she said. "That's because I'm stupid. If I was smart I wouldn't be happy when everything is so rotten."

"What's rotten?" he said at once.

"Oh, nothing, nothing," she said, waving to dismiss him. She flicked her long hair out of her eyes. It fell far down her back and she'd washed it the day before, somehow expecting him to come, so she knew it must shine in the sunlight. She knew she was pretty and now she wanted to be beautiful. "When things get better I will be beautiful," she promised herself. If Lowry would stand still long enough and she could climb up into his arms and sleep there forever, the two of them entwined and not needing to look anywhere else, then she could relax: then she would grow up, she would become beautiful. She was standing now on a large flat rock near the water, which flowed in a fairly rapid stream in the center of the river bed. She leaned over to see herself. There was a trembling vague image, not hers. She felt as if love were a condition she would move into the way you moved into a new house or crossed the boundary into a new country. And not just this one-sided love, either; she had enough of that right now. But the kind of love held out to her in the comic books and romance magazines she was able now to read for herself, which she and Sonya traded back and forth wistfully:

164

love that would transform her and change her forever. It had nothing to do with the way other girls got pregnant and fat as cheap balloons—that wasn't the kind of love she meant. The only real love could be between her and Lowry. You couldn't imagine any real love between Sonya, for instance, and her boy friend who was married. They never felt about each other the way she and Lowry would. . . .

"I remember you that night way back in Florida," Clara said. "I think about that a lot. Who were you with then?"

"Nobody special."

"Mrs. Kramer got sick and a doctor was out. They can't figure out what's wrong."

"Who's Mrs. Kramer?"

"Ginny's sister, her stepsister. But she's a lot older."

"What the hell does that have to do with anything—her getting sick?"

"I don't know, I just thought of it."

"Well, Christ."

"I just thought of it," Clara said stubbornly.

She had thought of it to get her mind rid of that memory of Lowry and everything that came with it: going back to his room with him. If she got her mind stuck on that she would be miserable to him, and maybe he was casting his mind around for some excuse to get away from her earlier—here it was about six o'clock and they would have to get some supper. Clara had told him she would make it herself. A tiny churning sensation began in her stomach and subsided at once, at the thought of the food she had bought that might still be there the next morning. She said, "I'm going to walk in here. It's cool." The stream of water was deep on her side. She could look right through to its stony bottom.

"You're going to wade in that?"

She kicked off her shoes. Her feet were tough from going barefoot so much in the summer. Clara stepped into the water and was surprised at how warm it was on top. "I like to wade," she said. "I used to do it when I was a kid." It was the kind of remark other girls probably said; Clara did not really think of herself as lying. The edginess in her voice must have made Lowry conscious of this, because when she glanced around he was looking at her. "What about you, did you play in cricks when you were a kid?"

"I grew up too fast," Lowry said.

She moved slowly through the water, staring down at her pale feet. Her legs were wet up past the knee. She pulled the skirt of her dress up higher. At first her legs were cool where they were wet, then the sun got to them and made them burn. She had to keep flicking her hair out of her eyes when she turned back to speak to Lowry. "I grew up fast, too. I'm just as old as you are if you look at it right."

He made a snorting sound.

"Damn you, don't laugh at me," she said. She bent to pull something out of the water—a barrel stave encrusted with scum and tiny snail-like things. She dropped it at once.

"Lowry," Clara said, "did you love your family?"

"I don't know. No."

"Why not?"

"I don't know."

Clara lifted one foot out of the water, gingerly. "I loved my family. I couldn't help it."

"Well, I was born able to help such things," he said. He shifted around, straightening out one leg. She thought there was something uneasy in his voice but she did not want to be so conscious, so meticulous with him. She walked farther out, gathering her skirt up around her thighs. Lowry flicked his cigarette out from him and it landed on the dry river bed. "I never could see what it was—things between other people," he said seriously. "I mean invisible things. Ties that held them together no matter what, like getting flung up on the beach and dragged out again and flung up again, always together. — Don't walk any farther out, you want to fall in? I'm not coming in after you."

"I'm all right."

"I'd like to have everything I owned in one bag and take it with me. I don't want things to tie me down. If I owned lots of things—like my father did—then they'd get in the way and I wouldn't see clearly. Once you own things you have to be afraid of them. Of losing them."

"I wouldn't mind that," Clara said sullenly.

He did not seem to have heard her. "If I have to kill myself for something, I want to know what it is, at least. I don't want it handed to me. I don't want it to turn into a houseful of furniture or acres of land you have to worry about farming—the hell with all that."

Clara glanced back at him. He was just far enough away so that she could not see whether those tiny wrinkles had appeared again around his mouth. "You're getting beyond me," she said, afraid to hear anything more that he had to say.

He was silent for a moment. Then he said, in a different voice, "Clara, are you about done messing around in there?"

166

She looked up at the sky, feeling her hair fall down long and heavy on her back. It did not amaze her to think that her eyes were floating up helplessly into the sky and could come to no end, could never find any boundary. In Lowry's voice there was something she had heard once before but now, in her wonder, could not quite recall. She closed her eyes and felt the sun hot against her face.

"Come on out from there," Lowry said.

"Go to hell. You're bossing me around."

"Come on, Clara."

"Now you called me Clara. How'd you know that was my name?"

"You're going to walk where the water's going fast, and fall in."

"I am not."

"Well, I'm not going to carry you out, ma'am."

"Nobody asked you to."

"We should be getting back. . . ."

"I'm in no hurry."

"It might be I am."

"You aren't, either," Clara said, letting one shoulder rise and fall lazily. But she stepped out of the water and onto the dried rocks, which had a curious texture now beneath her cold feet, like cloth. She spread her toes on the whitened rocks as if they were fingers grasping at something. Then she saw, between her toes, a dark filmy soft thing like a worm. "Jesus!" Clara said, kicking. She jumped backward and landed on the other foot and kicked again violently. "Get it off, Lowry!" she screamed. "Lowry—help—a bloodsucker—"

She ran at him blindly and he caught her. Everything was speeded up, even Lowry's laugh, and he was still laughing when he picked the thing off. With a snapping motion of his wrist he flicked it away. Clara knew that her face was drained white and that her muscles had let go, as if that bloodsucker had really sucked away all her blood. She lay back, sobbing, and when her eyes came into focus she saw that Lowry was not smiling any longer.

He bent down by her. "You oughtn't to have done that," he said, not smiling, and Clara stared bluntly into his face as if he were a stranger stopping out of nowhere. He kissed her, and while she tried to get her breath back from that he moved on top of her, and she remembered in a panic that he had done this before, yes, years ago, and it all came back to her like a slap in the face, something to wake her up. "Lowry—" she said in a voice all amazement, entirely removed from whatever was giving him such energy and half-trying to push him away—but everything that might have shot into clarity was ruined by his damp searching mouth and his hand thrust under her, getting her ready in a way she only now realized she had to be gotten ready. In amazement the blue sky stared back down at her, wide and impersonal, deep with the unacknowledged gazes of girls like Clara who have nowhere else to look, the earth having betrayed them; the blue shuddered with a panic that was not fear but just panic, the reaction of the body and not the mind. Her mind was awake and skipping about everywhere, onto Lowry and past him and even onto the Lowry of a minute before who had surprised her so, trying to figure out just what had happened in his mind to make him turn into this Lowry—filling out the gestures of her imagination without having to ask what they might have been. It would never have seemed to Clara that love could be such a surprise, so strange, that she could just lie limp and have it done to her and never be clear enough to anticipate any more even when she had tried to figure out what they would all be years in advance—then her amazement turned into pain and she cried out angrily against the side of his face.

She felt him pushing in her, inside her, with all the strength he had kept back from her for years. She pulled at his shirt and then at his flesh under the shirt, as if trying to distract him as well as herself from what he was doing. Lowry's hot ragged breath came against her face and she caught a glimpse of his eyes, not fixed upon her and not ready yet to see anything, and for the first time the kernel behind those eyes gave a hint of itself. She groaned and tightened her arms around his neck, hard, and Lowry kissed her with his hot open mouth and she gasped and sucked in his breath, squirming with this new agony and waiting for it to end, thinking it couldn't last much longer with a kind of baffled and staring astonishment—until Lowry, who was always so calm and slow and seemed to calculate out how many steps would be necessary to take him from one spot to another, groveled on her with his face twisted like a rag in a parody of agony, and could not control what he did to her. She felt as if her body were driven into the ground, hammered into it. She felt as if it were being dislodged from her brain and she would never get the two together again. Then everything broke and she felt his muscles go rigid, locking himself to her and waiting, suspended between breaths that must have made his throat ache. A soft, surprised sound escaped him that was

168

nothing Lowry would ever have made, and Clara let her head fall back onto his arm without even knowing she had been holding it up and waiting for him to stop.

He lay on top of her and his chest heaved. Now that the day was clear again she touched his hand, smoothed his hair off his forehead. Between her legs her flesh was alive with a pain that was so sharp and burning she could not quite believe in it. She felt as if he had gone after her with a knife. She felt as if she had been opened up and hammered at with a cruelty that made no sense because she could not see what it meant. That logic was secret in Lowry's body. In her imagination—lying sleepless in her bed at night, or dreaming behind the store counter—she had known everything Lowry felt and had felt it along with him, because that was part of her happiness; but when it had really happened it was all a surprise. He had made love to her and it was all over and she knew nothing about it, no more than this pain that kept her veins throbbing.

"Jesus, Lowry," Clara sobbed, "I must be bleeding—" He brought his damp face around and his lips brushed hers, but she pushed him away. She tried to sit up. The pain had shattered now into smaller pains that shot up toward her stomach. Lowry wiped his face with both hands and, still breathing hard, lay down beside her. He was like a man who has fallen from a great height. Clara lay back. Tears were running down both sides of her face, into her mouth. Whether the sky was in focus or not she could not tell. Lowry lay beside her, on his back. Her body burned where he had been. She thought that she would never get over it and that he would never be able to do this to her again. So she lay very still with her pain, as if what she felt had more power over either of them than any other feeling she had showed.

Finally Lowry said, "Now you're not a kid, sweetheart."

She wept bitterly. "I never needed to grow up," she said. "I never needed to be gone after with a knife."

"I'm sorry."

"What the hell made you do it?"

He laughed a little. He seemed to be asking her permission to laugh, by the sound of it. "I thought you loved me," he said.

Clara sat up and smoothed her hair back from her face. She took hold of it and twisted it up and back, away from her neck. The perspiration on the back of her neck made her shiver. She looked down at Lowry, who was lying now with his arms behind his head. He smiled at her, then his smile

169

broadened. Clara's face remained rigid. "If I said I loved you, could be I didn't know what I was talking about," she said.

"Could be you don't yet."

She bent her head back again suddenly to a look at the sky, but did not see it. In spite of the pain she felt a sensation of joy, something unexpected she didn't want Lowry to see yet. "So, after two years," she said. "You wouldn't ever do it when I was ready, or when I wanted you to or thought I wanted you to. That would have been too easy."

"I didn't want to do it, honey."

"If you find yourself not wanting to do it again, let me know," she said. There was a twist to her mouth she'd copied from Sonya. "I can get something else to do that day."

He smiled at her toughness. "It doesn't mean anything, honey."

"I know that."

"I'm serious. It doesn't mean anything except what it is."

"I knew you would go on to say something like that."

She tried to get up but froze. A sigh escaped her that was a sound of regret for everything, but not serious regret. The only thing that was serious was the pain and she knew now that it would not last long.

Lowry put his arms around her waist. From behind, he embraced her and pressed his forehead against her back; she could feel him there, and she turned a little as if she were listening to his thought with her body. "You are such a bastard," she said. "Do you know that?" His fingers locked together. He lay still. Clara looked down at her bare feet and blinked when she remembered how it had all happened—and there was the spot between her toes, pink from where the blood had been but now smeared around, a tiny dot of blood that was all that was left from the bloodsucker.

Lowry said, "I'm not going to marry you. You know that."

"All right."

"I can't think of you that way. Don't you think of me that way either."

"All right."

"I'm ten, eleven years older than you, sweetheart...." His words sounded sad. Clara glanced down at his fingers, which were making wrinkles in the cloth of her dress; but it was probably ruined anyhow. Her eyes ran along down her thighs to her legs and feet and back up again. She smiled slightly. She would have drawn in a great exultant breath, except

170

Lowry's embrace kept her back. "How do you feel?" Lowry said.

"You must have made me bleed."

"Does it hurt bad?"

"No, it's all right."

"No, really, does it hurt?"

He straightened up and turned her head to him. He kissed her and Clara made a slight gesture of impatience, mock disgust, then he held her head in his hands and kissed her again. She felt his tongue against her lips and smiled while she kissed him. She said, drawing away, "You never kissed me like that before. You're going to love me if you don't watch out."

"That might be," Lowry said.

It was late when they drove back to Tintern, between ten and eleven. Clara's hair was tangled and her face drawn with exhaustion; she lay with her head against Lowry's shoulder. She thought he was holding the steering wheel in a strange way, with a precise, almost drunken attention he had never showed before. Lowry said, when they were parked outside her place, "Are you going to go in or what? You want to say good-by?"

"No," said Clara.

"Or would you like to take a few days off and come with me?"

"Yes, Lowry," she said. It surprised her to see where they were, even though a moment before she had watched them drive up and stop. The stores on the main street were darkened; only the drug store was open. Someone sat in the doorway on a folding chair, and another figure was behind him. "Where would we go?" Clara said.

"Thought I'd take a drive to the ocean."

"The what?"

"The ocean. You'd like it too."

"All that way? Drive all that way?"

"I can do it."

"Without sleeping?"

"We could maybe sleep first."

"Yes," she said gently. She tried to open the door but could not pull the handle down hard enough. On her second try she succeeded. Lowry slid over behind her and put his arms around her, his hands over her breasts, and buried his face in her hair. Then he pushed her out and followed her upstairs.

When Clara woke off and on that night she felt no surprise

171

at all that Lowry was with her. It might have been that in her sleep she had been with him so much, that now the real Lowry was nothing to alarm her. Being so close to him was like swimming: they were like swimmers, their arms and legs in any easy position, blending together, breathing close together. Her toes groped against his. She thought, It's all decided now. I am a different person to him now. When he made love to her the next morning she began just at the point she had left off the night before, and she had already learned to feel past the pain to the kernel in her he was stirring that was like the kernel in himself he loved so well, that inspired him to such joy. She said, "I love you, I love you," in a kind of delirium, her ears roaring with the flow of her own blood and fit to drown out the silence that had been with her all her life.

At dawn they drove off in his car to the ocean some hundreds of miles away. She brushed her hair with her blue plastic hairbrush, languid and pleased as any married woman, letting her hair fall down onto the back of the seat. She hummed along with the songs on his radio. On the front of the dime store, for the manager she had left a note: "Have been called home, emergency. Will be back Thursday latest. Clara." It was with the little dictionary that Lowry had given her one time that she had looked up, by herself, the word "emergency." This had pleased him. Everything about her pleased him now. She lay back, comfortable in the sun, and thought that now it would be decided between them—what they were to each other, how they had to stay together—and she had only to wait for Lowry to explain it to her.

6

There were three sun-drenched days in a scrubby resort town far away that were going to remain in Clara's mind for the rest of her life; then she found herself back in Tintern with her brain still dazzled by everything that had happened and had not happened.

She thought of Lowry most of the time, but then switched onto things around her that had to be done and was able to get through them that way, as if by groping with her fingertips. She had the idea that she was beautiful now, that she had changed. Around her Tintern changed also, getting pale with dust by August, a small easily-forgotten clump of houses and buildings that were identical with other houses and buildings along the same highway. Against this background she felt herself glowing with something—beauty, health, awareness. She was radiant and buoyed alone by this happiness, which was more than the love comics and magazines had promised her.

"Then it's all decided," Clara thought on the first day, and on the second day of lying in the sun with him and lazily watching other people live out their lives—parents and children from nearby "cottages"—she had thought, "It must be all decided. He doesn't even think about it." Lowry would lie for a while on his stomach, and if she leaned over to stare at his face it would be like the face of a dead man, perhaps— nothing there to make you feel self-conscious. Then he would turn over and lie on his back with his knees bent and read, paperback books with covers showing scenes in deserts or jungles, until he'd finish the last page and sigh in a contemptuous way and toss the book off the blanket and onto the hot sand. At these times Clara felt most anxious. His mind had clicked off one thing and was about to latch onto another, and this hesitation bothered her because he did not naturally seem to turn to her. But after a moment he usually did. She liked to sit under his gaze and brush her long, long hair and look out at the ocean, which was so big that—like the land in the valley—it made people around it loom up like giants as well.

That might have been the way Lowry was so gigantic—a presence that was almost enough to cut off the sun from her. He had grown to fill her mind most of the day, and at night he was something she slept curled against and would have clung to had there been that need. "He must not be thinking of it, even," she thought, waiting to ask him what plans he had and whether he was keeping in mind that note she had left for Peltier about Thursday. Would that Thursday come, so naturally, and would she be back in the store? She could not believe it. But a part of her must have accepted it all along, because she felt no great surprise at ending up back in Tintern on Thursday, just as he had said.

The days at the shore were a flashing, blurred interruption of the summer, and all she had left of it were two pictures, one of Lowry and one of her, taken in an automatic stand near a roller rink: Lowry with that wary expression people use when seeing their own reflections (there had been a mirror facing him) and Clara's picture vague, with a kind of beauty never hers, her hair gleaming and falling to her

173

shoulders and the edges of the picture clouded, her face misty and softened by some mistake in the photographing process. Clara had hoped Lowry would ask for that picture, but he didn't think of it.

And she also had this tanned, satisfied body, and all those memories, and his promise of coming again in two Sundays—it was the earliest he could make it, and he sounded sorry—and a remote suspicion that her laziness about taking care of herself the way Lowry had demanded (he had bought the things in a drug store himself, not particularly pleased with her shyness) might have been a mistake after all. But she had no way of knowing this yet.

When Lowry had said, as early as that first day, "You sure as hell don't want to get pregnant," Clara had heard the word clearly enough but had dismissed it at once. She had not thought about it any more. It was as if the word, like all those unknown, mysterious words in the dictionary, would have no power behind it if it weren't believed in. Besides, Clara had the idea you couldn't get pregnant that fast. Sonya had said so. She said that some women tried to have babies for years and had no luck, that was the real truth. The opposite of it was just something said to scare girls. Sonya's lumbering, indifferent contempt for what people said—particularly women—caught on with Clara and gave her courage for a while. She could imagine Sonya's mouth stretching into a sneer, taking in the stupidity of all people who predicted trouble for others. (That was because she was involved with a married man.) Sonya was irritable all the time now and Clara avoided her, afraid she might hear something she didn't want to hear. The serenity of Clara's face might annoy Sonya, for with Sonya love made things jagged and troublesome and brought out blemishes on her face. Clara had softened. If her face looked empty it was because her mind was occupied, sorting out and arranging memories. In four days there had been less of them than she would have thought, because moments blended into one another and were almost the same moment. But she had certain images to love: Lowry doing this, Lowry looking at her in such a way. One day a man had said something over his shoulder to Clara, and Lowry had grabbed him and pulled him around, and the man had jerked away and told Lowry to let him alone, and Lowry had waited a second and then gone after him again, pushing him along with one hand and showing by the stiffness of his bare back that he was furious. When he came back to Clara she had been ashamed, not

174

because he had been so angry on her account but because he had been angry just for something to do. That was one of her memories. And all the times when she had said aloud to him, "I love you," the words tortured out of her by a force that was like a devil squirming inside her, lashing out in his frenzy. Sunlight in at the window—they stayed in a boarding-house that was clean but a little noisy—and certain water marks on the ceiling, and the eating stands and taverns, one after another, and Lowry squeezing her shoulders or swimming in loose circles around her: she had these things to think about.

As the days passed she began to think more and more of Lowry's baby. Her mind broke through to the surface of the day, shattered by the sunlight, and she was positive that she was pregnant—she knew it must be. But she waited. She fell into the habit of dreaming about Lowry and the baby together, as if the two of them were somehow one, and what had begun as a thought that frightened her turned into a daydream she looked forward to. If she had a baby it would be his and it would be something only he had given her, something he had left her with. After the first several times he had never again said to her, "Are you taking care of yourself, Clara?" because it embarrassed her. Sometimes they would fall asleep and he must have known she was doing nothing, but forgetfulness came down upon them like the lazy heat of the beach and told them that all was well. Clara thought that all was well forever and that the future would stretch out before them the way the ocean and the beach did, stretching out of sight but always the same, monotonous and predictable. She supposed it would be that way with Lowry once he settled down. She supposed that in his mind everything had been decided—that he was going to keep her with him from now on—but, back in Tintern a while later, she had had to give up that idea and start working on this new one.

On the surface of her mind was this worry, was she going to have a baby? Or could it be that her body was thrown off by Lowry? It was only on the surface of her mind, however. What she really felt came out when she said to Sonya, one day, "It would be nice to have a baby," and then stopped to think what she had said. Sonya made a contemptuous noise that was like something ugly kicked out before you, for a joke. This did not bother Clara. She felt like a plant of some kind, like a flower on a stalk that only looked slender but was really tough, tough as steel, like the flowers in fields that could be blown down flat by the wind but yet rose again slowly, coming back to life. Her first thought was, "Lowry will be mad at me for not taking care of myself"; then she thought, "It's his more than mine because he's older," and remembered the many times he had been gentle with her, drawing her close with a casual gesture that meant more to her than anything else. They came together at moments like that. On the beach his dreaminess had been a dreaminess that drifted out for miles, while hers was a dreaminess of motion content to remain still for a lifetime; but still they had come together at certain moments.

Ginny's children, especially the baby, drew out Clara's love. On Sunday she went to a charity picnic with them, just to have something to do while waiting for Lowry to come (he had said not before eight), and she kept asking to hold the baby even when Ginny said she didn't mind carrying it herself. Ginny was pregnant again. Her husband Bob had not found work yet and he and Ginny were living with her mother.

They walked slowly about together, a little group. Clara thought that everyone at the picnic looked different, special. The old women wore hats, round black straw hats with bunches of artificial flowers, usually violets. Many of the men wore suits, though they looked awkward and hot in them. Ginny wore a filmy long-sleeved dress that was already stained with the baby's milk, an accident they had in the car, but her face was freshened by the music and the excitement of the picnic and she did not seem to mind the way Bob walked a few steps ahead of them. Clara returned looks she got with a slow, dreamy smile, not surprised that people should think her worth staring at but rewarding them for it. She saw Sonya and her boy friend standing at the Volunteer Firemen's Beer Tent, the biggest tent of all, but she did not go over to say hello. Ginny nudged Clara and said, "Don't they have a nerve?" but Clara just shrugged her shoulders. She was in a warm, pleasant daze, trying to balance the secret she was now certain of about herself with the color and noise of the picnic, dazed by what she knew that no one else, not even Ginny, could know.

They stopped at the bingo tent and the two girls played a few games, while the baby whined and tugged at Clara's skirt and the boy tried to swallow the dried-up corn kernels they pushed around on the dirty old bingo cards. A fat lady, the wife of the man who owned the drug store, stood by them and chattered at the baby. She wore an apron with special pockets sewn in it to hold change. "Too bad you don't have better luck, you two," she said to Clara and Ginny. On the last game Clara had no luck either, and sat toying with the kernels of corn and staring down at the card with a small fixed smile, her mind already fallen beyond the noisy tent of bingo players and the shaking of the numbered balls and the recorded music to those days by the ocean with Lowry. But those days seemed already far away.... Then someone yelled "Bingo!" and as always, she wasn't ready just yet to hear it. Ginny said, "Crap," and pushed her card away. Clara swung herself around on the bench and let her legs fall hard. She thought, "Six or seven months and I won't be able to do that." This thought, which came out of nowhere to her, was more real than all the memories she had been reliving.

They found Bob at the beer tent, which was naturally where he would be, and stood around talking with people. There was just a slight wind and it picked up dust—the land was dry in August—and Clara sometimes reached down to keep her skirt by her knees. She wore yellow high-heeled shoes and no stockings, which was a mistake because a blister had begun on one heel, and a pale blue dress that reminded her of Lowry's eyes, though her own were about the same color. That morning, and every morning since Thursday, she had washed her face with cream in a blue jar she bought a the drug store (it cost 59¢) and stood dreamily massaging her skin in small circles, looking beyond her own eyes in the mirror. After she finished with the cream she washed it off her face carefully and then leaned close to the mirror and plucked at her eyebrows, until they were shaped in thin rising lines and made her look a way she had never looked before—delicate and surprised. She had always had the look of a girl standing flat-footed, but now she looked like someone else—it might have been the girl in that dime photograph she was imitating. Herself, but a better self. Whenever men glanced at her and their eyes slowed, Clara turned her head a little to loosen her hair just to give them something more to look at; being with Lowry had done that for her. She thought that all men were like Lowry in some way, or trying to be like him. At the beer tent Bob joked around and jostled her and then, when Ginny had drifted a short distance away, talking to someone else, he had taken hold of her upper arm and squeezed it. Clara looked at him as if she did not know who he was, doing such a thing. She had listened for months to Ginny's weeping over him, and she knew that Ginny was right, but now this hard, sullen young man confronted her with a look of trouble that was all his own and she could not really identify him. It crossed her mind that he too could have done what Lowry did to her, and the baby she might be going to have could be his baby, that it could be any man's at all—and the idea was astonishing. Except for Lowry, everyone was common.

She got away from him and caught up with Ginny, and was holding Ginny's baby and wondering at its out-of-focus eyes when someone approached her. It was Revere. She smiled at him and made the baby's hand wave at him, as if it were natural he should just step up out of a noisy crowd at the Tintern firemen's picnic. Clara chattered about the baby: "His name is Jefferson and this is his mother here, Ginny, and that's his father down there—where they're all laughing and carrying on. Isn't it a nice picnic?" Revere stood with one hand in his pocket, awkwardly.

"Clara, give him back. You go have fun," Ginny said. She sounded maternal and bossy, like her own mother, but it was really meant to be critical so that Revere could catch it: after all, he was here alone and he was married and hadn't he just fired Caroline's husband for drinking too much? She took the baby from Clara's arms and left Clara just standing there, facing Revere.

"You seem to like children," he said.

"I love babies especially," she said. She thought of Lowry and of any baby that Lowry might father—it would be half hers and might look like him around the eyes, and she would let him name it—and a sensation of faintness rose suddenly in her. She and Revere began to walk together. She felt this dizziness, this uncertainty that was not at all unpleasant, and wondered if she should tell this man about it. He seemed to have nothing to say and so she went on, chattily, "I'd like to have seven or eight children, lots of kids, and a big house and everything. Nobody is happy in a house without a baby, right?—I was just over visiting by the ocean, all that ways. I went with some friends and was swimming and out on the beach."

She turned to him with a dazed, dazzling smile, as if she were still a little blinded by the sun. But he did not smile with her. He looked uneasy. "A friend of mine is coming to visit me tonight," Clara went on. In her excitement she wanted to tug at Revere's arm to make him understand how important this was. "I have lots of things to do and have to get back home—I just came to the picnic with a friend—"

"Would you like to talk about them?—your friends?"

She thought this was a strange question. She glanced at

178

Revere and was a little slowed down by his eyes, which were fixed on her in a way she remembered Lowry's had been. The faintness swelled out inside her. She wanted to turn and get back to Ginny, where it was safe, even if Ginny was angry, and get rid of the time somehow until eight o'clock when Lowry would come. She said, "My girl friend Ginny—" but was cut off by some boys running past.

They strolled through the picnic grounds and at the edge of the parking lot. The "parking lot" was just a field where cars could park for the picnic. From here the music sounded thin and sleazy. Revere said, "I think I'd like to talk to you. I don't ask anything from you." Clara smiled nervously. She kept listening to that music and thought how far away it was, so quickly, and here she hadn't been with this man for five minutes.

"Yes," Clara said, "but my girl friend—I'm supposed to have supper with her folks."

"I can get you something to eat."

"Somthing to eat?" Clara said blankly. "But my friend is coming at eight."

"Is it a boy friend?"

She said cautiously, "Just a friend," and turned to him as if to get them on their way back to the picnic. But her gaze swung around past his chest and did not dare reach up to his face. She was conscious of his name. His name floated about him like perfume around a beautiful woman, touching people before he even came near, defining and fixing him in a way he himself could never know about. Lowry himself had known this man's name. . . .

They stepped through the weeds and went over to his car, which Clara recognized at once. She must have looked at it more closely than she knew. She said, "Someone told me your name is Revere," and he laughed and said, "I told you that myself." But she did not mean him.

"You look a little different than you did before," he said.

"Yes, I know it."

She got in his car. The seat was hot and burned the backs of her knees. "Maybe," she said weakly, "we could not drive far but just a little ways? Just a short drive?"

He drove out to the road, over the bumpy field. Some kids were playing around the parked cars. A boy with a toy cane stood on the roof of a car and waved his cane at them, calling something. Clara closed her face against them.

"What did you want to talk about?" Clara said.

He seemed a little embarrassed. She wondered if there

wasn't something resentful about him, about the way the corners of his mouth drooped in profile as if he were puzzled himself over what he was doing. "I should be back to have supper with them," Clara said, relaxing a little so that she could enjoy the drive, "they're real good friends to me. I don't have any family or anyone and they invite me over a lot. . . . I'm friends with a girl named Sonya too. But you probably don't know her. . . ."

He might have been waiting for her to get through with this kind of talk. Clara shrugged her shoulders in miniature at his silence, not for him to see. She thought of Lowry probably on his way driving to her, and of how they would make love that evening. She thought of the ways she might use to explain to Lowry what was wrong with her—unless it was just a mistake. She would have liked to talk to Revere about Lowry but did not know how to begin. Anyway, you should not confide in adults, especially men; it was better never to say anything secret to anyone.

They drove up the highway and kept going, not fast. Clara looked out the window and enjoyed it, though she'd had quite a bit of driving with Lowry the week before. Moving around and getting somewhere so long as you were more or less already on your way back always struck her as nice; it was nothing like riding on the crop seasons. She said, "I loved the ocean. I loved driving there and seeing everything. You can see more of the mountains on your way out. . . . Do you travel around much?"

"Mostly to Chicago."

"Chicago?" Clara said. "In this car?"

"By train."

"Oh," she said, pleased. She liked that expression, "by train." Anyone else would have said "on the train." She imagined him speeding through the countryside in those straight, relentless lines railroad tracks made, cutting through back country and eating up distance like nothing. She looked over at him as if he had performed a magic feat. "Mr. Revere, what was it you wanted to say?"

He brought the car to a stop as if he were far enough now from what had bothered him back there. They were at the top of a hill and could look down to some scrubby land where there was a narrow angular lake—"Mirror Lake"—dotted with trees and the stumps of trees on its north side. Young people swam here and had picnics, but today there were only a few couples; everyone was at the charity picnic. Clara could hear someone's car radio blaring, all the way up the

180

hill. The memory of those days with Lowry came back to her like a stab in her breast. Clara felt how far she was from them already, just the way Mr. Revere must feel far from those young people who were swimming and carrying on around Mirror Lake.

Revere rubbed his face. He might have been, like Clara, trying to wake up out of a dream. "There are some things I can't understand," he said slowly. His words were a little harsh. Clara noticed that they cut at the air more than the words of other people did; there was something impatient about them. "I don't think I can explain them. But—when I was your age I stayed with an uncle of mine who lived on a ranch in Dakota. I spent the summer there. He drove my cousins and me into town and it was hardly a town at all—much smaller than Tintern—just a muddy street with some stores. Back from the road there was a shack and a big family lived there. Nine children. There was a girl my age. She had long hair that was almost white and dressed just in rags and she was—like you. . . . She was Swedish."

"I ain't Swedish," Clara said suspiciously. "I'm American."

"She was happy," Revere said.

Clara wondered at that. She did not understand what this man was talking about. What he was saying had something to do with another girl, someone who was grown up now and old, lost, forgotten, someone Clara had never even seen. "That was nice," Clara said uncertainly. "I mean—her being happy."

"My first wife was from a family in the valley here," Revere said. "She was my own age. Then she died and I married Marguerite—"

"Yes," Clara said, "somebody said that was your wife's name."

He took no notice that someone had been talking about him. He said, "We have three boys but she's never really been well since before the first one was born. She's a fine person . . . her father was a fine man. It's all in her, behind her . . . her family. . . . But her heart is heavy."

"Why?"

He looked off to one side, as if Clara had asked a foolish question. "Most people are that way, Clara," he said.

Clara did not know what to say. Should she make a joke, or smile, or what? What made her uneasy was the knowledge that she would not be able to tell anyone about this conversation, especially not Lowry. She said, gropingly, "Your boys

181

are real nice, anyway the two I saw— There ain't something wrong with the youngest one, is there?"

"No."

"But—then—"

"There's nothing wrong."

"Is your wife sick bad?"

"I don't know."

"Does the doctor come out a lot?"

"Yes."

Clara thought about that. "It's nice he can come out a lot," she said. "A doctor looked at me once. He gave me some shots in the arm that stung a little. . . . My pa, though, was real scared. Grown-up men get scared sometimes too. But he wasn't scared of anything else," she said quickly. Revere was still looking out the window. Outside, some blackbirds were fighting over something on the ground. "Tell me," Clara said suddenly, "are there books in your house?"

"Some."

"Are they up on the walls?"

"On shelves? Yes."

"Oh," Clara said, pleased, "that's nice."

"Do you like to read?"

"No, but I like books. I like them up on the wall that way—I seen some pictures of it." She smiled happily at him. "If I had some kids I would like for them to read books. I would give them lots of books and they'd learn how to read just by themselves." She thought of Lowry reading those paperback books and giving her that dictionary; of course he would want his children to read. People who read were different from people who didn't. "Then they'd know things fast, before other kids. If I could of gone to school and learned things right, I'd be—I'd be different than I am now."

"Why do you want to be different?"

She colored a little. She laughed. "I guess I don't want to be different."

He looked at her for a while. Clara thought that Ginny and her people would start to talk by now and she wondered why Revere didn't think of it too. With his first and second finger he kept squeezing his lips shut, thinking. She could feel the resentment in the air about him, and something else too—the steady inflexible weight of his stare that meant she had been selected out of the whole landscape just for him to worry about. And Lowry was on the road coming to her, and in a few hours they would be together again—it wouldn't even be dark yet. In her purse were the two photographs from the beach and she had an impulse to show them to Revere. But she took out only the one of herself. "This is me, taken down by the ocean," she said. He reached out for it. The way he studied it disturbed her a little, because she hadn't meant anything special by offering it. After a while he said, "This doesn't look like you either." She shook her head no, obediently, but she was really thinking—What does this man know about how I look? She put out her hand for the picture but he was still looking at it. "It's very strange," he said. "I don't ask anything of you...." His voice was cold and she had the idea he was about to bend the photograph in two between his fingers. Instead, he put it in his pocket.

"I didn't mean...." Clara began weakly.

"Can't I have it?"

"All right."

"My first wife died having a baby," he said. His words were so harsh now that Clara wondered how anyone could listen to them for long. "The baby died too. That was so long ago, she was young enough to be—she could have been—my daughter now. They did everything for her but she died. Is your mother alive?"

"Yes."

"Where is she?"

"I guess down in Florida."

"Why did you run away from home?"

"My father hit me," Clara said. But suddenly an idea opened at the back of her mind. That was really not why she had left home; she had left home because it had been time. One day she and Rosalie had seen a flag and she had stolen it, and after that everything had just come along by itself. That was why she was sitting here in Revere's car this afternoon, on an August Sunday years later. She said nervously, "He used to get drunk and hit me and I had to leave."

"Your father?"

"He got drunk and hit me...."

"Did you love him?"

"Sure."

"Why?"

"I don't know. Is it all right if we go back now?"

"Why did you love your father if he hit you?"

"He was my father."

"But—so what?"

"He was my father," Clara said sullenly. She wondered if he was making fun of her the way Lowry did sometimes.

There was some picking, precise look in his eyes that reminded her of Lowry. "You don't stop loving somebody when
they hit you."

He thought this over. Clara half-shut her eyes and remembered that street, that house, that flag. She remembered
running up to snatch it and could see herself, as if all the
action had been done by another person. Then in the next
instant everything fell away, years vanished, and she was
sitting here with this strange man. What had her father to do
with it, then? But she could not explain this to Revere.

"Are you going to be married soon?" he said.

She looked at him. "How come you say that?"

"Are you?"

"I don't know. I guess not."

"But you might?"

She laughed shyly. "I don't think so."

"Is there somebody in mind?"

"Mister, can we go back now? Please?"

He looked at her the way he had looked at the photograph.
"All right," he said. "We can go back."

She sat up straight, with the docile alertness of a child who
may have done something wrong. The land back into Tintern
moved unhurriedy to them, and Clara measured with her
eyes the distance they had yet to go. And Lowry was on the
way to her and would be with her in a few hours. She felt slow
and peaceful, as if warmed by the sun. Revere was even
more of a stranger to this town than she was herself, she
thought. She stood between him and the ugly little clump of
buildings and the clearings that were only halfway cleared
and the dusty lanes with weeds growing in their centers; he
might have owned some of it or all of it but he was more a
stranger than she was.

When he let her out he looked tired. She thought he must
be almost forty; it was the first clear thought she had had
about him. "Take care of youself," he said, echoing Lowry's
words. Clara was a little shocked at that echo. She shook her
head yes, smiled yes, with her hand on the doorknob just
waiting for its freedom, waiting for his sad, heavy gaze to
release her. Why his resentment, why that bullying set of his
mouth? Clara wanted to tell him that she was free and
belonged to no one at all. And if she ever did, it would be to
another man. But she did not know what he wanted. She had
never met anyone like him, she did not know how to talk

184

to him. All she felt when she left was a sense of relief at being away from the pressure of his gaze.

When she climbed the stairs to her room she felt that relief ebb out of her. Revere's look stayed with her, the look her father should have given years ago if he'd known how—but of course he hadn't—and that would have kept her home, kept her from running. From Lowry too. And from this new, stunning knowledge—she let her hand fall against her stomach. Yes, it was true. Was it true? How could she know for certain? She stood at the top of the stairs breathing heavily.

She opened the door, half expecting Lowry to be inside, but the room was empty. The air was very hot. A few flies buzzed about when she entered, annoyed at being disturbed, then they quieted down. Clara sat on her bed and stared at the opposite wall for a few minutes, thinking of nothing. Then Revere's face returned to her, and then the knowledge about her life she'd had in the car: what had brought her all this way to Lowry and to what she thought she might be carrying inside her had just been an accident. Was that it? One thing led to another and then to another and wasn't it anything more than that?

She kicked off her shoes; her feet ached. She went to the sink and pumped water and splashed it on her warm face, not caring if she got her dress wet. Up on the window sill the new plant she had bought basked in the sunlight. The earth in the clay pot was hard and crumbly, so she watered it. She ran one finger along a leaf: it was so carefully made, so small and intricate. If you looked closely enough at anything it was carefully made, intricate, mysterious.

She would have liked to explain this to Lowry. And the idea she had had about her life. But it was hard for her to think. If she tried to think in any serious way it would be nothing more than an imitation of Lowry, who had taught her how to think. Was she going to spend her life imitating him, rehearsing their conversations before the mirror? That face in the mirror there—that body—were hers, all right, but the breathlessness belonged to him. He had done that to her. If she was beautiful, that belonged to him too. It wasn't what she had always supposed she would want—the kind of faces shown in magazines and on advertisements in the store for lipsticks and make-up. This had something strange about it, something that looked hurt. That was it, Clara thought: she looked like someone who is hurt or who is going to be hurt. That was what that delicate look meant. . . . When Lowry came she would tell him about all these things no matter how hard it was, and she would tell him about the baby too, and wait for him to make everything right by an airy wave of his hand.

She lay on her bed and lit a cigarette and waited. She thought of what she was going to tell him, which words to use. She would begin by saying. . . .

Her face went hard and blank at the thought that everything that had happened to her, even the baby, especially the baby, had fallen over onto her like something dumped out of a window. Why was that so strange, so frustrating? She could not keep hold of it. She did not understand her own thoughts. If Lowry were here he could help her, or he'd laugh them away—but he wasn't here and she was afraid he would not come. It was early yet but she was afraid. Clara went to check her face in the mirror; that was all right. What was going wrong was inside her head and wouldn't show. And she thought slowly, dully, that maybe she would have a child out of all this and it would be born the same way she had been born: just an accident. Things fell together or fell apart or knocked onto something else and overturned it, but if you tried to get up somewhere so that you could make sense of your life, all the things that had happened to you just stretched off past the horizon—fathers and mothers and grandparents and off into time so deep it made your heart sink. Was that why her joy had vanished? Revere had looked at her and seen some other girl, and his wonder at her happiness had begun to drain it, right then. Why had he followed her? What did he want? She walked around the bed, touching her hands lightly together and pretending that she was not really striking herself, punishing herself. Maybe he wanted everything from her, maybe he wanted to suck at her life, Clara thought. At that moment she was as old as she would ever get. Maybe he wanted Lowry's child and everything Lowry had made of her, beginning with the way he had washed her that night in his room. . . .

She wanted to be able to tell Lowry, "We should stay together now because we love each other"—but the half-formed knowledge she had had a moment before began to spread in her, like something cold and ugly. She had almost seen what Lowry knew. It came close, brushing against her, but she could not quite get hold of it—why was it awful that she and Lowry had been thrown together by accident, that she loved him by accident, and that everything that happened should follow from one moment, from her catching sight of that flag hanging by someone's porch? The hot dry air of the afternoon sank down about her, lethargic with failure and disappointment. If Lowry hurried—

But Lowry did not hurry. She practiced telling him about her trouble many times: "I'm afraid I got some trouble, Lowry," or "There's something wrong you need to know," or "I feel bad about. . . ." It might have been the ease with which she mouthed this that made her know she would never get to say it, that things did not go that easily.

After dark she somehow thought he could drive faster, that the roads would be clearer. Lying on her bed, she tried to make her mind calm, wondering why she was so afraid while at the picnic she had been so happy. The picnic had fooled her with all its noise. And Revere had come up out of it. . . . He remembered a girl from years ago: that girl had been like Clara. Clara was like that girl. She turned her head on the pillow and saw a vague image of another Clara up in the snow, up in Dakota—she knew more or less where that was and thought it must be cold all year round—dressed in rags, with her long hair free in the winter wind, and having to grin and laugh all her life. Revere had wondered why that girl had been happy. In Revere's brain many things were run together. He could go anywhere he wanted "by train," he owned so much land he could never walk over it all, he owned people, he had children. But he had wondered why that girl had been happy, not knowing that she hadn't a choice probably—what choice did you have? Revere knew everything but he could not know that. Lowry sped all over the countryside, back and forth, and left behind him all sorts of things damaged and wrung dry and thrown so far away from him he would never remember again. He was the opposite of Revere and Revere might wonder about him too—why was he never happy? She knew this about Lowry and that was why she was afraid. Then she pushed it all away and sat up and lit a cigarette, thinking she was crazy, this was all crazy. She had said he might end up loving her and he'd said, with no one forcing him, "That might be."

"That might be."

She heard it again: "That might be."

Why would he say that if he didn't mean it? Or did he know what he meant? Didn't people have control over the truth when they spoke, making it true just by saying it? Or could a true statement turn out to be false later on, with no one to blame?

"That might be," Lowry had said. Which meant nothing.

Clara wondered how she had lived through the two weeks.

187

And the picnic today. And that ride with Revere that had seemed to last so very long.

When he finally came it was late. Clara had taken off her dress but still lay on top of her bed, waiting. In the darkness she could see objects without bothering to figure them out; she knew where everything was. She lay with her feet curled up under her, half-sitting, propped up by a pillow, with an ashtray tilted on the bed. She was just lighting her sixth cigarette when she heard the unmistakable sound of Lowry's car outside; she hadn't known that she had known what his car sounded like.

He knocked and came inside. Clara had stood. "No, don't turn on the light," he said. He closed the door and she could hear him breathing hard.

"What's wrong?"

He seized her and pulled her over against him. "I can't stay, I'm in a hurry. I did something," he said. Though his voice was rushed, he was not frightened. "I'm on my way through. I can't stay. Are you all right, Clara?"

"What's wrong?"

"For Christ's sake don't cry—stop that," he said. He embraced her and lifted her off the floor. There was something reckless and joyful about him that terrified her. "Little Clara, it's all right, I'm not hurt or anything—just in a hurry— How the hell are you, kid? How's everything here? I missed you—"

He pushed her back toward the bed and sat her down. "Look, I can't stay. Maybe I could write you a letter or something—okay? Okay, sweetheart?"

"Did you do something?"

"Christ, yes, it's about time," he said. "I was fed up with this two-bit business, this two-bit goddam junk I've been doing. Next time you see me I'll be different. I'm sick to death of myself the way I am—what the hell am I?" He sat down heavily beside her. His released joy made his body heavy. "I'm going to Mexico, sweetheart."

"I'll go with you—"

"What? You stay here. You grow up. Do you need some money?"

"Why are you going away?" Clara said wildly. "What's wrong? Did you kill somebody?"

"I've never been down to Mexico, that's why I'm going there. I'm going to do lots of things— Look, do you need some money? How the hell are you?" He took her jaw in his hand and looked at her, this new, loud, strange Lowry. She could feel his anxious breath on her face and was paralyzed. No words came to her. "You're a sweet little girl but look, look, I never fooled you, did I? I never lied to you. I told you all along how it was. Okay? Are you okay?"

He lay back with her on the bed and held her in his arms. But she had already retreated from him, grown small. She felt small, and her body was numb and dead in his arms, something foreign to both of them. Lowry kissed her and kept on talking in that low, explosive way, his energy threatening to damage her with the very innocence of its joy, and she could not understand it. She had shrunken far inside her body and could not control its trembling and could not understand what was happening. Lowry said, getting up, "Clara, I've got to get going. I'm in a big rush. If somebody comes looking for me, tell them to go to hell—right? I'm only taking what's my own. If he follows me I'll smash his head in. Tell him that. Here, Clara, I'll try to see you sometime again—remember me, all right? Here's something for you. Remember me—I took good care of you, didn't I?"

Then he was gone. Clara lay still. When she finally turned on the light she saw money on the table, bills scattered carelessly as if the wind of Lowry's passing had blown them there by accident. It was some time before she could make herself get up to put them away. She moved slowly, woodenly. She wondered how she would live out the rest of her life.

7

The day Clara took her life into control was an ordinary day. She did not know up until the last moment exactly how she would bring all those accidents into control, like a driver swerving aside to let a rabbit live or tearing into it and not even bothering to glance back: he might do one or the other and not know a moment before what it would be.

She was sixteen now, and by the time the baby was born she would be seventeen. Every morning after Lowry had left she woke up to the clear, unmistakable knowledge of what had happened to her and what it meant. The dreaminess of the past two weeks had vanished. She stared long and hard at things. It might have been that she didn't trust them—that she wanted to make sure they stayed still, kept their shapes, identities. She thought about the baby all the time, and through it she thought of Lowry, who would be kept alive this way even if—down in Mexico or anywhere—he someday really did die. He would stay alive through it and its eyes might be like his, or its mouth or something about it—and it would answer her when she called it, come running when she called no matter how far away it was.

To people in Tintern she must have looked like their own girls, girls up and down the highway who have grown up too early but are anxious to grow up even more. The older people, those established enough not to have lost all their money and land in the trouble some years before, could not have distinguished her from other girls of the sort who were taken dancing, under-age, in neonlit roadhouses on the highway and who were from farms, their eyes hard and obscure with the knowledge that goes with so many years of boredom and excitement back to back, ordinary burdensome life and dangerous, frenzied life, days spent working on the farm and nights out on the highway or back in abandoned houses or barns with men they'd met the night before. Clara did not talk to any of these girls, though she knew how precariously she was set apart from them; she looked just as cheap as they did but she did not know what to do about it. She knew people were talking about her. When Lowry showed up they had talked and now that he did not show up they talked even more. Sonya's boyfriend had a fight and had been beaten up by his wife's brother, in another town, and people had that to talk about too. Ginny liked to chatter idly and cruelly about Sonya, and Clara's head ached to think that all this applied to her too, that she was worse than Sonya because Sonya had at least expected nothing from it all. But she kept on loving Lowry and wondering if maybe he wouldn't change his mind —Mexico was so far—and she noticed that the outside of her, her face, stayed the same. In memory of him she washed her hair twice a week and let it dry in the white-hot sun of late August, being able to forget in this heat the time that now stood between her and those days at the ocean. In such violent heat all barriers fell away.

She spent hours crying and then cursing herself for crying, just as she had for the past two years. It was the dry, painful hours when she had no more tears or curses left that hurt her most. It was like trying to throw up when you hadn't had anything to eat—just the awful gesture that brought no relief or end to itself. Lowry was a bastard, she thought, but it meant nothing to know that because he had been a bastard all along and had made no secret of it. He was everything else, every dirty name, and he would have accepted them all so they struck him and fell away, leaving him the way he'd

190

always been—just Lowry. She was exhausted with this love for him, this physical frenzy that was like a devil clawing and screaming inside her to get free. She would have gladly freed it—vomited it up—but it had hold of her and didn't really want to let go. It had nothing to do with the baby. That was something separate, something peaceful and waiting, that slept in her and was in no hurry. It took life feebly from her, tiny gasps of blood, but the devil she carried about with her to the most innocent places—even to church one Sunday when she couldn't stand the long ordeal of that day, alone— was a creature that reached and lunged out into every part of her body, prying, prodding, teasing, not content with anything feeble or gentle. It was all for Lowry, for his love. He would have been able to keep it down but he was gone and she supposed he would never come back.

"That son of a bitch," she muttered. She sometimes muttered to herself out on the street, trying to keep her lips from moving. She stared often at cars that passed through, strange cars, as if they might be bringing word from the outside, from a distant land, and those people received her look and took it with them. Sonya told her that her eyes looked bigger. She shouldn't lose any more weight or she'd be too thin, Sonya warned her, but she liked what Clara did to her eyebrows. Her own eyebrows had been plucked too much and expressed perpetual anemic amazement; then her eyes, slanted and heavy, expressed nothing. They had seen too much. Sonya might have sensed Clara's unhappiness, since Clara no longer chattered to her, but she was clumsy with affection and did not know how to be serious about anything that was personal. It was better to make cynical, sneering remarks about men, to show that men did not matter much. Clara kept forgetting to ask her to stay overnight with her, and Sonya kept forgetting to suggest it. They did not want to return to their close friendship because each had too much to keep secret. But Clara noticed that Sonya made no scornful references to Lowry, that "blond bastard thinks he's so smart." All that had stopped.

And Caroline, who came with her baby to visit her parents and then stayed on for a while, week after week, declared that Clara looked different too. Caroline herself had changed since that wedding day, was thinner, sadder, more nervous, and had a habit of touching Clara sadly, which Clara did not like. "You look funny sometimes," she said. There was no other way for her to express herself, though this was coarse and she knew it. "Is that bitch from the country school board after you again? What's wrong?" Caroline's baby was sickly and whatever was going on between her and her husband was kept quite secret from Clara, who did not especially want to know anyway. So she tried to avoid her friends. She tried to avoid everyone. Something was working along in the back of her mind and it could take as long as it needed, but she had nothing to say to Sonya or Caroline or Ginny any more and could not keep up the reckless indifferent banter with men the way she had at one time—when Ginny's husband came in the store to bother her she told him to go right to hell, not smiling, and he hadn't liked that. Then one afternoon, late, when she was out walking by herself along a back lane a mile or so from her room, she saw Revere's car parked and understood at once what she was going to do and what she had been planning for nearly four weeks.

It had been that long: four weeks. She thought it could have been four years. Clara had never paid much attention to the workings of her body, but after that trip with Lowry her attention had turned inward so violently and resentfully that she would never be able to think of her body any other way. Lowry had changed her. But she was healthy despite this. The trouble was that her body's health had nothing to do with her personally, with Clara; its workings and demands were not hers. She sometimes dreamed that Lowry was making love to her and her mind did not want this at all—it was disgusted and angry. She would press both hands against her stomach when she was alone, or even sometimes in the store, and think of how her body had continued in its way while her mind had tried hard to go in another; but in the end there was no choice. Time kept on passing, she kept on growing into it, drifting into it. There was no choice.

When she had nothing else to do she went out walking by herself. In Tintern there were always people walking, kids or old people or anyone at all, maybe attended by dogs that ran barking and sniffing everywhere. Some of the old men carried heavy branches to use as canes, some of the kids carried branches that were supposed to be weapons. Clara walked back the dusty lanes that led past closed-up storage barns and frame houses and fields that had never been cleared. She avoided walking by the creek because so many people hung around there, and she never went past the Tintern "hotel," where mill hands rented rooms or just hung out. One day she saw Revere's car parked up on the shoulder of the road; back a distance was a new building, a small office that had something to do with the lumberyard. It looked as if it had

192

been built out of new raw lumber just the other day. The lumberyard itself was large and not very busy. The sawmill, some distance away and facing another road, was noisy and crowded with men; Clara was afraid of it.

This was the very end of August. The air was motionless. Clara was used to perspiration on her forehead, her neck, her body, but she did not like it because it made her feel dirty. Lowry disliked dirt. So she wiped her forehead with the backs of her hands and stood at the side of the road and waited. If she stared straight ahead, she could see the tall ungainly buildings of Tintern, one of them the building she'd lived in now for over two years. Seen from the back, they looked hollowed-out and strange: women had clothes hanging up to dry, drooping from line to line, on the back porches. Two girls came from the turn-off of the Main Street, riding bicycles, heading down toward her. They were about twelve or thirteen and lived somewhere on the other side of the town, in those neat identical white frame houses bought by men who had managed to save money for twenty years or so in the sawmill or at the gypsum plant, doing steady work, therefore different from Clara and her people. She felt this difference now more and more often. When she had been with Lowry—no matter where his imagination had been—she had never noticed such things. She must have lived in a daze. But now she did notice, now her eyes had taken on the characteristic of narrowing shrewdly when she met someone, as if sizing up an enemy. The girls were laughing shrilly together and as they approached Clara they fell silent. Clara stared at their sweaty, smeared faces, their little mouths and eyes shaped for secret wonder and laughter about this strange blonde girl Clara, whom everyone knew and talked about, who didn't have any family, who lived by herself in that dump—!

The first girl pedaled faster and shot by Clara, saying nothing, then the other was by too. Once they were past, they giggled again. Clara watched them ride away—the second one had a boy's bike, old and battered—and wondered what they had been saying about her. She did not feel any bitterness. She did not feel anything toward them at all. She watched them ride down the lane and wondered why she had never had a bicycle, why she hadn't trained her legs to go up and down like that in tight controlled circles, so that the muscles of the calf showed, even on those skinny girls. They wore blue jeans that were baggy and faded, they stood up on the pedals in a breathless rigidity that waited to see where it

193

would be taken to, the girls calm and unalarmed by bumps and rocks in the lane. They zigzagged back and forth, calling out to each other, their words flattened now by the distance. The soft pale dust of the lane was marked by their tire prints, a vague blurred confusion of lines that no one but Clara could understand. Clara looked after them and felt how old she was, how far she had come while never having ridden down back lanes like this with a friend, on bicycles, before supper. . . . Then she heard some men talking and looked over to the office, where Revere and two other men stood. Revere was backing off from them.

He must have seen her because he backed away, still talking, and then turned and headed to her. She was serious when he approached her. She watched him come and saw how his eyes emerged out of the distance, fixed upon her. She had not quite remembered them. He said hello, but she hesitated, unwilling to say anything across that space of dirt, when here she had been standing and waiting for him so obviously—anyone could tell that.

"Is anything wrong?" Revere said. He brought a sweet, fresh smell of new lumber with him on his clothes. But it began to fade at once in the afternoon heat. "Did you want to—see me?"

Clara almost shivered, but she had felt it coming and controlled it. She must have been looking at him with a small, fixed, strange smile. Revere wore no suit coat today and no tie, and the sleeves of his shirt were rolled up. But he still did not look like a man from this country. Just as Clara, dressed up, looked like every other girl for miles, so Revere looked like no one else even when dressed like them.

"I was out walking and saw your car," Clara said flatly. She kept staring at him as if to force him into saying something, doing something. Revere was slowly folding up a slip of yellow paper, then he seemed to forget about it and held it between his fingers absently. "It's hot, it's awful hot. I feel all heavy and sick with this summer," Clara said. Her voice had gone breathless, amorous in a tired way, and her eyelids drooped as she spoke, not knowing at all what she was going to say. But she did not think she had to say much of anything. She was so aware of him standing there that her throat kept wanting to close up, to swallow in terror; his movements too were stiff. They might have gone through this before, many times. Clara did indeed feel that she had said something of this nature to him before, and that he had looked at her as he was looking now. Clara glanced down at

194

herself, as if to guide Revere's eyes, at her bare tanned arms and bare tanned legs, at her black ballerina slippers that had cost $2.98 new and were already run over and smudged and looked like hell. Everything she had, Clara thought, looked like hell sooner or later. She said, tossing her hair back out of her eyes, "Do you own this place here—this lumberyard?"

"Not all of it," he said. He tried to smile.

She still had not smiled and so she felt ahead of him. "You own lots of things in town, though," she said flatly.

"In Tintern? Yes, something. It isn't important."

"How do you get to own things?"

"What?"

"How do you get that way?—How would a baby end up like that? A baby that was just born and had nothing?"

"You look a little tired, Clara," he said. He came to her. Clara watched his hand approaching and thought, This can't be happening. He touched her arm. It was the first time he had touched her but it too seemed familiar. "Is something wrong? Have you been ill?"

"I must be ugly in all this heat," she said, turning away. She felt real revulsion. She brought one hand up to hide her face from him and he stepped around to look at her, the way a child or dog will press after someone who has retreated. He looked so strange, so uneasy and nervous, that she was afraid she would do something crazy just to end what they were going through.

"No, you're not ugly," he said.

"I'm tired—"

"You're not ugly."

He said it sadly. She did not want to meet his eyes. Her heart had begun to pound heavily. Revere pressed his hand against her forehead, just for an instant, a light, casual gesture that was meant to calm her but instead made them both nervous. Clara thought, Somebody is watching from the lumberyard. She thought, The whole town is watching. But when she swung her eyes around, as if trying for freedom, she saw no one at all. Nothing.

"I can drive you back," he said.

He waited for her to acquiesce. It took a moment or two. Then he pushed her gently toward the car. This was the way Lowry had pushed her—not a real push, but just a nudge, something to get her started and guide her a little, but really just an excuse for touching her. "You work too hard in that store. You shouldn't have to work at all," Revere said.

"Yes," Clara said, thinking of how she had worked all her

life and had never known any better, while other people owned the farms she and her family had worked on, and still other people owned the trucks that drove up to buy the vegetables and fruit, and others owned banks and sawmills and lumberyards and factories and grocery stores in town that sold the things she and her family had picked, and the children of all these people were free to ride bicycles up and down quiet dusty lanes throughout their whole childhoods, never growing old.

She got into the car and let her head droop down toward her chest, just for an instant. It was all she allowed herself. In the next moment she would know, she thought: it depended on which way he turned the car. If he drove back into town (the car was headed in that direction) she would have to start thinking about getting out of this place, but if he turned around and went the other way, she had a chance. Revere started the car and drove it a little jerkily up onto the lane, then backed up into the lumberyard driveway so he could turn the car around.

She knew they were talking to each other, even though they had nothing to say out loud. All she had were questions, questions. She was fearful of being injured, broken, dirtied beyond anything Lowry could ever fix up. But she had trained herself to think, "That bastard," whenever Lowry's name came to mind and the blood pulsing from her anger for him gave her courage. In a few minutes they had overtaken and passed the girls on the bicycles. The girls were standing and resting, their legs on either side of the old bikes, and Clara let her eyes brush past them with something like a forlorn, wistful affection—but they were just brats anyway, girls with fathers and mothers and families who dawdled around the dime store handling things and who stared a little too often at Clara and Sonya. In the instant Revere drove by them Clara wanted to catch their eyes and toss out to them a look of contempt, but when she turned, her look changed into one of confusion, of clumsy affection, as if she would have liked somehow to be nothing more than a third girl with them, on another bike, and not in this car heading out toward the country and whatever was going to happen to her out there.

He was saying, "I didn't know if you'd want to see me again. I don't want to get you in any trouble."

"Yes," Clara said.

"I mean with people in town."

"Yes."

196

"I stopped by the picnic to see you. But you belonged with those young people you were with."

Clara said nothing.

"It's strange," Revere said. His voice was not warm. "I didn't think I would see you again."

Clara looked out the window. The hot sun, facing them, gave her a vague reflection in the side window so that she could see herself. She rolled down the window and the wind poured in, whipping her hair back. She closed her eyes. After a moment Revere said, "There's a house I own out here. I bought some land and a house came with it. . . ." Clara opened her eyes and waited for the house to come into sight. She expected it to materialize out of nowhere. "I own this land here," Revere said. "There are two hundred acres to this. But the land's no good."

"No good," Clara echoed, not quite questioning him. She wondered why anyone would buy farmland he couldn't farm on, but she was too nervous, too oddly tired, to ask.

When they reached the house her face and body were damp with sweat that had turned cold. She did not bother wiping her forehead. Revere, helping her out of the car, touched her with a hand that was cold with perspiration too. She wondered what he was thinking or if he was thinking at all. They were some distance from the road, parked in the overgrown driveway. The farmhouse was probably a hundred years old. Clara saw feverishly that its roof was rotted in one part and that some of its windows were broken. Tall thistled grass grew everywhere. There were sharp weeds that brushed against her legs but she was too nervous to avoid them. Revere was indicating something, very seriously, and she turned and saw a few old barns, washed by the rain to no color at all. They went on toward the house. Clara was watching her feet. She did not want to stumble on the back steps, which looked wobbly. She thought that if she stumbled she would fall apart, everything would crack into pieces. Revere helped her up. Since he had first touched her back on that lane she had grown weak, as if she did indeed need help getting in and out of cars and walking up three or four steps. Revere pushed the door open and it moved away from his hand, opening by itself. Clara swallowed hard. In her body everything was pounding with heat and fear and heaviness.

Just inside the house she turned to him miserably, sobbing. He took her hands and tried to comfort her. She felt his pity, his own uneasiness, and that hard strength behind him that she had to count on now. She was giving herself over to him and it would be done the way Lowry would do something, thinking it through, calculating on it, and then going ahead. All her life she would be able to say: Today she changed the way her life was going and it was no accident. No accident.

"I'm afraid—I don't want—" she began. But Revere pressed her face against him, hiding her face. He was trembling. Clara shut her eyes tight and thought that she would never go through this again, not anything like this. She would never be this terrified again.

"No, don't be afraid. Clara. Don't be afraid, " he said.

Her teeth had begun to chatter. She thought of Lowry, that bastard Lowry, and of how he was making her do this, making her heart swell and pound furiously in her chest like something about to go wild. It was of Lowry she thought when Revere made love to her. They were in what must have been a parlor, surrounded by drifting bunches of dust and the corpses of insects and odd pieces of furniture hunched beneath soiled sheets. The ceiling was covered with cobwebs that swayed a little though there was no breeze at all.

8

By the time the first cooling thunderstorms came in late September, that house had been fixed up—the roof mended, the steps and porch strengthened, the inside painted and even papered with a special wallpaper Clara herself had picked out of a big book, pale pink with tiny rosebuds. When she was alone in the morning she would sit out on the porch as if waiting for someone to come, or she would stare off across the land that had come with this house, untended and belonging to no one really, since Curt Revere did not bother to put anything into it. She would try to think what she was doing and how this had come about: she tried to imagine the old people who had lived out their lives here, a couple who had built everything and worked the land and who had died and lost it so that Clara could sit on their porch and stare out with a stillness that she must have sucked in with the air of the old house, the intimate breaths of that old couple.

Revere had said of them: "They were eighty or more, both of them—the man died first. Their children were scattered and nobody wanted the old farm."

Clara thought that she had never heard anything so sad.

Sometimes she went walking out in the fields, carrying

herself as if she were a vessel entrusted with something sacred or dangerous, something that must not be jostled. As often as she thought of the baby—which was nearly always—she thought of Lowry, and even when Revere was with her she could gaze past his face and into Lowry's face, wondering what he was doing at that moment and if he ever thought of her, knowing that the energy she needed to keep hating him was more than he deserved. These long months were a kind of dream for her. Looking back, afterward, she was never able to remember how she had passed all that time. If Revere had allowed her to ask Sonya out, or if Caroline and Ginny had been able to come (their people forbade them), she would not have needed to drift about so in this sleepy confusion, waiting for the baby to be born. She was waiting for pain too. She could remember enough of what her mother had gone through to expect the same thing. The long, groggy months of pregnancy kept her heavy and warm, slow, a little dizzy with the awareness of what her body was going to accomplish and of the extraordinary luck she had had: where had Revere come from? He stayed with her for hours and held her in his arms, soothing her, telling her how much he loved her and how he had known this at once, the first time he saw her, telling her of all the things he was going to do for her and the baby; and out of all this Clara stared back at the way she had come and tried to figure out what was happening, but it always eluded her. She was like a flower reaching up toward the sun: it was good luck that the sun happened to be there, that was all. Like a flower she basked in the warmth of Revere's attention, never quite certain in those first few months how long it was going to last. When Revere stayed with her in the old house or when they walked slowly about the fields, talking, she believed she could hear past them the vast silence that had always followed her about, a gentle roaring that was like the roaring of the ocean when she'd been lying with Lowry out in the hot sun or like the monotonous rattling noise of the engines that had carried her and her family around for years. . . .

He bought her a car, a little yellow coupe, and gave her driving lessons. They practiced on the lonely dirt roads where no other cars ever appeared, once in a while a hay wagon or a tractor, that was all, or some kids on bicycles. Clara loved those lessons and sat very straight behind the wheel, throwing her hair back out of her eyes with an excitement that was nearly hysterical—she could have been thinking of the complex system of roads that led from there to Mexico, a system she might be able to figure out. A map told you one astonishing thing: no matter where you were, there was a way to get somewhere else, lines led there, crossing and recrossing, you just had to figure it out.

But when Revere didn't come she only drove the car around in the driveway and in front of the house. She couldn't go into town, where people would stare angrily at her—she figured it would take them a while to get used to her and Revere, so she would give them that time—and Revere would not allow her to drive over to Sonya's, and it was too far to go to another town; anyway, she did not want to leave. If she couldn't go to Mexico she might as well stay home. She had a home now that was all hers and no one could kick her out. She had someone to take care of her and she wouldn't ever have to worry about being slapped around or him coming in drunk—as far as she knew he didn't even drink, which was strange. She explored the old house so thoroughly that she accepted it as hers and no one else's, as if she had been living there all her life. For weeks she seemed to be sleepwalking through an immense warm dream that had the dampness of October in this part of the country but none of the clarity of afternoons when the sun finally broke through, and the passivity with which she had had to accept Lowry's baby inside her kept her passive about other things as well. Revere brought her anything she wanted: sewing machine, cloth, odd pieces of furniture. It was her home.

The birth of Lowry's child was coming upon her the way death had come upon the house's first tenants, a warm sullen breeze blowing toward her from some vague point in the future. Whatever Revere brought her or decided to do to the house, she accepted as if it had always been planned, as if he were just filling in an outline. When they walked out in the fields or along the old lanes, Clara pulling at weed flowers or sucking grass, Revere sometimes lifted his shoulders in a strange forceful way he had, as if arguing with himself, and Clara had only to close her eyes to see not Revere but any man, a man, the idea of man itself come to take care of her as she had supposed someone must, somehow. She did not think enough about the peculiarity of her situation to come to the conclusion that she was the kind of girl someone else would always protect. This would have surprised her. But Revere might have been a promise someone had made—that someone was Lowry—when he had taken her away to save her from the old life back on the road, in another world

200

now, and it would never have occurred to her to thank him for it.

He liked to frame her face in his hands and stare at her. He talked about her eyes and her skin; Clara hated this but put up with it, then it came to be something she expected Revere to do. If they were outside, she would smile up at the sky and let her mind loose from this place, wandering everywhere, and at the end return suddenly to this man who was staring at her—and she would be startled by the love she saw in his face. How could this stranger love her? Were all strangers so weak, no matter how strong they looked? But then, Lowry had been a stranger too, and so had her father, and everyone else. The only person not a stranger to her was Lowry's baby, the only thing she really owned. But each time she looked at Revere she saw more of him, until her shyness began to fade and she wondered if maybe she wouldn't end up loving this man after all, not the way she had loved Lowry but in another way. She knew that his mind did not flit around everywhere when he was with her; she knew he was looking at her and not through her at someone else.

"You're smart, Clara. You catch on quickly," he said, teaching her to back up the car. She had had no compliments in her life, and her face burned with pleasure when Revere said this. She took his hand and pressed it against her cheek. All this drew him to her, fascinated him, and it was only to be in later years that she would do it just for the effect. At this time in her life everything was new and spontaneous. She was hypnotized always by the wonder of her being here at all: how had it happened? Had she really done it herself, made the decision herself?

Out of the lonely, dark winter days in the house she had this idea: to make of Lowry's child a person to whom everything would make sense, who would control not just isolated moments in his life but his entire life, and who would not just control his own life but other lives as well.

They acted out two roles, not quite consciously: Revere was the guilty one, because he believed he had made her pregnant, and Clara was the victimized one, made softer and gentler by being victimized. She told him of her fears about having the baby, about the pain her mother had had each time, about the last baby that had killed her—this memory mixed up with a card game some men were having while, in another cabin, Clara's mother was bleeding to death. When she cried she was amazed at the sorrow she felt. She must have loved her mother in spite of everything, in spite of

201

really having no mother for many years—so she wept until her head pounded, wishing she could call her mother back from the grave and give her all these gifts Revere had given her; why hadn't her mother had anything? Revere soothed her, rocked her in his arms. The fact of her pregnancy meant that she was his and, like any stubborn, lucky strong man used to getting his own way, he loved what was his own. He talked of "making up for everything" and Clara listened, her eyes still glistening with tears, accepting his apologetic caresses at the same time she might be thinking about Lowry, if he might write someday and what if someone at the post office, just to be mean, got hold of the letter and ripped it up? At some point Revere's sorrow for having "hurt" her made her feel guilty and she said, "But I love it already. I can't wait to have it. I love babies," and by saying this everything would be returned to her, even the joy of having been in love with Lowry, though it had lasted only those few days. "But I'm not going to no hospital or anything to have it," she said. "I want to have it right at home here."

"We'll see about it," Revere said.

"No, I want to stay here. I'm not going away."

"We'll see."

She was fierce with love for her home. From her old room she had brought things along for her bedroom, which was the first "bedroom" she had ever even seen, let alone lived in. She had a bed and a bureau of good polished wood, and a mirror rising from it that was like no mirror she'd seen before, and a closet just for her clothes, though she hadn't many, and a chair with a pillow on it, and a table alongside the bed on which Revere put his wrist watch when he stayed with her. On the wall opposite the bed was a print of a sunset, all spreading oranges and reds like pain flicked carelessly into water, with trees starkly silhouetted in black— Revere never said anything about the picture, which Clara had picked out herself. If she sat and stared at it long enough, strange, sad thoughts came to her and she would begin to cry, for no reason. Never in her life had she bothered to look at a real sunset; she heard sometimes on the radio a twangy-voiced man singing about a world "beyond the sunset" that also inspired her to tears, but still she did not bother to look at real sunsets. Paintings and music were meant to turn things into other things, Clara thought, so that the sunsets in pictures could make you cry while the real thing had no meaning at all. How could it? Even the picture of a house in winter, banked by clumps of evergreens, on the cover of a box of candy Revere had given her, meant more to her than the frequent picture she had of her own home, seen from the lane or the road. She could be moved by such things but not by reality, which was something that just lay stretched about her, indifferent and without meaning.

And just outside her bedroom was a corridor that led first to the kitchen—a big old drafty room with a pump at the sink, which Revere was going to fix up and which had already been painted a bright yellow—and then the parlor with its high gloomy windows that could hardly be stirred to life by the sun shining through them, then to another room that was left empty. There were heaters in three of the rooms. The house had an attic, but no one had bothered to fix it up; there were old boxes of junk—clothing dampened and mildewed, and Christmas ornaments of a wispy silvery type, many of them broken, and ugly furniture. Clara had been through everything many times. She felt closest to the old people when she looked through the Christmas ornaments, fingering the bulbs and the prickly lengths of trim that left silver flakes on her hands, thinking how unfair it was to those people that the things they had loved so ended up with Clara, a stranger. Then she put everything back carefully, as if she expected the owners to return and make their claim. Left alone in the attic, in sunny air or air heavy with gloom, she tried to think whether Revere was coming that evening or not. Sometimes she could not remember what he had promised.

One day someone drove down the lane in a rusty station wagon and Clara ran out onto the porch. It was November now and cold, but she stood waiting for the man to come up to her, her face set for a surprise, for something pleasant. But the man was about sixty, cranky and nervous. He said, "If somebody lives here now there's got to be a mailbox out front. Why ain't there a mailbox?"

Clara looked out toward the road as if checking to see if one might be there. Then she said, "There's nobody going to write me a letter."

"You need a mailbox regardless. Are you gonna get one?"

"I don't need none."

"What's your name?"

"Clara."

"Clara what?"

"Just Clara. I don't have any last name," she said sullenly. She stared down at the man's feet. Of course he knew who she was and that Revere owned all of this, but he kept at her

203

with his eyes and his angry voice until she said, turning away as if she were a married woman with other things to do: "Oh, go to hell!"

Through the parlor window she watched him turn the station wagon around and drive back out, fierce and in a hurry. She thought with a kind of slow nervous power that maybe Revere could take that man's job away from him if she bothered to complain. But when Revere came out that day she said nothing. It was too shameful—she remembered the way that old man had looked at her, as if she were dirt, and how it was like everyone would look at her if they got the chance.

After a while she began to think about Revere's wife, who fed him meals on those days when he didn't eat with Clara, and the same sensation of power she had felt about the mailman rose up in her. What if. . . ?

She sometimes said, "What does your wife say when you're not home for supper? Does she get mad?"

Revere could signal her to be quiet without ever saying a word himself, but at times she chose not to understand his gestures. She would lean against him and let her head droop against his shoulder as if overcome with thought or worry and he would always answer her. "This has nothing to do with her," he would say finally. Clara did not like this answer but she did not believe it, either. She would smile into Revere's face as if she knew better. He sometimes said, a little coldly, "You shouldn't worry about her. She's a very strong person."

"What do you mean, strong?"

"Strong. Like her family."

He never wanted to say much about his wife but Clara drew it out of him gradually, over the months. She did this with an actual picking gesture, touching his arm or shoulder and drawing something away from him, bits of lint or minute hairs she would hold between her fingers for a second and then discard with a deliberation that had nothing to do with thought. He must have been fascinated by her, by her words or her face, something, because she noticed how he would always answer her questions in the end. He seemed always to see another Clara, not Clara herself. "She isn't like you, Clara," Revere said once. "She isn't a happy woman." And Clara had stared at him, wondering if he thought *she* was happy—then she decided that of course he did, what did he know about her hours of being alone and thinking of Lowry, always Lowry, and her fear of what might happen in child-

204

birth? He couldn't guess any of this. She was a girl who had been walking one day in the middle of a muddy road, dressed up, proud, excited, waiting for a man but not the man who had driven up behind her and stopped to give her a ride. Or she was the girl at the firemen's picnic, dressed up again but too excited and too reckless to know anything about how she should look, or about how people should look at her. Or she was the girl who ran out to meet Revere on the porch of this house, or òut onto the hard frozen grass, shivering so that he would scold her as he embraced her, and so far as he knew her life had begun that day on the muddy road after someone else's wedding and had its reality only when he was able to get free and drive over to see her. So it was no wonder he thought she was happy; and she knew she would have to stay happy if she wanted a last name for Lowry's baby.

"But why isn't your wife happy?" Clara said, pretending surprise.

"I don't know. She isn't well."

"How bad is she sick?"

"She isn't sick. But she isn't well."

Clara would pretend to be baffled at this, as if such complexity lay beyond her. She was learning to play games with him to take the place of the passion she had felt for Lowry—you had to do something and say something to a man, and what was there to talk about that made any sense? Everything that was serious about life had to be kept back because Revere could not know about it. He could never know. Even if someone in Tintern hinted to him about Lowry, about another man involved with Clara, he wouldn't believe it. He did certainly think he had discovered her and that he had almost seen her born, that he was almost her father in a way. "She isn't like you," he would tell her. "You're very beautiful, you don't worry about anything. . . . You're just a child."

"I'm not a child," Clara said.

"You enjoy everything in life. You don't worry," he said.

That winter he began to bring a cousin of his over to visit her, a thin, lanky man who had not yet married, who was in his thirties. His name was Judd. While Revere sat with his feet out before him on the heater, firm and confident, Judd was restless and made Clara want to run to him and calm him down. He had a bony, earnest face that might have been handsome if something hadn't gone wrong, some angle pushed out of shape by his prominent cheekbones.

She listened to the two men talk about horses and the

weather and their families and business contracts; evidently Revere had forced one of his competitors out of business. Clara sat listening, not quite knowing what they were talking about but sensing that Revere wanted her to stay on the periphery of his life, except when he crossed over to her of his own accord. She did not mind. Life out in the country had infected her with its silence; she imitated that cat Revere had brought her from home, a long-haired gray cat with a shabby, gentle, lazy face. The men talked, Revere more than Judd, about people Clara would never know, some of them living far away, others already dead. "Yes, sir, he is asking for trouble. He is asking for someone to sit on him," Revere would say, but smiling. Judd would make a flicking motion with his fingers, as if dismissing this person. A minute later Clara found out they were talking about the governor of the state. It made her smile in alarm, to think she could listen to a conversation that tossed that man's name about so casually; she felt a strange surge of power, as if Revere's quiet, bemused strength might someday turn into her own. But all she did was pet her cat, who lay sleeping at her feet and paid no attention to them at all.

They taught her to play card games. Revere always won; he was an apologetic winner. Clara made mistakes because she could never remember the rules. She thought card games were silly but they belonged to the world of men, so there must be some point to them. Staring at a hand of cards newly dealt to her, trying to make sense of the numbers and suits, Clara understood that her brain could go so far and no farther. She was limited, like a dog tugging at a chain. Somehow the two men could work these cards, toss down combinations right in the middle of talking, but Clara had to work hard every second. Perspiration came out on her forehead, tiny beads of sweat because she was ashamed of being stupid. She did not want to lay down her hand for them to see because it would be like opening her brain to the daylight and revealing how limited she was.

From Revere and Judd she got a picture, gradually, of a vague web of people, the generations mixed together and men present in their talks simultaneously with their grandfathers, and Revere and Judd as children; it was like a great river of people moving slowly along, bound together by faces that looked alike and by a single name. How wonderful to be born into this name and to belong to such a world. . . . Clara thought of Lowry's child among them, even if she herself could never quite make it. She thought of this child pushing its way through, appearing before the legs of aged people and pushing them aside, impatiently, with somewhere to go. Her child would be strong, Clara thought, like Lowry. It would be like Lowry. It would push its way through like Lowry did and yet it would be happy, while Lowry had never been happy, because it would be born with everything Lowry had been seeking. It would have a last name and a world and want nothing. . . .

They alluded now and then to relatives, in an oblique, glancing way that was difficult for Clara to follow. She gathered that the most wealthy of the Reveres lived in the city, in Hamilton. She gathered that there was some kind of quarrel between the city and the country Reveres, but that it would be straightened out. Revere's father had been a great fat man who'd died at the age of forty, knocked off a horse that ran under a low-hanging branch; he had been drunk at the time. Clara could not reconcile this with Revere himself. That story about his father was almost a joke, but nothing about Revere himself was a joke. And they mentioned a cousin of theirs, an older woman who traveled everywhere and never came home. She lived in Europe. Revere screwed up his face to show disgust for her. Judd defended her, saying, "People can't help what they believe. She says she just can't believe in God." "She'll believe in hell, though, fast enough," Revere said coldly. Clara sat leaning a little forward, her eyes lowered. She was learning. In those love magazines she used to read there were many stories of girls screaming at married men who had promised to marry them but never did marry them, and the point of the stories was that you got nothing by screaming but might get something by shutting up. Clara was learning that that was so.

During the long days when he was traveling or could not leave home, she talked to the cat and carried it around in her arms until it struggled free, or she worked at the sewing machine or tried to cook. She wandered through the rooms and looked out the windows at the snowy fields where white lay upon white out to the very horizon of the mountains. She cried out in silence for Lowry to come back to her, but nothing happened, no one came except Revere and once in a while his cousin Judd. She learned how to be still. Her hands would fall innocently upon her stomach and rest there, and she could not remember what she had done with her hands before. Kneeling on the sofa and staring out into the heavy winter sky, she thought: "I will not think about him. I will think about nothing all day long. Nothing. Nothing." The cat was so lazy it made Clara sleepy, so she slept during the day and felt that it was good for her. Then she and the cat sat in the kitchen together, she gave the cat warm milk, and talked to it off and on.

Because she was alone so much, she looked in the mirror often, as if to seek out her reflection as company. She liked to look at herself. She wondered if this was the face Revere saw, or did he see someone else? Her face was fine-boned, her eyes were slanting, like pale blue glass, eyelashes thick and innocently pale, almost white; she had a sleepy, lazy smile that could come out of nowhere even if she never felt like smiling again in her life. She held the cat up to the mirror and tried to interest it in its reflection; it did not respond. "Mighty strange, not to see yourself in a mirror," Clara said aloud, feeling sorry for the cat. What if people couldn't see themselves? It would be like living in a vast desert. The cat's name was Rosalie. When Revere and Judd sat in the parlor talking, she held the cat on her lap, her own expression shaped and suspended like the cat's, sleek and sleepy at once, so that Revere could stare at her with that look she was beginning now to control; she thought, "He fell in love with me the way another man falls into a swamp," and was able to think of herself as this swamp, something Revere could sink into and lose himself in. And if Lowry ever saw her again, she thought, he too would sink and drown; she would get him.

That bastard Lowry, she thought, clear-eyed and awake when Revere dozed off beside her, his heavy arm around her to keep her still and close to him. Sometimes she lay sleepless until dawn, when the night turned into day abruptly and awkwardly as light shot over the ridge of mountains—and where all that time went she could not say. She could watch Revere's face define itself into the face she now knew and was beginning to love: the lined, stern forehead, the eyes that did not seem to relax even when closed. Clara's long hair would be twisted with sleeplessness.

She thought of Rosalie, the first Rosalie, and how that girl had had a mistake happen to her and had not known where to run with it, on whose lap to dump it. Clara had known what to do before she had even known she would have to do it.

She thought of her mother—all those babies gouging themselves out of her, covered with blood, slippery and damp as fish, with no more sense than fish and no value to anyone.

And how her mother had died!—she knew more about that night than she had ever let herself think about.

And she thought of her sisters, and of her brothers—lost somewhere—and of her father, who would probably be on the road right now, as always, drinking and fighting and going on, getting recruited on one crew after another, and that was going to be all. Had she betrayed them by running out? What did she owe them or anybody?

Her hands fell onto her stomach and she thought fiercely that she would betray anybody for this baby; she would even kill if she had to. She would do anything. She would kill Lowry himself if she had to.

In the morning she drank a cold glass of water to help keep her nausea down and felt the bright new coldness fall inside her as if there were nothing to stop it. And she would stand in her bare feet, shivering on the rough kitchen floor, and look out the window past the rust- and snow-flecked screen that was still left on it from last summer, to the barns that were stark black against the snow and past them to the decrepit orchard and as far as she could see to the horizon, to the sky, and hear silence easing down to her.

One day Revere drove her down through the valley and across the river and into the city of Hamilton, which she had heard about but had never seen. It was a port at the branch of two great rivers. Clara saws its smoke rising far up into the winter air for miles as they approached the city, driving on smart paved highways and passing cars that were often as good as Revere's. Back from the highway were the occasional shanties with their tar-paper or tin roofs, abandoned or filled with some hint of forlorn life, and along the highway were pieces of thrown-away junk, iron scraps, rusted mufflers that just fell off cars, sometimes even automobiles, and the frequent unsurprising signs for Royal Crown Cola or hotels in Hamilton with rates for the family or Lucky Strike cigarettes, everything sad and misty in the gray air. That soot on the edge of the signs, Revere told her, was blown out from the city they were coming to.

They crossed the Eden River on a high gleaming bridge. It was the same river Clara had waded in while Lowry watched, so long ago, and she thought grimly that it was really a different river this far out of Tintern and at this time of the year. It wasn't the same river at all. The bridge was high and new and Clara's stomach cringed to think of how high they were. She stared down at the water far below, winding tightly between two bright banks of ice covered with soft powdery snow; she was afraid she might be sick. She wondered if this trip might be a trick and if Revere might be going to abandon her somewhere, six months pregnant as she was.

They kept on driving for some time. The sun tried to shine through the gray, misty air, and finally they were driving in traffic and Clara looked out narrow-eyed at girls her age waiting to cross streets, their arms loaded with books. They wore bright wool socks that went up to their knees, and plaid wool skirts, and coats that hung carelessly open as they stood about with a vague purposeful air of having somewhere to go but feeling no hurry about it. It was about noon. There were many trucks on the road. Everything brightened and Revere turned off onto a winding street that led down toward the river. He said, "This is upriver from Hamilton." Clara tried to think what that meant; was it something special? Upriver, they maybe didn't get polluted water.

The homes here were set far back from the street, on hills that faced the river. Great immense homes with rows of windows that caught the sun and flashed it out indifferently, bounded by spiked iron fences and gates or high brick walls. The houses gave no sign of life. Clara stared out at them. Revere slowed his car in front of one of the hills. "Look at that," he said. It was nearly hidden from the street, high behind clumps of evergreens, a dark gray-stone house with columns. "Does someone you know live here?" Clara said. "One of my uncles," said Revere. Clara's jaw muscles involuntarily tightened as if she were biting down hard on something, unable to stop, and she could feel the baby hard and tight inside her, demanding this already—the house and the columns and its heavy brutal look. She said, teasing, "Are you going to take me up to visit?" but he was already driving past. He didn't like to joke about things like that. "I thought you were going to take me in," she said. She did not call this man by any name. She certainly did not call him Curt nor did she even think of him by that name; she did not think of him by any name at all. If she had needed to call out for him to come to her she would have said, "Mr. Revere!" like everyone else.

"Someday, who can tell?" he said, trying to match her own tone.

He drove on for a while until they passed over into an area where the homes were closer together, all on a level, and Revere's surprise was a visit to a doctor—Clara had been against doctors all along. She had thought his silence meant

210

he agreed with her. So she sat in the car for a while, trembling with anger while he talked to her. Then she gave up, close to tears. "All right, goddam it," she said, and allowed him to get her inside the waiting room so that she could sit with him, without a wedding ring, in this room filled with women and their husbands who stared at her as if she were on display. "I hope it's born dead, just to get back at him," she thought, imagining Revere's sorrow and her own righteous hatred of him for what he had caused. She clasped her hands together, turned away from Revere to refuse his murmured conversation, and stared fixedly at the feet around the room—boots and rubbers and women's boots tipped with fur and unhooked farmers' boots (these were Revere's) that were leaving a small puddle on the floor. Good. It showed they were from the country, making a mess, and her without a wedding ring (and she would not hide her hands), while a skinny scarecrow woman with hair like straw looked up from her magazine at Clara, and a man with a round pumpkin face watched her too. There was a glassed-off partition behind which a nurse sat, answering a telephone, and in this glass Clara could see a vague reflection of herself. When they had come in, Revere stooped to talk through the hole in the glass; he had said, "Clara Revere," as if this were really her name, as natural as anything, and he didn't expect anyone to be surprised, not even Clara. She had wanted to interrupt and say, "Clara Walpole," but had no nerve. So she sat now and waited, and when that strange name was called—Clara Revere—she got up and refused to look at Revere as the nurse led her out.

When she came out again she must have looked awful, because Revere got right up and came to her. He took her hands. Clara was certain everyone thought he was her father and of course they had noticed she had no wedding ring— every woman had seen that in the first instant—so her face flushed with the shame of this situation he had gotten her into, just as it had flushed with shame before the doctor. The doctor called Revere inside to talk to him and Clara put on her coat and sat sullenly in it, thinking of nothing. Her feet were out loose on the floor, ankles turned out the way Lowry had sat that day on the river bank, as if he had abandoned walking forever and would have been content to sit there doing nothing the rest of his life.

Revere came back out in a few minutes, his boots flopping, and Clara stared at them as if they were objects she could not quite place. Out in the car she cried with that hopeless, inflectionless passivity that cost her the least effort, while Revere talked to her, saying everything that was sensible and reasonable and that Clara would agree with in time but not right now. She was struck and weakened by his love for her, which was crazy, out of focus. "And I'm not going to a hospital. I'm not," she said. "Nobody I ever knew went to a hospital and they were all right. . . ." After a minute or two she sensed that she should carry on no longer, that he might lose patience, so she wiped her eyes dry and was quiet.

"I wanted to get you something," Revere said apologetically. This was downtown, where the traffic fascinated and frightened Clara and the buildings were taller than any she had seen. On the sidewalks women walked past quickly in high-heeled shoes, as if they were used to wearing them on an ordinary weekday. They passed a big dirty-gray building with a statue out front: a horse rearing up toward the sky, a military man on his back, both of them tarnished a hard dead gray-green. It looked like something fished up from the bottom of the ocean. Revere parked the car and put a coin in the meter; Clara tried not to look too hard at the little flag that jumped back inside it. She had never seen that before. The air was frosty and impure here but no one seemed to notice. "Along this way." Revere said, not touching her. She walked along slowly, staring. Her lips were parted. Revere brought her to a small shop with only a few yards' coverage on the street; it was a jewelry store with a sign bearing a long foreign name Clara could not read.

There were no other customers in the store, which was narrow and deep, consisting of one long counter that led to the back. Clara stared about at the gleaming clock faces and silver plates and tea sets, placed out in the open so that anyone could steal them, and down past the flawless clean glass to the jewels on dark velvet. She felt dazed by what she saw.

"Maybe you'd like something here," Revere said.

An old man waited on them. He was servile and smiling; he wore glasses. Clara stared down at the man's fingers as he brought out rings for her to look at—this could not really be happening, she thought. He indicated she should try a ring on. She slid it on her finger and saw how her hand was changed by it. "What's that, an emerald?" Revere said. The man said yes. Revere took Clara's hand and stared critically at the ring. "Well," he said, releasing her, "pick out any one you want. It's for you."

"But I don't know—what kind they are," Clara said. She

stood flat-footed and awkward. She had a terror of picking something too expensive, or something Revere thought was ugly.

"Take your time. Pick out something pretty," Revere said. He stood a little apart from her. He was not uneasy, not quite, but Clara saw that there was something guarded in the way he spoke. She picked up a ring with a purple stone and tried it on.

"I like this one," she said at once.

"That's an amethyst," said Revere. Clara wondered what this meant.

"I guess I like it," Clara said shyly.

"Look at the others."

The old man pulled out another tray. Clara's heart beat in confusion and alarm at everything she had to see, touch, think about. Her instinct was to take the first thing and have done with all this awkwardness, all this pain. But in Revere's world, evidently, you stared hard at everything before you made your choice. The stones sparkled at her and their settings were intricate and beautiful, gifts from another world she had no right to and that she was stealing from those who really deserved them—not girls like herself but women who were really married, who were not choked with shame in a doctor's office. She was stealing from them and from Revere's wife, who should be here in Clara's place. Her fingers went blindly to another purple ring with a gold setting, placed high and cut into a dazzling intricate shape with many facets, and she turned it over and saw the price tag—just the number 550 in dark ink—and this did not register at once. When it registered she put the ring back. There was an ugly roaring in her ears. She would be able to wear on one finger something worth more money than her father had ever had at once, something worth more than anything her mother had owned, ever, and it was all coming about with no one showing any surprise except herself—the old man behind the counter wasn't surprised, maybe he was even bored, and Revere looked as if he did this every day. This was how life was.

In the end Revere wanted her to take that one. It was a little large for her finger but she said it was all right, she didn't want to bother anyone. All the way back home she stared at her hand, looking off at the colorless countryside and back at her finger, at the rich deep purple stone, her mind so overcome by it that she did not think of it as something she had stolen—from Revere's wife or her own people or anyone. It was hers. Clara brought the ring up and touched her face with it, then raised it to her eye so that she could see the sharp tiny reflection of the moving countryside in it, shadows and blurred forms that were like the passing of time in a world you could never get hold of.

"I thank you for this," she said to Revere.

The baby was born in May, a few weeks overdue by her reckoning, but that was lucky: it was just on time, according to Revere. And what she went through turned out to be no great surprise—it was not as bad as the times she had suffered along with her mother, having to watch helplessly. Revere drove her in to Hamilton, to a hospital, because this was what he had wanted and in all things that did not really go against her wishes she would give in to him; and the son she had, hers and Lowry's, was delivered over to Revere forever.

9

As soon as she became a mother with a baby to care for, time went quickly for Clara. She learned to live by the baby's rhythms, sleeping when he slept and wakening when he woke, fascinated by his face and the tiny eyes she imagined were like Lowry's eyes, coming so slowly into focus and one day looking right at her. Revere named the baby Steven, and Clara said that was a fine-sounding name, but her own name for him was Swan; she liked to whisper "Swan, Swan" to him, and sometimes when she fed him her hand would come slowly to a stop and she would sit leaning forward, frozen, staring at this creature who had come out of her body and had now taken on life of his own, putting on weight as if he knew what he was doing—and there he was, looking at her. "You smart little baby, darling little Swan," Clara would sing to him, hurrying around barefoot when it was warm enough at last, taking in the air of spring with a joy she hadn't felt since Lowry had left her. She made up tuneless tireless songs about him:

> *He's going by train and by airplane*
> *All around the world. . . .*

Revere was a little shy with the baby. "Why do you call him Swan?" he said. Clara shrugged her shoulders. With the

214

baby born, she had work to do now—she did not bother fixing herself up for Revere but sat wearily or with a pretense of weariness, her long bare legs outspread and her hair tied back from her face carelessly, interested only in the baby. When Revere held him, Clara could hardly tear her eyes from the baby's face to look at Revere and to listen to his words. "I like the name, I picked it out myself. It's my baby," Clara said stubbornly. But she knew enough to soften anything she said, so she leaned forward to touch Revere's hand. She said, "I love him and I want lots of babies all like him."

She could tell that Revere didn't know how to hold a baby or how to feed him, it was just a nuisance to have him around, but she kept quiet about how she felt. She could outwait anyone, outlast anyone.

She would never have known what people thought of her from just the things Judd said if she kept asking him, except one day in July, when she thought Swan was sick, she drove into Tintern by herself. She had the baby bundled in a blanket, lying on the front seat beside her, and as she drove she kept leaning over to touch his face; she was sure he had a fever. "Don't fall asleep, that scares me," she said. "Swan, you wake up." She heard her voice climbing to hysteria. So she stopped the car and picked up the baby and pressed her face against his; then it struck her that this was crazy and that she should have called Revere on the telephone, hunting him up wherever he was, instead of taking the baby out into the heat. "You're not going to die. What's wrong, why don't you wake up like you used to?" The baby looked drugged. Clara began to cry, then she stopped crying and put the baby down and drove on, and when she got to Tintern the dusty little town opened up before her eyes like a nightmare picture someone had made up just for a joke. She thought how dirty it was, how ugly and common.

When she ran into the drug store, barefoot, a few people at the counter looked at her. They were sipping Cokes. "Mr. Mack?" Clara said. A fan was turning slowly above the counter, making noise. "Where is Mr. Mack?" Clara said. "My baby's out in the car sick. I need help for him." Her voice accused those people who stared at her as if they were complete strangers and hadn't lived in the same town with her for two years. The woman behind the counter, Mr. Mack's niece, looked at Clara for maybe ten seconds and said, "He's takin' a nap an' don't want nobody botherin' him."

215

"My baby's sick," Clara said. She went past them and kept going. "Mr. Mack?" she called. At the doorway to the back she hesitated, her toes curling. There was a beige curtain pulled shut across the doorway. She did not push it aside, but said, "Mr. Mack? This is Clara here— Can you come out?"

He was not an old man but he had always looked old, and in the while she had been away from Tintern he had grown to look even older. No more than forty-five, but with a reddened face that was pale underneath its flush, and hair thinning meekly back from his forehead: he brushed the curtain aside and looked at her. She saw how his eyes narrowed, remembering her.

Clara's words came out too fast, tumbling over one another. "My baby's sick, out in the car. He's got a fever or something—he don't wake up right."

"Take him to a doctor."

"What doctor?"

He looked behind her, as if making out the face of a doctor somewhere in the distance. "In the city. Don't your man take you to a doctor in the city?"

"I need some pills or something," Clara said. She was trying not to cry. "He's real hot. You want to come out and see him? He's in the car—"

"How much money do you have?"

"I don't know—I—I forgot it," Clara said. They faced each other silently and Clara thought in panic that she should have brought the baby inside, not left it out there, or was she afraid to pick it up? At the counter people were watching. And there was some noise outside that meant her little yellow car had attracted attention already; but she did not turn around. Finally Mr. Mack said, in a voice that let her know what he thought of her:

"All right. Just a minute."

Clara hurried back out, past a big mannish woman with great shoulders she had seen once or twice before—a farm woman—and those two girls of maybe thirteen who had ridden past her that day on their bicycles. She did not look at them. After she had passed and was out the screen door, she heard someone laugh. "Bastards," she thought. "Sons of bitches, I'll get them." But this took only a second and already she was lifting the baby out. His eyes were closed, milky-pale, and she bent her face against his to see if he was breathing—but she could not tell—and her heart stopped beating for a moment as she wondered if she was standing here with a dead baby, out in the sun with people drifting

216

over to look. There were some little kids across the way; they called something out to her.

Mr. Mack took his time coming out. His face was furrowed like an old man's. "Remember, I ain't no doctor," he said. "Let's see him."

"He's hot, ain't he?"

"Take him out of the sun," the druggist said. His face showed disgust. Clara wished he would look at her, acknowledge her. They stepped back against the building. Mr. Mack touched the baby's forehead with the back of his hand, as if he were afraid of catching something from him.

"Look, I'll get money," Clara said wildly. "You know I can pay for it; just take care of him. It ain't none of that baby's fault—"

"He's got a fever."

"Is that bad? How bad is that?"

Mr. Mack shrugged his shoulders.

"What if he dies?" Clara said.

"He won't die."

"But what if—"

"Then he dies."

Clara stared at him. "Look, you give me some pills or something. You better give them to me."

"I'm not a doctor, I don't prescribe."

"Please, mister. Give me some pills or something—"

"All right, just a minute."

He went back inside. Everything was silent. Clara did not look around to check out this silence. The baby's eyelids fluttered as if he were struggling to get awake. He choked a little. "What's wrong?" she said. "You wake up, now. Why don't you cry or something?"

Mr. Mack returned and handed her a bottle. "You can rub this on him," he said. He wiped his hand on his thighs, uneasily, indifferently. Clara stared at the bottle's label: Rubbing Alcohol. "Give him some of these, too. Can you read?" he said. He handed her a little bottle of children's aspirin.

"I can read," Clara said.

"All right. There you are," he said, glad to get rid of her. He was about to turn away but Clara stopped him.

"How much do I owe you?"

"Nothing."

"Why nothing?"

"Forget it."

He turned away. Clara forgot the sick baby and said, "My money's good enough for you!" Mr. Mack did not acknowledge this. He let the screen door slam after him. Clara wanted to run to the door and yell something out, something to make them all sorry. . . . But she put the baby in the car and tried to get quiet. He was fighting at the air now, kicking. She took that for a good sign. "What the hell do we care for these people," she muttered. She wiped the baby's mouth on her skirt. She opened the blanket and unbuttoned the baby's shirt, and using her skirt again she dabbed some of the alcohol on his chest for a minute or so. Then she wondered if maybe this was a joke, that Mr. Mack had played a trick on her. . . . But she guessed it must be right: it said Rubbing Alcohol. She had never heard of it before; she thought alcohol was something you drank.

Across the street the kids were saying something. "Gonna give us a ride, Clara?" one of them yelled. He was big and had a familiar face: one of Caroline's brothers.

"What the hell are you asking?" Clara cried.

She climbed in the car and closed the door behind her, awkward in her haste, suddenly panicked by the children there and the other faces attracted by the commotion—someone was coming out the drug store door to watch. She felt how they were all together and how she was alone. "I'll tell him and he'll kill you," she muttered. She was thinking of Lowry; Lowry had maybe killed someone already and he could do it again. She tried to start the car but the engine must have been flooded. It was very hot. One of the boys yelled again and Clara did not look around, remembering how she and other kids had yelled at people, making fun.

A pickup truck turned the corner and approached slowly, driving down the middle of the street. Clara sat with her head bowed over the steering wheel and saw through a mass of hair one of the local farmers driving the truck. Some farm boys were in the back, their legs dangling over the edge. She felt heat push in on all sides of her and tried to start the car again.

"You havin' trouble, you want a push?"

The driver stopped right by her, leaning out his open window to look into hers. He had a broad, thick, tanned face, and hair everywhere on his body that you could see—Clara's face went hard just to see him. "Little Clara, huh?" he said. "You want a push·somewhere in your new car?"

"Go to hell," Clara said.

The boys in the back thumped against the roof and shrieked with laughter about something. Clara saw the farmer's face break into a happy grin and she did not bother to

218

listen to his words, but cut through them viciously: "Go to hell, you fat old bastard, you fat-assed son of a bitch of an ape! You monkey's ass!" They were silent for a moment just out of surprise. Clara fumbled with the ignition and this time got it started.

"Whose car is that?" someone yelled. There was a rising, buoyant joy in everyone but Clara; she could sense it. "Whose baby is that? Whose baby?"

Clara got the car going and it leaped ahead, away from the truck. She saw heat glimmering over the road like figures dancing to distract her. In a minute she would be out of this and safe. Nothing like this would ever happen again. Those bastards, she thought, her mouth like a slit outraged by pain, and as she turned the car into the center of the street to get out of town she felt and heard something crash against the roof. A clod of mud burst there and fragments flew to all sides. Her first instinct was to press down on the gas pedal, but something made her look back—she could not help herself. Caroline's brother was running after her with something else to throw, and while she looked right at him he slammed another heavy clod of mud against the back window. People laughed. The boys on the pickup truck had jumped down. Caroline's brother ran at her, yelling "Shoo— shoo! Scat!" as if he were chasing chickens out of the yard.

Clara sat frozen, the engine idling, her body twisted so that she could see them all—these boys and those young men, running after her car, drawn by something feverish and hunted in her face. "Shoo! Get on home—you stink! Clara stinks!" the boy yelled, pounding his fists on the side of the car.

She must have had a moment in which to think, to choose, but at once she opened the door and got out of the car. She ran right at the boy, running into him. He was about twelve years old and as tall as she was. She surprised him so, butting him like that, that he fell backward and his mouth jerked open. "You little fucking bastard!" Clara screamed. She kept on screaming and pushed into him, digging at his face with her nails. The other boys stood around, amazed, and Clara kept striking at Caroline's brother with her furious blows, and when the boy recovered enough sense to fight back she was ready for him and met the blow with one of her own, pounding the soft inside of his arm with her fist. "I'll teach you! I'll kill you!" Clara screamed. Something kept her going —rising in her like madness, pushing her forward and running her into the boy so that he never got his balance, but only

219

yelled at her in desperation. She had the feverish vision of his face streaked with tiny bands of blood, then she lunged at him again and caught hold of his hair with both hands and swung him around. She kicked him as hard as she could between the legs and let him fall groveling in the street. "There! I told you!" she cried. She turned to taunt them all, her hair loose and wild about her face, and all their faces were just one blurred face to her—then she was back at the car and pressing down on the pedal. They let her go.

If Revere ever found out about that he said nothing to her and she certainly said nothing to him. Sitting on the floor with the baby, playing with him, Clara could forget her humiliation in his face and the clumsy motions of his hands, fascinated by how everything was diminished in Lowry's baby that had been so hard, so strong in Lowry himself. If she had been insulted because of the baby it was nothing—she could go through it again and again, what did she care? "What the hell do we care?" she murmured to him.

She sang:

> He's going by train and by airplane
> All around the world....

She imitated the baby's patience, the cat's long sleepy patience, the turning of the days into nights and the relentless trance-like motion of the seasons, feeling herself sinking down to a depth that was not quite unconscious but where all feelings, emotions of love and hate, blended together in a single energy. She remembered her father's anger that had never been directed toward anything that made sense and Lowry's insatiable yearning, a hunger that could take him all over the world and never give him rest; these impulses belonged to men and had nothing to do with her. She could not understand them. The most she did was ask Revere about his house sometimes, innocently: "Is it drafty like this house? Is there a special room for a baby?"

She got the impression of something vast and unexplored, a big stone house with elms around it, the house a century old and in better condition than new houses—everything must be perfect there. Judd had told her the barns had the name REVERE painted on them in big black letters; Clara had been struck by that. She closed her eyes and tried to imagine what that might be like, to see your name written out like that. It was hard for her to put together the man who sat in the kitchen of this old farmhouse, watching Clara and the

220

baby playing together, and the man who had barns with his name on them: how could he be the same person? How could a single man be so expanded? Or how could it be that a name on a barn, something so big, could be diminished into this man who was tall and strong but weakened by his love for her?

She asked Revere: Did the boys have anywhere special to play around that house? Were they getting big? Did the house have a porch where you could sit out in the summer at night? Did the house have lightning rods? Was there a nice garden? Was there a fireplace? Was the kitchen nice and clean, or was it big and drafty like hers?

That winter passed by and in the spring she began to dream about Lowry again. She had the idea he might be coming back. There were hours when she wandered around outside with the baby, staring off toward the road and waiting for someone to appear without knowing what she wanted. If she understood what she was waiting for, she rejected it angrily; there really was no room in her life for Lowry now. She would give up nothing of it for him. But she kept looking and waiting and there were times at night when she rose dizzy with sleep and tried to get her head clear, wondering at the power of her body and at the deep vast depths of herself where there were no names or faces or memories but only desires that had no patience with the slow motion of daily life.

In the summer after Clara's eighteenth birthday, Sonya died and Clara went to her funeral. Revere was gone away to Chicago and so Judd was good enough to come and watch Swan, and Clara drove by herself to the little country church ten miles from Tintern where Sonya was going to be buried. She had forgotten Sonya for some time and the news of the girl's death was at first something oblique and impersonal, like a newspaper item. Then it began to eat into Clara and she thought of the many times they had been together— already years ago, in what had been left of their childhoods; but even then they had not been children.

Everyone was silent in church. Clara saw Sonya's mother and a few kids who were Sonya's brothers and sisters, and some relatives, old women she had never met before, sitting up in the second pew wearing black and looking sick and heavy. There were not many people in church. Clara recognized some of the faces and sensed that these people could look at her today without any special hatred, believing that she was like Sonya and therefore destined to be punished for everything sooner or later, like Sonya. And it did happen, Clara thought, that you were punished sooner or later. It happened whether you did anything wrong or not. So she sat in a black cotton dress with a wide-brimmed black hat on her head, pulled down a little over her forehead to hide bangs, and watched the coffin as the minister talked over it, wheedling and prodding them into thinking about a strange invisible world of God that was somehow simultaneous with this world but never found in it, until she wanted to cry out to the man that he should shut up—what did all that have to do with Sonya? "There are some bastards that don't do nothing but talk, talk all their lives," she thought.

No matter what he might say, trying to turn facts into something that sounded better, Sonya was dead and that was that. The top of the coffin was closed. Sonya had been her best friend in those days before Revere came and changed her life, they'd slept in the same bed and talked all night long, but now Clara sat healthy and erect in the pew and Sonya lay dead while everyone stared gloomily up at the coffin as if a little put out that they had to be here on this beautiful day. Clara could see the side of Sonya's mother's face—a pale hawkish profile that showed no grief. Everything eroded downward in that face and whatever happened that was ugly just etched the lines in deeper, convincing her she had been right all along. But then, Sonya's mother was supposed to be a little crazy; she wouldn't know what to feel. How did you know what to feel? Sonya had been strangled by the man she'd been living with for nearly a year, and now the man was in jail waiting to be killed himself and his wife was going around making trouble everywhere, drunk half the time—so how did you know what to feel? Sonya just hadn't gotten out in time, that was all.

The ceremony came to an end. Clara heard the minister's words stop a moment after they had actually stopped; she had been so wearied by them. Everyone stirred and the church felt hot again. Sonya's oldest brother and some other young men went awkwardly up front and picked up the coffin. Clara flinched when they lifted it into the air, feeling the sudden heavy weight of Sonya's body on their shoulders—but they picked it up with no effort and walked out into the sunlight and around back, their young faces grim and faintly sullen in this company of women; they were out of their own world. Everyone else filed along behind with that pretense of hurry that disguises a confused reluctance. The outdoors made everything different—a little unreal. Clara smelled sun-drenched, sun-burned corn and wheat, and her eyes moved involuntarily to the sky where the future lay eased out forever, without boundaries. There, anything could happen: you need only be alive. The pulsing of her veins and the slight trembling of her body made her feel light, while Sonya in that coffin must be heavy, gravitating already down toward the dry earth. It was not fair, Clara thought, but she was alive and Sonya was dead. Something gleamed and caught her eye: the amethyst ring Revere had bought her.

The grave was ready. Clara caught up with everyone and then stopped still; there was nowhere farther to go. She stared from face to face at those people on the other side of the open grave, and felt tears at last coming into her eyes. She could not quite believe that Sonya was in that box. She had not seen Sonya for many months, for a year. What had she to do with Sonya? Everything was unreal, faintly incredible—the soft warm air and the hard black coffin, the songs of birds and insects invisible all about them and the minister's droning voice, the hole there dug right out of the earth that was so peaceful on all sides, with its ancient tilting gravestones and weeds and forgotten, forlorn flowerpots with dried-out plants in them like tiny skeletons. . . . In the middle of all this, while the minister went on with something he had to get said, Clara thought quite clearly and desperately of Lowry. She could not live out her life and die and never see him again. She could not die and be buried, like Sonya, with strangers standing around who did not give a damn or who believed God's will was being done, sin punished, while Lowry was somewhere else—or maybe dead himself, buried by people who also did not give a damn and who could not have known who he was. Something wanted to claw its way out of her, made wild by this thought. She covered her face and wept.

Then it was over. People turned to leave, relieved, their eyes skidding away, breaking up into little clumps—family, mainly. Those people who hated one another and fought every evening in their homes banded together comfortably out of loyalty, or habit, or spite; Clara was the only person who was really alone. The minister would have walked with her, to prove something or other, and to make Clara think seriously of her own future—as if anyone was ever going to strangle her! But she walked fast to avoid him. She said nothing to anyone, not even to Sonya's mother. She had nothing to do with these people. She had nothing to do with Sonya either, now that Sonya was dead.

223

She drove quickly away, not even glancing back to see the cloud of dust she made and to wonder what they thought of her—frowning, disapproving eyes, waiting for her to get punished the way Sonya had. As she drove she cried silently, feeling the tears run hot down her face. She was thinking of Lowry. Her heart churned inside her at the memory of him. She pictured him, she tried to remember how he talked; her head jerked a little as if in silent conversation with him. Outside, the land flowed by without her noticing it. She did not know which direction she had taken. Whatever road it was, it wasn't the right road; it was some dusty country road that led nowhere. She drove for quite a while, faster and faster, with the tears now burning her eyes and her mouth set sullenly against the pressure that would make her turn the car around and drive back home.

About an hour later she approached a town: FAIRFAX pop. 2500. She had never seen Fairfax before. It looked like Tintern except it was on a hill, jumbled and awkward. She let the car slow down to drift through the town, and she noticed a gas station. It was an old, small building painted green some time ago. There were just two gas pumps, giant ugly things, and the drive was all dirt, bleached pale by the sun. Clara turned into the station.

She sat breathing hard, her heart still pounding. An attendant came out of the little building, hurrying toward her with his head bowed, or with his body shaped in the pretense of hurry. Behind him she caught sight of another man standing in the doorway. Something rushed in her, a sensation of drowning, choking; but the man was a stranger. His height and his slouched shoulders had made her think of Lowry and she hated herself for that. . . . The attendant hurried around to her and she said sullenly, not caring what he thought of her reddened eyes or windblown hair, "Give me some gas, some expensive gas." She picked up her purse as if to indicate she had money, then let it fall back on the seat. The attendant was a skinny man in his forties with a dull, freckled face. Clara got out of the car. She let the door swing open. Her heart was still pounding, everything seemed about to tilt around her, and yet she did not know why—it could not still be on account of Sonya, who was gone forever now, and why should it be because of Lowry? She hated him. She did not give a damn about him.

The sun was hot and bright about her. She walked around the car as if testing her legs. She looked at her bare arms, at her wrists and hands, at the ring that gleamed so darkly in

224

this rich light, and only after a moment did it occur to her that she was doing all this for the man inside the building. She looked over at him. He was just lowering a soft drink bottle from his mouth. She saw him wipe at his mouth with his sleeve, and a smile began to itch at her mouth. He stepped down onto the packed dirt and tapped to check his cigarettes in his pocket, some little ceremonious gesture that meant he was conscious of her, and Clara let her head fall back as if to dry her eyes in the sun or to show off her face. He walked right up to her car and put one foot out against the fender, as if appraising it; then he looked sideways at Clara.

"Somebody's been drivin' fast," he said.

Clara brushed her hair back from her face with both hands. She felt cunning and lazy; what had been wild inside her a few minutes before was now waiting quietly. She said, "You work here or something?"

"Hell, no."

He finished the bottle of lime pop and turned to toss it back against the building. It struck the side and left a white streak. "What are you doin'?" the other man said, up front by the car hood. The man just laughed. Clara smiled and saw him watching her and as he watched she let her lips move slowly back to show her teeth, the way a cat would smile if it could smile. He had dark, damp hair and he wore a pull-over shirt with something faded on its front, and blue jeans old and faded with grease; Clara saw that his face was young and impatient. He took hold of the radio antenna of her car and bent it toward him slightly, then let it go. He looked at her. Clara kept on smiling. He wiped his forehead, then his mouth, and his fingers closed into a loose fist while he watched her.

"You ain't from around here, that's for sure. Where're you from?"

"Driving through," Clara said.

"Where're you goin'?"

She lifted one shoulder vaguely and then let it fall. "Somethin' happened maybe?" he said. "You been cryin'?"

Clara turned away and said to the gas attendant, "How much is it?" He told her and she reached inside the open window to get her purse, one leg raised from the ground to balance herself, and then she took the dollar bill out and handed it to the man; the other man, the one who had been talking to her, had come up close so that she could see a small white scar almost lost in his eyebrow. She said to him,

225

"If you live outside town and want a ride home, I can drive you."

She said this so dreamily, staring right at him, that he had no time to let his gaze drop somewhere so that he could think—instead, he said at once, "Fine with me," and nodded once or twice. Clara ran around the car and got in and he was already beside her, his long legs awkward, smelling of perspiration, glancing sideways at her with the same kind of taut calculated smile she herself had.

She drove down through the town and out from it, out into the country again. "You like living here?" she said to him.

"I'm goin' in the Army next month," he said.

"What if they go in with all them people fighting?" Clara said. She knew only what she overheard from Revere and Judd: fighting in Europe. The young man made a sound that expressed contempt for the war and for her question. "You maybe could get killed," she said.

She glanced over at him and saw that he was maybe twenty-two, twenty-three, and that if he was going to die shortly he would need her now. He was watching her as she drove. His face was damp again, though he'd just wiped it and his shirt was soaked through; on his hard muscular upper arms the sweat looked oil-slick. "I thought you were somebody else, the first sight I had of you," she said. She spoke softly and coaxingly. He said, stirring as if he were uncomfortable, "Sorry I ain't that man." "There's no need," Clara said. "Yes, I am real sorry," he said. She stopped the car and they sat for a moment, not looking at each other, then they got out of the car and seemed almost to be testing the ground with their feet. He came around to her side, dragging one hand across the hot hood of the car. Right next to the road was a thick woods that was posted. Clara said, "You think they're going to get the state troopers out if anybody walks in there?" He took her arm and helped her across the ditch. He lifted the barbed wire for her to go under, holding it up as high as he could. Clara ran through and into the woods with her hair loose behind her, feeling something pushed up to suffocate her, almost, in her chest and throat. It kept pushing at her, goading her into a wild feverish smile she turned toward the woods but not toward the man.

He caught up with her and took hold of her as if he had been waiting for this for hours. Clara heard his breath come brokenly. They lay down and he was ready for her so fast that it seemed this must just be another dream, Lowry's face

226

obscured from her while she gripped him around the neck, tensing herself, the cords in her throat getting taut and anxious. "Come deep. Deeper," Clara said. Then she stopped thinking and abandoned herself to this man, sinking down to that great dark ocean bed where there were no faces or names but only shadowy bodies you reached out to in order to calm yourself; nothing came before and nothing came afterward. She shut her eyes tight and had no need to think of Lowry, who was with her in this stranger's body, and at the end she moved her teeth hard against the bone of his jaw to keep from crying out. Afterward he didn't roll off her but stayed where he was, holding her down as if she were a prize he had won by force, and he kissed her to make up for what they had not done before. His chest was heaving, his body drenched with sweat. Clara brushed his wet hair back off his forehead and framed his face with her hands while she kissed him. She felt as if she were drowning in the heat of his body, in the heat of everything wet and drugged that she could not control or get clear in her mind, and that she loved whoever had come to her like that, she was lost in love and would never get out of it.

When she got back to the house it was early evening. Revere's cousin Judd was playing with the baby in the front yard. Clara saw that he had a weak, vulnerable face and that something in the urgency of his look meant that he had been worried about her. She got out of the car and looked down at her wrinkled dusty dress and her dirty bare feet, and for no reason at all she set the black hat on her head and came over to meet them. She picked the baby up and kissed him, closing her eyes with gratitude. The very earth before her feet seemed to her solid and transformed; the baby's happiness was her own happiness; her body had not been like this since those days with Lowry. Seeing Judd's look she said, "I got lost somewhere," and pressed her face against the baby so that she would not have to look at Judd.

10

"Honey, where are you? Swan?"
Clara was working in the side garden and it occurred to her that the boy had been gone for a while. She let the hoe fall. "Swan? Where are you?"

Revere said she fussed over the boy too much and she knew it, but it was partly just loneliness; anyway, she liked to talk, and if Swan wasn't with her she couldn't talk without thinking herself a little crazy, like a few women in the vicinity she could name. She looked around the garden and out toward the orchard, letting her eyes move easily from thing to thing, all her possessions. She had been living here for four years now; she was twenty-one. If she thought of the time behind her, she felt no regret, no doubts at all. All those years when Revere came to visit her and occasionally stay the night were kept here in the look of the land he had gifted her with, the slightly shabby farm with its tilted and moss-specked barns, the wild grass that to Clara was so beautiful, the wild flowers and weeds and bushes sprung out of other bushes like magic—all this was hers.

She tilted her head back to let her hair fall loose. Her hair was warm and thick, too thick for August. Sometimes she wore it pulled back and up, in a great clumsy knot that fell loose all the time and made her feel childish; most of the time she let it fall wild. It was bleached by the summer sun, like her boy's, almost white, a pale gleaming moon-colored blond that seemed to be kin to the burnished tips of certain weeds and the way the sun could slant its light off the tin roof of the old barns. Clara said, "Swan?" without bothering to raise her voice and went through the garden toward the back of the house. It was a large garden for just a woman to handle, though Revere and Swan could help her. But it was her garden and it bothered her to have someone else working in it. A year ago, before his marriage, Revere's cousin Judd had put in some large petaled roses for Clara, and in a way she had minded even that—though she had not let on. Now, since his marriage, Judd never came to see her. His wife would not allow it. So it was Clara's garden and no one else's, and when her eyes moved from plant to plant, pausing at each dusty familiar flower and occasional insects she'd flick off with an angry snap of her fingers, a feeling of accomplishment rose up in her. The garden was as much of the world as she wanted because it was all that she could handle, being just Clara, and it was beautiful. She did not want anything else.

Her mother had never had a garden, Clara thought. If her mother were still alive she'd maybe like to sit on the back porch and look at this garden, and be pleased at what her daughter had done.

To Clara it was all transformed by the sunlight that bathed

228

the land every day, changing those old rotting barrels out back and the dilapidated chicken coop and everything her eye might come across into things of beauty. Even the most dwarfed of the pear trees could be beautiful: she only had to look at it with that fierceness of satisfaction that had now become part of her. And if Swan should run back there with the dog, jumping and playing in the grass, she would stand transfixed, as if she were at the threshold of a magic world.

Clara came through the back yard. Revere had bought a few chairs for it from a store in the city—tubed metal, painted bright red (the color Clara had thought she wanted) and glaring like splotches of paint dashed right on the land itself. She paused to look through the back screen door, thinking he might be in the kitchen somewhere. "Swan?" she said. On either side of the back stoop were great lilac bushes banked up close, not in bloom now but heavy with leaves. Over the house elms seemed to be leaning, like people watching Clara, and she thought of how quiet everything would be except for Swan's dog and how the world had moved back from her—the worry and bother of which old person was sick now in Tintern or what Ginny would do with that boy of hers whose teeth had to be pulled, all of them— all rotted—and who would win the war over in Europe, so far away from her on this land and impressing itself upon her only through the few signs she saw nailed on trees and in town: JOIN NAVY, RED CROSS, WORK AT GARY, WORK AT DETROIT, WORK AT WILLOW RUN, GIVE BLOOD. "Give Blood" made Clara think hard; it was the only sign that got to her. She went into town as much as she wanted now, no one bothered her—most of the men were gone and quite a few of the families, following their men down out of the mountains to work in the defense factories, disappearing. Many old people were left and the mail now was everything to them; they were jealous over one another's letters. The world had suddenly opened up the horizons falling back far beyond the ridge of mountains that had seemed at one time to be the limit of their world. And so nobody cared about Clara now; after four years, she was almost as good as Revere's wife, and so they did not bother her.

"Give Blood," those signs said. Clara sucked at her lip to think of what that meant, why it was nailed up everywhere. Men were dying, drained of their blood; did it sink into sandy soil, or into dust, or into mud, across the ocean where Revere would never have to go?—when you owned what he did you went nowhere, you stayed home and managed things, even

Judd did not have to go, but that was for a different reason: nerves. But the husbands and sons and brothers of people in town, Caroline's husband and Ginny's husband (though Ginny's husband had already left her) and anyone you could name, many of them were not just gone now but dead or reported missing, which was the same thing. Clara could not keep this in her mind and there was the remote, haunting idea that she should keep it in mind and think of it all the time, that someone needed to be thinking of it—it was so strange, this sudden opening-up of the world. But she put it all out of her life and thought instead of Swan, who was a child and therefore safe. When she went to town and someone cornered her, some woman, she listened with her eyes lowered as she heard about some young man or boy who was "all right," didn't she think so, because everyone knew they were treated well in the prison camps? She thought instead of Swan.

Out here, north of Tintern and south of the Eden River, in the slow gentle slope of the valley that encompassed so much land, history had no power for her. It was hardly real except if you listened once too often to one of those old women. Clara kept up her house and sewed for herself and the boy and worked outside and made supper for Revere and took care of him when he came to her, telling him what he wanted to hear and letting him love her and say to her what he always said, as if he were kept young by saying these things, pressing his face against her body and losing himself in it. Out here time might pass, but it was just weathertime or daytime, seasons blending into one another or days turning into night, nothing that got you anywhere: she was older than before, maybe, but she looked better than she had ever looked in her life. Time had nothing to do with her.

The dog was barking. It rushed around the corner at her eagerly as if it had something to tell her, a dog of no particular type Revere had bought her one day. Clara ran around the house and saw first a car parked out by the road and thought, "That's strange," and then she saw a man at the end of the drive, just where it branched off to go to the barns and back along one of the old pastures. Swan was standing by this man. He was facing him and the man was bending a little to talk to him, his hands on his thighs. Clara approached them and the dog came up behind her and overtook her, barking. Once or twice she had been bothered by strangers and one winter morning she had even discovered footprints out in the snow, under her windows. . . .

The man was Lowry.

As soon as she saw that, she stopped. She stopped, panting, her hand against her chest as if she were stricken with pain. They looked at each other across the patch of scrubby grass, and the boy turned to look at her too. When she got her senses back she walked to Lowry, slowly, and he came to meet her. Clara said in a voice that was too faint, "What the hell do you want?"

Lowry looked the same. Or maybe not: something was different. He wore a blue shirt and dark trousers and shoes smudged with dust from the walk down the lane. His face was the same face, with its thick firm jaw and that expression that played for innocence, as if he'd been gone a week at the most and why did she look at him like that?

"Mommy—" Swan said.

She wondered, staring at the boy, if Lowry knew. But how could he not know? She let Swan push against her, he was frightened; in another minute he would hide behind her legs. "It's just a visitor," she said, a little sharply. She wanted him to be brave in front of Lowry. "You go over and play with the dog."

The air between her and Lowry must have been choked with heat. He kept looking at her, smiling. No one should be able to smile that way, Clara thought. But she could do nothing in return, not make her face ugly or hard against him. She felt rigid, as if a small ticking mechanism inside had suddenly failed.

"Well, what do you want? What do you want?" she said.

"I came to see you, that's all." He held out his hands, not to suggest an embrace but just to show that he was carrying nothing, had no surprises.

"You—you dirty bastard," Clara said. She looked over to where Swan was playing, pretending to play, then her eyes shot back to Lowry. "Why did you come here? You want to ruin everything for me? Didn't they tell you about me?"

"Sure."

"You asked them in town?"

"I asked them in town."

"Well?" Clara said shrilly, "what do you want, then? He isn't here now, it's lucky. You want to see him?"

"Why should I want to see him?" He leaned toward her and laughed. She heard the familiar laugh but saw something flash from inside his hair, something flat against his skull; this frightened her. It might have been a scar around which hair

231

wouldn't grow. "I just came to see you. I thought you might want to see me."

"I don't know why in hell you thought that," Clara said, trying to make her words hard enough to keep down her trembling. She turned away from him suddenly to stare out at the fields that ran to the road—thick with dandelion fuzz that was white and fragile as she felt. Out there his car was parked. "Why did you leave your car out there?"

"I don't know."

But she thought it was strange. He had come back to the house on foot. "How did you find me?" she said.

"They told me. But they didn't think I should come."

"Well—what do you think? What do you want?" she said. She stared at him and felt in this instant that she was too young to go through such things, that this moment was terrible for her because she knew what he wanted and what she would say to him, as if everything had been rehearsed in her dreams for years without her knowing about it.

"Honey, I came back for you," he said. He took her hand. He slid his hand up to her wrist and jerked her a little as if waking her. "He's a real cute little kid," he said, nodding over toward Swan. "I knew he was your kid right away—he looks like you. I knew I was at the right place then."

"But—what do you want?" Clara said.

"Do you love him, this Revere?"

Clara wanted to say something but could not. Her lips parted but Lowry's eyes had too much power over her, they wanted too much. She felt that she would fall helplessly from him if he released her wrist.

"I said, do you love him?"

"I don't need to love anybody."

Lowry laughed. His face was not as tan as one might think, this late in August. "Aren't you going to invite me in? Have supper or something—what time is it?"

"Suppertime almost, but I don't have anything fixed—I—"

"Don't you want me to stay?"

She looked around to where Swan was kneeling with one arm around the dog's neck. They might have been whispering together or crying together. The impulse to tell Lowry that this child was his was so strong in Clara that for a moment she could not speak at all. Then she said, "You can come in. I'll feed you. He isn't coming over tonight."

"That would be real kind of you."

"You're probably hungry."

"I'm hungry."

232

"You look tired—you've been driving a long time."

"That's right."

At the door her foot slipped and Lowry had to catch her. "Swan, come on in," she called. The boy was waiting on the path, his clever, silent face turned toward them. Then Clara said, confused, "No, never mind. You don't need to— it's hot inside." She started to cry. It had something to do with her foot slipping on her own doorstep—mixing her up, frightening her. Lowry laughed and put his hands on her waist and pushed her up into the house.

"This is nice," he said, "but Revere could do better for you."

"I know that."

"Don't you mind, then?"

"I don't want anything else. I told him to stop buying me things a long time ago."

He walked through the kitchen and looked into the parlor. There Clara's plants were everywhere, on the window sills and on tables—broad, flat leaves, ferns, tiny budlike leaves, violets you might almost miss if you didn't look closely enough. She was Lowry looking at them. "You have a house all your own now," he said.

Clara followed him into the parlor where it was cool. She was still crying, angrily. Lowry turned and said, "I see you got grown up."

"Yes."

"When did that happen?"

"After you left."

"Not before?"

"No."

"They said you've been with him a long time. Four years, maybe? That's a right long time, it's like being married."

"Yes," Clara said.

"You like him all right?"

"Yes."

"What's this here?" And he reached up to take hold of the small gold heart she wore on a chain around her neck. "So he gives you nice things. This is expensive, right?"

"I don't know."

"What about his other wife?"

"He's only got one wife."

"What about his other sons?"

"I don't know."

"They don't mind you?"

"I suppose they hate me—so what?"

233

"Doesn't it bother you?"

"Why should it?"

"Being out here like this—for him to come visit when he wants."

"You used to do that too," Clara said, pulling away. He let go of the heart. "I suppose you forgot all that."

"I didn't forget anything," Lowry said. "That's why I'm here."

Then the trembling started in her, a rigid violent trembling that began far down on her spine and passed up her back to her shoulders and arms, a feeling she had never known she could have. All those years with Revere were being swept out into sight and considered and were maybe going to be swept out the back door, as if with a broom Clara herself was whisking about impatiently.

"Let me get you a beer," Clara said.

"Are you cold?"

"For Christ's sake, no," she said, looking away. "It's summer out." She felt the shivering start again and made herself rigid. Lowry sat down and she went to the refrigerator and got two bottles out. At the window she saw Swan by one of the barns, alone and lonely, a child without other children, with a mother who was now about to desert him and betray him, just as she must have always known she would. And the worst betrayal of all would be her giving him this father who had come down the lane without even driving up, apologizing for nothing and already bossing them around. She saw Lowry through the doorway, his legs outspread and his hands fallen idly across his flat stomach.

She sat on the arm of his chair. Drinking together like this made them quiet, quieted something in her. Lowry said, "I went to Mexico and got married."

"You what?"

"Got married."

Clara tried to keep her voice steady. "Where is your wife, then?"

"I don't know."

"Well—that's nice."

"We got rid of each other before the war. She was trying to teach down there, just for something to do. She was from Dallas. I guess," he said, closing his eyes and pressing the bottle against them, "I guess we were in love, then something happened. She kept at me, she kept worrying. She was afraid I went after other women."

"What was she like?"

"I don't know. What are people like? I don't know what anyone is like," he said. "She had dark hair."

"Oh."

"This was all a while ago. She divorced me."

"Divorced?"

The word was so strange, so legal, it made her think of police and courthouses and judges. She stared at Lowry as if she might be able to see the change this divorce had made in him.

"Are you all right now—are you happy?" she said.

Lowry laughed. She saw the lines at the corners of his mouth and wondered for a dazed instant who this strange man was.

"That depends on you, honey."

"But what do you want from me? You son of a bitch," she said, bitterly. "I'm a mother now, I have a kid. I'm going to be married too."

"That's nice."

"I am, he's going to marry me."

"When is this going to take place?"

"Well, in a few years. Sometime."

"When?"

"When his wife dies."

Lowry grinned without there being anything funny. "So you're waiting around here while she dies, huh? They said in town she was sick but she'd been sick for ten years. You want to wait another ten years?"

"I like it here."

"Stuck out here by yourself?"

"I'm not by myself, goddam it. I've got Swan. I've got Revere too," she added. "There was nothing else I ever wanted in my life but a place to live, a nice place I could fix up. I have a dog too and some cats. And all my plants—and my curtains there that I sewed—"

"It's nice, Clara."

"Sure it's nice," she said. She drank from the bottle. "You're not going to take this away from me."

"You could just leave it, yourself."

"What about Swan?"

"He comes too."

"Where do you think you're going, then? You're so goddam smart. You always had plans, you always knew where you were going," Clara said. She bit at the neck of the bottle, hard. Lowry was watching her as if he felt sorry for her, suddenly, after all these years, and as if the emotion were a little surprising to him. "You came and went, you drove up and you drove away, I couldn't think of anything but you and so you went away and that was that— The hell with me. You never thought about anybody but yourself."

"Don't be mad, honey."

"You're a selfish bastard, isn't that true? You go off and leave me and come back, what is it, four years later? And I'm supposed to love you, I'm supposed to go with you—to the beach again maybe for three days. Then you'll give me and the kid a ride back and kick us out—"

Lowry sat back in the chair. He looked tired.

"I didn't think about you like that, honey," he said. "I mean—the way I thought about the woman I married."

"You don't need to tell me."

"I wanted something else, honey. I couldn't talk to you."

"But you could to that woman down there, huh?"

"Yes."

"Is that why you left her? If you like her so much go on back and find her," Clara said furiously.

"I don't want her."

"Why the hell do you want me?"

"I'm tired of talking."

"What? What does that mean?"

"I'm tired of talking, of thinking the way she did. I'm tired of thinking."

Clara raised the bottle to her mouth again, trying to rid herself of that trembling she hated so. She felt that her body was moving off from her, going its own way and paying no attention to what she wanted.

"I joined the Army, honey," he said. "I came back to the States and enlisted just in time."

"You what?"

"I've been over in Europe, you know where that is? I want somebody who doesn't know where that is," he said. He was not smiling. He caressed Clara's arm and she did not move it away; she watched his hand moving on her skin. There were tufted blond hairs on the backs of his fingers and she thought that she remembered them, yes, she remembered every one of them. His fingernails were thick and milky, ridged just a little with dirt. Lowry was staring at her. "You've changed quite a bit, Clara. You really are a woman now."

Clara looked away.

"I know why he loves you. I don't blame him. But he's already married and he has a family—he won't be able to do anything for you. You know that. You could never fit in with

236

those people, you're nothing at all like them. He won't marry you."

"Shut up about that."

"Clara, you know I'm telling the truth."

"He loves me. And anyway this is none of your—"

"But sitting around here waiting for someone to die—a woman you don't even know—"

"I don't know her but I hate her," Clara said viciously.

Lowry was amused at this. "How can you hate her if you don't know her?"

"He'll marry me after she dies," Clara said.

"You'd really like to be his wife?"

"I would."

"I don't believe that."

"Go to hell then! What's wrong with you? You want everything handed over to you—even a son like that, a kid given to you. Right?" She drew her breath in sharply, watching him. She felt as if she were on the brink of something terrible.

"If he's your kid. . . ." Lowry said. But his answer was just vague enough to lessen the tension between them. "He's a quiet boy."

"He's strong and growing fast. He's smart too."

"I could see it was your boy right away. . . ."

"Lowry, why did you come back?"

"I was meaning to come for a long time. I sent you a letter, didn't I?"

"What letter?"

"A letter from Mexico."

"I never got it."

"Sure you did."

"I never did."

"Didn't that bastard give it to you . . . ?"

"No." Clara rubbed her hands against her eyes. "What was in it, news about your wife? A wedding invitation?" Then she stared at him. "Or did you really write a letter, really? I don't know whether to believe you or not. . . . You were married and everything. . . ."

"Honey, don't be so jealous. You're still jealous after all this time."

"I'm not jealous. I really don't give a damn."

"I thought I wanted a different kind of woman, that's all. You and she are nothing like each other—honey, a man wouldn't bother looking at her if you were around. But I thought I wanted something that it turned out I didn't."

"Now you want somebody stupid, somebody who can't talk or bother you," Clara said. "Somebody to make love to and forget about, right? And you know you'll always be welcome when you come back, so what the hell? *She* threw you out right away."

"No."

"What the hell kind of a marriage was it?"

"Clara, don't be so angry."

"I'm not angry."

"Drink your beer, finish it up."

"I don't want it, I feel like puking."

Her being like that, being vulgar, was just enough to make him laugh a little. She could not trust herself to look at him too steadily. It was like staring at a light, at something blinding; in a few seconds the center could fade away and she might see nothing.

"So I left her and went back to the States and enlisted. I went to England for a while, then over to France. Someday I'll tell you about what happened."

"You were over there all that time?"

"For two years."

"You really were in the Army?"

"Sure."

"And I didn't know it. . . . What if you were killed?"

Lowry laughed bitterly. "There were a few of us who got killed."

"But Lowry, you couldn't die. What if— You—"

She ran out of words. It was so close to her, this knowledge of Lowry and Lowry's death, a possibility Lowry himself maybe could not see. He took her bottle from her and set it down and pulled her into his lap. "Would you have worried about me, honey?"

"Yes, Lowry."

"You didn't get that letter?"

"No. Never."

"Did you miss me?"

"Yes."

"Did you wish I was here?"

"Yes."

"What about Revere, then?"

"He loved me, he took care of me—"

"Do you love him? Did you?"

"I don't know—"

"Was it hard for you, having the kid like that? Without being married?"

238

"No. I didn't think about that."

"You didn't care?"

"No."

"You wanted the kid, huh?"

"Sure I wanted him."

Lowry smoothed her hair back. He looked at her as if she were really some distance away. After a moment he said, "He isn't my kid, is he?"

Clara's lips parted in shock. "No."

"Does he look like Revere?"

"Mostly he looks like me."

"I used to know Revere," he said. "I didn't tell you this but my family was like yours—except my father did farmwork. He went from farm to farm, always getting kicked out. Finally he took off and left us, and my mother took the kids back to her mother. I was fourteen then. Once my father worked for Revere. . . . I didn't tell you that."

"But I thought—"

"We're like each other, you and me, except I went places and tried to find out some things and even got shot for my trouble. while you camped down and got everything you wanted. Those are real nice plants, honey," he said. He kissed her. "I can't tell you how much I like them. I like this house. If I hadn't been told whose house it was—"

"Lowry, I thought—I thought your family—"

"Just white trash, honey."

"But you had a nice car, and had money to spend—"

"I was helping somebody run whisky. My family was all gone by that time."

"Run whisky? Was that it?" And she could not keep the flat surprised sound of disappointment out of her voice.

"I pulled out and tried to get something going in Mexico, I had a few thousand dollars I'd taken from this bastard I worked for, and I wanted to start something—some business —but nothing turned out. I didn't know enough. I met her then—"

"Your wife."

"She was sort of bumming around but she was a teacher too, she had a job she could point to. Her family kept sending people after her, trying to get her back home—she was staying with me then—and she maybe married me to get back at them, to make them shut up. She told me I was fooling myself with my life, running around and never getting anywhere—She was right, but what the hell."

"No, she wasn't right—"

239

"What the hell."

"Did you say somebody shot you?"

"Nothing much, just in the leg here."

Clara touched his thigh. "Is it all right?"

"It's all right now."

"Did it hurt awful?"

"I don't know."

"Lowry, for God's sake—"

"What?"

"You were in the war and everything, you got shot—I never knew about it—"

"Lots of people get shot. They're getting shot right now. Or bombed to pieces, that's even better. I don't want to talk about it."

"Were you in a hospital?"

She saw his mouth jerk as if he had to taste something ugly, so she let that pass. He was quiet. She was not angry. She said, "Were you surprised about me?"

"No. Maybe."

"What did you think?"

"I didn't think you'd still be around here. Or I thought you'd be married."

"This is the same as being married."

"Not quite."

"I have a kid."

"Revere doesn't live with you, honey. How often does he come over?"

"When he can."

"These days he's a busy man. How much money do you think he's making off the war, him and his people?"

"I don't know anything about it. He never says."

"They say he's making money off it. Why not? All the trash from around here and all the hillbilly backwashes in the country that didn't get shipped over to die are working their heads off in the factories, making lots of money. Or so they think. Your friend has investments in things like that."

"He never says—"

"Why should he? When he comes to you he forgets about it. But I knew you first, I brought you here. For two years I've been thinking about you. I didn't even think about her—my wife—I thought right past her to you."

"Did you?"

"I thought about you all the time. I thought that if I got back here and they let me out—"

"What?"

240

"If I got back I'd come right here and get you and we'd go somewhere. Even if you were already married I was going to come back and marry you."

"Marry me?"

"Now I'm going to do this: I'm going up to Canada, to British Columbia. They're giving away land there, practically. Thousands of acres. I have a little money and we're going to get clear of everything except the outdoors, we'll have a farm, I can learn how to work on one again—"

"Lowry, you're crazy—"

"Why am I crazy?"

"I don't know, it's just—I—"

"Why are you afraid?"

Clara pushed away from him and got to her feet. Her teeth had begun to chatter; she felt that the very air about her had turned brittle. "I don't want to hear it," Clara said. She closed her eyes and shook her head slowly. "Don't say anything to me. I'm afraid what I might do. How can I change. . . ? Once there was a man that looked like you, in a gas station—"

"And?"

"He made me think about you all over again."

Lowry got up. "Honey, everything is beautiful here. This old house is beautiful. Out the window there—those trees— it's all beautiful. We'll have a place just like this in Canada, by ourselves."

"Lowry, no."

"You don't know what you have here, how beautiful it is. You don't understand what it is," he said. "Over there I thought about you all the time, Clara. You were at the center of what I was trying to think about. I remembered how it was by the ocean, and down by the river that day—how nice you were to me— Nobody was ever as nice to me as you were, Clara. I know that now."

Clara went out into the kitchen and stood at the screen door. She heard Lowry following behind her. Her fingernails picked nervously at the screen, at tiny rust-specks or dirt embedded there. Outside, Swan was digging a hole by the fence that cut off the orchard from an old pasture. "Swan?" she called. "What are you doing?"

He looked around. "This here," he said, his small clear voice a surprise to her. He lifted the spade. After a moment, staring at her and at Lowry behind her, he turned away self-consciously.

"Suppose that was your kid, what then?" Clara said.

"It wouldn't matter, I would want him with us even if he wasn't," Lowry said. And that answer, that should have sounded so good to her, somehow didn't; she had wanted something else. "I'm thirty-two," he said. "I had my thirtieth birthday over there and I never thought I'd get that old. Now I'm back here and I could maybe forget about all that, if I could begin everything over."

Clara stared at him. She did not understand.

"You're worried he's going to come?" Lowry said.

"No."

"What are you worried about?"

She pushed past him. "I've got to fix supper," she said.

"Forget about supper."

"You've got to eat, and Swan—"

"Forget about it. Come back here with me."

"Lowry, I can't."

"Come on."

She stared miserably at the floor. Everything was draining out of her, all her strength, all the hatred that had kept Lowry close to her for so long. It struck her that she had fed on this hatred and that it had kept her going, given her life. Now that he was here and standing before her, she could not remember why she had hated him.

"You bastard," she whispered. "Coming back here like this—You—"

"Let me make you quiet," Lowry said.

She looked up at his smile, which was exactly like the smile she remembered.

"That boy is still outside playing," Lowry said. From the bed he was leaning to look out the window. Clara, lying still, watched the long smooth curve of his back. "Any other kid would come bothering you, but he doesn't. How does he know that much?"

"Smart, like his father."

"Why is he so quiet?"

"He isn't quiet. He was afraid of you."

"He shouldn't have been afraid of me."

"A strange man coming up the lane, walking up the lane like that. . . . I was afraid of you myself."

"Are you afraid now?"

She wanted to say angrily that she would always be afraid of him, that there was nothing she could do to keep herself from him and that this was terrible, this power he had over

242

her. But she lay still. Her hair was tangled around her damply; she felt soiled, bruised.

"I'm sorry if . . . I upset you," Lowry said gently.

He pressed himself against her again, hiding his face against her, and she felt how soft even a man's flesh can be, lying so delicate on top of his bones; and if it had all been blown apart, shot apart, what then? If the bullets that had shot about Lowry in the dark, over there in Europe, across the world in Europe, had hit him instead and stopped dead in his body, what then? He would not have come back to make love to her. Lowry's body, which was all of him that she could see and touch, would be rotted over there in a ditch in a place she would not even known by name, could not even imagine because she would not have the power to do so . . . and what then? She caressed his back and her hand came away wet with sweat. That was all she had to go by. She felt how weak they both were, she and Lowry, how the terrible power he had in his body and in his hard muscular legs passed over into this weakness that was not at all like the weakness before sleep but was something heavy and close to death, like lying on the bottom of an ocean of sweat, their bodies still trembling from all the violence they had suffered. She felt as if a wound had been viciously opened up in her, secret in her body, and that all her strength had drained away through it and left her helpless again.

"What is Revere going to say when I tell him what we're going to do?"

"He's got a wife."

"But he loves me," Clara whispered. "He wants to marry me."

"The hell with him."

"He loves me."

"I don't give a damn about another man's love."

"He loves Swan too. . . ."

"Well, I don't give a damn about that either."

"What if you get tired and leave me again?"

"That won't happen."

"How do you know?"

"I know."

They fell back into silence. Clara listened to his breath, felt his breath against her. She said dreamily. "But you . . . Lowry, with you everything is just what comes into your head. It comes out of somewhere like in a dream and you want it and then you get it, then that's over. . . . People or places to go to or things to do. The world is just spread out

243

as far as you can see or feel it. I could fall out of that world, get pushed over the edge or something. Then what?"

"Clara, don't talk crazy like that."

"And the kid too. He might get forgotten. You're in such a rush. . . ."

"No."

"I'm not just a kid now, Lowry. I'm afraid what you'll do to me this time."

"I always took care of you, sweetheart."

"Oh, Christ—"

"You just wanted more from me than I wanted to give."

Clara sat up. She did not want to look at him. It was as if they were criminals together, weak and suspicious together, not happy with each other the way she'd been with that man from the gas station—who had made her feel Lowry inside her without having to really be Lowry. The air was warm and sultry. This bedroom, which Clara had always loved, now seemed to her someone else's room. It was not just Lowry who did not belong in it, but Clara herself.

She let him embrace her again. Her mind stumbled backwards to other embraces of his, and back all the way to that night in Florida years ago, when he had taken a washcloth and cleaned her up to suit him, to make her good enough for him. Or was she wrong about that, was she judging him wrong . . . ? She remembered that Lowry and she remembered herself, as if she had been outside her body all along and watching. He was the same man and she wanted him just as violently; making love with him cost her everything, every agonized straining to give life to that kernel of love he would always keep inside her. She would never be free of him. But she knew what she was going to say just the same.

"No. I guess I'm not going with you," she said.

"What?"

"I'm not going."

He touched his forehead with his fingertips—a strange gesture. He was stunned. Clara closed her eyes to get rid of that sight. She felt sick.

"You're not coming with me?" he said.

Clara got out of bed and put her housecoat on. It was made of pink cotton, rather wrinkled and not too clean. She went to the window and stared out. Lowry had not moved. After a while she looked over her shoulder at him, narrowing her eyes against anything she might see that she would not want to see. Lowry was tapping at his teeth with his fingers, watching her.

244

"You changed your mind?" he said.

"I never really thought any other way."

She let her head droop. Her hair moved about her face languidly, lazily. She knew she must have the look of a woman in a picture who had everything decided for her, who had never had to think, whose long complicated life had been simplified by some artist when he chose one instant out of it to paint: after that, the hell with her.

"You want to spend your life waiting here for another woman to die?"

"If I have to."

"Does your kid know about that?"

"I don't know what he knows. He's just a baby."

"Maybe he knows more than you think."

"Maybe."

"And what about Revere, what if somebody told him I was with you?"

"Are you going to tell him?"

"Suppose I did?"

"If you want to, go ahead."

"Suppose I told him about before, too. Four years ago."

"Go on and tell him."

"Don't you care if I do?"

Clara looked down. "You won't tell him, Lowry."

"Why not?"

"Because you won't tell him. You won't do that."

They were both silent. She raised her eyes to his, narrowed.

"Why won't I?" he said.

"Because you know I love you. Why would you want to hurt me?"

"If you love me, why the hell—"

"I'm not like I was!" she said. "I'm different now—I'm a mother, I'm grown up— I had all this time to think about things—"

"Clara—"

"There's all these things you think about that I can't understand," she said. She spoke softly and quietly, trying to keep her voice still. "You always go past me. That was why you wanted another woman, and you'd want one again—"

"If that's it—"

"No, that's not it. I'd go with you anyway. I'd take that chance if it were a few years ago—what the hell would I care? But it's different now."

"Clara, you could do so much for me if you would."

245

"I can't do anything for you."

He was breathing hard. "It wasn't just being shot that hurt me, it was other things," he said. The way his mouth twisted showed how he hated to say this. "I had some trouble for a while. I was in a hospital over here, in Washington. They had to keep me quiet— try to keep me quiet—"

"My God," Clara whispered.

"I don't want to go back to it, I mean I don't want to think about it," Lowry said harshly. "Up in Canada we could start over again, and the kid too, a kid is so young he doesn't know anything—and we could have other kids—"

"Lowry—"

"I can't understand things. Life," he said. He shut his eyes tight, as if to get rid of something flying around him, at him. "I don't mean around here. Here, everything is quiet. Your garden here. . . . It stays in one place. But over there— Nothing stays still long enough for you to understand it. How do you know what you're doing, what's happening? I can't live that way."

"Lowry, please."

"I can't live that way. It would kill me."

"Lowry, I just can't go with you."

He waited a moment. "All right," he said.

She went out in the kitchen to wait for him. Swan must have caught sight of her because he came up on the porch. A slender, shy boy, with his father's face and Clara's hair, standing out on the porch and looking in as if he were on the precipice of time, not really born yet. He waited shyly out there. Clara looked at him as if he were a stranger. There was only this child between herself and Lowry: without him she would throw some things together and the two of them would run out to his car and drive off, and that would be that. Whatever happened—Canada or no Canada, more babies or not—she would not have given a damn.

But the boy was out there, watching. She said, "Swan, come inside, I'm going to fix up supper."

He hesitated.

"That man's leaving," Clara said.

The boy came inside. He remembered to shut the screen door without letting it slam. His eyes moved carefully, almost shrewdly around the kitchen, as if looking for things out of place. Clara touched his head and let her hand fall a little heavily onto his shoulder. He flinched a little but said nothing. They waited for Lowry to come out. "Did you dig some nice holes?" Clara said. "Did Butch help you?"

He shook his head, no.

Lowry came out. "I'm going to fix up some supper, you stay for it," she said.

"I'm not hungry."

"Everybody's hungry," Clara said. She did not mean her voice to be so harsh and hopeless. Lowry and Swan looked at each other, both of them strangely shy. In Lowry there was something stunned and withheld, in Swan there was the kind of timidity Clara hated in all children, especially boys. "For Christ's sake, people have to eat," she said. "You want something or not?"

"I said no."

She and Swan followed him out onto the back porch. "You got a few more hours before it gets dark," Clara said. "Do you expect to drive far, or. . . ." They kept up this kind of talk in front of the boy, Clara feeling herself pushed forward farther and farther toward that precipice, so that she wanted to scream at Lowry to get out of here before it was too late and everything was ruined. If he said just the right thing, if he looked at her in just the right way—

But he did not know this. If he had known, he might have changed her life; but he was exhausted, he had given up, something had drained out of him and left his face ashen. Instead, he took hold of Swan's chin and bent down to look into his face.

"You ever killed any snakes or things, kid?"

Swan tried to jerk away.

"Let go of him!" Clara cried.

"I just want to ask him: you ever killed anything?"

Swan shook his head no desperately.

"You're lying. I can see in your face you killed something already and you're going to kill lots of things." Lowry's own face twisted into something ugly that might have been there all along, through the years, without him or Clara knowing of it. Clara saw how his mouth changed, how his grayish teeth were bared. "I can see it right there—all the things you're going to kill and step on and walk over."

And he released Swan. He straightened up, stepped back. The boy ran to Clara, too terrified to cry, and she stood without bending to embrace him and watched Lowry walk away. He walked out along the side path to the lane and out along that, taking his time. The last she saw of him wasn't even him, but the dust that rose behind his car as it moved out of sight.

"You forget about him, you hear?" Clara cried. "Don't

you think about him again—he's going and he won't be back! You're going to get things that he could never give you, you're going to get a last name, a real name, and a whole world to live in—not just a patch of a world—You hear me? You hear me?"

She had to be careful or she would go crazy, Clara thought. She had to be careful. The boy's face, drawn and strangely old, seemed to her suddenly the one thing she had to hate, the only thing that had lost her Lowry.

THREE

Swan

1

The man said to be Swan's father had shoulders that stooped a little, as if to minimize their obvious strength. His hair was gray, a mixture of many shades. All his life Swan had been seeing this man, but today, when he looked at him, his vision seemed to blotch, as if trying to protect him from some mysterious injury. He was a child, seven. His vision would pound and tiny nerve-like veins around his eyes pulsed a warning to him, but a warning of what? He was seven now and getting big and had no patience with babyish fears; he himself could measure how fast he had grown this year by the limb of the apple tree he had never been able to reach before.

That morning they had been driven to the man's house many miles from their own, in the man's car. It was a house Swan had never seen before; but he had heard his mother talk about it. Everything was strange and confusing. Revere sat in an old-fashioned chair with a soft scuffed cushion in the parlor of this house and drew Swan to him. Clara said, "Don't be afraid of him, Swan. What's wrong with you?" Revere stared down at the child's blank, frightened face with the look of someone confronted with a message he cannot understand. "See what it is for him to be afraid?" Clara said. "What did I always say? I said it was awful, a shame. Him to be afraid of his father and in his father's house for the first time. . . ."

Swan's face must have shown what he thought of his mother's words; he was embarrassed and angry. His mother knew this but did not care. She was energetic and excited, *she* was afraid of nothing. She had never been in this house before but she looked around, with her calm, narrowly interested gaze, at the furniture that was so heavy and polished and nothing at all like the things in their old house, and she was not afraid. In the very air of this great stone house there was an odor that could never have belonged to their own house—an odor of weight and darkness and time, of things oiled and cared for. At one end of the room there was a great fireplace, big enough for Swan to stand in if he wanted, and above it a mantel with silver candlestick holders on either side. He knew what silver was, more or less. His mother had some silver things. And she had a golden ring and a golden necklace too, gleaming, delicately glittering things that lay so gently against her tanned skin that you might worry about their getting lost or being thrown aside when she was in a hurry. Once she had lost a little heart Revere had given her, and Swan had hunted for it and found it in the weeds by the back door.

But they were in this house now. Clara said, looking around, "Your sister really keeps this nice. Why are those chair legs twisted?"

"That's the way they are."

"Is it supposed to be nice or something?" Clara said. "I mean, is it old, is it an antique?"

"Yes, it's French."

Clara narrowed her eyes. Swan waited to see if she would say she didn't like it, but she went on instead, "That man's nice in that picture there. Where'd you get that?"

"It's a painting of my father."

"Your father?"

Clara jumped up and ran over to the painting. She stood with her hands clasped before her, staring, while Swan and Revere watched. The man in the portrait stared down at her out of a dark cloud of brown that might have been smoke or fog obscuring his body beneath his shoulders. A white, cold light illuminated that face, which put Swan in mind of a sharp, clever dog's face. Clara looked back at Revere, comparing the faces. "He was heavier than you," she said. "Are you going to look like him when you get that age?"

"I'm older than he was when he died right now," Revere said. He made a sound that might have been an embarrassed laugh. Clara drew back her head as if trying to figure this out. She turned to them slowly, carefully, conscious of her new, expensive dress and her long silky legs. She drew her skirt down over her knees when she sat.

"Ah, well," she said, "people live and people die. It keeps on."

She let her legs stretch themselves out. She was lazy and comfortable even today, even in that pale blue dress, while Revere sat stiffly, as if listening for something from upstairs or outside that he was afraid he might hear. He wore a dark suit. He smelled of something harsh—maybe tobacco—while

Clara smelled of the perfume in the amber jar Swan had always loved. He would sneak into her room and hold the jar up to the light to look through it. Through that glass the back yard became mysterious and fluid with a grainy, fragrant light. The ugly old pear tree, dying on one side, became serene and frozen in the glare of that special light—even if there were those pouches of cloudy cocoons filled with worms high up on the tree, it did not matter. Swan could look at them without disgust through that bottle.

"Steven," Revere said, "What is your last name going to be now?"

Swan looked up at him. This man's natural expression was muscularly pleasant; his smiles faded easily into one another. He had big squarish white teeth that seemed to smile too. He was a man who belonged outside, not in this parlor. He had already tried to take Swan hunting with him, out behind Clara's house, and his strides through the grass had drawn him away from Swan, who hurried along nervously and could not look away from the grass for fear he would trip over something and the gun he had would go off. It was out of the high grass the pheasants and quail flew, and their flight terrified Swan so that he had burst into tears. He remembered that.

"Tell him," Clara said, nudging him with her foot. "What's your name going to be? Don't be so shy, kid."

"I don't know," he said.

That was bad, a mistake. He sensed their impatience. "Don't you know?" Revere said. He smiled. "It's Revere. You know that. Say it now—Steven Revere."

There was Clark, and Jonathan, and Robert, and now Steven: all brothers.

"Steven Revere," Swan said softly.

He wished he had another name to blot out this one, to take its place, but he had nothing. His mother always said with a laugh that she had no last name—it was a secret—or better yet, she had forgotten it—she had been kicked out by her father, she said.

"Steven Revere. Steve," the man said slowly. He peered into the child's eyes as if trying to locate himself there. Swan stared up shyly—he had the feeling for a moment that he could love this man if only he wouldn't take him out hunting and make him handle guns and kill things. Why was there always so much confusion and danger with men?

He edged over toward Clara but she was talking to Revere about other things. They talked about people who were coming, about the house, about Revere's sister. Swan, who spoke so little when he was with anyone besides Clara, tried to force the dizzying flood of words and impressions into coherent thoughts—this was all he could do. The only power he had was the power to watch and to listen. His mother could pick things up and toss them out in the garbage; she could slap him, spank him, hug and kiss him; she could yell out the window at some kids crossing through their property; she could sit smoking in the darkened kitchen, smiling at nothing. She was an adult who had power, and because Swan was a child, he had no power. This man here, this kindly man with the strong hands and the urgent, perplexed look—he too had power, the power suggested by this large house and the barns and land behind it, the enormous sweep of cultivated land that belonged to him while so many people owned nothing at all. He could walk confidently across his land and know that he owned it because he was a man, an adult, he possessed the mysterious power of strength that no child possessed, even those boys at school who pushed Swan around. But even those children had no real strength; adults owned them. Everyone was frightened by someone else, Swan thought. It was a thought he did not quite understand.

"Well, what do you think?" Revere said, smoothing down Swan's hair. "You're not worried about the boys, are you? They're good kids. You'll all get along."

"They'd better be nice to him," Clara said.

"They won't bother him," Revere said. "They're good kids."

"I know what kids are like. . . ."

"Don't worry him, Clara. You know better than that, Steven," Revere said, leaning to him, "you know your mother will take care of you. There's nothing to be worried about. It's just that now we're going to live together in one house. We've been waiting a long time for this. And you'll have three brothers to play with—you won't be alone any more."

"He never was alone," Clara said.

Swan knew these "brothers." His terror of them was based on the fact that they had never spoken to him but only looked at him. They were big—ten, twelve, and fifteen—and had their father's heavy squarish shoulders, the dark hair, and the dark quiet blue eyes. They seemed to be waiting for him to speak, to do something. The times Revere had brought them to meet Swan, Revere had done all the talking and even Clara had been silent. Revere had talked about them hunting together, fishing, playing with the horses. He had talked about doing chores together. He had talked about school. . . .

But the boys had said nothing except what was dragged out of them by Revere and those words had no meaning.

"Look, everything will be fine. You know that," Revere said to Clara.

She shrugged her shoulders but she smiled. She had taken out a cigarette and now she leaned forward so that Revere could light it; Swan, forgotten for the moment, watched in fascination the burning match and the tiny flickering glow at the end of the cigarette, as if he had never seen these things before. He wanted to pay attention to every small thing in order to keep time going slowly, because something important was going to happen that day and he was afraid of it.

"It isn't good for boys to be . . . without a mother," Revere was saying.

Swan had always watched people closely when they were around his mother. He saw how they caught from her a certain catlike easiness, no matter what anger they had brought with them. Even this big Revere, with his squarish jaw and his wide, lined, intelligent forehead, was squinting at her now as if something misty and dazzling had passed between him and Clara. Swan looked quickly at his mother as if to see what it was that Revere saw in her; but he did not see it, not exactly. His mother smiled at him, showing her teeth. It was a special smile, for him. It told him, right in front of this man whose big hands could have hurt them both, that they were here at last, here they were, what good luck!

"I know what you need around here," Clara said. "Some windows open and some airing-out. Some of this old stuff cleaned, right? What's that thing you're sitting on, honey? I can see the dust in it, eating right down. Doesn't your sister care about the place?"

"She isn't well," Revere said clumsily. Swan saw how the man's gaze faltered; Clara must have been frowning. "It's only been a month since the funeral, after all. She just hasn't gotten over it yet—they were like sisters."

Swan looked at the man's shoes: black stiff-looking shoes without any mud on them, not even a faint rim of dried mud around the very bottom.

"They were a lot alike," Clara said softly. "People said so. Your sister is older than—than your wife, though." The child stood between them, listening. He took everything too seriously and had not learned to laugh; he knew that, didn't his mother tell him so every day? But he had the idea that he must watch and listen carefully. He must learn. Living was a game with rules he had to learn for himself by watching these adults as carefully as possible. There had been one other adult in his life—not the schoolteacher, who didn't count, but one other man, almost lost in his memory, a strange blonde man who had touched him and who had vanished. . . . Once in a while he found himself thinking about that man, trying to remember what that man had said to him. But it was fuzzy and lost. He had been too young. Now the memory of that other man, awakened by Revere's attention, swept down upon him like one of the big chicken hawks everyone hated, with its dusty flapping wings and its scrawny legs, and Swan could almost smell the fetid odor of that breath. ("Never say a word about him," Clara had told him, just once. She did not have to tell Swan things twice.)

"Look—Esther was like a sister to her too, not just to me," Revere was saying. Swan knew that their attention had moved completely away from him; he was relieved. "Out in the country like this, and not ever getting married—she liked Marguerite better than she liked me, really. She never caused any trouble. She never came between us. But she has nowhere to go now, she's too proud to ask anyone. The house is just as much hers as mine—"

Clara made a disgusted sound.

"Our father left it to us both."

"Who keeps it going? Who has the money?" Clara said breathlessly.

"She has money of her own, that's not it. I don't care about that. Anyway, she doesn't want to live in Hamilton, she doesn't like it there and I don't blame her. She doesn't like my uncle. My sister and I have never really been close, but. . . ."

"How she must hate me!" Clara said.

"She doesn't hate you, Clara."

"She never told you?"

"No one ever said anything, all these years."

"They were afraid of you, that's the only reason. But they hated me anyway and they'll always hate me. Are they really coming today?"

"Yes."

"Every one of them? Really? The women too—Judd's wife too?" Clara said greedily.

"They do what I ask them to."

Swan sensed something brittle and dangerous in the air about them. A faint warning began in his stomach, as it did when he was inching out on ice, but his mother must have

256

felt nothing, for she went on teasingly, "Your wife didn't do what you asked."

Revere shook his head. "That's finished."

"If she'd done what you wanted," Clara said, "you and I would be married now. Not like this, with the kid seven years old and us going to be married finally—what a laugh! But no, no, you can't budge a woman like her. From a good family with a good German name, is she going to give a divorce to a man to make him happy? Never! She's going to sit tight with her nails dug in you to keep you as long as possible."

Clara made a vague spitting gesture; then, to soften the movement, she frowned and picked a piece of tobacco off her tongue. "So your kid here has to be taught his last name, and he's afraid of you. Your own boy afraid of you. Are you proud?"

"No, I'm not proud."

"Men are always proud, they think more of that than anything. But not women," Clara said. She crossed her legs. The blue silk dress was drawn tight about her thighs in tiny veinlike wrinkles. She had lean, smooth legs; because she was wearing stockings today the curve of her calves was not shiny as usual. "Women have no pride. They do what men want them to do, like me, and to hell with it. If some bastards turn their nose up at me, let them. I never asked for any of them to like me."

"After today everything will be all right," Revere said. "The past is over. Marguerite is dead. I can't think anything bad of her now."

"I don't think bad of her either," Clara said quickly. She had the look Swan sometimes saw on her face when she was about to throw something down in disgust. "I don't think bad of the dead. She was a good woman to give you three sons—I don't think bad of anybody dead. I never knew her. And when I'm dead myself I won't give a damn if they're still talking about me."

"After today it will be different," Revere said.

Clara smiled a smile that could mean anything: that he was right, that he was wrong.

Today was a holiday; his mother was going to be married. Swan knew all about it. She had told him the night before that nothing really would be changed and he shouldn't worry; she was doing this for him. "We're going to live in a nice big house, not like this, and there's even a woman to help in the kitchen—think of that! And Revere, he likes you so. He loves you. We're all going to live together starting tomorrow. How will you like that?"

Swan said, "I'll like it," but he meant that he would like it if she did. It was clear his mother liked the idea. She liked everything. If something in the house made her angry she would break it or throw it out, if the dog bothered her she'd chase it away, but nothing had the power to disturb her. Nothing could get that far into her. It was like the mosquitoes that bit Swan out in the fields—he would watch anxiously as the little white swelling formed, sometimes in strange shapes, but after a while they just flattened out and disappeared. Things touched his mother like that, just on the outside of her skin. That was why she could move so quickly from place to place and why she had time to comb out her long hair, slowly and fondly, while other women always worked. Swan knew a few boys from school and he knew that their mothers worked all the time. His mother had her own car and drove it anywhere she wanted, to town or anywhere. She had nice clothes and she liked to stand in front of the mirror and look at herself. Her hair was pale, almost white, and sometimes it lay down on her shoulders and past, straight and fine; but sometimes she had it twisted up somehow on her head in a way Swan did not like. He liked her careless and easy, running barefoot through the house, swearing at him for doing something wrong or muttering to herself about work she had to do; he liked her hands gesturing and arguing in silence, and her face screwed up into an expression of bewilderment as she tried to decide something—with her tongue prodding her cheeks and circling around to the front of her teeth, hard, as if Swan were not there watching her. Swan felt that he could spend his life hurrying after his mother, picking up things she had dropped and setting right things that she almost knocked over, and catching from her little grunted remarks that he must remember because she might forget. Now, sitting on this strange couch in a dim, airless parlor, she stared past Swan to Revere with that look of vacuity—her blond hair thick about her head, pulled up in a great swelling mass and fastened with innumerable pins, her neat, arched eyebrows rigid with thought, her eyelashes thick and confused—and Swan had a moment of terror in which he thought that she would not remember this man's name and that she would lose everything she had almost won.

But of course she would not lose. She began to smile, slowly. "Yes. After today it will be different. I'm really going to be your wife, and when I think of that nothing else matters."

Revere smiled nervously, laughed a short, breathless laugh. He was staring at Clara.

Swan looked down at Revere's shoes. He resented them not thinking of him, not even remembering he was there. He was getting big now. He noticed things more than ever. That strange straight look of Revere's, directed right toward Clara—he noticed that look and it made him want to close his own eyes.

"You hear that, Swan? Nothing else matters," Clara said. She leaned forward to embrace him. "Your father will take care of you and will change your life—my little Swan will grow up like his father and be big and strong and rich—"

"Why do you call him that, Clara?"

"I like that name, that's my name for him."

"What's wrong with Steven?"

"Steven is his name on the paper, but I call him something else. So what?" Clara said. "I saw in this magazine a man named Robin, he was a movie star, so handsome, so much money—that was when I was pregnant—and I thought of what I would call the baby if it was a boy. I would call him Swan because I saw some swans once in a picture, those big white birds that swim around—they look real cold, they're not afraid of anything, their eyes are hard like glass. On a sign it said they were dangerous sometimes. So that's better than calling a kid Robin, I thought, because a swan is better than a robin. So I call him that."

"They call him Steven at school."

"Sure—what do I care what they call him?" Clara said. "I call him Swan. Nobody else can call him that."

There was a moment of silence. "The kids call me Steve," Swan said.

"Steve. Steven. I like that name," Revere said. "That's the name I picked. God, it's been a long time, hasn't it? All those years—"

"He's seven years old. Yes, it was a long time."

"I didn't think it would ever happen—you coming here finally—"

"You mean her dying. It took her so long to die," Clara said. She rubbed her cheek against Swan's and it was so strange: that she could feel and smell so soft but be so blunt. Swan closed his eyes and smelled her perfume, wishing they were both back in their house, safe, alone, just the two of them. Only she and Swan really lived there, not Revere. That house wasn't much, and sometimes animals crawled under it to die—but Swan liked it better than this big dark house with the rock on the outside. What if lightning struck it and all those rocks fell in on them while they slept . . . ? "It was a hell of a thing. After we're married we won't say anything about it, huh?" Clara whispered. "Because then I'll be in her place and it would be bad luck. In her bed. But right now I can say that it was a hell of a thing. I wanted her to die, but—but I wouldn't really want anybody to die, you know? I just wanted to be with you. I couldn't stop thinking about it even if it was bad, in my dreams I thought of her gone off somewhere and me with you in this house—and Swan with us, like now—with his own father like a boy should be. I couldn't help that. Is that my fault, that I dreamt those things? Is that bad of me?"

He took her hands as if to comfort her. "We both wanted the same thing," he said.

"But look, I don't like anybody to die!" Clara said. "I don't want to be married with that behind me, I'm not like that. It was love that got me into this. I fell in love with you. I didn't ask for that, did I? Did I want somebody else's husband? And your poor wife, what could she do? None of us asked for this, it just happened. She had to die thinking of me all the time, and when you came home to her from me, what did she think? Christ, that's awful! I'd kill any man that did that to me. . . . What could I do to make it any easier for her? I fell in love and that was that. . . ."

She was staring up into Revere's face. She was both passionate and submissive and there was something urgent, something straining in her voice. They sat in silence for a while. Then Revere muttered, "I know, I know. . . ." He looked at Swan and seemed just now to remember him. A slight coloring came to his cheeks. He said nervously, "It's getting time. Esther must be ready by now, and. . . ."

"Where are your kids?" Clara said.

"Outside."

"Outside all this time? Why don't they come in and wait?"

"They'll be all right, Clara. Don't worry about it."

They took Swan upstairs, the two of them walking on ahead and talking about something in their new rapid, hushed voices. Clara, in this house, had already taken on the characteristic of walking with her back very straight and her head bowed, nodding in agreement with whatever Revere said, whether she really agreed with it or not. "I spent my nights in here when I was home," Swan heard Revere say to Clara.

"She was sick then. . . . Steven," he said turning, "This is going to be your room. Come here." He came. He looked into the room and his mouth went dry at the thought of it, a room of his own in this house, with its smooth empty walls and the window at the end with a curtain on it. After today he would be alone. He would sleep here alone and the door would be closed on him. If he had a bad dream he could not run in to Clara; she already belonged to someone else.

"What's this, one of the kid's rooms?" Clara said, opening a door. She looked inside briefly, as if all rooms now were hers to look into. Revere walked along the hall just ahead of her. He tapped at another door and said that that was Clark's room. At the end of the hall he opened a door and Swan's legs worked fast to get him to the door before Revere forgot about him and closed it again, leaving Swan alone out in the hall. "Is that—where we're going to stay?" Clara said, pleased. She looked in and seemed to hesitate, her back very stiff. Revere was saying that all "her" things had been taken out and the room had been painted; it was all new, all clean. Clara nodded. Swan stood a few feet behind them, unable to see past them. He did not care. This was to be the room they would live in and the door would close on it, and he would not be able to run in if he was frightened. He did not care about it. As Revere talked, Swan saw behind this tall dark-haired man another man, vague and remote but somehow more vivid than Revere, whose presence seemed to be descending over this house like a bird circling slowly to the earth, its wings outstretched in a lazy threat. Revere talked, Clara talked. They spoke in quick, low voices, as if someone might still be in that room listening to them. Swan half shut his eyes and could almost hear the voice of that other man, that man who was a secret from Revere and who had gone away and had never come back. . . .

A woman was waiting for them at the stairs. Swan had never seen her before. His eyes shied away from adults, as the eyes of animals sometimes refuse to focus upon human eyes, out of a strange uneasy fear; he felt that this woman's eyes also shied away from him and Clara both. She was introduced to Clara and the two women touched hands. She was an old woman, much older than Clara, so old that just looking at Clara must be awful for her. They talked fast. Both women nodded, and Revere nodded.

"—your Aunt Esther," Revere was saying to him.

Everyone smiled. Swan smiled too. He wanted to like this woman, this Esther, because she had the look of a woman nobody else liked. She was tall and gaunt with a face like Revere's, but older, narrowed, and her hair was white and thin so that Swan could see the stark white line of her scalp where her hair had been parted. This white line and the way her gaze dropped, nervously, made Swan understand that she had no power. She was an adult but she did not have any power.

"—Judd should be here, and the boys—the boys are outside," she said breathlessly.

"Don't tire yourself out, Esther," Revere said.

The old woman's hands were like leaves stirred restlessly by the wind. You would think they were at last going to lie still, they were so limp, but then they would begin to move again in jerks and surges they could not control.

"Let me go in the room for a minute," Clara said. "Are they outside already? Are they here? I have to fix my hair—"

"Clara, you look fine—"

"No, I have to fix it," she said nervously. She turned, and Swan was afraid for a second that she would forget and leave him here with these strangers. But she glanced back and said, "Come with me, kid. We'll both be downstairs in a minute." She took his hand and they hurried down the hall together. They left Revere and the old woman behind, and outside a dog was barking, which meant someone was driving up, but when Clara pulled him away he was all alone with her and they were like conspirators together. "You got something on your face—what the hell is that?" she whispered. "Christ, what a dirty kid!"

She opened the door to that room and went right inside. She went right in, pulling Swan with her, and closed the door behind her as if she had been doing this all her life. A big, sunny room. The walls had been covered with light green paper and there were silver streaks in it that dazzled Swan's eyes. "Silk wallpaper, what do you think of that," Clara said. There were four great windows with filmy white curtains that distorted the land outside and made it dreamy and vague; the curtains moved gently in the wind. Clara stood for a moment in the middle of the room, breathing quickly.

Then she said, "Where's that hairbrush? Goddam it—" She picked up a little suitcase that had been set inside the door and let it fall onto the bed and opened it. Swan wandered around the room, staring. He went to the windows first. His own window, back home, looked out on the back yard and that was all—everything ran back to a scrawny field and ended. He could not see the horizon. Here, so high in the air, he could see the fields and a big woods far away. He was not high enough to see the borderline of mountains, but, in this house, he knew they were there and for the first time he felt pleasure in this knowledge. He leaned against the window and looked down. An automobile had driven up. People were getting out. Two dogs ran at them, barking with joy.

"Oh, here it is," Clara said angrily.

Swan did not turn to look at her. He touched the window sill; it had warped a little from rain. When you looked closely at the room you saw things like that. There were a few brown water stains in the ceiling, like clouds—nothing anyone else would bother to look at, only Swan. And the big bureau that looked fine and polished, that had some scratches on it; he saw them too.

"Come over here, will you? You want to fall out that window?" Clara said. That showed she hadn't been watching him—he could not fall out the window, Swan thought with disgust. "I got to fix you up. You want to look better than his kids, don't you?"

She wet her finger and rubbed his forehead. Swan submitted without struggle. This room was fresh and sunny, not like the corridor outside and the parlor downstairs; and he had caught a glimpse of the big kitchen with its iron stove and wooden table—that had looked gloomy too. But up here, in this room that would belong to his mother and Revere, everything was fresh. There were even yellow flowers in a vase on the bureau.

"Did somebody die in here?" Swan said.

"His wife died in here a month ago," Clara said. "So here we are." She smiled a half-angry ironic smile at him. "Now, don't worry about anything. Do what I tell you. If they make trouble for you, tell me about it first, don't tell *him*—men don't like that. Tell me if those little bastards bother you. I know what kids are like, I had brothers of my own. Kids are all alike. But you, you're different. You're going to take everything away from them someday and kick them out of this house, so what the hell if they push you around now? Remember that. Someday you'll get back at him—you'll be his best son."

"I don't want to be," Swan said sullenly.

"The hell you don't," Clara said, yanking his hair. "Do what I say. Keep your mouth shut. Why do you think I'm here, except for you?" He stared at her. He was afraid she would say something terrible that she would not be able to get unsaid again. He felt panic for his mother, suddenly. How could she make her way among these people without being afraid? What if she lost everything after coming so far? "What the hell are you looking at?" she said, drawing back from him. She went to the bureau mirror and looked at herself. Automatically her hand came up and patted the back of her head, caressing the hair as if it were something fragile that might break. The image in the mirror seemed to be leaning toward her. Blond hair, tanned, healthy skin, a blur of eyes and lashes, and parted lips about to say something—Swan's heart began to pound in terror for her.

"So we got here after all these years, what the hell is wrong with you?" she said angrily. Her eyes were suddenly sharp, staring at him through the mirror. "You look like you're going to puke or something."

"I . . . I don't like it here," Swan said.

"You'll like it," she said in a soft, dangerous voice.

She threw the hairbrush down on the floor. A nerve near Swan's eye jerked at the noise. "You'll like it. You'll like it, goddam you," Clara whispered. Swan had seen her cry many times—she began to cry now. Her face got harder and harder and her lips parted. It seemed that she was crying because of what he had said, but he knew she was not. When she cried it was not for him. Sometimes she slapped him in disgust, sometimes she embraced him, but she did not really notice him. She cried only for herself.

"What could I do, what else? I don't mind waiting for something like this. That money! All this land! Gypsum mines—wheat—he's got horses, for God's sake, horses you just look at or ride around on and don't do work with. What was I to do, what else? Don't look at me like that with your goddam eyes! When we go to the minister's this morning and he marries us, you're getting a new father. You're getting a name. That much I'm doing for you; all your life you'll be a Revere!"

She was walking back and forth before the mirror, her arms at her sides, muttering. Swan wondered if she remembered him. He saw the familiar hot tears, and the bulge of a vein at her throat. . . . it was all so strange, her dressed in that blue dress and her legs silky and smooth, the legs of a lady in a magazine. . . .

Someone knocked at the door, too loud. "Clara? Can I come in?"

"Wait a minute, just a minute," she said. "I'm fixing my dress, I'll be right down to meet them——"

"Can I come in?"

"Oh, all right. . . ."

He opened the door and came shyly in. Clara turned to him with her face twisted, still crying, and Swan wondered why she had done it—why had she let him in? Was she going to tell him the secret she and Swan had? "Clara?" he said. His stooped shoulders, his lifted hands, his stiff-legged walk as if he were in the presence of something sacred—these made Swan love and hate him at the same time.

"Steven, go outside. Wait outside," Revere said.

"Yes, go out. Go out!" Clara cried.

Swan stared at her as if trying to get her into focus. He did not see Revere. He had not even understood her words, but he thought he understood that look. "Get out, get out!" she hissed, gesturing him away with quick, nervous jerks of her hand. He backed to the door. It seemed to him that as soon as he left, the two of them would change—Revere's stiff look and Clara's arched, poised impatience.

He left. If it was a trick of hers she would call him back, but she had not yet called him back. He pulled the door to behind him, quietly. He was in the hall. Swan did not turn around to look at the closed door but walked fast along the hall, getting away from the door, staring at a window at the far end. He did not want to hear anything behind him in that room. He pressed his hands against his ears, so that he could not have listened if he wanted to. He pressed his hands tighter. Something began to throb and pound.

At the window the sun was blazing; he could hardly see the sky around it. Everything was hot and still except for the throbbing in his ears. He would not be able to run to her in the night now, because she would never be alone again. That man would always be with her. They would close the door the way they'd closed it at the other house, but this time it would really never open again. And his "brothers" would be waiting for him. . . .

With his hands still pressing hard against his ears, he shut his eyes and leaned against the window. An odor of soap, paint. Everything was clean in this house and he hated it. He could hear and see nothing, and yet that void was filled with jiggling, dancing stars and a roaring sound that was worse than any sounds he might overhear through a door.

"You're going to take everything away from them some-day!" Clara had told him. Her words awakened in him other words, but he could not quite remember them. That was going to happen, yes. He would make it happen, he thought.

Because he would know all along what he had to do while his "brothers" would know nothing. He would wait and he would grow up. Having watched adults for so many years, he knew he would grow up soon—in his brain he was already older than Clark, even. Nothing could stop him.

He took his fingers away from his ears and opened his eyes: maybe Clara had called him. But there was nothing.

And he knew the adult he would grow into: not Revere, but someone else. That other man had a face Swan could almost see but he did not worry about not quite seeing it, because he would recognize it if he saw it again and in any case he would grow into it without trying. One day that man had come up the drive and Clara's face had had gently bluish circles under her eyes, and Swan had wanted to cry out in terror at how Clara changed just in the instant when she saw that man—no one, no one anywhere, had such power over Clara as that man. Swan would not have believed anyone could do that to her. And there he was, and there he stood, and later on he had gone off again and Clara had been trembling violently . . . no one was able to do that to Clara.

So Swan understood. Revere was going to be his father, but his real father was someone else. He felt that suddenly. He and his mother had a secret no one could make them tell. He would die with that secret. He would protect his mother from anyone who threatened her, he would never tell, never, he would grow up and take care of her and do everything she wanted and even Clara herself would never know that he knew. He had years to do it in. He would take his time. There were sounds outside, maybe another car driving up, and dogs barking—and Swan looked down as if surprised that there was land beneath him, ordinary sloping land. For a moment he was confused, called back from the depthless land of the sky to this hard, familiar ground. There was an excitement in him that was like breathing in the glare of the sun itself, something too big and too strong for him but filling all the same.

In his lifetime he could do anything.

2

That morning Swan had not been able to sleep much past dawn. He lay awake listening to the crows outside. Their harsh, frightened cries were close by, they might have been

266

mixed up with his sleeping. He thought, We are going to a funeral today. All the way to the city for a funeral. The sound of the word, which he whispered to himself, mixed in with the crows outside that must be rearing and darting up out of the orchard below. Outside, in the fields and the woods, all the creatures were like that—they started up for no reason, they stared at you with hard bright terrified eyes, paralyzed with fear or beating the air with their wings or tearing blindly through the bush, anything to get away. Swan listened to the crows, whose cries were fainter now. They kept moving from one field to another, on and on, and maybe the same crows came back the next day, but who could tell? He wondered why all the birds and animals were so afraid.

In the two years he and Clara had been in this house there had been funerals but Swan had not gone to them. Clark had gone to all of them—he was seventeen now, a big boy. Jonathan had gone to one. Swan and Robert had stayed home that time and waited, almost friends with the thought of funeral and death to bring them together; but when everyone came back Robert had forgotten about him. Today, he thought, he would be riding all the way to Hamilton in the front seat of the car, between his mother and Revere; he would have the best seat in the car. He knew this would happen. Only Jonathan and Robert bothered to quarrel over places in the car any more, and most of the time Jonathan didn't really care. But Swan knew that Clara would have him sit up front with her, and the three boys could ride behind, whether they liked it or not. Aunt Esther would be too old to go, again. She couldn't ride in the car because the car made her heart flutter.

The crows had awakened him, and he carried the shrill surprise of their calls along in his head, downstairs to breakfast. Every morning they ate breakfast in the big kitchen. Revere sat at one end of the table and Clara at the other, and when Aunt Esther was well enough she sat somewhere in the middle; this morning she did not come down. Revere sat drumming his fingers on the table, thinking. His hair was damp from combing; it looked a little thin. Swan watched him. He sat quietly. "If somebody steals that muskrat trap I'm gonna know who it is," Robert said to Jonathan sourly. "Yeah?" Jonathan said. He was fourteen now, a narrow-faced, dark boy with blemished skin and not enough weight on his arms and legs. He sat across the table from Swan and never looked at him. Now he was drawing his lips back to make a face at Robert, counting on his father not bothering to look. But at the last instant his face went blank, meaning that Revere had looked. The boys were silent. Clark sat closest to the stove, watching Clara. She wore the heavy pink robe, made of silk, that Revere had bought for the boys to give her on Christmas morning. It was quilted and there was a deep pink bow at the neck. Swan liked to hear the sound of breakfast food frying and he liked to smell it; it was mixed up with the smell that Clara had about her, sometimes powdery and sometimes like the back garden where she worked.

"When Mandy comes I'll have her take something up to Esther," Clara said. She leaned back against the stove, waiting for the eggs to fry. She yawned. "I feel sorry for Esther."

"She always was sick," Clark said.

Jonathan opened his mouth in a sideways motion, as if he were about to say something that could not be said out straight. But he stayed quiet.

"Lots of women are like that," Clark said. "It ain't just because they're old. How come you ain't like that?"

Clara smiled but Revere said, "You'd better be quiet."

Clark's face reddened slightly. He was a big thick-shouldered boy, almost as big as his father. Swan thought of him as a man. There was something heavy and swerving in him, the same idle lumbering gait you might see in bulls that are safely penned. "I didn't mean nothing bad," Clark said, puzzled.

Revere did not reply. He sat staring toward the window, but whether he was looking out, Swan could not tell. He was dressed to go already, with a white shirt and necktie and a dark coat that made him look like one of the salesmen who sometimes drove up the lane in the summer, braving the dogs to get at Clara with their suitcases filled with polishes and brushes. The nicer she was, the more things she bought, the more salesmen would come the following week; it was as if all the salesmen worked for the same place and knew one another.

"If it's too crowded in the car I could ride with Uncle Judd," Jonathan said. His eyes narrowed slightly as he said this; he looked sideways down the table to his father.

"We will have enough room," Revere said.

"Yeah, but—"

"We will all ride in the same car."

Swan sat with his elbows on the table and watched his mother. In the long thick robe she looked lazy and slow, but

268

at a certain moment she would begin moving quickly, lifting the pan, stirring the eggs with a fork. If she made a mistake and something burned, she would let the pan clatter onto the burner and suck in her breath sharply. Swan hoped she wouldn't make a mistake this morning and say "damn" or "hell." This would bring Revere's eyes around fast from the window, and this morning it would be all wrong, this wasn't the morning for it. "Mrs. Taylor, that's the one in Tintern, she's always sick or something," Clark said. "I feel real sorry for Sammy. He has to take off from work and drive her to the doctor and there ain't nothing wrong with her, anybody can see that."

Everyone was silent. Swan guessed by the silence that Clark was saying something wrong; he was maybe making them think of something they shouldn't. Even Robert, sitting with his head bowed a little, said nothing. Jonathan's sneer was fastened onto the table right in front of him, a small spot he wouldn't look away from. Whenever there was this silence it meant that they were thinking of their mother, who was dead. She had been dead now for two years and more, and they never talked about her, never, except Esther, who sometimes said her name in such a way that Revere would draw his breath in slowly and painfully, but he was always too polite to tell her to stop. The boys did not mention her. They all went to see her grave, the boys and Revere too, but Swan and Clara did not have to go. Swan did not understand why no one would talk about that woman—what was wrong? Clara just shrugged her shoulders. "That's their business," she would say. It could be like groping around with your foot on an iced-over pond, these times when they were together: if you said the wrong thing you fell through and no one would help you. Clark was always saying the wrong thing, old as he was, and the rest of them pretended they didn't hear.

Clara yawned again at the stove. She shook her hair out about her face in a gesture that meant the tension was over; she smiled and said apologetically in that way of hers that meant she was pleased with herself anyway, "I feel so sleepy, I didn't sleep right last night. All kinds of things went through my head."

"You should have waited for Mandy to do breakfast," Revere said. He spoke gently. When his voice came out gentle you knew it was aimed toward Clara. Jonathan looked down at his plate and smirked, just a little. That was the way he smirked when he whispered "bastard" to Swan as they were filing in their pew at church or when he passed by

269

Swan's desk at school. At other times, when no grownups were around and everything was open, just when you would think he might say anything, he did not even bother looking at Swan.

Swan thought that if Jonathan liked him, then everything would be all right—Robert did what Jonathan told him to, liked what Jonathan liked. Clark was too old to count. He maybe even liked Swan, but he never paid any attention to him. He was out of school now and working for Revere somewhere in town; he had his own car. Robert was using muskrat traps that belonged to Clark and Clark didn't even know about it, that was how much he cared. Swan watched Jonathan, waiting patiently for the boy to look at him.

"Don't worry, Clara. He was an old man and everyone expected this to happen," Revere said.

This made them uncomfortable, when Revere talked to Clara as if the boys weren't around. Even Swan felt it. But he felt most uncomfortable because Revere talked about things that Clara wasn't even thinking of, and what if she gave herself away by looking surprised? She was working at the stove, not really bothering to listen. She was placing tiny sausages on paper napkins to soak up the grease. When she turned and brought his breakfast to him first of all, before any of the others, he felt a lurch of his heart that was hunger and pride at the same time. "Eat it all, you're going on a long ride," Clara said, touching his head. Sunlight flooded the room and lit up the burnished pans that hung on the opposite wall on pegs worked into the brick. Behind Swan there was a big window, a new long window like the kind Clara had seen in newspaper and magazine advertisements: and one day this "picture" window had been put in so that they could all see outside. Clara had wanted that window for quite a while. She had made curtains for it herself, bright yellow curtains with flowers on them. She had made curtains for the living room out of a thin gauzy white material with red dots in it, and Aunt Esther had begun to cry. The old woman had stood in the doorway to the living room, crying, until Clara had taken the curtains down, her face flushed and angry. Swan did not understand why. He had thought the curtains were nice. Like Clara, he had felt pushed and herded around just by that old woman's helpless sobbing, and it was strange, but at that moment when Clara had given in, who had the most power, Clara or Esther? But Clara had all the old furniture up in the attic. It was too "old-fashioned," she said. They had a long low modern sectional that was mint green; Clara had seen it advertised on the back of the Sunday comic pages.

They ate breakfast. Swan felt a strange excitement in his stomach. The funeral was something special, a long ways away, but going there would be important too. He had never been all the way to Hamilton. And how did you look, how did you act at a funeral? Robert and Jonathan leaned over their plates as if they were starved for Clara's food, and grinned with their mouths full and poked one another if they saw their father wasn't looking, just as they did every morning. Clark ate fast. He was always hungry. He was not worrying about the funeral or anything else. Clara, her hair still down and her eyes still sleepy, was thinking about nothing. She happened to see Robert reaching over to pinch Jonathan and said, "Better sit still, kid."

This was a mistake: it made Revere look up. "What is he doing?" Revere said.

"Oh, nothing," said Clara.

"What's going on?"

"Nothing," Robert said nervously.

Robert had clear skin and eyes that were flecked with hazel; he was the nicest looking of the three Revere boys, but something about him made Swan think of a rabbit, a fattened rabbit locked up in a pen. Swan liked Robert and when they were alone they talked together. They played together. It was only when Jonathan came along that everything was changed. Walking to school, Robert and Jonathan were together even when Swan walked right beside them, and even when they did not speak for a long time. There was always something that kept Swan apart and he could not understand it. It wasn't just that he was the youngest, or that he was afraid—he had wept when Jonathan threw rocks at a squirrel one day, killing it—but it seemed to have something to do with his fair skin, his fair hair. He waited always for Jonathan to look at him and to talk to him. He would be patient. Now he caught Robert's eye and saw that Robert was afraid of Revere, and he was glad that they had this fear in common.

"Sit still at the table," Revere said to Robert.

"He wasn't doing nothing," Jonathan said.

There was silence. Revere lowered his fork. Nobody talked back to Revere and at the table the boys said only certain careful things; most of the time they were silent. Revere stared at Jonathan until he squirmed in his chair.

But the moment passed and Clara began to talk. They

listened to her talk without exactly hearing her words. Her voice addressed itself to Revere but was for all of them; she leaned over the table, her coffee cup in her hand, and talked—about Aunt Esther, about Mandy who was always late, about the back garden, the trip to Hamilton, anything. Two years ago, when they were new to this house, Swan had sensed something strange in Revere and the boys when Clara talked. They seemed to be straining to listen, leaning forward to catch something in her voice. She just talked, chatted, she did not think. Jonathan had said once, "Why does your mother talk so much?" His mouth had been mean and spiteful, like a mouth about to twist into a sob. But Jonathan always listened too, his ears reddening, and if Clara touched him when she took his plate he would remain still, holding his breath; if she fussed over him his eyes would narrow until they were almost closed. Once, when he had cut his hand, Clara had made a bandage for it, and he had sat with a queer dreamy smile while she fixed it on his hand, saying nothing, as if he liked the pain he felt. Swan had seen that. When Clara spoke to Jonathan her words went in just one direction and kept going; Jonathan did not acknowledge them. At night sometimes Swan thought of this and wondered why Jonathan hated him and his mother. He thought that if he knew the answer to that, he would be able to change Jonathan and make him happy.

Mandy came in when they were finished in time for the dishes. She was a short heavy woman, older than Revere but not as old as Esther, who lived in an old house that was just a shanty, a mile away. Her hair was thick and greasy, wound about her head as if she wanted to hide it, not bunched out and up the way Clara's would be when she fixed it. Swan sometimes heard her mutter to herself. She paid no attention to him, as if he were just a neighbor boy hanging around. Of the boys, she liked only Robert, but since he was getting bigger she seemed to forget who he was from time to time; she kept them all out of the kitchen. "When are y'all coming home," she said without interest. Her arms hung loose and ready for work, her big hands restless by her sides. Swan was a little afraid of her. "Probably this evening," Revere said. "If Esther wants anything bring it up to her. Then you can leave."

Her face did not indicate that she had heard this. She stood by the sink, her arms waiting, and it was as if they'd already left—she did not look at them.

"There's some grease in the pan there," Clara said. She

272

shot this woman a hard sideways glance; Swan knew that Clara hated her. "Don't save it, I don't want it around. I don't want it in the refrigerator. It makes me sick to look at it."

"That's good grease."

"The hell with it, good grease. It makes me sick to look at it."

"All right."

"Throw it outside or something, but get rid of it. Don't pour it down the drain."

"All right, Mrs. Revere."

Clara paused at that, focusing her gaze upon something past Swan's face. But the hesitation lasted only a moment. Then she rose and put down the coffee cup, slowly, her heavy sleeve falling down her arm all the way to the wrist. "I wish we didn't have to go," she said to Revere.

"Nobody likes funerals, Clara."

Back at the sink the woman waited for them to get out. Swan hated her because of the way she looked at Clara, or didn't look at her. He would have liked to say to her, You're ugly! You're old! You never were like her! You don't know what it's like to be her. . . .

Before they left, Judd and his wife drove in, just for a moment. They stayed in their car and talked with Revere. Swan was already sitting in the car. It was a new car and the boys were all proud of it. In the back seat the three brothers talked about something. The smell of the new car—a mysterious, sharp, leathery smell—was made stronger by the coolness of the day. Swan listened to the boys behind him and to the adults a few yards away, trying to saturate himself in the ordinariness of everything they were saying. He did not want to let the excitement he felt get too strong. It was bad of him to feel this way when someone had just died. When anyone died you were sorry for it, no matter who he was and no matter how far from you he was. If you felt excitement it had to be kept hidden.

He thought the word "funeral." He was going to a funeral. Then Judd drove off, waving at Swan and the boys. Swan liked Judd but he did not like Judd's wife. Judd swung his car around and passed quite close to Revere's car, so that Swan could see his wife looking out at them—a luminous pinkish face, fair, nearly invisible lashes about her eyes, the mouth pursed and set, and around all this a strange black hat that fitted her head like an old-fashioned stovepipe. Her face and her body were plump, with the suggestion of blood pulsing close beneath the skin, but her eyes and mouth gave the impression of something rigidly doll-like and rubbery.

"She's a bitch," Clara was saying. "She's a goddam bitch, never even looks at me." Clara opened the car door for herself and got in next to Swan. She brought an air of the outdoors and of anger in with her. Whenever they sat three in the front, Clara always pushed him over, no matter how much room he had made for her to begin with. She pushed him a little now, settling down. Revere was outside by her door, holding it open as if he had opened it himself; now he closed it gently.

Swan heard one of the boys behind them make a short, humorless noise with his mouth.

Clara looked around. Her lips were parted. Swan felt danger for her, some strange hesitating fear he could never understand, when she turned so openly to people who hated her and did not seem to know what she might see. The powdery, soft odor of her clothes filled the car, thinning out the leathery smell. Her hair had been brushed out and piled up, fastened in an elaborate knot. She wore a blue hat with a soft brim that was bent down irregularly about her face, nothing like Judd's wife's hat, but none of this could protect her. She said, in a voice they didn't expect, "Are you all set for the ride?"

"I'm gonna maybe sleep," Clark said. "If I can't drive I hate going places."

"If you want to drive—"

"No, it's all right," Clark said quickly. Revere was about to open the door on his side. "Don't ask Pa."

Revere got in and they drove off. Swan could tell by the jolting of the car that Revere was not really in a hurry to get anywhere but had to be doing something fast. Clara lit a cigarette. Swan rested his feet on the hump in the middle of the floor, ready to look out at everything. Even the familiar orchards on either side of the lane were a little different today because they were going to a funeral.

After a while the sun disappeared. Clara leaned back and smoked, saying nothing. She had taken off her hat already and put it on her knee; her legs were crossed. Her white gloves too were off and one of them had fallen onto the floor. She sat back, smoking, both her hands limp in her lap. She said, "The worst funeral I was ever at was this friend of mine, a girl. She was murdered by somebody."

274

It was as if she had opened a window and something nasty had flown in.

After a moment Robert said shyly, "A man was killed down the road a few years ago. I remember that."

"How was he killed, then?" Jonathan said, challenging him.

"Shot with a shotgun."

"You don't remember that."

"I do too."

They were silent. Revere's driving was steady and hard. The bleakness of the day seemed to weigh soundlessly upon them; Clara yawned often. Swan felt the tight hard curl of excitement in his belly, waiting to be set free. Clara's leg pressed idly against his, but he could not move over because he did not want to touch Revere. His father. He did not want to touch him and even Clara's touch was oppressive, keeping him still. He did not know what was going to happen in the city but he did knew that something strange and wonderful awaited him.

"I wouldn't want to be no man splayed out with a shotgun," Clark drawled. "You wouldn't hardly know who'd been there, right?"

"That's awful talk," Clara said.

They were getting far from home now. Swan did not think he had seen these fields before. The highway was a narrow road mottled with lines of tar that had run in the summertime but now looked fierce and hard. They gleamed like leather in the gray light. There were ruts in this road and the reddish dirt at the sides fell down in jagged little ravines to a big rain ditch that was partly filled with water; Swan shivered to think of what would happen if the car swerved off the road. They were passing shanties sometimes, old abandoned gas stations and farmhouses, cornfields that had been parched out by the late summer sun and were now just no color at all, bleached out and killed. The cornstalks looked as if they were made of paper. They went by an old farmhouse some family had taken over: here was a mattress on their drooping front porch and a junked car in the yard. A water tank that was all rust leaned against the side of the house.

"Lookit that dump," Jonathan snickered.

The house reminded Swan of the house he and Clara had lived in, except theirs had been nicer. It had been far away from the road. A garbage dump was smouldering not far away from this house, and Swan smelled something sharp and sickish.

"Who lives there?" he whispered to Clara.

275

"How should I know?" she said, irritated.

They were going downhill all the time. At times Swan could feel it even when they weren't on a hill, a peculiar unsettling feeling in his stomach. They were falling slowly, falling down away from the mountains behind them. If he were to look around, the ridge of mountains would have already become faint and insubstantial in the mist; what was ahead of them just looked like nothing. The highway turned onto another, larger highway, but with the same regular streaks of tar along the center of the road and horizontally across it every eight or ten feet.

They approached a small town where a mud-splattered sign said SPEED LIMIT 25. Revere did not slow up. Swan felt the approval of the boys in the back seat. There were no cars in the town except one or two parked off the road, so old and junky they might have been just scrap cars. Swan saw a child playing in the mud near a shanty. A few men stood about an old garage, watching Revere drive by. They had blank, dark faces that could have been hiding anything. In a field just on the other side of the garage there was a strange assortment of junk—old rusted cars, bedsprings, barrels, broken glass. The field had been the site of an old house, now fallen in or burned down. Gray stones marked its foundation. A muddy lane led back from the highway to four houses perched up on cement blocks; they were sided with asbestos all bought from the same store.

"The name of this town is Alfred," Clark said.

They were through it and past suddenly. The road just turned away and prepared to descend a great long hill, and they forgot Alfred. There were a few shanties balanced precariously on this hill, for no reason that Swan could imagine—junk lying all around them, wood rotted black, roofs caved in years ago. Everything gray and black and abandoned. Behind them, the leaves of hickories and poplars were beginning to turn; leaves had turned back home a few weeks ago. But these gave no autumn colors to the scene, they just hung limp and tired, as if rain had beaten them down and bleached out most of their yellow.

They were on their way into the valley now. A few more intersections with other roads, and the highway branched out to four lanes—made of some new-looking light concrete, already cracked but not so rutted as the other roads. Revere drove faster here. There was more traffic, pickup trucks and speeding cars, some of them new like Revere's. Swan sat up tall and watched these cars coming up from the distance,

276

wondering who was in them and where they were going, anxious to see the license plates. The cars made a sharp swishing noise when they passed by Revere, going in the other direction.

"California plates," Jonathan said.

"I seen one from Canada once," Clark said.

At the next intersection there was a big gas station with pumps different from the kind Swan had been seeing all his life. These were short and sleek, white and red and black, and the driveway was all paved, not dirt, and the garage itself was extraordinary—plate glass on its front, as fancy as Clara's kitchen window, and its walls made of some kind of red, slick substance that shone. It matched the gas pumps. There were several cars waiting to be gassed up, and men in uniforms to take care of them. Across the highway was a restaurant made of fake logs with a big statue of an Indian in headdress leaning out over the door.

"Could we stop there?" Robert said.

Revere did not slow up.

"I mean the restaurant. I'd sort of like to—"

"We don't have time to waste," Revere said. "You can wait."

A trailer truck was ahead of them, going too slow for Revere. He swung out to pass it. Swan stared at the automobiles perched up on the apparatus, hoping they would not tumble over onto Revere's car. These cars were brilliant and new, newer even than Revere's. Swan stared at the driver, who turned out to be a tired-looking man with a wool cap pulled down onto his forehead. He did not glance over at this Revere who was passing him so skillfully.

"You like to drive fast, don't you?" Clara said, pleased. "I never knew you liked to drive fast."

When she talked to Revere in a certain way, all the boys were embarrassed: they were not accustomed to hearing women speaking to men that way. Because the man was Revere it was all the more strange.

"Lookit that," Clark said. A stripped-down car was turning off onto the highway just in front of them—driven by a boy no older than Clark. The car was squat and ugly, painted black with a number thirteen in red on its side. "He thinks he's good, with a junker like that."

"Probably faster than yours," Jonathan said.

"Like hell."

The car lurched out onto the highway, making a loud

277

noise. It veered for a moment and then steadied itself and drove off in a hurry.

Traffic got heavier. Swan was accustomed to abandoned roads, to stretches of lonely pavement. He was a little nervous. There were men and boys not much older than himself hitchhiking along the road, and the red-dirt shoulders beside the highway were built up here, the ditches protected by short white stumps with wire between them. In some places these stumps were knocked over and the wire broken. Back up in higher ground you never saw hitchhikers unless they were people from nearby, wanting a ride of a mile or two, and then they were broken down. These people—the kids in their jaunty-colored jackets and their tight jeans and boots, the men defiant and humble at the same time in dirty old clothes, with shoes caked over with mud—looked as if they spent all their time hitching rides and were not ashamed of it; in fact, they could make you feel ashamed for driving past them if you let them catch your eye. Clara yawned and stretched, turning to the window lazily, and one of the men stared hard at her face as Revere sped by.

"Where do they think they're going?" Clark said. "I wouldn't give no dirty old bum like that a ride."

"No, don't you ever do it," Revere said.

It was the first time that day he had spoken in an agreeable tone. Everyone was pleased.

"I sure wouldn't do it," Clark said at once. "You pick up a bum and what's he got to lose if he kills you and steals your car? Nothing."

"Maybe you're going to be a bum yourself," Jonathan said. "Then what?"

"I ain't gonna be no bum."

"They never thought they was either."

Suddenly Swan was tired. There was so much to see, to keep track of. He remembered the crows waking him that morning and now he was this far from home, speeding somewhere that was farther away than he had thought. He had never really thought how far away another place might be. Some kids were standing on the side of the road, inching out and ready to dash across after Revere passed, and Swan wondered what it would be like to live down here, so far from the mountains you couldn't even see them. Those kids— one of them his own age—belonged to something entirely different from what Swan belonged to. His head ached with the thought that Revere, who owned so much and had power over so many people, did not really own very much at all.

There was a great vast world that even Revere could get lost in, if someone took his car and his money away from him and let him loose on the highway to hitch a ride.

"Honey, are you thirsty or something? You want to go to the bathroom?" Clara said.

"Okay."

"Let's stop up here," she said. She touched Revere's arm as if she weren't sure he would hear her without this. "That looks like a nice place. No, wait, it looks dumpy. There's a place across the street—"

"We have some distance to drive yet—" Revere said.

"That looks like a nice clean place," Clara said.

It was a glassed-in restaurant that looked to Swan like something in a magazine. He would have been terrified to go in it alone. Revere hesitated, slowing, then swung out into the center lane and waited to turn into the restaurant drive. "You kids all want to stop, don't you?" Clara said, just remembering them.

Inside, everything smelled hard and stale. The floor was slick and not very clean. Swan stood beside his mother at a counter and they waited while the breezy-looking girl made them hot dogs. Kids were sitting in one of the booths, laughing and carrying on; the jukebox was playing music that was all thumping and no tune that Swan could make out. Revere sat out in the car, waiting. He hadn't wanted to come in; he said he didn't want anything. The three boys were back in the restroom, and Clara was busy looking at herself in the thick plate glass that made up one wall of the restaurant. Swan said, "Is this how places are in the city?"

"I don't know," she said. "Don't you like it?"

"No."

She glanced around, standing with one knee on a stool. "I guess it's dumpy," she said. "It's *common*."

"What's that?"

"Where common people come."

Clara laughed, showing her teeth as if showing Swan a secret. She bent to him and slid her arms around his neck. He wanted to step away but couldn't; but she only hugged him just once and then straightened up and forgot about him. He saw the kids in the booth watching Clara. The other booths were empty, but one of them was still dirty from people who had eaten there. "How much is this here?" Clara said, pointing to a piece of cake under a glass. The waitress told her. Clara bought it and had the girl wrap it up, "for Swan, for later on."

279

Clark appeared from the side, wiping his hands on his jacket. He wore a light canvas jacket, a drab green. He had combed his hair so that it went back from his squat forehead in slick wings. "I smell something good," he said energetically. He sat on the stool beside Clara, turning from side to side. "It's a good thing you asked him to stop. He wouldn't of done it for us."

Hearing his drawl, one of the boys in the booth laughed, and the others joined in. Clark stared over at them.

Jonathan and Robert came out. Jonathan hung behind, watching the grill where the hot dogs were being fried. "Don't pay attention to those stupid bastards," Clara said. She took the piece of cake from the waitress and put it in her purse. If the kids in the booth heard her, she did not care; her voice came out warm and friendly and loud. Clark turned himself around on the stool one complete turn, as if stunned. Jonathan stared at the floor. The waitress brought them the hot dogs in little cardboard boxes already stained with mustard. She watched Clara closely. The boys hurried outside with the hot dogs, afraid to start eating inside the restaurant, and Clara followed in no hurry. Swan waited for someone to call out to her. What if one of those boys said something? Could they pretend not to hear?—but Clara would not pretend. She went out past them watching her, their straws bent in their bottles and their eyes quizzical and hard.

"That was a common place after all," Clara told Revere. "It didn't turn out to be nice after all."

They were groggy from the ride when they reached Hamilton. Swan stared about him at the rain-washed girders of bridges, disappointingly old bridges, and down into sudden valleys where railroad tracks ran far below, bordered by patches of weeds. Revere was driving more slowly now. Streams of traffic had joined them and the pavement was slick with rain. The sound of horns came remotely to them, forlorn and faint with rain. "Is that your factory? That one?" Clara said. Revere told her no. In the distance—a confused, jumbled distance made up of patches of open space and crowded frame houses—a few smokestacks were silhouetted against the gloomy sky. Haloes of light glowed about their tips.

"Are they on fire?" Swan said.

"That's just how they are, Steven," said Revere.

Rain fell lightly on the windshield of the car, the drops being swept aside by the wipers and the smooth spaces abruptly mottled again by more drops. Swan sat up straight, trying to see everything. There were men at the side of the road doing something, wearing white helmets that glowed in this off-light: a terrific drilling noise that made Swan's teeth jar. "Jesus," Clara said. Revere drove on. The street was wide here, but the houses and buildings looked strange—they were right by the sidewalks. Many of them were boarded up and people had put posters on their blinded windows or doors, bright yellow, rotted posters advertising circuses and cigarettes. One frame house was lived in even though there were boards x-ing out windows: there was a refrigerator on the front proch, and a Negro woman stood barefoot looking out at the rain.

"Are they all black people here?" Swan said.

"Just around here."

"Are we going to stop here?"

"No," Clara said, and laughed.

After a while they came to an intersection again and this time turned onto a wider road with a divider in its middle; grass and shrubs and trees grew there. Swan stared at everything. "I like that house there," Clara said, pointing. The boys in the back seat had begun to chatter. "Look in that store window," Clara said, reaching over to touch Revere's arm. "I never saw a dress that nice. I never did." There was a faint, furtive pleading in her voice, a begging she was not quite aware of but that Swan understood; he felt a little embarrassed. Later on, hours later, Revere would say that she could buy whatever she wanted—and it would be a surprise to her, because she would have forgotten the dress. So much came to Clara like that, as surprises.

They were passing through a neighborhood where the houses were as big as Revere's now. The lawns went far back from the road. Swan's excitement had begun to make him shiver: the boys' talk, his mother's chattering, the look of these homes with their blank, still, ornamented fronts—everything was foreign and indecipherable, exciting. He thought again that they were going through all this to go to a funeral, to see a dead man.

"You drove real well and real fast," Clara said to Revere.

They were going downhill again, but this time Swan could see why: there was a river or a lake in the distance. Everything led down to it. The street was made of brick, glistening in the rain and clean the way nothing could be clean out in the country, and all the houses had been built to face the water. It was gray today, and choppy. You could not be sure where the water blended into the sky, or whether that was just the opposite shore. "How do you like this, Swan?" Clara said.

"Please call him by his right name," Revere said.

"Steven," Clara said. There was no conviction in her voice; she poked Swan to let him know this was a joke. "Steven, how do you like where your father's people live, huh?"

"I don't know. . . ."

"Wouldn't you want to live here someday?"

"I was here lots of times," Clark said. He sat forward to lean against the back of Clara's seat. Swan resented that. He did not want to share anything with him. "There it is, their house. I don't like that color, myself."

Revere turned onto a bricked drive that led up past a wall to a gray house of an enormous size. There were columns in front that made it look like a building like the kind seen in books, photographs of places you did not really believe existed. Clara took out her compact and dabbed at her face. She stretched her neck and looked down at herself, her gaze skimming along her nose and cheeks. "God," she whispered, "I look like hell from this ride." She put her hat on her head carefully, groping about with her long nervous fingers. Her nails were colorless and a few were broken off quite short. Swan could sense her excitement.

A man in a tan raincoat came down the front steps. Clara rolled down her window and they heard him call out: "You all can park around back." He signaled to Revere, a brief cheerless gesture of recognition; when he turned, his coat opened and you could see how well dressed he was. Swan stared at the high blinding clumps of evergreens around the house, banked so high some of the windows were cut off. There were many windows in the house, too many. Even the third floor had its own windows. To one side was a garden and what Swan thought at first to be people turned out to be statues, gray and startling. Autumn flowers were blooming, but other patches were burned out and abandoned. There was something soft and shabby about the garden, accented by the rain. Swan thought that there would probably be a musty smell around this house.

He was right about that: it smelled that way in the kitchen. This room was not like Clara's kitchen at home, but something divided into three parts, with a high ugly ceiling. There was a kitchen table in one part, just a rough wooden table with knife scratches on it, and cupboards that were ugly and smudged. Clara looked around suspiciously. A Negro man in a white uniform came up to talk to Revere. The boys took off their jackets, not knowing what else to do. Clara was standing by the refrigerator—this was brand new—and was about to open it, maybe, but thought better of it. There was an older refrigerator next to it, smudged and chipped, and an ugly old stove that looked big as a train engine. Clara kept looking around, frowning, as if she thought someone had fooled her.

The Negro man took their coats from them. Clara smoothed her hair back from her face again, nervously. They followed the Negro out into the next room, which was a narrow pink room with more cupboards, showing plates inside and cups and various dishes, all in a jumble. Another table was pushed back against the wall and on it were more dishes; Swan could see that they were chipped. "In here," the Negro said quietly, opening the next door for them to pass through, waiting for them to pass, and now they were in a glassed-in room that belled out onto the garden; here a long shining table and chairs sat heavily upon the polished floor. Swan had never seen a floor like that. It was made of small ornamental squares, each glowing with light.

"It smells funny in here. It smells like rotting flowers or something," Clara said to Revere.

Swan's heart began to hammer. He felt that there was something about to happen, something hidden in the depressing richness of this house that he had to face. Clara tried to take his hand but he moved away. She had put on her white gloves again, and one of them was a little soiled. Swan was angry to think that the Negro man had probably seen his mother's soiled glove and was thinking something that no one could stop, and he had probably noticed the awkward way Swan walked, as if he knew he did not belong here. From somewhere in the distance came the sound of voices and footsteps on a stairway. Swan hung back.

"Steven, come," Revere said.

He followed behind his mother. Just then Jonathan leaned over and mimicked Revere in a whisper: "Steven, you little bastard!" Robert, right by them, started to giggle, he was so surprised, but when his father looked around at him he quit at once. He seemed to suck the sound he had already made back inside him.

Now they were in another room, hurrying on, and there was a great piano here that Swan saw mistily, and vases of flowers—a sickly sweet smell—and a fireplace with dark marble around it, and furniture he did not more than glance at, it was so heavy and rich. The curtains at the windows were flimsy, the color of ghosts, and the air was saturated with moisture—sluggish but not lazy, sluggish but nervous all at once. A woman in a gray dress was coming toward Revere. She walked across a large foyer, whose ceiling opened up high, all the way up to the second floor where there was a stained-glass window: Clara looked up at this and almost forgot to say hello to the woman. The woman looked young at first, but then she looked old; she had her face made up bright and pink but part of it had smudged, and when she stood alongside Clara she looked tired. "Is this Steven?" she said. "Steven?" Her eyes were damp. She was about to embrace him, this woman he had never seen before, but she hesitated for just an instant, so that when she did embrace him it meant nothing. Revere was explaining to Swan who she was but Swan could hear nothing. His heart was still hammering. He wanted to keep his eyes fixed on the woman's talking mouth, or on the great heavy rug—or whatever it was—that hung from one of the walls, or on the vases that had taken Clara's attention, anything to keep from thinking about what might be going to happen. More people appeared. They were like Revere; they walked like him. The men joined them with the easiness of relatives who have no particular interest in one another. They were softened, slowed, made tolerant by this death, but they were accustomed to it and were ready to talk of something else.

"This is my wife Clara—"

"This is Steven—"

They were introduced around, in whispers. The women were perfumed and sad. One of the men stood rubbing his chest, absentmindedly, as if he had felt pain a moment before and had forgotten about it. "Yes. Well," someone sighed.

They were moving slowly along and Swan moved with them. Clara walked a little apart from them all, different somehow from the other women: maybe that blue was the wrong color to wear. She was too young, Swan thought. The smell of the house and the lines in the women's faces made Clara too young for what she was doing. Swan stared up at the ceiling so far above them: down from that ceiling came a chandelier made of crystal on a heavy chain. Everything was polished and heavy and oppressive.

Then they were in a room like a hall, where chairs had been set up. Many people were there. Swan's eyes darted at once to the front, and there he saw it—a shining black box. The coffin. He stared at it; he stumbled into Robert, who pushed him away. Robert too was frightened. "Do we hafta look?" Robert said to Clara. She said no but he tugged at Revere's hand and said, "Pa, do we hafta look?"

Revere did not hear him. He was pushing out a little ahead. People gave way for them to pass, and it was like Swan's first day of school: seeing the eyes turning onto him, waiting breathlessly for someone's voice to snicker a taunt, getting no help from his brothers or anyone else. His "brothers." Swan's mouth was dry with the smell of death. He was bitter to think that Clara, walking right beside him, could not help him because she did not understand. She was looking, maybe, at a woman's hat or at a lampshade; for her the coffin was just the reason for being there.

"Here. Sit and be quiet," Revere said. He was quite pale.

They stopped, bumping into one another. Even Clark was nervous. He was awkward and oversized, too big for the aisle. Clara brushed a strand of hair back from her cheek. Swan saw her gaze move about the room, a little guarded, but moving steadily just the same. "I want Swan to come up with us," she said. She did not bother to glance down at Swan. Revere nodded as if he had only half heard her. She touched Swan's shoulder, her grip in the white glove only looking soft. Swan felt dizzy. He saw Robert and Jonathan staring at him, Jonathan's narrow sallow face strained, and in that instant he felt closer to Jonathan than he had ever felt: he saw that Jonathan felt sorry for him.

Then they were walking up the aisle, the three of them. The rug was soft underfoot. Swan's excitement began to boil sickeningly, to swirl inside him as if it had been waiting for this moment for hours: the long ride, the miles and miles of countryside and city, everything unwinding to bring him here today to this room and this sweet stifling odor.

And so there was someone dead in the room, he was in the presence of death. Revere was ahead of him and his mother, his shoulders bent slightly as if to protect Clara and Swan from seeing anything too fast. Swan could not really see the people behind and around them but he felt their softness, the restrained self-conscious whispers that meant so much, and the brief silences as the three of them passed. Were they looking at Clara, or at Swan? What was it about his mother and himself that made people stare, their lips pursed thoughtfully, their eyes narrowed? Even the women's painted lips were nervous about Clara. She walked along, she walked through their watching, she really did not see anything though she might be able to look anywhere, just as Swan saw everything without having to look. His breath was coming quickly and shallowly. He felt faint. He thought of the hot dog he had eaten, and the cake Clara had given him, and the excitement in his stomach was about to turn into something else. He fought it down. "Here, honey," Clara said. Her voice was remote. She touched his shoulder again, guiding him along, and then suddenly he was there: he was looking at the face of an old man who was lying on his back, while everyone else in the room was standing or sitting up. . . .

His eyes pounded. The old man looked like Revere: he was Revere, another Revere. The long stiff white hairs had taken him over, cropped close about his thin face and forehead. His eyes were closed. There was something resentful and bitter about his mouth, and from it wrinkles fell angrily down and away. The old man's neck was a mass of wrinkles and this was the only way you could tell he was really an old man. Swan stared at him. He did not feel Clara's hand on his shoulder any longer. It seemed to him that here was a secret, here was something for him to know—but what did it mean? He felt transfixed, hypnotized. It was the kind of transfixion he felt before he vomited. But this had nothing to do with his stomach, it was something in his head, buzzing and roaring through his head—words that tried to get to him, to make him hear. He glanced over at Revere. His father, his *father*, who stood with a face just like this dead man's, eyes heavy and even a little sullen, as if annoyed by death—

And just then he had a glimpse of his other father: a pale blurred picture that jerked in and out of his mind.

The man in the coffin might have moved. But he had not moved. His eyes were closed and they were not going to open.

"Ma," Swan whispered, terrified.

She was about to nudge him aside. He stood fixed, paralyzed. He stared at the dead man's lips, at his nose. His nose was perfect. It had nothing human about it; it was waxen and perfect. Swan felt his own nose and wondered why it was so cold, it was like a dead nose. Revere was bending to him. He said something, he said the name "Steven." Swan heard this name but did not connect it with himself. It was the name of someone else, another boy whom he did not know any more than he knew Robert or Jonathan or Clark or Revere.

Something blinked, not the dead man's eyes but something else, and he shook his head to get rid of it: his other father's face. A blue empty sky behind that man. An odor of the outside. What had that man said to him? He could hear the words as if through a door, muffled and teasing. Something

286

about "death." Death, dying, and the dead: here was a dead man, but what did it mean? Did it mean more than the dog dying, than the cats being squashed because they slept up under the car fenders? Did it mean more than the death of the muskrats Robert wanted so badly? Why did it mean anything more?

Clara pulled at him. He did not move his feet, he felt heavy and strange. He was as heavy as that coffin. The flowers banked so solicitously about the corpse were banked about him too, leaning over onto him, and it must have been their odor that made his brain so dizzy.

"Steven, come away," Revere said.

"Come away," said Clara.

He looked up at them and wanted to ask, Why is the man dead? Clara was pale but her lips did not tremble. He knew she was a beautiful woman. Revere, beside her, was like the dead man in the coffin and only Swan could see that—but then he looked again at Clara and saw the jutting of the bone at her cheeks, made a pale, pale pink by her excitement, and he saw how straight and perfect her nose was, just the kind of face to die and be sealed up for good. He understood that she was going to die too and that she did not know it, and Revere was going to die and did not know it. Swan's eyes burned. He let Clara pull him somewhere, he stumbled against her and got going right, but in his head he still had the picture of the dead man and a voice that might come out of it at any moment, maybe late at night when he was trying to sleep or in his dreams when he finally did sleep: faint and teasing him to understand, words gifted him by that other father whom Revere had never seen and Swan himself had seen only once. The excitement of the day was turned to something rotted and sweet that lay on his tongue, and he could not spit it out because everyone was watching.

3

At dawn of that day when Clara had her miscarriage—she had been about three months pregnant—she woke to see her husband dressing in the dark. He stood off to one side, dressing stealthily, and she lay very still, as if he were an intruder who had not yet noticed her. Her eyes were vague and gritty with sleep, her hair lay tangled over the pillow, and her heavy inert peace contrasted with Revere's quick movements. She saw as he turned to pick something up that his chest had grown heavy; his waist was thick. She could hear his breathing. The air was a little chilly—it was September and beginning to get cold at night—and the window behind him glared silently with light, everything slowed down as in a dream and having that strange elasticity of a dream, so that it could belong to any time.

She remembered him without those lard-pale ridges of fat: a younger man undressing before her, trembling with excitement for her.

She thought of Lowry, his face passing in and out of her mind as it always did, not upsetting her and not even blotting out Revere's kindly, hardened face, the look of precise concentration he was giving now to buttoning his shirt. The pregnancy with Lowry's baby had been uncertain, she hadn't known exactly what was going to happen; but this time everything was certain. There was nothing for her to worry about or even think about, except that she wanted a girl. So she looked at Revere in the half-dark and thought that he was a good man and that she did love him, she loved him somehow.

"Were you going to leave without saying good-by?" Clara said.

He glanced around, startled like a thief. "Did I wake you up?" he said.

"I don't know, it's all right." Clara stretched her arms and yawned. "When are you coming back, I can't remember. . . ."

"Tuesday."

She remembered then that he had told her that.

"Are you going to miss me?" Clara said.

He had been buttoning his shirt. She saw how his fingers hesitated—he had thick, strong fingers. It occurred to her that those fingers and everything that was his belonged to her and had belonged to her for ten years now. "I wish you could go with me," he said. He sat on the edge of the bed but was careful to keep most of his weight on his feet. "You used to enjoy train rides. . . ."

He stroked her hair. Clara liked to be touched; she closed her eyes. Somewhere a dog was yipping excitedly. "Those people don't like me and I can't talk to them," she said. She was not exactly complaining. "That time I bought that yellow dress . . ."

"Haven't you forgotten about that yet?"

Revere's flashes of anger came vertically upon her, out of nowhere, never addressed to her exactly but to attitudes of hers. She felt that she had the power of this man's anger but that it was not a comforting power. "She was just a white trash bitch," he said. "Anyway, you don't need to go shopping. You could stay with me."

"I get tired of the city with nothing to do. I can't talk to the people you meet, and anyway ... there's a lot for me to do here. . . . The garden, and the boys. . . ." Revere leaned over her and pressed his face against the side of her face and her hair. She felt his warm breath; it was a little stale from sleep and she wanted to move away. His hand was heavy on her stomach. She put her own hand over it and thought that he would be leaving in a minute, in just a minute.

She loved him but it was easier to love him with other people around. He was a big middle-sized man, the type that looks hard, wiry, solid, walking without any hint of grace or bother with it, without knowing what it was; he got whatever he wanted. The front of his body and even part of his back were covered with matted dark hair, and on his arms and the backs of his hands were softer, finer hairs. As he grew older all this was turning gray. Soon he would take on a delicate look and when his muscles did finally turn to fat he would look sad, puffy, discarded. Clara could think of this with a remote impersonal regret, the way one mourns over the death of former presidents and generals, men of public life who reveal their private degeneration all at once and die at that moment—up until then they are not really men and require no sympathy. She could hold him in her arms and look past him, as if looking from the present time into a vortex of no time at all—the Clara who had always been at the center of herself, whether she was nine or eighteen or twenty-eight, as she was now. Whatever else happened, that Clara never changed.

"Are you warm enough? How do you feel?" he said. He kissed her throat. She turned her face so that he could kiss her mouth, not because she wanted him to but because it had to be done. His other wife must have been dog-sick with pregnancies, she thought, the way he fussed over her; he did not seem to believe in her strength, which she took for granted. Nothing bothered her. If she had cramps occasionally it was nothing to keep her in bed, she liked to be up and doing something, anxious not to miss whatever was going on. She hated to be sick and idle, mooning around a sickroom— she had never been sick a day in her life, she told people. She would be healthy until the day she died. But most of all she liked to know what was going on, even if she could not

289

always understand it. Now that Revere had these new interests there was much happening, but it was a man's business—complexities of partnerships she liked to be told about even if she could not grasp their meaning. She could understand money, however, and Revere had enough of that. She believed vaguely that he had much more money than he had had in the old days when he had pursued her, but it was difficult to tell, and certainly it would be difficult to make it clear to people in the neighborhood: what could you buy, past a certain point? She had magazines that showed enormous startling houses and her own house would imitate these (she was having a back porch added) but it took time, time; she had good clothes but nowhere to wear them, and what did people in the country know about these things? All they could understand was something flashy, like her car; Clark's little foreign car, which had cost more money than Clara's, probably was lost on them and looked like a toy. They knew nothing, what could you do with such people?

"When I'm away I miss you very much. I'm afraid you might not be here when I get back," Revere said. Anything lured out of him by her softness or by their intimacy was something he would regret later; he was not that kind of man. Judd was a talker, but not Revere. So she felt uncomfortable when he confessed these things, not because they meant anything in particular to her but because she had no real interest in the private side of this public man's life. She touched his arm, the clean stiff material of the shirt Mandy had fussed over, and felt his warmth inside, a warmth that was alive and pleading but nothing she could respond to as a woman. She loved him about as much as she loved Clark and Robert—she did really like them—and a little farther behind was Jonathan, who seemed to resist her but who had such fine eyes, who was almost as smart as her own son. What she felt for Revere was confused on one side with his boys and this house, and on the other side with the man whose name was so well known and who could never be a private, intimate human being, but only a person committed eternally to fulfilling his name.

When she opened her eyes he was still leaning over her, staring hard, and something in his face discomforted her. Men were men but they had faces, individual faces, they came when you called them and stayed more or less consistent from one time to the next; but there was a layer in them hard as concrete that was their manliness, their secret unchangeable nature. "I'm very happy. Don't worry about me," she said. She laughed at his seriousness. He smiled. It was clear that for all his love he didn't quite trust her, but still he smiled. Clara could push serious things aside with just the right gesture: when he scolded his boys, which was frequent now, when Esther had made that last awful scene before going to the nursing home, when Swan came in crying from being teased—"teased"—she did not know what to do but she knew how to take it. "You're too serious, don't worry about me," she said. She lifted herself up on one elbow and seemed by this to be getting free of him. He moved aside. "We're going to have a little girl and she'll be as healthy as I am. Don't worry, all right? Now, you don't want to be late."

"I have enough time."

She did not like his talk but she didn't like his silence either. "Well, what do you want?" she said. The weight of his love was sometimes burdensome. She did not like having to walk about inside the circle of his infatuation for her, which was nothing she could understand or admire. To Clara, a man's love was no sign of his strength but rather of his weakness, something you wanted from him but then had to feel a little sorry about taking. "I'm not mad about the other night, that hunting business," she said. "If that's what you mean."

"I hope you aren't still angry. . . ."

"You're right, it's good for Swan to go hunting. Fine. That's fine. I agree." She brushed her hair back and in that instant wanted almost to cry out for something—for escape, for someone to help her. But the impulse subsided at once. She was at home here, warm beneath the covers, safe and protected by Revere and his world. He might seem to be a stranger at times but he was at least a stranger she could handle. "I asked him why he didn't want that gun—that's a real nice gun you bought him—and he told me something, but it didn't make sense. He likes dogs and cats and things, you know, and he doesn't want to shoot rabbits either. He doesn't like the loud noise, he said."

"He has never tried to go hunting," Revere said quietly.

They were tugging over something. Clara felt this, understood it perfectly, and knew enough to give in. "Well, I told him what you said and he said he'd go with Robert, he likes Robert. Robert's nice to him sometimes," she said, wondering a moment later why she had said that "sometimes," which didn't sound good. "He said he'd go today if it was nice. Him and Robert—he and Robert, they get along real well together if they're alone." She paused. All these jagged edges had been covered many times in the last few years, many times. She could run over them smoothly without really drawing his attention to them. "He'd tell you, but he's afraid."

"Afraid of his father?"

"He loves you but he's afraid. A boy should be afraid of his father a little," Clara said cunningly. She tried to remember her own father. Had she been afraid of him? What had he been like? He stood there, at one end of her life, as if at the opening of a tunnel, silhouetted against the light, barring her way back to her childhood: a tall lean man with a narrow face, blond hair, squinting suspicious eyes, a big mouth. Yes, a big mouth. Thank God, she thought, that Revere did not swear in front of women—not much, anyway; that he did not paw and grunt like an animal, the way Carleton had with her mother and then Nancy and who knows how many other women; that he did not drink too much. She awoke from this to hear Revere speaking quietly and she touched his smooth-shaven cheek, feeling a surge of tenderness for him, wishing there was something more of herself that she could give. "He's younger than the other boys, remember," she said. "He's afraid of them, you know how kids are. They don't bother him or anything," she said carefully, knowing of course that Jonathan hated Swan and bothered him all the time, "but you know how kids are. Give him time to grow up."

"Yes," he said.

Clara kissed him. "He'll use the gun. I promise he'll shoot something."

"And, Clara, you should let him alone more. You shouldn't fuss over him."

"Okay, fine. I agree with that."

"My boys never got much attention from their mother because she wasn't well. They aren't used to it—I don't mean they don't like it but they don't know what to do with it. You confuse them. And Steven needs to be let loose more. He needs more freedom."

"You don't know what it's like for a kid to run loose," Clara said. "I do."

"He has to learn to take care of himself."

"But that's what I don't want," she said. She rubbed her cheek against his, wondering how much longer he would stay. She listened to him always and agreed with him in words, and then went on to do whatever she wanted to anyway. She had learned this technique from Nancy, years

292

back. "I want him to be different from other kids. I want him different, I don't want him like—the way I was."

After he left she tried to sleep again, thinking mainly of Swan and of Lowry behind him, another figure silhouetted at the end of another tunnel, Swan's tunnel; but he could not really remember Lowry. He had been too small to remember anything. And it seemed to her that the relationships between people and their fathers were like thin, nearly invisible wires . . . you might forget they were there but you never got rid of them. She was sure that her own father was still alive somewhere: maybe he had finally gotten a real job, settled down somewhere with Nancy and the beginning of a new family, and there he was right now if she wanted to look him up. With her money, she would look him up someday. She could help him out, maybe, if he'd let her; but he might not let her. For Esther, who had grown old and helpless so fast, she felt almost nothing—she was just a stranger who hadn't liked Clara and had gone to pieces when Clara had moved in. It was good she was out of the way. But for her own father, who was getting old by now, she felt a confused, generous sympathy, blocked up because she had no way of freeing it. In a few years, maybe. There was no need to hurry.

When she woke again it was lighter. The sun was out, the air smelled good. She went downstairs and Swan and Robert were about to go outside. Swan was standing in the doorway to the side shed. "He's fixing up the guns," he said. Clara saw tiny flakes in the corners of his eyes but did not rub them out for him. He didn't like her to do that when anyone else was around.

"Did you both eat?" she said.

"Yeah, we ate." Behind Swan, Robert was cleaning his shotgun. He looked up at Clara, frowning. The gun in his hands made him look older. He was thirteen on his last birthday and a handsome, solid boy, with slow eyes and hands. Swan waited in the doorway, pretending to be at ease. He was still a little slight, though she thought he would be growing fast one of these days. He had Lowry's pale, clear blue eyes and something remote and unfathomable in his face, like Lowry, but his silence he had gotten from neither Lowry nor Clara. He had the air of a child perpetually listening to voices around him and voices inside him. Clara wanted to slide her arms around his neck but she knew this would just embarrass him.

"You kids be careful, huh?" she said.

"I'm used to it. I go out all the time," Robert said.

"What about Swan here?"

"I might not shoot anything," he said nervously. He did not look at her. "I might just go with him."

"He don't need to shoot anything the first time," Robert said.

They pretended that Swan hadn't gone out the week before with his father and come home crying.

"Is Jonathan going?" Clara said.

"He's with Sandy," Robert said evasively. Sandy was Jonathan's horse. Clara had the idea that there was some tension between the boys, that maybe Robert had been talked into this and Jonathan had not been talked into it—but from Robert's polite, slow face you could tell nothing. He was really polite, this thirteen-year-old, and Clara was always surprised by it. He handed Swan his heavy gun and the boy took it, his shoulders drooping just a little in surprise—he didn't remember how heavy the gun was—then he turned away, ready to go out into the shed.

Clara said uncertainly, not knowing if she should say it or not, "Your father never meant to holler at you, Swan." She was speaking past Robert as if he didn't exist, to Swan's back. Swan did not turn. "If you don't want to shoot the goddam thing you don't have to."

The words were so clearly Clara's—they could never have been condoned by Revere—that Robert lifted his eyes to her. He did not quite smile. "He's gonna be all right," Robert said.

Swan went outside with him, not looking back. Clara forgot about them and went into the kitchen, where Mandy had left things rinsed but not washed. She lit a cigarette and stood at the window, and after a moment the boys crossed the back yard on their way out. Then she made herself some coffee and sat by the window, looking out the way the boys had gone. Her cat jumped up beside her and rubbed against her. She spoke to it with affection though she did not bother to look at it. Then she poured some orange juice and went out into the sun porch—which she called the "garden room," since that was the name given to such rooms in magazines—and spent some time looking at the plants. She had known the names of all of them at one time, but now she was certain only of the African violet (which was dying) and the avocado plant (which had to be cut back again). This took a while, and by then Mandy was back. Clara told her what to do. She was not certain which walls had to be cleaned, which floors, clothes, anything, so she spoke idly and pointlessly, knowing that Mandy would do what needed to be done and only asked Clara for the politeness of it. Mandy was the kind of back-country, mannish woman in whom politeness is bred only out of hatred; she was never polite to anyone she liked.

"That old bag," Clara had called her once, and probably Mandy had heard. You could never make it up to anyone like Mandy, so why bother?

She made breakfast for herself and ate in the garden room, still in her bathrobe, her tanned legs stretched out in front of her. She was glancing through magazines devoted to interior design and "additions" to homes. She had a large pile of these magazines and kept looking through them over and over again, as if she did not remember anything she saw. At about nine o'clock she got tired of this and put her dishes in the sink, ran some water on them, and went upstairs to dress. She looked out the windows in her room and would have gone to look out the windows at the other end of the house, but Mandy was working there. She thought she heard some shots, off in the distance, but around here you always heard noises like that—half heard them, since they faded so abruptly. She tried to imagine Swan with his shotgun and she felt a tiny stab of something—sorrow, or fear—because she could imagine him so easily, just as she could imagine Lowry with a gun, though she had never seen him hold one. There was a certain kind of man (the quieter, the better) to whom a gun was natural, almost an extension of his hand or fist, to get where he himself couldn't reach or didn't want to take the time to reach. Revere's oldest son Clark was just the opposite: he was big and friendly and uncomplicated, he was the nicest of the boys and in his hands a gun would look strange, out of place. So she listened while she dressed, trying to make herself feel that this was nothing to worry about. She never worried about anything, so why should she worry about this?

And on that morning, what else had she done before Judd drove over? Later, in trying to remember the day, she would linger over what had pleased her most—that quiet breakfast, the sunshine on her bare legs. And Judd. On his way into Tintern he had to drive right past this house and so he usually stopped in. Sometimes he stopped in on his way back too. Like Revere and also like men out of work, he could come and go when he wanted. It was only a certain kind of man who had to work at a particular time and could then stop; Revere never had to begin at any special time and never had to end either, the result being that he worked or at least thought about working all the time. Men too lazy or too sick or old to work had the same kind of freedom, but it got into them and sickened them to death; nobody wanted such freedom. No man, anyway. Clara liked idleness, the way any cat or gentle, lazy animal would like it, but she believed that men needed work or they died.

Judd came around eleven, when she was out in the garden. She recognized the sound of his car. He came around back, his hands in his pockets, smiling at her. Clara straightened, shading her eyes, and they said hello. She wore a stiff green straw hat to protect her hair from the sun. "He got off to an early start this morning," Judd said, not quite questioning, smiling at her in his nervous, friendly way. There were lines going out from his eyes because of all that smiling. He was a tall, loose man, not at all like Revere. You could say anything to him and it didn't stick, not exactly, where with Revere any stray word might be kept forever. Clara thought it a shame that he was homely, almost ugly, and it was a worse shame that he was married to that fat old bitch of a wife—a woman who had never once bothered with Clara though she lived five miles away—because she would have liked him single, hanging around as he had some years ago.

They sat in white lawn chairs under the yellow tree and Clara poured him some orange juice. He talked. She listened beyond their conversation to those gunshots, trying to keep her forehead free of the tiny little lines she sometimes discovered on it; one day she wouldn't be able to rub them away with cold cream. Judd sat in his chair as if he had nowhere to get to, nowhere to get back to. His legs were out and his arms hung down so that his fingers played idly with the grass.

"Your hair is grown long and it looks nice," she said, half teasing and half serious. He brushed his hair back from his forehead as she said this. She talked at Judd in this fashion, enjoying his company but not worried about it, because he so obviously admired her but would never do anything about it. "How's your little girl?" she said, thinking at once of her little boy who was not so little any more. "When are you going to bring her over? I like little girls. . . . this next one is going to be a girl." And she touched her stomach. Judd looked away, strangely fastidious. He said something about his daughter, whose name was Deborah. She was five years old. Clara took little interest in children who were not immediate to her. She could not quite believe in them. So she listened vaguely, inclining her head toward Judd. Her gaze

296

moved on to her legs, which were stretched out in the sunshine, and she saw that Judd looked at them now and then too, as if accidentally, bemusedly. They fell silent. Clara sighed. Then Judd began to talk again, about a problem of his. Revere accused him of being slow and lazy and too kind, but what could he do? It had something to do with business and Clara did not respond. Then he asked her about the porch and she brightened. "Clark is going to do it for me. I made all the plans. Now that my husband owns the lumberyard, all of it, I can get anything I want. . . ."

"That's very convenient."

"Clark likes to help me. He's a good boy. Then, next, we might have a swimming pool."

Judd nodded pleasantly.

"They all go swimming in that lake," Clara said. "There are snakes and bloodsuckers there. Lots of junk. Carp. They could cut their feet and get lockjaw; it happens. A swimming pool is best."

"I suppose so."

She paused. She said, "Swan is out hunting now."

"Hunting?"

"Yes, I think it's good for a boy to go hunting."

Judd shrugged his shoulders. "I don't know. I never liked it."

"You didn't?"

"Why should I? Shooting rabbits, birds— What's the point of it?" He looked over at her without smiling. "I don't like blood. I like things to go on living, life is precarious enough as it is. . . ."

Clara thought this over. She said, "Swan talks to you sometimes, doesn't he? Did he ever say anything about hunting? Or about—food he eats?"

"What do you mean?"

"Once he began telling me about why he didn't like to eat, but I laughed at him. I shouldn't have done that," she said slowly. "He said that when you pull chicken meat away from the bone you can see how the chicken was put together. Then you can't eat it. He said something like that," she said, narrowing her eyes at Judd. "Do you think that makes sense?"

"Maybe."

"Do you know what he means?"

"I think so."

"But I don't know," she said. She listened, thinking she had heard another gunshot. She heard nothing. "I don't understand him when he talks like that, I think he's crazy or something. I don't want him to be crazy. Swan is smart, the teacher says so, he's smarter than Jonathan—and Jonathan is fifteen now. It used to be Jonathan who read all the time, up in the attic, but now it's Swan. He loves to read. I want him to read," she said dreamily, reaching across to touch Judd's arm with a blade of grass for no reason. She just wanted to touch him, to touch somebody. "I want him to read but it makes him so quiet. Is he thinking all the time? I wonder what he thinks about—if he thinks about how he was born, the way I was living. . . ."

"He's a very intelligent boy."

"But what does that mean?" Clara said sharply. "I want to know what he thinks. When he was little it was different, he used to tell me. Now he's ten and that isn't old, he's just a baby yet, but he won't tell me things and I know enough not to ask. You can't push kids. I know he loves me but it doesn't let me know what he's thinking. I want to know."

"Why are you so worried?"

"Because—there are some things I don't want him to remember."

She tossed the blade of grass away. Judd was lighting a cigarette and he offered her one. She supposed he was thinking of her living alone, supported by Revere, but really she was thinking of Lowry.

"I want to understand him when he talks," she said. "I don't want to be just a stupid woman, just a mother. They used to make fun of Esther because she was so slow. She never caught on. Well, I don't want that! But the kid is smart, he reads all those things— Over there, under that chair, is a book he was reading. I brought it out to read myself."

"What is it?"

"I don't remember," Clara said, a little embarrassed.

Judd leaned over and picked up the book. "*A Natural History of Animals*. It sounds like a good book."

"Like I told you, he likes animals. He drew some deer once. So he said he didn't want to shoot them, but can't you draw deer sometimes and shoot them other times? My husband says it's for the deers' own good, they'd starve to death. Is that true with rabbits and pheasants too? Rabbits are a nuisance. . . . But what did Swan mean, that you shouldn't eat meat? I want to know what he meant by that."

"You might ask him again."

"But I laughed and told him he was crazy. . . . I'd never tell my husband the kid said that. He wouldn't like it."

298

"Is Steven still so afraid of him?"

"He isn't afraid," Clara said sharply.

"I mean—"

"No, he isn't afraid."

They fell silent. Clara looked over at Judd and after a moment she smiled, fallen back into laziness, trying to convince herself that nothing was wrong, that people—even children—kept on and on without changing, that there was never any point at which you had to say, What has happened? When did it happen? In the speckled sunshine Judd did not look homely so much as meek and ravaged, not by time but by kindliness, thoughtfulness. She would have liked to put her arms around his neck, making a gift of herself to him the way she would have liked to make a gift of herself to any man, wanting nothing out of it except to give pleasure, to make someone happy. "I just don't like it when I can't understand my own boy," she said softly.

"Don't feel bad about it," Judd said. "You can live with a person, have children, but it doesn't mean very much. It doesn't mean you know any more than you ever did. . . . Having children doesn't change you."

"I think it does change you," Clara said.

"No, it doesn't change you, you just want to think that."

Clara frowned. He spoke in such a flat, unsurprised voice that there was no room for her to get at him.

Judd rubbed his hands over his eyes. "My own experience has been that nothing changes except to get older. I don't know any more now than I ever did. Nature runs one way. Everything I think about doing has been done for me, ahead of me, by better people. I don't have your husband's energy, maybe I know too much. I've always thought I'd like to clarify at least one thing, set one thing in order—I'd like to write one book, get everything into it. But I haven't begun it yet."

"Write a book?" Clara said, narrowing her eyes.

"One book. I haven't begun it yet but I think about it sometimes. In a few years. . . . I'd like to travel too."

"To Europe?"

"Everywhere."

"Why don't you go, then? Maybe we could all go."

"Yes, maybe," he said, without enthusiasm.

"I've seen pictures of Europe. I'd like to see Paris," Clara said. "You don't need to speak French, do you? Do you think in Paris they'd be different from the way they are here—

people in stores and restaurants? I mean, they couldn't tell one American from the other?"

Judd stared at her. "Maybe," he said.

"Because in this country people who are important talk one way and the rest of us talk the other. I can't talk the way you and my husband do. I can't learn it. If I think about the way I talk I can't say anything, I stumble over my words, I'm like a kid. . . . There was this bitch in a store where I bought a dress, she thought I was just back-country dirt until I paid cash. The dirty bitch! In Europe they couldn't tell, could they?"

"My wife doesn't like to travel."

"Oh, the hell with her. Leave her home," Clara said. She looked over to see how shocked he was at this, but she went on, "My husband is busy here, he can stay home too. You and I could go and take Swan; he'd like it."

"You're joking."

"I want him to go to a good school, not that crappy one outside Tintern. That high school. He's too smart for the teachers there. He'd like to go to Europe, see things, do things other kids don't do. . . . And I'd like it too, to see lots of places. Wouldn't you? Aren't you listening? You could take care of us—"

"It's out of the question for Curt to go."

"Why should he buy anything more? Doesn't he have enough?"

"He couldn't go now."

"Then he can stay home! Why the hell does he want more money? He won't let me see the bank books. I have one of my own and he shows me others but I know there are more. I know it. What the hell is the secret about? Does he spend money somewhere, is he giving it to that bastard what's-his-name, going to run for senator? I know that's it. Well, I don't give a damn what he does, it's his money, but he could let me go to Europe. . . . I could buy some clothes there, and nobody would know how I talked. . . ."

Judd stared at her. "Aren't you happy here?"

She felt sullen, heavy. With this pregnancy she had hardly gained any weight yet but she felt burdened; it was strange. "Why don't you make me happy instead of asking about it? I want things now and then. I want things my husband can't give me, he doesn't understand about—like other men. If he wanted other women I wouldn't give a damn, but I don't think he does. He loves me, he'd always be thinking of me if he went with somebody else—"

300

"Why does that make you angry?"

"Am I angry?"

"You know he loves you very much."

"I know it, so what? What can I do with it? And you, look at you," she said contemptuously, "all that time when I was living in that house you'd come around and you wanted to go to bed with me but you didn't dare—you think I didn't know that? I knew it, I knew everything! And you could have married me too because I wasn't married and Revere was married to that bitch of a wife of his, it took her ten, fifteen years to die and she fought every minute of it—but you didn't dare. You didn't dare. Every day almost you come over here and look at me, but the hell with you—"

"For God's sake, Clara—"

"Oh, the hell with you," she said.

They sat in silence. She felt a wave of excitement but she could not focus on it. She did not know if she was happy or unhappy, did not know what she had said. Judd sat with his face in profile to her, shocked and still listening to what she had said. He turned to look at her and just then the shot rang out. It was too close to the house. Then a long moment of silence followed; the silence that rang out around the gunshot joined with the silence between Clara and Judd. Then they heard the screaming begin.

4

Hunting was strange to Swan—in a way it was like walking, except there was something precarious and deadly about it. It was boring too. Swan stumbled along behind Robert as if only Robert knew the way and the faint, familiar track through the woods that he had walked hundreds of times was a path that belonged now only to Robert. He carried his gun the way Robert carried his: they were both men, playing at being men. Swan sucked in his breath and tried to think that this was what he wanted, this was good; more than anything else he wanted to grow up as fast as possible and be like Revere and learn everything that Revere could teach him, learn it faster than his brothers and go on and find out what even Revere might not know. There was no other way for him to be at rest. Then, when he had all this knowledge and was traveling with Revere on those trips he took all the time, arranging things for his father, sorting out things that right now he couldn't even understand—then he could sit back and rest and look around. Then he would be able to think about himself.

"Well, he didn't hit you and he hit me lots of times. Jon got it too, lots of times," Robert was saying over his shoulder. He was trying to get Swan not to feel bad about being hollered at by Revere, but Swan did not allow himself any opinion about it. He did not allow himself any opinion about his father. "Once Clark got whipped, and I mean whipped. God!" Robert laughed. Swan saw the flash of the boy's teeth: like a domesticated rodent, a squirrel or a rabbit, something they might be going to shoot down dead this morning. "He was whipped with a real whip, some old thing Pa had out in the barn. He was bleeding too. I forget what he did—fooling around with some girl or something, and him only fifteen then. He was always running after them girls when he was younger than that but Pa never knew. I like to told Pa myself, because there's something nasty about it. Don't you think so?"

He spoke shyly, uncertainly. Only when he was with Swan did he speak like this. Swan's silence, his look of turning things over carefully in his mind, drew Robert out. Robert was all right when he was alone. "Our Ma told us there was something bad about it, it was Clark she was talking to mainly," he said. "I don't like them Seifried girls at school. Do you?"

"No," Swan said, catching in his mind an image of those plump, nervous, giggling girls and getting rid of it at once. He had other things to think of. Somewhere around them pheasants might be hiding, ready to fly up, small silent animals might be hugging the earth, a few minutes from their deaths: if he had to shoot anything he might as well shoot now and get that over with. Then he could maybe forget about hunting for a while, until Revere brought the subject up again.

"How come Clara likes them, then? Your Ma was teasing him about some girl. How come your Ma don't get mad—don't she care?"

"What?"

"Don't she care about it?"

There was something Robert was trying to get at, but Swan had no interest in it. His hands were sweaty on his gun. He kept his mouth closed, rigid, as if he were a soldier stalking a lively enemy who had him already in his gunsight. He said, swallowing, "How far do we need to go?"

"We just take our time," Robert said. "The idea is to take your time." Swan could tell that he was repeating something he'd heard an adult say.

Swan kept on. If he was to start thinking about what he meant to do, he would maybe get sick and have to turn back. So he would not think about it. He would sweep angrily out of his mind the memory of his father and another man returning with deer draped over the pickup truck fenders and more in the back—dead, heavy bodies still bleeding. Those bodies were strangely heavy. He would not think of that. Or of the mess of fish the boys brought back from the bridge, those round staring eyes your own face could be reflected in, if you got that close—something you surely wouldn't want to do. And the white paper-thin flesh at the mouth torn by the hook. . . . And the pheasants and the chickens, their own chickens, dead and ready to be picked of their feathers, with that warm sickening odor rising about them as Mandy worked, whistling. The guts in the bucket. They put the chickens in the oven and browned them some and there they were, right on the Sunday table with its white tablecloth and the candlesticks Clara had bought in Hamilton, everything clean and fancy—and in the middle of it the dead chicken, roasted. Out came their guts, which were changed for stuffing now and spiced up, and their hearts and liver and gizzard and whatnot, and everyone's mouth watered.

Swan spat sideways, like a man. He tasted something ugly in his mouth.

And sometimes it wasn't all the way roasted but would be red and run red, thin trickles of watery blood that got into your potatoes. When they had steaks it did that sometimes. Revere ate that blood, picked the soft helpless meat up on a fork and ate it, and so did Clara, whose teeth could eat anything, and all the boys, who were always hungry, and anyone who was a guest. Only Swan sat there alone and stared and felt his stomach turning over, getting itself ready for what was coming. In his mouth the strands of meat were each vivid and clear; the patches of gristle, fat, muscle, stray flecks of bone. It was all real and all alive. Clara had said, shivering, "What if the heart comes alive and starts beating in your mouth?" and they had all laughed, even Revere had laughed a little. Only Swan had sat there staring as Clark ate the heart. Of course he might be crazy and he had better shut up about it. Clara had told him that.

But. . . .

But if he had to kill something he would do it and get it

303

over with. He was ready. He would never be more ready. If a bird flew up he might as well shoot, he could close his eyes at the last moment. He would let Robert tell him what to do. And Revere had already told him. So when he pulled the trigger it would not really be he himself who did it, but his father or Robert, someone else. And what would the dead bird care about it?

"You think it hurts them awful much, to get shot?" Swan said.

"They don't feel nothing."

"Should you shoot more than once?"

"I'll tell you everything to do," Robert said, a little embarrassed. He was maybe unused to all this—this questioning and talk about what he had done for years without thinking about. He kept glancing over his shoulder, back into the woods, as if he hoped Jonathan or someone was running to catch up with them. At first they had walked stiffly, alertly, but as time went on they began to relax. Swan thought that maybe nothing would happen after all. It could be put off to another day. Around them everything was quiet except for the high invisible birds and the insects, invisible all around them. Swan liked the woods. He liked the sunlight falling sideways, breaking up into patches, showing the moss and the mossy fallen logs as if picking them out just to be shown— things you might miss if you didn't look carefully. Robert walked right through some wood violets. His feet left marks on the humps of moss and broke down weed flowers, and he did not bother to notice how everything smelled: the end of summer, the beginning of fall, with hot winds coming up from the lower valley, rushing up the slopes toward the mountains and unloading on them the rich complex odors of sun-blasted weeds and clover and sweet peas. Swan liked all this. When they came out to the edge of the woods they could look back and down, they could almost see the house and the barns off there in the distance a few miles away—but maybe they weren't seeing them at all, only imagining. It was hot now, outside the cool of the woods. "Christ," Robert said, wiping his forehead. "Everything is sleeping and hid. They know enough to stay out of sight when it's hot." He whispered. Swan liked that; he liked the thought of the birds and animals sleeping, hidden, smart enough to stay out of sight.

Once or twice things scurried away. Rabbits probably, Robert said. He aimed his gun but did not shoot. Swan could not imagine the sullen quiet of the woods really being disturbed. "You could maybe shoot at anything, to practice," Robert said. "There's a nest on that limb—go and shoot." But Swan did not want to shoot the gun, not yet. He licked his lips nervously. Robert said, "I was afraid to pull the trigger the first time, myself. I got over it fast, though."

"I already pulled a trigger," Swan said.

"Sure. That's so."

He seemed always to be walking away from Swan. He walked with his gun barrel pointed down, and Swan did the same. Swan felt dreamy and quiet here in the woods, these were his woods more than they were Robert's or anyone else's, because he spent more time in them. He had explored them. The woods were not just something to walk through, looking for animals to shoot. He wanted to explain this to Robert but Robert seemed always to be straining away from him, hurrying ahead.

They came out after a while by the side of a hill. They sat down and waited. At the bottom of the hill was a gully, red clay split into millions of cracks, hard as rock. There were rocks too, that looked as if they had been tossed down there and forgotten. Swan could see no reason to them, no place for them to have rolled from. In spring the gully would be rushing black with water, propelling along trees and roots and the stiffened bodies of animals, but now everything was sun-baked and dead. Lazy dead, not the kind of death you sometimes saw in animals on the road, buzzing with flies and maggots, that looked as if they had been run to death and fell over still running. Swan hated to see animals dead. And that man dead in his casket, all the way over in Hamilton—he did not like to think about him. But this oversweet lazy deadness, the death of the inanimate world—rocks and boulders and drooping vines and split earth, eroded red clay, the same kind of hard indifferent death you saw everywhere in wintertime, when the snow drifted high against everything—this was something else. It did not make you sad. There was nothing in it to make you sad. On the farther bank, rising high above it and running out of sight in a torrent of vines and leaves, was a dirt road no one used any more—Swan had walked along it but there was nothing there. A lot of dust. And higher than that was the beginning of the mountains, rising misty behind what was sharp and clear in the foreground—those complicated shelves of green, different shades of green. But there it was cool. It was not deadly still and then gusty with hot, rich, drunken winds smelling of rotting things, the way it was down here, where anything could be driven into your face and up your nostrils, making you dizzy with it. Even in broad sunlit places, in meadows, the air could die down still one minute and in the next rise up hot again, fast and hot, smelling of dead things or things gone overripe and rotten—grapes on invisible vines back in the woods, pears and plums and honeysuckle and worm-ridden apples and elderberries and chokeberries—all these things that made so dotted and immense the world he had been born into but was not yet ready for.

They walked on again, a little slower. Swan was sorry that Robert had nothing to say to him. Robert would rather be with Jonathan or one of his friends. Those boys were just like him, they should have been brothers to him instead of Swan, who didn't know how to talk right and never wanted to do anything. Swan never wanted to play games at school, and when he did play he got hurt—he was always watching himself play and couldn't let himself go. They played pom-pom-pull-away and he hadn't the nerve to run right into the kids and make them let go their clasped hands, so he always ended up losing; nobody wanted him. He knew he could do better, but something always stopped him. Even the girls were stronger than he was. . . . They yelled and stomped and ran in the cleared-off, packed-down dirt that was their playground, and why couldn't he imitate them if he tried? He just did not want to, not yet. He had so much thinking to do, there were so many books yet in the schoolhouse and at home—so much to think about, sort out in his mind, get memorized and set down so that he could go on to something else. Sometimes he felt shaky, his knees and hands trembled, and he didn't know why. He felt as if he were edging out onto ice that might crack at any minute, and he did not know why he was edging out or who there was to watch him if he turned back. . . .

He was like that now, in spite of what he'd thought so firmly to himself. He was nervous, shaky. He hated that shakiness that seemed to begin in his stomach and spread out everywhere, right down to his fingertips. How could he aim a gun if his fingers were trembling? Just then Robert said, hissing: "Lookit the chicken hawk!" and he raised his shotgun. The blast made Swan's head jerk backwards. His ears rang. Robert was already running through the brush, yelling out, and Swan stood with his heels heavy and stunned in the mossy earth, waiting for his heart to get back to normal.

"Got the dirty old bastard," Robert chortled. "You need to shoot them whenever you can. Dirty old chicken killers." He was kicking around in the thicket and his voice was bright and enthusiastic, as if he were talking in front of older relatives, aunts and uncles. Swan did not join him. He was staring at Robert's happy, sweet face, suntanned and healthy, a little dirty, and thinking: Please don't bring it over here. Please. He knew he would throw up if he had to see the bird.

"Holy Christ," Robert said, stooping. A few dragonflies were buzzing around him as if nothing had happened. Their bodies glinted fiercely in the patches of sunlight and they looked like dangerous chinks of metal suspended in the air and ready to dart. Swan felt dizzy looking at them, his eyes dancing along with them. Robert was bent over the dead bird and kicking at it. "It's really a mess," he said. Swan stopped looking at him and stopped listening. He walked a short distance away, into the woods, and thought that the cool dead-white toadstools and the moss that covered everything like a rug would help his trembling. High above, killdeer were calling one another. From the misty sweet sound of their cries no one would guess that the silence of the forest had been blasted into fragments only a minute ago. There were many birds around, suddenly—the noise might have woke them up. They were coming to see the dead chicken hawk. Now it was probably a bleeding mass of intestines and flesh and bone. What else? Grackles were crying out over-head too. They were smart birds. Crows were smart too. Swan felt a rush of hope for them; maybe they wouldn't all be killed. But of course they were killers themselves. They killed other birds and insects and anything smaller than themselves, anything they could kill they certainly did kill, and pluck its eyes out, and eat. . . .

That was how it was.

But that chicken hawk had reminded him of something. Of someone. The way those birds soared up into the sky, so effortlessly, their black shabby wings outstretched in a threat that was in no hurry to get to you. A sparrow hawk or chicken hawk, whatever they were called. . . . He could imag- ine that bird come back to life and circling high above them, calling down contemptuously at them, at Swan, laughing at him for being so weak: why are you such a baby? Why are you ready to throw up your breakfast? Robert was saying something to him. Then Robert was approaching him, still talking.

"Might as well leave it here," he said, pleased with himself. "There's one goddam old dirty bird won't bother nobody again."

307

"You got it real good," Swan said shakily.

Robert snickered, not at Swan but at the dead bird: when something was dead it had to be laughed at.

They walked along again. Swan's head had begun to ache. He was ready to be sick, but he had not once thought of asking Robert to turn back. It did not occur to him. So he followed Robert, staring at the boy's dusty shoes and watching them move up and down, up and down, watching the soft marks they made on the forest floor. The day grew hotter. They had to cross a meadow and here the sun blasted them. Swan's eyes ached as a flood of dragonflies sped before them, gleaming and glinting like bullets, and he had the idea that he would be happy to stay out here in this quiet, indifferent, heat-drenched land, he would be happy to lose himself in the sucking noise made by all growing things as they tried to breathe—he could almost hear this noise, or maybe it was his own breath—anything so that he did not have to go back and confront his father. This land sped off forever in all directions, boring downward far into the earth and rising into the sky, making the boundary between earth and sky unclear, even in the hot broad sunlight of noon; it was like time speeding backwards and forwards. You could be lost in it and not have to think. This vast sweep of land and sky was something that could hide you. Even the dead white of winter could hide you, flaking gently over you, and nobody would need to put a tombstone up to keep your name remembered because there would be no name to be remembered: like the chicken hawk, you could come to an end.

But he would have to go back. And in a day or so, when Revere returned, he would have to face him. That was how it was. Swan's love for his mother was so great that he never thought about it, the way he did not think much about the body he owned that was evidently going to be his for a long time: these things were so close you couldn't think about them. So it was Revere's love that counted. It was Revere's love he had to have, but he did not know how to get it except through draining the blood of birds and animals, blasting them into soft bleeding bits.

In his brain there was a bird fluttering to get out. He was aware of it in his most helpless, frantic moments, or when he was exhausted. Its wings beat against the walls of his head, pounding along with his pounding ears, and would not give him peace. As he followed Robert and slid without thinking down mossy hills, over polished pine needles that covered the ground, he could feel this bird struggling to get free. It was like the hot round ball of nausea in his stomach, something that had come up out of the depths of himself and which he had to get rid of.

"Too bad you couldn't get nothing," Robert said after a while.

And Swan realized, by something in his voice, that they were headed home.

"I can go again. Tomorrow," he said flatly. Robert did not bother answering. They were both hot and tired. Swan knew from the way Robert was straining ahead that he had failed again and that even if Robert—who was only thirteen, after all—did not exactly know this, he felt it and that was what mattered most. It was something in the air between them. Swan smelled it. His sweat itself stank of failure, embarrassment, shame. But he had not thrown up his breakfast, he thought. Nobody could tease him about that. . . .

They crossed an open meadow shortly, heading toward the woods back of the barns. Jonathan was riding his horse at one end and came galloping over to them.

They watched him come. "He rides real good," Swan said. Robert ran out ahead and had not heard, or did not indicate that he had heard. He was waving at Jonathan.

"Gimme a ride, Jon?"

Jonathan had sharp, nervous eyes that glittered in the sun. The horse's eyes were like his: they kept jerking, moving. This horse was a mare, its body supple and clean in the sunshine, its hard living sides shuddering with the effort of breathing. It pawed the ground. Jonathan said, "You two didn't get nothing, huh?"

"I got a chicken hawk," Robert said.

"Like hell you did. Where is it? And *him*, he didn't get nothing either." His words came in a harsh, humorless sing-song. "What's wrong, you afraid to pull the trigger? You need your ma to do it for you?"

Robert laughed and did not look at Swan.

Jonathan broke away and circled around, at a distance, to show he had no interest in them. Swan watched him with envy. Swan's face and body were bathed in heat and shame. "Hey, you little bastard!" Jonathan called over. "You, I mean you. Think you could shoot a horse? Think it's big enough for you?"

"Come on," Robert said to Swan.

"Think you could shoot a horse, huh? Betcha can't shoot a horse! Little fucking bastard—baby!"

309

Swan hurried after Robert, without looking back. His legs worked fast. He heard the horse's hoofs pounding behind him and Jonathan's voice rising up, out of breath and pricked with something more than daring, with a desperate recklessness. "Hey, little Swan! Little Swan! You afraid to fire a gun without your ma?"

Swan grimaced, going rigid against the pounding that was now right behind him. He supposed that Jonathan would run over him and there was nothing he could do about it. He would die. But Jonathan galloped past, laughing, and Swan was safe. Jonathan did not turn back. They watched him ride off and around to the lane that led to the barnyard.

"Oh, Christ, he was only kidding. He wasn't going to run you down," Robert said, disgusted by Swan's look of fear.

Robert approached the fence behind the woods. They would cut straight through instead of going the long way around by the lane. The meadow was spiky with cut grass; it hurt Swan's ankles. He kept his eyes on Robert's back, wondering what kind of face Robert would turn to him. At the fence he ran to catch up with him. "Why does he hate me?" Swan said. He was sweating profusely. His heart was pounding. This was the kind of thing he knew he should never say, but the words forced themselves out.

"Jesus Christ," Robert said, rolling his eyes. "Forget it."

"Why do you all hate me?"

"Shut up about that."

"How come you all call me names?" Swan said. Something was moving up into his throat; maybe it was vomit trying to get free. He felt wild. "I ain't a bastard. Nobody's going to call me that!"

"I said shut up!"

"Goddam you," Swan said, and he realized, suddenly, that as soon as Robert climbed that fence and jumped down they would be home; here, in the back meadow, they were still out hunting. He lunged forward and struck Robert on the back with his fist, hard, and shoved him forward sideways against the barbed wire. Robert's gun went off. The noise was so close that Swan almost heard nothing. Then, when he was able to see again, he saw what had happened to Robert—the great gaping tear in his shoulder and throat—he stumbled backwards as if struck himself by a fist sharp on his chest. Robert began to scream. The scream came out in a high, thin shriek, like a girl, astonished and beyond pain, while Swan stood staring at him in a sun-drenched vacuum he could not move out of.

310

He could not move. He could not speak. Robert's screams rose higher and higher out of that face blasted by pellet, and Swan saw the blood streaming out and running onto the prickly grass where it floated along and lifted chaff with it, then disappeared. The air rang everywhere with the boy's screams. Swan had hold of his own gun, his fingers had frozen to it as if he needed it to protect himself against whatever had happened to Robert. Then he saw Jonathan, running on foot, and he saw his mother and Judd coming through the field; he thought that they had lost time coming that way, all the way around the lane when they could have cut through the woods. . . .

Clara's face had gone white. She did not even see Swan but ran to where Robert lay and tried to pick him up. Blood spilled over the front of her dress as if it were tipped out of a pitcher. "My God, Judd!" Clara screamed. "Get the car around! Get the car back here, we'll drive him—"

Judd faltered a few yards away. He looked sick.

"Get the car around!" Clara cried. She tried to pick Robert up again but he was too heavy. He stared up at her as if he were astonished by something, trying to think of how to say it, how to explain it. Swan saw now that his arm hung to the shoulder by something thin and limp and that blood was pounding out. Clara began to scream over her shoulder at Judd. "Get the car, goddam it! Judd! Jonathan! Get the car around here, you goddam stupid son of a bitch! You want him to bleed to death? What are you doing?"

It was Jonathan who finally drove the car around. Everything took time. Swan stood where he had been standing all along, watching them with his breath a solid column inside his body, not understanding what had happened or how he was related to it. It passed slowly, dreamily. He did not cry or think about crying. He still held the gun Revere had given him. Clara got Robert up, dragging him, and got him into the back seat of her new car. She was still screaming, yelling. Swan could not understand her. Jonathan, his face struck white, was behind her trying to help, but his hands did not quite reach Robert. They were all afraid of Robert, everyone except Clara, who was still screaming. Swan dropped his gun at last and pressed his hands over his ears. Judd was somewhere else, further down the fence, leaning against it like a man trying to wake up. He could not get awake. Clara said to Swan, "Get on the telephone and tell him we're coming! Call the doctor!" She drove the car off, bumping through the field, Jonathan reaching out with difficulty to close the back door, and Swan still stood there with his hands pressed over his ears.

He was left alone with Judd, who was being sick, and that great shining patch of blood on the ground; and Robert's gun, which lay fallen against the barbed-wire fence.

But Robert died in the car, not five minutes from the doctor. Later on they burned the car because it was soaked with blood in back and Clara wanted it burned. She was to talk about that ride for years angrily, sarcastically, as if there were something in the car and the road and the very remoteness of that doctor that had deliberately taunted her. "And Judd—big goddam puking baby!" she would say, showing her fine white teeth. Many days later, when she was well herself from whatever had happened to her—Swan did not quite understand and no one would explain it to him—she finally said to him, not touching him, "Did you shoot him or what?"

He had told them all a hundred times how it had happened: Robert climbing the fence and slipping.

He had explained it until he was sick with explaining it and they were sick of hearing it.

"Did you shoot him?" she said.

She kept looking at him, cold and unsmiling, her face smooth as wax and her hair pulled back.

Swan said finally, "I don't know." He was trembling when he spoke and he almost expected that she would take his trembling from him. If she touched him, embraced him, she could make him still again. But she did not. She sat looking at him for a while.

"Did you shoot him?" she said again.

"I don't know."

"When are you going to know?"

He stood helplessly. His brain buzzed as if alive with those fine brittle dragonflies he had seen that day; but he had no answer.

"What you don't know, keep your mouth shut about," Clara said harshly. "You understand me?"

5

He understood her. For some months he did not stop thinking about it, and for months after that he would not have been able to stop thinking about it even if he had tried.

312

Then, in the years that stretched out between Robert's death and his own eventual death, that memory was to return to him from time to time, as jagged and bright as on the day Robert had bled to death.

"You don't need to use that gun, that's all right," Revere told him. Swan knew that it had not been his gun but Robert's that had killed him, but this made no difference. He had wanted to give the gun to a boy at school, but his father took it from him and put it away. Revere had a habit now of breaking off his words in the middle of a sentence, staring at something up on the wall or in the sky; then he woke up and forgot what he had been saying. Swan was uneasy before him. It was as if he had opened a door suddenly and there his father was, unexpected, a different man from the one who had always sat so stern and straight at the table and who watched Clara with his strange, heavy stare, with an air of possession that did not make any attempt to listen to what Clara was saying.

On Sunday evenings, Revere began reading the Bible to them. He told them that his own father had done this.

In the winters those evenings were long and hot, because they sat down by the fireplace. Fire choked inside the big fireplace and its fumes spread out into the room. Sparks leaped out angrily onto the rug and Clara had an excuse to jump up and rub a smouldering spot with her foot, muttering "God!" under her breath. Revere sat by a humped hurricane lamp with fierce, dazed colors that seemed to rotate around its globe, and the rest of them sat around the table and listened until it was their turn to read.

Swan listened to those stories from out of a lost, crazy past, liking the Old Testament better than the New because nothing made much sense back there and things were yet to be decided. In the New Testament everything was finished and history was ended. Revere, reading the story of Moses or the various confused tales of people visited by punishments, would breathe quickly and deeply, his voice taking strength out of the grotesque violence itself. Swan would narrow his eyes and see in his father's blunt, graying head a shadow of God Himself. He felt excitement listening to those words, knowing that in a few lines the story would end with death or reward, it hardly mattered. Lurking over everything was the spirit of God, restless and haunting; it would swoop down now and then like a bird of prey, like a chicken hawk, and seize someone in its beak. Swan had the uneasy knowledge that he would be one of those siezed by the throat if the

313

world he and Clara now lived in belonged to that God—
which of course it did not—"God" was a word in a book like
many words in many books.

When they were alone he said to his mother, "Did you
ever talk to God or see Him or anything?"

"Are you crazy?"

"Like those people in the Bible. . . ? How come *he* talks
about it so much then?"

Revere was *he* to Clara and Swan; it was an impersonal
pronoun that always remained impersonal. It was true that
Revere talked of religion more now. Of "God." This had
crept up on them slowly enough, the way baldness, chronic
headaches, arthritis creep up on people. Clara showed by her
smirk that she was embarrassed of her husband in front of
her son, and this made Swan sorry he had asked. "Just shut
up and listen; do like me."

"But why do people take the time to believe it?"

Clara had been glancing through a magazine, staring at
full-page, colorful advertisements. She looked at Swan. "Believe in what?"

"God, and angels, and people like Moses. Why do they
believe it?"

"Honey, how the hell would I know?"

"They're not crazy, are they?"

"People have a right to their religion," Clara said, turning
a page. "He wants to think Robert is in heaven, maybe.
That's all right."

"How can he be in heaven?" Swan asked softly.

Clara turned another page.

"I wish he could be in heaven," Swan said.

"All right. Maybe he is. You can go there yourself someday and see him again," Clara said. Swan wanted to protest
that Robert's face was all ruined—all shot away. How would
he know Robert in heaven or anywhere else? He waited.
Leaning onto the table—it was one of Clara's new tables,
inlaid with marble, bought in Chicago and shipped all the
way out—he watched his mother's serious, blank face as she
pretended not to be aware of him. Sometimes, thinking of
Robert, he felt his stomach curdle as it had that day before
anything had happened but when the feeling of something
happening had been with him; he had not been able to shake
it. Because Revere never spoke of Robert after the funeral,
never said anything, Swan felt a sweaty, panicky need to
keep thinking of him. Robert became "Robert" as the months
passed and Swan could catch the boy's face only at acciden-

tal moments when he tried to recall him. Most of the time he could remember only a vague form without a face. He tried faces onto that form—those of boys from school, Jonathan, Clark. The death of Robert was not quite real to him but he felt that Robert would die again, would die forever, if he stopped thinking of him.

"Why do they get so mad about it?" he said suddenly. "Reverend Wiley gets mad, and other times he cries."

Wiley was the minister at the Lutheran church, six miles away. He was a small trembling man who put Swan in mind of a carrot—fluffy hair that stood up on top, a face made inanimate by thick glasses, a body that dwindled down uninterestingly into nothing. Someone said that Reverend Wiley had got stuck out here in the country and hated everyone and would never forgive God, but maybe that was a joke. Swan felt nothing for the man or for church except boredom.

"He's got nothing else to do. Anyway, it's his job," Clara said. She smiled at him. "Why are you so nosy?"

She picked at him, teased him into smiling. Clara never liked serious talk. He would have liked her to touch him but she didn't, so he felt a little resentful. He went on, frowning, "But God is real to them. He's watching them all the time. Do you think that's maybe true?"

"Oh, hell. There's nobody there."

"But—"

"But me no buts," she said. She turned a few more pages, singing under her breath. Swan heard words like "loveless love," "careless love," and he wondered what this had to do with his question. "Forget it, sweetheart," she said vaguely. Around the house now she wore soft, shabby sweaters of bright red or yellow or blue. They were supposed to be shabby, fuzzy. She looked very young. Sometimes she wore lipstick, sometimes she didn't. When she wore no lipstick and her face was shiny she looked like one of the girls at the high school. Swan was in sixth grade and in another year he could take the bus into Tintern along with Jonathan so that he could attend the consolidated school. There, in one big ugly building, were six grades of students—from seventh grade to twelfth. The oldest students were adults to Swan. He could imagine Clara dawdling down the hall with them but he could never imagine Revere there. Revere was different. He had never been that young. Swan had seen pictures of women dressed like Clara in her magazines, except they were thinner and their faces were like boys' faces. Clara's face was oval and full.

315

Clara finished the magazine and closed it with a flourish. She smiled at Swan. "Honey, are you still thinking about that crap?" She reached out to grab him, half wrestling, half tickling. Swan eluded her; then, when he saw she wasn't going to get up and chase him, he let her catch him. She coddled him and pressed her face against his. She sang in a husky, breathy voice: "Twas in the merry month of May, when green buds were . . . blooming. . . ." But when she sang her words came out absent-minded and vague.

"You don't think He's watching us?" Swan said.

But when Revere had him read from the Bible on Sunday evenings, Swan did not think of how crazy it all was. His spine straightened with pride as he read those strange, remote tales, and he felt surges of excitement as the words came alive and shaped into sense. He was sorry when his turn was over. And when Jonathan read it was unpleasant, because Jonathan stumbled and paused as if he had trouble with his tongue or maybe his eyes. They sat quietly, waiting. He read a line, hesitated, stuttered the first letter of a word, then plunged into the word and on down the line and on until he ran out of breath; sometimes he would swallow in the middle of a word. Swan did not look at his brother or Revere, but he could feel Revere looking at Jonathan. They sat quietly and listened, wishing themselves somewhere else—Swan and Clara and Clark—while Jonathan stammered on and Revere sat, his head bent a little with the concentration of listening, trying to get hold of the story somewhere behind his son's faltering voice.

Sometimes he said quietly to Jonathan, "Read that verse again."

And Jonathan would blunder through it again.

Sometimes Revere would even say, very quietly, "Read that again."

If Swan glanced at his mother to see what she thought, he discovered her face secret and closed. She did not seem to be listening after all. She was thinking about something else and Swan wished he could know what it was. Clark sat with his elbows on the big round table, frowning, his slightly blemished forehead prickled with lamplight and shadow. He was big now, over six feet tall. He had big shoulders and arms and a round, hard jaw; on this jaw and up onto his cheeks nearly to the soft skin beneath his eyes, there was always a dark beard, the glimpse of where his beard would be if he didn't shave every day. Swan looked at Clark to see what he thought and saw that Clark was thinking of nothing except getting away. After the Bible reading he would go out in his car to see a friend and he'd come in late that night; he was thinking about that.

So Jonathan blundered on. Swan thought that he could remember Jonathan reading school lessons to them, a few years ago, and Jonathan at that time had read without any mistakes. Something must have happened to him. Now he read like the dumbest kids in Swan's class; he might have been seven instead of fifteen. Swan thought this was strange. He did know that when it was his turn he seemed to be buoyed up by the poorness of Jonathan's reading and he was inspired to read even better himself, imitating the inflections and pauses of Revere's voice and of Reverend Wiley's voice. Clark read too fast and his words were all on one level, as if he were reading foreign words and could say only their sounds, not their sense. Clara said that she didn't like to read out loud, it was too slow that way, so she didn't have to read. Revere had asked her only once and she had grown flustered, her face had reddened, and she had told him in a fast sharp voice, she didn't like to read. "It would sound better in a man's voice," Revere said. When he asked Clara to do something and she refused, he met her refusal with silence and then added something to it, something to soften it where Clara hadn't bothered or hadn't known enough to bother.

Those were their Sunday nights.

Swan had lots of cousins but he didn't like most of them. At Christmas and Easter and the frequent occasions when people got married or died or had babies, the big Revere family got together. There was Judd's family, and Eric's family (he had six children and two old people living with him), and two or three other families with children Swan could not keep track of. Swan had always liked Judd, and his Uncle Eric was a bald, big man who talked too loud and was mainly interested in farming, so Swan liked him well enough. He liked and trusted adults because they left him alone.

At these big gatherings the kids ran wild and Swan had to stay close to Clara. If he'd gone out with them to play down by the creek, what might have happened? One time his cousins had ambushed him when he stepped fearfully into the hay barn, urged in by their pleads and promises. They were going to show him a new colt, they said. But when he stepped in the dark barn with its dry hot air slit by countless cracks of light, they had hit him with dozens of green pears and bloodied his nose. Then all the kids, including Swan, were blamed for picking pears from the orchard trees. So he stayed close to Clara no matter how people snickered. He did not mind. "Look how big he's getting," she would say, dragging him forward for some woman to glance at him. "He eats all the time, he's real healthy. Smart, too." Then she'd push him back a little and he could sit down again, forgotten, and wait patiently until it was time to drive home. He would have hated these gatherings if he had thought he might have an opinion about them. As it was, he thought of them the way he thought of blizzards, mud slides, any kind of bad weather or bad luck. If he was lucky he had a book to read. If not, he sat and waited. There was a great deal to listen to and try to understand in this aimless, meandering talk of adults. He discovered one thing: that people's talk went all over, started and stopped and started again, but that if someone had something to say he got it said—it just took a while. The important things were not the things said most often, but things alluded to quietly. Their talk was like a complex sloppy weaving. And he discovered another thing as the years went by: there was a vast territory conquered by these people and now wholly possessed by them, by their network of names and relationships, occasionally tied in with someone "in the city." The city people were admired but not trusted; when they were mentioned, it was often with a cynical smile, a sneer. Their world consisted of land and certain holdings, but more than that it consisted of people spread out everywhere, all the way to Europe—innumerable cousins, many of them girl cousins who were always getting "engaged." Swan had a sense of something holy and terrifying. As he sat listening, hunched over and shy, humble, patient, his need to be one of them and to share that name rose up in him like a wounding, deadly blossom opening inside his body. He had to be one of them and to understand and to possess everything. . . .

"Oh, farming, wheat and cows—dear God—" one of the younger women would say wearily and sweetly: someone's daughter, anxious to get out of the country. Or someone's young wife. There were two or three wives around here now who were younger than Clara; they were not shy but pushed right in conversations, crossing their legs and tugging down their skirts. They were not as pretty as Clara but they seemed not to notice. When the women talked together, Swan had to sit off somewhere because it would not look right if he was with them (Revere hated that), but he tried to hear what

318

they said. He tried to hear what his mother said. Bent over a book, pretending to read, he would flinch with shame when he sensed that Clara had been snubbed again. It was even worse because he could not be sure that she herself had sensed it.

His cousins ran outside, through the barns, through meadows, down to the inevitable creek that meandered through everyone's property. It was necessary to have a creek, Swan knew. All good farms had creeks. The kids occasionally chased cows until their milk ran dry, teased the horses until they stamped with rage in the stalls, threw stones at chickens, taunted the roosters, chased the cats, climbed apple trees and fought in the highest branches, started someone's car going downhill, stole cigarettes and smoked them in the barn, of all places, dared one another to feats of courage, usually jumping from ten to fifteen-foot heights. Robert and Jonathan had always run with them (Clark was always too old to care; sometimes he didn't even come to the gatherings) but Swan himself had stayed inside where it was safe. He did not mind them teasing him. "Little Swan! Little baby!" they called. After Robert's death, the teasings stopped. Swan felt lonely and brittle then. He was grateful for them leaving him alone but somehow he was not quite happy. He would like to have glanced up to see Robert somewhere, even if Robert had only come to tease him. . . .

There was only one cousin he liked, a girl. The other girls were loud and tough as the boys. "Revere" girls had reputations in school for being able to take care of themselves. But this girl did not run with them because she was "sickly," according to Clara. She was Judd's daughter Deborah, who was years younger than Swan. She too sat with the adults, with the women, but it did not look so strange with her. She had long thick brown hair and a small, pale, doll's face; she liked to read and she and Swan traded books. She could read anything they gave her when she was only five, her mother bragged. That mother was the woman Swan hated, so he did not think this was true. But when Deborah was alone he would approach her and ask her what she was reading.

"Grandma's old schoolbook," she would say.

She was a child but she did not act like a child. He had the idea she was more intelligent than both their mothers—there was a deep stillness to her eyes that fascinated him. She sat reading, on the periphery of the circle of chattering women, or by a window sill, as if she cared about nothing else. There were a few strands, come loose, of her long brown hair lying on her tiny shoulders.

Outside the window their cousins ran, shouting. Swan would say to Deborah, "How come you don't want to play with them?" She would look at him as if she saw nothing special where he was standing and say, "Because I don't want to." If he waited around she would not say much more; she would rather read. He could not decide if he hated her or liked her. He had the idea that she hated him the way all his cousins did, but that it had nothing to do with Robert.

One day when Clark drove Clara out to buy something, he talked to her in a way he had never talked before.

"Jonathan doesn't act right any more," he said. He was crude and knew it. He had to focus his big, clumsy gaze down to fit Clara's face and get his voice down soft enough for her to listen to. "I don't want to tell Pa because he'd get mad and I don't know what the hell'd happen. Jon's acting real funny. I don't know what he's going to do."

"Acting funny how?"

"He hangs around with a couple of guys—Jimmy Dorr's one of them, you know him? He was in the Navy and came back, nobody knows why. Jon hangs around with him and another guy. I heard some things about them."

"What things?"

"Just things," he said vaguely and sadly. He looked at Clara. "I think it might be because of Swan."

"Steven," Clara said. The name "Swan" now embarrassed her; it was not a good name. It was no name at all.

"Yeah, Steven," Clark said. His face had begun to redden. "Sw—Steven gets along better than Jon, he's smarter at school. I guess that's it. It used to be always Jon was the smartest in the whole school and everybody fussed over him."

"Well, whose fault is that?" Then Clara paused, as if realizing how bad she had sounded. She went on, "It's too bad. But he gets along with me all right."

"Maybe."

"He gets along with his father all right."

"Well—"

"What about it?"

"Sometimes he tells me how he hates Pa. He tells me that."

Clara looked at him sharply, as if he were confiding a precious secret to her without his exactly knowing it.

"He was like that a few years ago, when Ma was dying. I

mean, he was bad. He used to spend all his time reading, laying on his stomach on the floor, and Pa wanted him to go outside and do some chores," Clark said vaguely. He was rubbing the dirt-encrusted steering wheel of his expensive car. He and Clara watched the dirt peeling off. "That was before you came up.... Because we all knew about you then. I mean, everybody knew. How us kids found out was from some other kids at school. Robert wasn't in school yet. They told us things about Pa and were real nasty and I had to beat some of them up, then Uncle Judd told us about it and how we should keep quiet. That was then," he said, wondering why he had brought this up. "Jon was bad then for a while. He stayed away overnight in somebody's barn, then came back in the morning. Pa whipped him that time. That was the last time Pa whipped him; Jon got sick from it. He ain't strong like me. You ever see how his ribs show?" he said, glancing at Clara and screwing up his face so that Clara nodded, the two of them secure in a fleshly, healthy kinship that belongs only to those with handsome bodies. "Well, now he's getting that way again but he goes off more. He stays away."

Clara said softly, "I'm sorry to hear this. I like Jonathan."

"Yeah, he's all right. He's all right."

"I think he likes me—"

Clark said nothing.

"Everybody likes me," Clara said. "If I want them to like me I can get them—why not? Why shouldn't everybody like me?"

"I don't know." Clark smiled at her. "Listen, if they don't like you they're just jealous."

"But why shouldn't they? Why shouldn't Jonathan like me?" Clara said. She was very serious. Clark was accustomed to her teasing—she liked to taunt him slyly about his girl friends—but he saw that she was not teasing now. When she was serious there was something flat-footed and solid, even heavy, about her.

When school let out for Christmas vacation, Clara took Swan with her to Hamilton to visit for a week. She spent two days packing, walking stony-eyed with speculation back and forth in the bedroom, holding a dress on a hanger pressed against her. Swan lay on the bed. He did not particularly want to go to Hamilton, which he had seen just once; he hadn't liked the city and it had been raining then. But vacations were depressing out in this house, with Jonathan turning quietly away from him and Clara busy with new curtains or measuring floors for new expensive rugs she ordered by mail. And there was Revere, whom he thought of all the time as if there were something in that man he had to figure out and settle: he loved his father but was afraid of him, was nervous when his hand groped onto his shoulder with a vague, cold affection that might have once been directed toward someone else. He was hungry for Revere to love him but when that love swung onto him he wanted only to be somewhere else.

So he was glad to leave and, like Clara, was able to pretend sadness when they said good-by. Clara did not drive, but they went by train like people out traveling across the country with nothing special behind them or in front of them. Clara was restless in her seat, crossing and uncrossing her long legs, squinting at the faint reflection of herself the window gave. Swan read a few of the books he'd taken from his father's library at home—a library in the attic, a chaos of old books in boxes and trunks—but the rolling of the train distracted him. He was excited but had no object for his excitement. The books he read told of explorations in India and Asia, but this trip he and Clara were making seemed to him more exciting. Now and then Clara caught his eye and grinned, as if they were conspirators.

"It's good to get away," she said, nodding.

She ate chocolates, potato chips, limp sandwiches she'd packed for them, pickles and olives together in a little jar. Revere had warned her that food on the train was too expensive and was no good. Swan had no appetite, so she ate the sandwiches she had made for him too. "Don't say anything about us eating from a paper bag," she said, licking her fingers. "I mean to your aunt or anyone where we're staying." It was not that she and Revere were cheap, but that they hated to waste money. That was the only point the two of them really agreed upon—Swan, who was only ten, had noticed that himself. Money fell into his hands from Revere's relatives and occasionally from Revere himself, when Swan got up at five to help him with chores, but Clara gave him nothing. He saved these dimes and nickels solemnly, taking them out of his drawer to look at them, piling them up. He tried to keep them secret, as if he had the strange idea that Clara might take them from him. She might say, "What the hell do you want with these?" and sweep them away. . . .

When they arrived in Hamilton in a dark, crowded station, someone was waiting for them. A middle-aged woman in a fur coat and a younger man with a fat, pale face. Swan had never met these people before, but they talked to him as if they had met him; maybe at that funeral. Clara and the woman chattered together during the ride to the house they were to stay in, as if each of them was trying to imitate the other. Swan did not know which one was the imitation. Both talked lightly, cheerfully, leaning a little toward the other. Clara sat in back, the woman in front. Swan saw thin bluish crescents on the woman's eyelids. He heard about his father, who was "Curt" to these people, and about his brothers and himself, and the farm, and Clara's new rug—things he now saw from a new angle, surprising him. He had not known his father had been fighting a cold for weeks, and he had not known that Jonathan was growing up. He heard himself discussed fondly as if he were a pet or a piece of furniture. Yes, he was big: he was a little thin but tall for his age. He was five-one. Swan knew that was tall because other kids his age were shorter. He was able to listen to this without showing his irritation. He stared out the window at the sleek, icy streets, watching people hurry the way they never hurried out in the country.

"He's handsome. He'll be a handsome young man," the woman said. She had white hair that fell in gentle, lacy bangs onto her wrinkled forehead. Swan had not yet looked into her eyes, but only at her.

"I'm afraid I can't stand smoke. I just can't stand it," she said.

Clara put out her cigarette. "I'm sorry."

Swan wondered, had he ever heard her say she was sorry before?

They stayed at the same house the funeral had been at, so he must have met these people. He had no clear idea who they were, though it had probably been explained to him; he was not interested. Grownups did not interest him because nothing they did was of any interest. They certainly would not hurt him. Clara explained that the boy was a cousin of his and he was surprised to hear that man called a "boy." "He's only twenty or so," Clara said. Swan made a noise to indicate that twenty was old; Clara glared at him and pretended to be mad. She had one bedroom and he had another, but they were linked by a door. They were on the second floor but it was a higher second floor than back home, and Swan could look down a long white hill to the lake. The lake was frozen so there were no boats on it. He would have liked to see boats sailing across that white expanse, but nothing came—it was empty. A sense of oppression settled on him,

323

not scattered but made more intense by all the surfaces in his room that reflected light. Many polished arms, legs, expanses of wood. A heavily ornate bed with a crocheted white cover, a chest of drawers that looked as if the worms had gotten to it, a desk of a queer useless kind with wobbly legs, vases and candlestick holders and even doorknobs that gleamed. He had his own bathroom and for some reason this fact frightened him. He did not want to be so alone.

While Clara showered in her own bathroom he waited for her, sitting on the edge of her bed. The mattress was hard. One of her suitcases was opened and some clothes looked as if they had flung themselves out and fallen on the edge of the suitcase. Having nothing else to do, Swan folded them up and put them back inside. Then he sat and waited. He wished the two of them were back home.

Clara sang while she kept him waiting. The door was open and steam came out. Swan lay back and thought of their home, of his own room and his dog—though he didn't much like the dog because it was too vicious, it gobbled field mice and then vomited them up—and his father and brothers. It seemed to him strange and unlikely that he and Clara had really come from a home like that. Maybe when they went back there would be no such place, or Revere wouldn't let them in the door. He would say, "Who are you?" Clara came out barefoot, smoothing her slip down over her thighs. She wore a black slip. Swan watched her and felt something warm in his blood like shells that seemed hard but became transparent and then dissolved away.... "Too bad there aren't any other kids around here," she said. Swan did not know what she meant by this. She pulled the clothes back out of the suitcase in a heap, not noticing how he had straightened them. "What am I looking for?" she muttered. Her hair fell heavily across her face and she brushed it back. She found what she wanted—some stockings. Swan saw that she was warm from the shower and that already tiny droplets of perspiration were forming on her forehead. He saw the white powder dabbed on her shoulders and chest get coarse.

"Oh, you little pest," she said, "why don't you make yourself useful? Find my hairpins, they fell all over inside the suitcase. Goddam them...."

When they went downstairs, Swan smelled food and his mouth reacted violently. But supper did not come for hours. He had to sit through a long, long session in the living room, while people he had never seen before and hated talked to Clara and pretended to talk to him. After a while they stopped pretending. He sat glassy-eyed, waiting to eat. He had no idea who these people were or where they had come from, but he wanted to shout at them to get home so they could eat. The tiny crackers and junk the woman with the lacy bangs passed around were just half a mouthful apiece, and after he had taken a few of them Clara looked at him to indicate he should stop.

The adults had drinks. They talked. Clara was wearing a dress that was silky, black and white, and the nervous arch of her back made Swan know that she was happy. She sat with him on a strange off-white sofa that wasn't really a sofa because it was too short by one seat, and after a while she had turned her back on him. He saw people watching her. They smiled, they liked her. Or did they like her? He wondered if she laughed too much. She accepted another drink, maybe that was wrong. A woman in a dark dress laughed loudly too, but maybe she was better at it than Clara. There was one other woman, an old woman, and the rest were men: Swan's cousin, that "boy" with his fat serious face; a man with glasses; a man who kept tapping his fingers on a shiny-topped side table. Another man came in after a while. Swan was drugged with boredom when they finally went in to eat. He was surprised that the rest of the company came along, as if they didn't know enough to go home when people had supper.

In the dining room Clara said, "Oh, that painting is beautiful." The woman with the bangs smiled and linked her arm through Clara's. That had been a right thing to say. Swan was glad for his mother. At the table there were more things that gleamed; his eyes ached. He must have fallen asleep in his chair because, some time later, Clara leaned over to nudge him awake. "Steven? Sweetheart, are you tired?" She would never have spoken so gently to him had they been alone, so when he jerked awake he did it with the consciousness that someone besides Clara must be watching him.

The next morning Clara had to go somewhere with the aunt to a luncheon and Swan stayed behind. A colored girl made him lunch but it wasn't enough, just a sandwich and some cookies. He sat at the long shiny dining-room table, hunched over. Outside the big windows snow was falling and he thought of how it fell on Revere's land on the grave that was Robert's out behind the Lutheran church. Not far from it had been another stone, a bigger one, with the name Revere on it too; it had been a woman's name. And then, when you looked up, you saw Revere everywhere—a garden of them. He said his name, Steven Revere, and then a quieter voice said his real name, which was Swan Walpole. If they put him under a stone with the name Revere on it, who would care? He wouldn't care.

He had found out that his name was Walpole because one day he'd looked through Revere's papers and found a marriage license. Clara Walpole, Curt Revere. Some dates and information. Along with it was a photograph he had never seen before, of his mother and father on their wedding day maybe, Clara smiling too broadly so that her cheeks dimpled and her eyes narrowed, Revere stern and drawn back as if he were fighting a sneeze. Swan had put the things back carefully and closed the filing cabinet drawer. When he left the room he had been trembling.

He said his real name out loud so that he wouldn't forget it: it was Steven Revere.

Clara came back and the aunt was with her, breathing a little hard. She hugged Swan and told him they were going to the museum now. He remembered something about a museum from the night before—the man with the tapping fingers had told him about it. The museum was something he would like and they shouldn't miss it. The aunt told them good-by.

So they went there in a taxi. Clara was very excited. Her cheeks were flushed; Swan noticed how the taxi driver stared at her, and it made him feel strange. She smelled of perfume like flowers. She opened her compact and looked at herself in the mirror, turning her head from side to side. She rubbed her front teeth hard with her tongue, back and forth in a sideways motion. Talking to Swan in a rapid, quiet voice, she kept looking at herself, as if that tiny face in the mirror was the face she was really addressing.

"It isn't like the last time. I knew I should try again. Revere is crazy not to like them, he doesn't know how to talk. He's just a country—he's just from the country. He doesn't know how to talk with people like them."

Swan had never known that his father didn't know how to talk. He wondered what Clara meant.

"They know so much, they talk about so many different things. At this woman's house there were maybe ten, fifteen women—she had them all for lunch—luncheon. All those women! It must have cost fifty dollars, I bet. We all sat at the table and everything was beautiful, she had silver—I guess it was silver. Everything was of the highest quality." She spoke quickly, excitedly. The word "quality" was like liquid gold rolling from her tongue.

The museum was so big it frightened him. She took his hand and pulled him up the long dirty steps. "This is good for you, you can tell your teacher about it," she said vaguely. It was snowing and a few flakes fell onto her hair. Swan hoped the museum was closed but it was not. A guard, an old man with a face like gray crepe paper, was leaning against a counter in which books were for sale. He smiled at Clara and tipped his hat. "Now, that over there—that's some armor or something," Clara said, showing Swan some armor. "They wore them over in England a long time ago. Isn't that queer?" They ascended a few more steps and Swan looked at some armor. It was tarnished and must haven been for a child or a dwarf. It baffled him; the headpiece was no higher than he was.

"These things were all for soldiers," Clara said.

"But you could shoot right through it," Swan pointed out.

She pulled him on. He saw spears, hammers, strange blunt things on chains. Tarnished shields. Everything had to do with fighting and made Swan shiver. "Why's that so little?" he said, pointing back to the armor. Clara had walked on and did not hear. Her high heels made too much noise on the marble floor and the sound echoed everywhere. Swan followed along and glanced into dimly lit rooms and up at the high, incredible ceiling that was decorated with gold and blue; then out of one of the side rooms a man came. It was the man who had tapped on the table the night before.

"I'm sorry I'm late," Clara said, smiling.

He said hello to Swan. Swan saw that he was younger than Revere; he wore a dark overcoat that was not heavy like Revere's, but looked as if it would not keep much cold out. He had unbuttoned it so that it swung open.

Clara sent Swan off to look at some things. He walked fast and did not look back, hating her, then he found himself in a room of statues that caught his attention: bulls, bears, lions. He liked their heavy, dangerous look. He stroked the back and head of one of the lions. You could almost feel the muscle beneath the iron or whatever the statue had been made of. It was a small statue, no longer than his arm. He pressed his forehead against it. He stood like that, imagining he could hear the heartbeat of the little iron animal. It was crouched like that forever, waiting. He stroked the sleek hard shoulder muscles, admiring it, not thinking about the man who had made it but only about the animal itself somehow trapped within the iron—it was a real animal but something had happened to it. He could understand that. That made sense, because sometimes he himself felt that he could change into iron, get hard and solid and unafraid. Inside the hard iron that kept the animal quiet there were the same old muscles and the pounding of blood and the appetite for small, shrinking animals that it had always had. Swan could understand that.

He walked aimlessly. There were few people in the museum that afternoon and they were startled to see a child appear out of nowhere. His eyes began to ache and he wished he were home. Just when he thought he was lost, he walked through a doorway and saw his mother and that man, sitting on a marble bench talking. He backed away. The man sat with his elbows on his knees, bending forward as if he were talking very seriously. Clara was leaning back, her legs crossed, smoking a cigarette. She had unbuttoned her coat so that it swung open. Swan could not hear what they said and he did not give a damn.

The next day she took him out "shopping." They went to a dark store with junk piled up in it and Clara bought something. Swan looked at a price tag on an old ugly candlestick that was tarnished; the figure said $50 but must have been a mistake. Clara wore white gloves and Swan could guess, by the skeptical way the shopkeeper looked at her, that she would be buying quite a bit. He had a foreign accent. Swan looked at himself in a cracked yellowish mirror and did not especially like what he saw. That mirror was priced at $285 and must have been a mistake too.

"What's that?" Swan said, pointing.

"A fruit dish. I bought a fruit dish," Clara said. The man was wrapping it up. The fruit dish was like something his aunt had, the one with the feathery bangs. His aunt's dish was a little junkier than this one so he supposed his aunt would be embarrassed by Clara's purchase and he wished she had not made it.

The taxi driver was a different man, but he looked at Clara the way the first driver had. She had done something to her eyes—there were thin silvery-blue crescents on her eyelids. Her lashes looked longer. "Mister, where's the library?" she said. "Isn't there a library or something around here?" They found the library: it was made of the same wet-looking gray stone as the museum and the house they were staying in. Swan did not understand at first what Clara meant when she told him she had something to do and he would like that library; there was nothing like it where they came from.

"All by myself?" he said, swallowing.

"The books are going to eat you up?"

"How long?"

"Look, I thought you liked books so much. Out where we come from there isn't anything like this, right?"

It must have been serious, to make her say "out where we come from" in front of the driver. After a moment Swan got slowly out of the car. He went slowly up the gray steps and into the library, not bothering to look back when he heard the cab pull away. Once he was inside the building, he smelled the rich warm odor of leather and books and felt that he might be safe for a while.

He sat by himself near a fireplace. The fireplace was empty. An old man sat at the next table, half asleep. Swan read about rockets and all the planets. The librarian approached him and he smelled gum. "The room across the way is for children," she said, staring at him.

Swan didn't want her to hear his accent because he knew it was so back-country she might throw him out. So he nodded politely and slid out of the chair and went across the way.

A few children here, with mothers. They did not linger. He brought a pile of books to one of the glass-topped tables and read through them one by one. He read about a boy of fifteen who owned a stallion, but that boy did not talk the way Jonathan did or even the way Swan himself did. He read about two boys who solved a mystery. He read about a boy who stowed away in a rocket ship and went to Venus. Behind these stories something pulsed furious and dark, content to wait for him to acknowledge it.

Finally he whispered, as if the word had forced itself out of him, "That bitch."

It got to be three o'clock, then three-thirty. At four-thirty he had stopped reading and sat with a book just open in front of him. The book had large type and its pages were soiled by children's fingerprints; dozens of children must have been picking their noses over this book. It was about frogs who went to school.

At a minute to five the lights flicked off and on, so Swan guessed the building was closing. He slid out of his chair at once and put on his coat while he hurried to the door. He and the old man walked out together, anxious to show they belonged somewhere else, had somewhere else to go to. Once outside, the old man arched his back against the wind and hurried down the steps but Swan followed him only a short distance.

Swan waited until the doors were locked and the library darkened, then he came back up the steps and sat down with his back against the wall, in a corner. The wind did not bother him too much here, but his bottom got cold. He waited. After a while another taxi pulled up and Clara got out. He saw her stand for a moment on the sidewalk, quite still. The wind had blown her hair loose; she wore it piled high up on her head. Her fur coat was soft and gentle, rippling in the wind. After a moment he got to his feet, grunting with the effort like an old man, and she saw him.

When they were in the taxi she said, "I hope you don't catch cold."

He had to sit through the drinking session again and through dinner. The man with the tapping fingers was back again; Swan stared at him bitterly. He thought he could take one of the little forks they used for shrimp and drive it into that man's throat. The man smiled right back into Swan's bitterness without noticing it. Clara sat nowhere near that man, but Swan was aware of them listening to each other— he could feel them listening to each other, almost feel the tense cords in his mother's neck in that instant before she laughed joyfully at something that man said.

After dinner he was able to get away and go up to his room, where he fell asleep without undressing. He did not understand where adults got their strength. Sometime later Clara came in. "Why aren't you in bed the right way?" she whispered. She kicked off her shoes and sat on the edge of the bed, beside him. He woke up slowly, confused. The light had been left on overhead and it hurt his eyes. At first he could not remember where he was.

"So, sweetheart, you're mad at me?" she said. He could smell her perfume and something else—the liquor everyone drank downstairs, perhaps, or the odor of her secret life, what made her laugh so happily at that man's jokes and what made her backbone so stiff with wonder. "Don't be mad at me, I'm so happy . . . so happy. . . . Tomorrow we're going home and I'm happy to go home. I'm happy here and I'm happy at home." She began to cry. Swan was frightened. He did not want to look at her. Finally she said, "I can't help it, I'm just so happy—I feel so good. Nobody has ever felt like me, nobody has ever been happy like me."

For the first time in his life he did not share her mood. He looked away from her, sullen and a little shaky; he remembered that name he had called her in the library, that name he had said to himself. But he did not regret it. He wanted to punish her and that name was a punishment, even if she did not know what he had done.

330

6

When Swan was twelve and in seventh grade, he took the bus to Tintern along with the older kids. The school bus was painted a mustard yellow and had black letters on it: Eden County Consolidated Schools. The bus driver was a thin, empty-eyed man with a wheezing cough. Right behind him sat his "girl friends," day after day, and whatever he said would cause them merriment that was energetic and loud. They were plump, freckled, awkward girls, blemished in some way even if just by their large, lipsticked mouths. They were curious about Swan but did not bother him.

There were three or four other Reveres on the bus—"Reveres who don't count," Clara said—but they avoided Swan. Jonathan sat at the very back with the biggest, loudest boys. Swan would not have dared approach him. He sat as near the front as he could without getting too close to the bus driver's girl friends, in a kind of limbo where kids no one liked sat: a fat sad boy, a girl said to be "loony," though Swan thought she was just quiet. On the rides back and forth Swan read through his lessons, and if something was thrown onto his lap or struck him on the back of the head, he would try to laugh to show that it was a joke, he knew it was just a joke, but he wouldn't ask who had done it.

If he could get through these years, he thought, gazing at the smudged obscene words scrawled on the steam of the bus windows, he would be safe.

When Jonathan bought his car, Clara asked him why he didn't want to take Swan along to school. Why should Swan take the bus with all that trash? Jonathan looked like a cornered rat; he said he had pals to pick up, miles away, and he had to leave early. Swan wouldn't like his pals.

"Steven," Clara said.

"Steven wouldn't like them," said Jonathan.

"But he's your brother, you should be glad to take him along," Clara said. "He says he hates the school bus."

"It's my car," Jonathan whined.

"He's your brother."

Jonathan looked as if he were about to refute this, but he said nothing. Swan, embarrassed, stared at Jonathan's pale, pimply face and wondered what had happened to him. He hadn't grown for the last two years or so and he was getting bad grades at school. There was something shy and hunted and ratlike in his eyes, no matter when you saw him: he was taking on the look of those kids Clara called white trash. Loudly as they shrieked, wildly as they laughed, they always looked hungry. Swan could not believe that he had ever thought Jonathan strong and confident—he remembered the first day he had seen Jonathan, on his mother's wedding day, and it was a mystery how Jonathan had changed.

"I can ride on the bus," Swan said.

Clara did not seem to have heard him. "It's a nice car, Jon bought it himself and he should be proud of it," she said. "He wouldn't want his brother to ride that crappy school bus."

After two months of seventh grade, Swan was skipped into eighth. This only meant crossing the hall, being assigned to another desk. These kids were older and there was only one Revere in the room—a long-legged boy who smoked cigars out behind the school. He must have told his friends strange things about Swan, because they stared at him with a kind of suspicious curiosity, never getting too close. Swan knew enough to stay away from them.

He sat near the front of the room, in a desk directly before the teacher's desk. Since he could do his work faster than anyone else, he always finished first and then sat drawing pictures in his notebook. He drew a picture of the teacher, who was a woman of about forty, forty-five, aged and ancient to Swan but likeable; he would never say the things about her the other boys did. She wore her hair cut short and straight about her face, so that she looked like a dog. Swan thought of her as the only person of value in the room, the only person he could learn from. So when she spoke, he sat straight and listened as if he would have liked to drain all her words right out of her and keep them for himself. He did extra credit assignments in math and English, he read the books she lent him, he lingered after class to ask her questions. . . .

"You don't want to be late for lunch," she would point out. Or, after school: "You don't want to miss the bus."

After some months she said, in an awkward nervous way no adult had ever spoken to Swan: "Did you ever—did you have an accident of some kind? With your brother?" Swan felt his face get red. He nodded yes; a hunting accident. The teacher paused for a moment. Then she said, "Of course it was an accident. I'm sure it wasn't what those boys say."

But he realized after a while that she was afraid of him.

And Jonathan too: that was the greatest surprise. Jonathan gave in with a sigh and said he would drive Swan to school; what else could he say? He might have been thinking of that old whip his father still had somewhere in the barn. Or he might have wanted to give in to Clara, holding out for a while and then giving in with a helpless expulsion of breath, his keen unsteady gaze moving up onto her as if dazzled by what he saw—and when he said yes, Clara had slid her arms around his neck and hugged him. And that night she had made his favorite pie, which was pumpkin pie (and Swan didn't like that at all), and he ate three big pieces of it, as if ravished by hunger.

What happened was that one day in early winter Swan found a jackknife in the mud near school. No one was around so he picked it up, wiped it off, and put it in his pocket. Clara did not want him to have a knife and he had never thought about getting one either, there was something dangerous about a knife—you might suddenly jab it into someone's throat just to see how it felt. But this old knife was rusted and dull. So he kept it and forgot about it and that afternoon when Jonathan was driving home he thrust his hand into his pocket and there it was.

Always he tried to talk to Jonathan. He tried to offer him something, anything. So now he took out the knife and said, "See what I got?" and the very inflection of his voice was that of any boy's—he was imitating the boys he heard all day long in school.

Jonathan looked over at him. He saw the knife and his face went white—Swan even heard his breath being sucked in.

"I found it in the mud," Swan said. "I don't know who lost it."

Jonathan's car swerved just a little, enough for them both to notice, then he straightened it out and began to drive faster. After the first moment he was not afraid, but he had been afraid for an instant and both he and Swan knew it. "It's just junk, I don't want it," Swan said shakily. "You want it?"

"I don't want nobody else's shitty knife," Jonathan said viciously.

So Swan opened the window and threw the knife out, just to show Jonathan he meant no harm. How could Jonathan think he had meant harm? He was only twelve and Jonathan was seventeen. . . .

"I just found it in the mud," Swan said.

Jonathan said nothing.

The next morning Swan took the school bus again and never bothered Jonathan about a ride. Clara, who had cared so much about this a few months before, now did not care at all. "Yes, maybe it's better, you can meet some kids to play with, and some girls," she said vaguely. Her kitchen was being done over and everywhere canvas lay harsh and gritty underfoot.

Once he was freed from Swan, Jonathan drove off and spent the day any way he liked: the hell with school. He was still a junior, he hadn't been passed on. So he drove a few miles down the valley and picked up two other kids and they went fishing or inspected motorcycles and used cars in a big slummy lot out on the highway, or, after a while, they got to certain corners before the school bus arrived and drove certain girls to school, though the girls didn't always have time for school.

If Revere was out of town, Jonathan wouldn't bother coming home for supper. They ate in a diner out on the highway, fifteen miles away. He knew that Clara would not tell on him. When the notices started arriving from school asking about why he was absent so much, Clara talked seriously with him and he said that he hated school, he hated the teachers and kids. He was defiant and on the verge of tears. But Clara touched him and said, after a moment, "I know how it is." So she did not tell Revere. He could trust her.

"She's a goddam filthy bitch," he would say to his friends. "I'd like to slit her up and down and hang her out to drain." And he spat onto the ground, his face contorted with disgust. One of his friends was over twenty, in and out of the Navy already (he had been let go), and he always asked about Clara: did Jon ever see her undressed? Did she walk around without all her clothes on, ever? Jonathan flushed at his questions, embarrassed and angry. Clara ran around the house any way she liked, barefoot and with her hair wet and loose down her back, dripping onto her blouse, and at night she made popcorn for herself and Swan, wearing one of her many robes and not always bothering to see that it was buttoned—but he was not going to tell anyone about this. It was nobody's business what Revere's wife did.

"Why the hell do you want to know?" he sneered. Skinny as he was, no match for this guy, he had no care for how arrogantly he talked—it might have seemed he was asking

334

for a punch in the mouth. "You wouldn't ever have no chance with her, so forget it."

"Wouldn't be too sure of that," his friend said.

So Jonathan laughed scornfully and nastily.

The girls they drove around were the same girls who had been on the school bus for years with them. Now, suddenly, everyone was older. Some girls had already quit school, were married and had babies. It went so fast—the years went so fast, Jonathan thought. He drank more than anyone else because he had more to push out of his mind. They drank for fun but he drank for serious reasons; then, after a certain point, he forgot the reasons and was able to have fun. They drove twenty, thirty miles to get beer and liquor, knowing in mysterious ways just where a certain roadhouse was, what its prices were, what its manager was like. They knew everything, yet no one could have said how they knew; it was mysterious knowledge, breathed in with the air around them.

They went to all the outings and charity picnics. But when the Lutheran church had its outing Jonathan stayed home alone, he didn't say why. While Clara and Revere and Swan and Clark went, he stayed around the house, acting strange. The idea that just a few yards back in the cemetery his mother and brother were buried made him sick: how could people wolf down hot beef sandwiches and all that beer, those barrels and barrels of beer, when out back bodies were rotting and stinking in the soil? Didn't anyone know that?

So he stayed home, feeling shaky, and played poker with the few hired men who hadn't enough money to go out. When Revere and the others came home that evening, he was sitting on the porch steps as if waiting for them. He knew Revere liked that. Or he had liked it, in the days when he still liked Jonathan. It was after dark, so he had taken down Revere's flag and folded it up right.

Clara had talked Revere into buying that flag. She had said that she was proud of being an American, and didn't he want a flag? So they bought one and were American. When Jonathan wandered back from the woods with his gun, he had the desire to shoot the flag into tatters, he didn't know why. What would happen then? What would his father do to him?

He didn't sleep well at night but not because of dreams. He had the idea he never dreamed. He had nothing to dream about.

Clark had warned him about the girls he went out with: "They're pigs, so be careful. You know what I mean."

Clark knew everything, he knew about all the girls. Twenty

miles away they'd heard of Clark and were surprised that Jonathan was his brother. But any girl so sluttish that Clark would have nothing to do with her was just right for Jonathan, he thought; she would have to like him. Who else could she get? They weren't ugly, exactly, he and his friends, but there must have been something wrong with them—the prettiest girls ignored them. They had enough money, or at least Jonathan did and he could lend money to the other boys, but still the best-looking girls avoided them and they were always crowded by a certain kind of heavy, lipsticked, sly girl who liked them well enough and laughed uproariously at their jokes. These girls were always impressed by Jonathan's car and the remote prickly excitement of knowing he was a Revere—even if he himself was a disappointment, too thin, and with skin that was never clear. Wasn't he a Revere, might there not be a chance of catching him? Clark went out with a pretty, long-haired girl from Tintern who worked in the drugstore, and this girl certainly wasn't good enough for Revere—he would never let Clark marry her—so the girls Jonathan was able to get were so low that Revere would not even have spat on them, and he felt satisfaction in this.

Maybe he would bring one of them right into the house someday and announce he was marrying her: she was pregnant and that was that. He would stare into his father's face to see what he thought. "I'm not the only one in the family that can marry a whore," he would say to his father.

And what would his father do? Whip him again?

The most he could do would be to kill Jonathan.

He thought about getting a job, since his friends had "jobs." They worked part-time in a service station. By now, his father would have given him a job somewhere if he was ever going to; he had given Clark a job when Clark had been only sixteen. So that was out. He was not going to ask his father about it because it was evidently settled that he wanted no part of Jonathan. Or he might be waiting for Jonathan to straighten out. But it came to the same thing. So he thought vaguely about finding a job somewhere, but he had no skills, knew nothing, could hardly change a tire. He hated the smell of gas, so how could he work in a filling station?

He thought, the hell with getting a job. He didn't want one anyway.

He had a year and a half of school yet to go but he did not go back in the fall. As far as he was concerned, he was finished with it forever. Since he was stupid, there was no point in bothering—he might as well be dead. "Did you ever wish you were dead?" he asked Clark. But Clark, running off to his girl friend, had no time for him. "Did you ever wish you were dead?" he said to his Uncle Judd, whom he resembled closely; but questions like this made Judd nervous. Since that time in the back meadow—the accident with Robert's shotgun—Judd had seemed more nervous. Or was Jonathan just imagining it? Sometimes he himself could hear that blast, then the screaming. . . .

(He had jumped off his horse and run back, and at first he hadn't seen anything at all. Then he saw it. He saw what the shot had done to Robert and how what had been Robert was shattered forever. Just like that. It did not matter that he died later, because he was dead right then. You couldn't fix up anyone who looked like that. . . . A few feet away Swan had been standing.)

"Did you ever wish you were dead?" he said to one of his father's men during harvest. The men all worked hard and were paid well, so they had to like Revere. They saw him rarely enough, so it was easy to like him. Jonathan supposed that they did not like him but he was so scrawny, so punky, that they couldn't be jealous, at least, because he was a Revere. The men thought he was crazy and all they asked him about was Clara—when he told them to shut up they lost interest.

The night he ran away and disappeared, he was out with a girl from a small farm some miles away. She was only fourteen but she looked older: she had a big, sturdy body and long bleached hair that fell past her shoulders. She wore pink lipstick and her fingernails were painted to match. They got beer from a roadhouse and drank it for a while on the back porch of that place until the manager said they'd better leave, some state troopers were probably going to drop in, so they drove around for a while in the dark drinking it while the girl complained about her mother, and finally they parked and finished what was left of it. In the back seat of the car Jonathan wrestled around with her and she teased him, giggling drunkenly, and when she finally gave in he felt that something dangerous was approaching him. He could feel it coming as if he were standing on a railroad track and it had begun to vibrate. For years he had fooled around with girls like this, it meant nothing to him, it was nothing more than going to the bathroom—almost the same thing—but now he felt icy with fear. He tried to make love to the girl but something was wrong. He went cold, dead. Then, when she

337

tried to get up, he began hitting her. He screamed into her
face.

"Slut! Filthy bitch!"

He bloodied her face and punched her in the stomach and
breasts. He wept with the ferocity of his hatred. Then he
pushed her out of the car and left her, his tires kicking up
pebbles and dust behind him as he pulled away—and that
was that.

7

Outside the high school building it was a cold, clear
November day. Many boys had skipped school to go hunting;
that was against the "law," but the principal was a cheerful
manly man who would not expel anyone. So there was a
strange sense of holiday or half-holiday in the air—the usual
girls had come to school but only about half the boys had
showed up. Swan liked the relative peace in the corridor
around his locker. The girls chattered and giggled the way
they always did, but it was not quite so high-pitched, so
self-conscious. There were no boys nearby to hear them
except Swan, who did not count.

He was only sixteen but a senior already, and he must
have carried this fact around with him without knowing it
like a stamp or tattoo on his forehead that identified him as a
freak. In the locker room he could not approach any group
of boys and join them, because he didn't know how, nor did
he want to know how; out in the corridors or on the stairs or
outside in the parking lot, he could not sidle up to any girl
and tease her in that certain winning way, because he did
not know how and he supposed he did not want to know.
Revere had told him about girls and that he should be
careful of any situations that might lead to temptation.
"Temptation." It was a word out of the Bible and Swan
bowed his head in admiration for its holy and ancient useless-
ness. These days, Revere spoke a little loudly but you had to
pretend nothing was unusual. He was hard of hearing, Clara
explained; that always happened to men. But she thought it
better to let someone else tell Revere about it. So he instructed
Swan in a loud, slightly embarrassed voice that he should
avoid temptation. He was not yet old enough to understand
the complexities of his own body, and when he was old

338

enough, Revere would explain it. For the time being, he should just avoid temptation.

When he'd been only twelve, Clara had told him all about it. He had gotten the idea from her that it was something he would be doing sooner or later, preferably sooner because then he could "grow up better," that it always made a girl happy, but only if she was the right kind of girl. Clara was emphatic about this. "Someone like your cousin Debbie—no. Nobody around here. Nobody on a big farm. But some of those people that live down by the river in those dumps— with all the junk around them—and any time you see a girl standing round a bunch of boys and they're all laughing together—probably she's all right. You understand?"

He respected Revere's standards but he supposed that his mother was right and Revere was wrong. So he stopped thinking about it. He had so much else to think about that he would have to put off anything like that for a while—when he got older, and when Revere had explained to him everything that he had to know, then he would have time for himself. He would then have the rest of his life for himself.

So he did his homework in free periods at school and at home he did additional work and read books that were related to his courses. He did not let these books interfere with his teachers' teaching, though. He could respect their kindly limitations. And he went with Revere on small errands, to Tintern and to other small towns and once all the way to Hamilton, sitting beside his father in his father's new big black car and inclining his head toward him, listening to what his father had to say about money, taxes, buildings, land, wheat, gypsum, and men that had to be hired for the lowest possible pay. He could feel his head filling up slowly. At times he woke to the fear that his head would burst, that facts and ideas were being squeezed into his brain too fast, before he was able to make room for them. But he kept on studying and working at school and at home, he kept on listening to Revere and to the men Revere talked with. His ears were like holes in his head that sucked in information and stored it away, useless as it might seem to be at the moment. Everything he heard was sucked in. He never forgot anything. Along with the important equations he memorized in physics and chemistry were jumbled conversations he had overheard between his mother and someone's new wife she was trying to befriend, or vicious oaths spat out on the cramped litle gym floor when the boys were playing basketball, or the sweetly sickish popular songs the girls hummed to themselves out in the corridor. He never forgot anything.

That day he felt a sense of holiday too, but it made him apprehensive. He did not trust unusual feelings. In English class, half the desks were vacant and it was easy to figure out that the toughest boys weren't present: just Swan and two or three boys who would never succeed at anything, especially not at being boys, and a dozen girls. Swan despised this English teacher because she was so like himself, so uncertain. She was a new teacher, just graduated from college the spring before, and he had to turn his pencil round and round in his fingers as she spoke, to find some outlet for his own nervousness. She looked around the room, fearful of seeing something out of place, and finally, ten minutes after each class began, her gaze would come to rest timidly on Swan's face; she could sense that he was different, like herself, he was quiet and that maybe meant he was shy; at least he was intelligent and the rest of the students were stupid. Stupid. Of course they were all stupid, who would expect anything else? Swan did not dislike them for being stupid, he was grateful to them. Whoever was stupid was beneath worry or thought; you did not have to figure them out. This eliminated hundreds of people. In this life you had time only for a certain amount of thinking, and there was no need to waste any of it on people who were not threatening.

Swan sat in the outer row near the windows. A few feet away the window was open a crack, slanted downward, so that the fresh hard air eased onto the side of his face. With one part of his mind he listened to the teacher and with another part of his mind he thought about what he was going to do. Clara talked more and more about living permanently in Hamilton, and he would have to help her with that. It would take them a few years to convince Revere. His father spoke vaguely of how Swan and Clark were to take over everything of his someday, when he got "old and worn out," as he put it—with a special forlorn grin that meant he was joking, he'd never get old and worn out. Swan thought about that. Clark was twenty-four and that meant he was eight years older than Swan. He talked to Swan only the way you'd talk to a child. He would always talk to Swan that way, he would never be able to accept Swan as an equal. . . .

"Steven?" the teacher was saying.

Swan answered the question. He felt the girls looking at him, then back up to the teacher to see if he was right. But of course he was right—they were tired of him. They sighed, they exchanged glances. Swan wanted to snarl across at them, "I didn't ask to be smart." But he sat still, turning his pencil round and round. It had got to be that whenever he was sitting or standing still he had to keep some part of him moving, usually his fingers. He didn't know why. Sometimes he jerked his toes around, hidden safe inside his shoes, so that no one could see; sometimes he tapped his fingernails lightly on the desk. But he could not sit perfectly still. He had the idea that his brain would burst if he did not direct energy away from it.

The bell rang and they filed out. Swan came to the front of his aisle in order to cross over to the door, lowering his gaze. He avoided his teacher's eyes. It was not that he was really shy, as they thought, but that he hadn't time to worry about his relationship with them. He hadn't time to assess and catalogue anyone else. So when he saw the English teacher hurriedly put some papers together, he supposed she wanted to talk with him—about college again—and he walked with shoulders hunched forward out into the corridor where he would be safe.

But he was just outside the door when he heard her say, "Steven?" So he had to wait. She caught up with him, a tall ungainly woman in thick-heeled shoes, with a voice always gentle when she wasn't teaching. "Have you talked to your parents any more about college? What did they say?"

Swan had talked to no one. He wasn't going, he couldn't leave home. He said, "They want me home for a year. My pa is sick."

"But—"

She had nothing to say. Swan waited politely for her to let him go.

"I'm sorry to hear that," she said finally. She sounded bewildered. Swan nodded, made a clicking sound with his teeth that indicated he knew nothing, he was confused, that was the way life was. Before turning to leave he let his gaze rise up to flick across hers, which was only polite. Then he was safe.

Study hall was his next period. It was held in the school's dingy little library, which was just another classroom. The walls were lined with ragged old books and there were two long tables for students to sit at. It looked quite empty today. In this room the cheap fluorescent lights were always flickering; Swan saw with disgust that they hadn't been fixed yet, and they had been broken for a week. He sat by himself at the very end of one of the tables, with his back to the window. A few girls filed in and let their books fall at the other end of the table, sighing and whispering. They looked down at him with their bright, penciled little eyes, then looked away. One leaned across to whisper to another and her black hair fell across her face. Swan narrowed his eyes and watched her secretly. He was prodding the soft flesh about his thumbnail with the nail of his forefinger.

He thought of how nice it would be to be alone with that girl, to hold her in his arms. He thought about kissing her. But she sat back, flicking her hair back, and he saw she was chewing gum. Her name was Loretta Stanley and she lived in Tintern. As soon as she sat back, she looked vulgar and cheap; just to be with her and to touch her would be cheap. It was only the thought of her that fascinated him. . . . He opened his math book and looked at the problems. There were additional problems at the back of the book that he always worked out and might or might not hand in to his teacher. He began to work the first problem, leaning over his paper. The fluorescent lights flickered. A girl on the far side of the room giggled. The teacher in charge of study hall got to her feet; there was a sense of daring and danger. Swan kept on working. When he finished the problem he turned to look out the window, as if this were his reward. Fresh, clear air, not air sullied by the odor of gum and cheap cosmetics and hair spray. . . . But the sky beyond the gritty window had turned gray, the color of slate. In this land the sky changed rapidly and violently. If it was spring he would worry about a tornado, but it was only November, early winter, so they were safe. Because this room was on the second floor of the building, he could see nothing out the window except the sky and an ugly black smokestack that rose from the part of the school building that had only one floor. Out past this, miles away, the land rose to ridges and hills and then, at the horizon, dissolved upward into that higher ground that was called mountains. Somewhere between the mountains and this building lived the Reveres. He felt as if he were an alien in this room, waiting patiently for the time to come when he could return to his proper place. He had nothing to do with the smell of chalk dust and wet leather, the whisking sounds of girls hurrying by in the hall, the louder sounds of teachers' heavy heels on the old wood floor. His head ached and he pressed his hands against his eyes.

All I want, he thought, is to get things straight. Put things in order. Then, after that—

He took his hands away and blinked dazedly. After that?

He could envision no future beyond the long years that awaited him, of struggle with Clark and then with other Reveres, probably his uncles, and after that the many-faceted struggles Revere had always taken on with such energy in the past: with men like himself in other cities, with workingmen, with unions, with builders, carpenters, merchants, trucking concerns, trains, and on and on out to the farthermost limits of Revere's world, which stretched out endlessly and was a universe of its own. The only way out of it was the way Robert had gone, by accident, or Jonathan had taken on purpose. Swan understood that and perhaps that was why his head ached and he feared his brain might burst.

He put down his pencil and went to the front of the room. The teacher was an old, mannish woman with a sour mouth; she taught history. "May I go to the rest room?" he said. No one here said "may" but Swan said it anyhow, to show that he knew he was different, but what the hell? Out in the corridor he walked with his head drooping. He could smell all the familiar odors of the school—his eyes took in the streaks of pale light reflected off the dented lockers that stretched out before him. All this was old, familiar. He saw someone's lost mitten and that too was familiar. He had lived a hundred years here. He felt that his mind could take it all in—the teachers as well as the students, the seldom-used closets and corners no one else ever glanced at—but that his mind could do nothing with it. It remained ugly and inert and confident, a building that had been already overcrowded and outdated as soon as the last fixture was screwed into place. He could take in his classmates and the students in lower grades, those his own age, and he believed he could predict for them all unsurprising and unpromising lives, but he had no power over them to help or befriend them, to answer any questions they might have. They had no questions and they had no idea what questions they might have.

He went across into the annex where the junior high rooms were. This period was study hall and there were no classes. He went to Deborah's home room and looked in, making sure the teacher could not see him. Deborah was sitting up at the front, just as Swan always had, these strange and perhaps frightening children one never knew what to do with except to keep them in clear sight—protected from the healthy coarseness of the other students. Deborah was writing in a notebook. The notebook was twisted at quite an angle; she had this queer stilted handwriting that slanted far to the left. Swan watched her and was happy that she was sitting so close to the door, that she hadn't seen him and knew nothing, did not suspect she was being watched. He would have liked her to sit straighter, not to let her shoulders hunch over the desk like that. Sit up, Deborah. Sit back. But of course that was the way Swan sat too—as if pressing against the desk top and the book that lay opened on it, trying to get closer, a little farther ahead. She'd been sick with pleurisy last spring and had missed weeks of school; Swan had felt a rush of possession toward her, as if, kept home with her ugly mother and her weak father, she would be safe from all "temptations" and could truly belong to him. She had the look of a child who would never be quite well. Her skin was smooth and pale, but the paleness was underlaid with an olive hue. Her eyes were big but a little too big, too intense. Her small lips were pursed together with concentration; other mouths hung half-open, in the aftermath of slack grins. Swan fitted the edge of his thumbnail into the crack between two of his lower teeth and worried it up and down for a few seconds, watching her. She was his cousin and he thought he might love her. Of all the Reveres and the families married into them, she was the only one he liked—even though she did not return his friendship.

She wore a blue wool jumper with a gray kitten made of felt for a pocket. Swan thought he had never seen anything so beautiful.

When he returned to the study hall, however, he felt depressed. He came in and the air seemed to suck at him, eyes lifted to take him in without interest and discard him, those cunning adult eyes of girls who waited out the school hours until they could be free, and who were waiting out school years until they could marry. Loretta stared at him as he passed her and he looked at her with a heavy, contemptuous droop of his eyes. Then he was back at his seat. He rubbed his eyes again, reluctant to continue the problems. Why was he here, what was he doing? The floor was old and polished in spots where feet never reached; between the boards cracks seemed to be growing wider every day. Black cracks through which insects or pencils might fall and never be seen again. The sun came out briefly. Swan crumpled up a piece of paper and let it fall to the floor, into the patch of sunlight.

Then it struck him that he had to stop reading. He had to stop thinking. If he could lose himself in Deborah or Loretta or in that ball of paper, that harsh clean white against the worn old wood, he would be safe. But he could not under-

344

stand why he felt this way. He was seized with panic as, lifting his eyes, he saw shelves of books he had not read, and the ghostly shelves and shelves of books he remembered in that Hamilton library, books he would never get hold of and whose secrets would be lost to him forever. He had not time for it all, and if he couldn't do it all, then what was the point in doing any of it? He could not go away to college because he was terrified of leaving this land, of relinquishing what he had won in his father. And he was terrified that he himself might forget the strange, almost magical air of Revere's world, those vast acres of land that lay beneath the magical name—if he should forget all he had learned, all he had been born for, what then? He did not understand the sensation of panic that began in his stomach. If he kept reading, his mind would burst, but if he pushed his books aside and rejected everything, he would never learn all he had to learn—for knowledge was power and he needed power. He could feel his insides aching for power as if for food. Between the two impulses he felt his muscles tense as if preparing themselves for violence. Something fluttered in his head and he dug the tender flesh around his thumbnail until it was raw.

He stared up at the walls of books. Then, in the foreground, the familiar heads and faces of his classmates took form. They were not going insane. Did anyone go insane who didn't want to? No, he was safe. He was not going crazy. The girl sitting beside Loretta, Sharon Cornish, unzipped a red patent leather pencil case and took something out—a tube of lipstick. She dabbed pink lipstick on her mouth. Loretta, her eyes slanted sideways, caught Swan's look past her friend's upraised arm, and the two of them smiled in that jerky, surprised way people smile who are not prepared for it. Swan felt immediate relief. If she smiled at him and, better yet, if he smiled at her, wasn't he safe? Reading and thinking were dangerous because they made too much of everything. In the real world there were only faces to be encountered, smiles exchanged, lessons studied, and problems worked out. That was all. In his father's world it was the same thing exactly, but on a larger scale. When he solved problems he extended his power over people, whereas Swan's book-problems extended Swan's power only over that book. But it was a beginning.

After class Loretta lingered by her books until he came by. She lifted her sooty eyes to him and was prepared to smile. "Don't you like to go hunting, Steven?" she said.

"No," he said.

"I don't either," she said. "I agree with you."

They looked at each other. Swan understood with a rush of feeling that she was the kind of girl Deborah would never be—she had that oval, hard, knowledgeable kind of prettiness that could be wiped off with a thumb or at least smeared around. But she had it. Her pale, freckled forearms were exposed by the pushed-up sleeves of her red sweater in a way that was both glamorous and prim. Swan reached out and with his forefinger tapped a fake gold ornament on her purse. He felt drawn to her perfume and her tawdry primness but he would not have known what to do with her.

A few days later he went into the diner across the street to buy some cigarettes. He had begun smoking to give his hands something to do, but he never smoked at home. Clara would not have cared and Revere would probably not have noticed, but he wanted to keep it secret just the same. He thought that if he was growing up, changing, he would keep it to himself for as long as he could.

The kids who ate in the diner were of a different crowd from those who stayed safe in the close, milky-smelling cafeteria room at school; they were not necessarily older but they were louder, more sure of themselves. Swan liked the crowded smoky atmosphere into which he stepped bringing a flurry of snow in with him. The pneumatic device above the door hissed and the door closed very slowly, so that he had the impulse to pull it shut behind him. A group of high school students stood around the counter, making noise, and all the booths that ran along the front of the diner were filled. There was a floor-stomping, shrieking anonymity here that Swan never felt back in school, where everyone was still named as precisely as they were on the teachers' seating charts; here the country music from the jukebox filled in any gaps there might be in conversations or thought. Swan went to the counter and asked for a package of cigarettes, any brand. He was confused and lonely in this place and would not have been surprised if his classmates—these brassy adults who, in the world of the diner, clearly knew everything important about life—turned to stare contemptuously at him. No one looked.

When he turned, opening the cellophane wrapper, he let his gaze run along the row of booths. Those faces and even the backs of those heads were familiar to him, yet at the same time strange. Was it possible that Swan, who supposed he knew so much and had never had any choice about it, really knew very little? He had always been aware of his classmates but he had never thought seriously about them. Even back in the country school, the boys who tormented him had existed on the periphery of his real life, which was his life at home. He was on a kind of voyage with them but their destinations were far different; when the voyage ended he would get off to go his way and they would go theirs. He had not hated them because he had not thought that much about them. There had been the whole Revere family to keep in his mind: uncles, aunts, cousins, new babies, new wives, the legends of older men now senile or crippled or dead, his own father, his father's father, the table-thumping accounts of spectacular successes that were legal, but not so legal they had no sensational surprise to them. And all that land, so much land, tended and tortured into a garden so complex one might need a lifetime to comprehend it.... His classmates had seemed to Swan to whirl about in their own trivial little world that had to do with the friendships and hatreds of one another; that was all. As soon as he had come into Tintern to eighth grade he had been aware of a central group in his class—an amorphous but unmistakable unit of boys and girls who seemed omnipotent in their power. They had only the power to give or deny friendship, to include or exclude, and Swan had not cared about that. He had not cared. Though he had no interest in them he had been overhearing for years the tales of their weekend and after-school exploits, their parties and hayrides and wild nightriding out on the highway, and, as time went on, their romantic alliances and feuds that marked them as adult, mysterious. He thought their bright clothes and loud voices drab enough, trivial as the high school classes they all disliked, but he could not help admiring something about them—their blindness, maybe? Their complacence?

He was crossing the street and heading back toward school when he heard someone behind him. "Steven?" she said. Loretta was hurrying toward him, her head ducked. She wore a bright blue kerchief to protect her hair from the snow. Swan saw how her hair bunched out and made the kerchief puffed and bouncy; a lot of work had gone into that hair. The windows of the diner behind her were steamy; above her head a big sign ran the length of the building, cracked and peeling. Crossroads Luncheonette—Truck Stop—Drink Coca-Cola. Swan had never looked at that sign before.

"If you're going back I'll walk with you," she said.

347

They walked along. Swan lit his cigarette and then offered her one. He thought: If she takes it that will mean something. She took it and he lit a match for her, the two of them pausing in the snow. Flakes had dampened her hair on top, on her thick puffy bangs. She had a hard, smooth, carefully made-up face. She could have been any age until you saw her eyes; then you knew she was young.

"I s'pose they're laughing at us back there," she said, alluding casually and with brittle humor to something Swan was expected to know about. "But I really have to get back early. I really do." They walked along self-consciously. Loretta wore drab little boots with gray fur on top that looked like cotton; it was thick and had separated into bunches. Her coat was plaid, blue and yellow. Cheap. Everything about her was cheap. Swan felt sorry for her but at the same time knew that in the high school world he had to enter every day she was superior to him—not only a year older, but superior because she "knew" things he didn't; she ran around with the right people while Swan, Steven Revere from up the valley, ran around with no one. He shivered, thinking of her as she had been that day in the library, her dark glossy hair falling over her shoulder and swinging free. . . . He had always been aware of Loretta but had not bothered to truly look at her, just as he had been aware of all his classmates. Somewhere inside his brain, stored away with other useless, foolish knowledge, were faithful records of all their alliances and loves, going back to the eighth grade passions that were expressed by scribbled notes and inked initials on the backs of hands.

"I didn't see you in there when I went in," Swan said, as if he had been looking for her.

"Well, I saw you come in. I didn't know you smoked."

He had no answer to that. They were walking up the driveway to the school—cracked pavement with crumpled-up papers and junk in its gutters. The air was very wet and not cold. Neither Swan nor Loretta dared to look at each other, but were fascinated by everything around them. Swan said, pointing to one of the orange-yellow buses parked forlornly out in the lot, "That's the bus I take." Loretta nodded with interest. He was aware of her beside him, the silhouette of her head. She was several inches shorter than he. The girls who were loudest, most confident, who had bright red lips that might say any word and show no shame, always turned out to be short and modestly proportioned. Swan shivered again and was so nervous he had to keep wiping snowflakes out of his eyes just for something to do. They were so vivid and real, he and this girl. It was not a bright day, but the sullen air glared about them, setting them apart and dissolving everything else back from them—the school building with its gray concrete blocks, the withered evergreens at the corners of the school. Even their voices sounded harsh and loud. A whisper would have carried everywhere, to every corner of the school, Swan thought. He had no idea what to do with this girl, who seemed to be pushing against him—even when she was several discreet feet away—and offering her face up to him, her big pencilled eyes and face caked with pink-toned makeup. He did not know the style of language and behavior the other boys knew instinctively. He did not know what to say or do and the knowledge of his stupidity depressed him.

After they had been having lunch together in the diner for a few weeks, they idled by her locker one day—the old locker tumbling and crowded with books, papers, old scarves, tissues, a mirror with a yellow plastic frame, and her sweater and coat—he tried to talk with her as he would have talked with Deborah. He told her of his nervousness, his need to smoke. As he talked with her, leaning in with one arm up over her head in the classic pose all his classmates used and which he was consciously imitating, he tapped lightly on the thin metal of the locker with his fingertips. Loretta smiled as if he had begun to tell a joke or a complicated story. He went on, uncertainly, to say that he did not think his father would like her because he didn't like Clark's girl Rosemary, and she was something like Rosemary; and at last she began to listen, her eyes getting keen and sharp. He thought the irises were like tiny pebbles, like pellets. "So what are you saying?" she said, standing back flat on her heels. The sockets of her eyes were fiercely shadowed by the dimness of the hall. Swan understood then that he could not talk to her and if he tried he would only distrub her. He could not talk to his mother either, and of course not to his father, and never to Clark and never to his teachers, and it made sense that he could not now talk to Loretta, who walked so close to him and smiled dazzlingly up into his face as if these gestures of intimacy had nothing at all to do with Swan himself and his problems, but were just conventional gestures everyone used. As soon as he understood this he was all right. He was even relieved. When he encountered Deborah he could say things to her, certain things, and she understood, even if she offered him no friendliness and certainly no intimacy. But Loretta was another person.

"Nothing, I'm sorry," he said.

"I know your father's a big deal, so what? You trying to tell me something?"

"I said it was nothing. Forget it."

He had caught on to something arch but at the same time pliant in her—her edginess could always be caressed into softness if the caress had a harsh enough sound to it.

Loretta lived half a mile away and he could never walk her home because he had to catch the school bus. He felt juvenile and degraded by this fact, but Loretta did not seem to mind. She stood out back with him in the crowd of kids from the "country"—which could mean anything from the scrubby lower section where families lived fifteen to a shanty, to the vast rich farms of the Reveres off to the north of Tintern—and she cradled her books against her chest, standing with her back straight and her shoulders ready to shrug up in a coquettish gesture, while Swan smiled down into her pretty, ordinary little face and felt somehow illuminated by her presence, made special, important. He could not understand why she liked him. He could not understand why she had singled him out, abandoning some other boy or boys in favor of him, and he had abdicated to her the complete privilege of choice—it would never have occurred to him to turn to another, more intelligent girl. He would never be able to approach his cousin Deborah with the casualness he approached this Loretta, whom he scarcely knew even after weeks of lunches and huddled talks, though he felt that he knew Deborah thoroughly and that knowing her was like coming across a splinter of himself. But he could touch Loretta and slide his arm around her; in the precarious safety of an emptied stairway he could kiss her; he could bump his nervous forehead against hers secure in the knowledge that she knew how to do this: she was smiling and conspiratorial, she was never embarrassed.

They met out in the corridor during classes, each asking to be excused at the same time and exhilarated with the idea of such fraud, such daring—seeing her come shyly out of a classroom down the hall made Swan wonder dizzily who he was to have such power. He led her down the back stairway past the double doors to the cafeteria and past the first floor (there were no classrooms at the rear of the first floor) and down the basement, the last flight of stairs absolutely forbidden to all students and generally of no interest to them—where, in a dim alcove under the stairs, surrounded by the mysterious comforting hum of machinery and the permanent odor of food from the cafeteria, they could stand pressing against each other, kissing, and Swan felt so strongly how nice she was—he could think of no other word—that he had to keep telling her, telling her. He felt that they drifted out from themselves, from Swan and Loretta, into a sweet mild anonymous world where there was only the gentleness and kindliness of affection, simple affection. He felt how easy it was to be good and how intoxicating this girl's warmth, which was never a threat to him, asked nothing of him but only wanted to give; he wondered if the men who had come to Clara's arms had discovered this sweet entrancing silence and if all men discovered it sooner or later.

Some months later, when Clara tried to talk to Swan about her, he was uneasy and avoided her eyes.

"But why, what's wrong?" she said. He thought her too eager, too simple. What business was it of hers that he had a girl friend? That he had turned out to be less freakish than everyone suspected should not have surprised her. "Why don't you want to talk about her? Clark says she's cute, he knows both of her brothers—"

"I'm not interested in Clark's opinion of her," Swan said.

"But Clark says she's nice. Why don't you look at me? There's nothing to be ashamed about."

He flinched as if she had struck him.

"A boy your age should have a girl friend, there's nothing wrong with it. Why don't you want me to tell your father? Clark always went out with lots of girls, even Jonathan did—I guess—and it didn't mean they were going to marry them. All your father is afraid of is you or Clark marrying someone below you, that's all, but he knows how it—"

"He doesn't know anything about it," Swan said.

"There's nothing wrong with her—is there?" Clara said.

Swan tapped his fingers impatiently on his desk. Since his mother had come in his room he couldn't leave; that would be a mistake, it would be admitting defeat. She sat on the edge of his bed, her legs crossed at the ankles, as if she owned everything in here, including him. After a moment Swan said, beginning quietly, "You think it's all so simple. You think it's just two animals together and that's that—no,

351

don't interrupt me. I know what you think. But it isn't like that. I don't act with Loretta the way you think and there's nothing wrong with her. I don't do what you think."

Clara stared at him. "What the hell are you talking about?"

"When I was thirteen you told me about girls . . . and how it would be all right if I, if I . . . ."

"I did?" Clara laughed. "Why did I do that?"

He saw that she did not remember. How had he been able to remember every word and gesture of that conversation while she had forgotten?

"Tell me what I said. I must have made you mad, right?"

"No, you didn't make me mad."

"But you're mad now? Because you have a girl friend you have to turn against your mother?"

"I haven't turned against you," Swan said.

"Look around at me, then. Why do you look so sad? What's wrong?"

"I don't know what's wrong," Swan said helplessly.

She brushed his hair back from his forehead as if she wanted to see him more clearly. Her fingers were cool and deft. He thought that if she stayed by him, this close, or if Loretta pushed up so perfumy-close against him, he could escape the sense of alarm and depression that was like a puddle of dark water moving steadily toward his feet.

8

But Clark ended up marrying his Rosemary, that birdlike, short little girl with plucked eyebrows and hair dyed black to set off her white, white face, white as flour and just as softly smooth to the touch. To escape Revere's anger he moved out the day he announced his plans, and he and the girl were married a week later. The Revere women and women in Tintern generally began counting months and weeks, staring at Rosemary's trim little stomach whenever they saw her, but nothing happened. Their first baby wasn't born until a year later and by then it was all forgotten and Clark's place with his father was settled: Revere was speaking to him again and he was given a good job, in a few years he might be managing the lumberyard if he did well, but he had been lost forever to the vastness of Revere's schemes and fortunes. He and Rosemary lived in town upstairs in a two story white frame house, on one of Tintern's better streets.

He began putting on weight along with his wife when she was pregnant, a plump, serious, worried young husband. In a year or two he would be able to bring her out to the house, maybe, but in the meantime her family took them in and crowded about them and loved them dearly, as proud of their son-in-law as if he had come down from the mountains to wed Rosemary and had been able to take her back up again.

A week and a day before that wedding, Clark had driven to the railroad depot to pick up a package for Clara. It was a long, heavy thing—another rug from an Eastern import store. He had taken off from work at the lumberyard to get the rug before the depot closed, and he had just enough time to drive by the drugstore to say hello to Rosemary; then he was off on the drive home. It was early April now. He felt a sense of elation that had nothing to do with spring or with Rosemary, whom he loved sweetly and simply and whose petite body seemed to him vastly exciting, but with this package he was bringing home. It was a present, a gift. He was proud of bringing it to Clara, who showed such gratitude and such surprise over everything, though her attention did not last long.

When he got home the old dining room rug had been dragged out. Clara wore jeans and an old shirt; she was barefoot. "God, it looks big," she said. "You think it's the wrong size?" The dining room furniture had been pushed out into the other room and Clark was a little surprised that Clara had done it all herself. "I want to get it all fixed up for your father. I want to surprise him," she said.

They struggled with the wrapping around the rug, grunting and sweating. "If Swan was home he could help," Clara said. But Swan had his own car now and took his time about coming home; and anyway Clark was glad he wasn't around. He felt a sense of possession toward this rock-heavy rug in its awkward packaging, as if it were something he had picked out for Clara himself.

When it was unrolled finally, the rug astonished them with its colors. They felt a little shy before it. "My hands are dirty, I shouldn't touch it," Clark said. Clara was bent over the rug, staring at it. She bit her lower lip thoughtfully. But Clark, who was embarrassed by beautiful things as if they were an affront to his manhood, broke the silence by saying: "Guess I'll drag all this junk back in." The "junk" was the old, good furniture that had belonged to Revere's first wife, reclaimed from the attic by Clara. She had discovered that its graceful lines and mellow wood were exactly the kind of thing she had been seeing in her magazines.

Afterward they sat at the dining room table but with their chairs turned around, so that they could look at the rug. They drank beer and talked quietly, aimlessly. Clara sat with her knees hunched up and her bare heels just on the edge of the chair; she kept staring at her new rug and as she did, her lips would turn up slowly into a smile. Clark was oddly pleased. "When you get married I'll help you with your house," Clara said. "I can tell if things are quality or not."

"Who says I'm getting married?" Clark said.

"Oh, you. You're a nuisance," Clara said, waving at him.

After supper Clark drove down the road to a tavern just for fun. Usually he did not go out alone but tonight he felt like doing something different; he was restless. In the tavern he stood at the bar and talked loudly and seriously about politics with the farmers who came in. He could tell that they liked him. He warmed at once to anyone who liked him and his magnanimity sometimes puzzled them; they were not accustomed to such friendliness from a Revere. But they did like him. At about eleven, one of his friends came in, a young man who had been married for maybe five years now, who wasn't doing well and had been avoiding Clark. But in ten minutes they had made everything up, Clark had won the man's friendship again, it was all right. They were both the same age, twenty-five. Tears came into Clark's eyes at the thought of them knowing each other so long. The young man said he had to call his wife to say why he was staying out so late, and Clark went over to the telephone with him. They were both quite drunk. After the man hung up Clark called Rosemary's house. Her mother answered and said she was in bed, was it important? Clark said yes, it was important. When Rosemary came to the phone he told her that he loved her, how was she? Tears had come into his eyes again. When the roadhouse closed he had to drive his friend all the way home because the man had passed out, then he had to drive home by himself, taking the turns as precisely as possible. Sometimes he drove fast, sometimes slow. He did not seem to know what he was doing except when he tried to make a turn then he could tell by a weak queasy sensation in his stomach if he was going too fast. When he got home it was quite late and the house was dark except for the back porch light. He turned off the ignition and sat smiling toward the house. He was too lazy and content to move.

He must have fallen asleep, because he woke up to Clara shaking his head. She had hold of his hair. "Wake up, come on," she said. She was whispering. "You want your father to know how drunk you are? Drunk like a pig?"

He felt a surge of nausea, then forgot it. He was very sleepy and peaceful. A long gap of time seemed to pass and then Clara jerked him awake again, bent low to hiss something into his face. "I'm okay," Clark muttered. "I can sleep here. . . ."

"Come on, please. Wake up. You don't want trouble."

Her hair was loose. She shook him again and strands of her hair flew into his face, stinging and tickling him. Clark did not remember her opening the car door, but it was open. He tried to step out but it was like stepping out over a chasm; everything was dark and strange.

"Clark, please—come on," Clara said.

She took hold of his head and shook it hard. Clark seemed to be working his way up through a heavy, warm pressure of water. He woke suddenly to see Clara bent over him. Behind her was the clear night sky and the moon, just a chunk of the moon, and he wondered why she looked so worried. He reached out and his elbow just brushed the horn—it almost made a sound—and he took hold of her. "Don't be so mad," he said sleepily. He pressed his face against her. Clara made a noise that might have been a surprised laugh, then she pushed against his forehead with her hand. "You're real nice," Clara muttered. "Wait—don't—"

He shut his eyes tight and held her. His mind stumbled backwards away from this woman standing here in her half-open bathrobe and her bare feet to that earlier, younger Clara who had come home one day with his father. Just a girl. For years he had heard about her and one crazy time he had even gone all the way over to her house, risking everything, that whip of his father's or worse, just to stand by her windows and try to look in. . . . Now he had hold of her and dreamily, dizzily, he thought that he would never give her up. It seemed to him that he had struggled a long way to get to her.

"You're crazy, let go," she whispered. Clark pulled her down and tried to kiss her. He felt her hesitating—he was sure of that—and then she dug into his neck with her fingernails. "You son of a bitch, let go! Let go!" she said. Clark fell backwards but did not really fall: he was still sitting in the car.

The next morning, before Mandy made up breakfast,

Clara called him out into her "garden room." She was already dressed. Her hair had been pulled back, skinned back, and fastened with pins. On her right hand was the old purple ring she hadn't worn for years. Clark started to tell her how sorry he was, how miserable he was. "Yes," Clara said. She did not seem to be listening. Nor did she seem to be looking at him, exactly. "What you have to do is get out of here. You know that. You can't stay in the same house with me now."

"All right," Clark said.

"You just can't," she said, and her face, caught in the morning light that flooded the windows, was not the face he had loved and wanted the night before—there were fine feathery lines on her forehead and by her mouth. She was still a beautiful woman but the woman he had wanted was gone now anyway: that young girl Revere had brought home to marry.

"Do you understand?" she said. Her gaze was flattened and remote, like a cat's gaze. Then it sharpened upon him and he could see that she was a little frightened. She tapped at his arm and then let her fingers rest. "I'm sorry you did it. I didn't know—I never—But you can't stay here now. Go and marry her and that's that."

Clark bent to hear her better. "Marry who?" he said politely.

9

On Swan's eighteenth birthday he rode in with his father to Hamilton, where they met Clara and had dinner at a hotel restaurant. Clara visited the city often, usually staying in a hotel, but this time she was at a relative's house. When Revere asked her what she did she was pleased and vague, explaining she had to shop, had to check out stores, had to see people. It was not clear whom she saw, but Revere did not ask. He distrusted his city relatives; he thought they looked down on him.

Revere had come in for important business—his aunt's estate was being settled. Swan was disturbed by his father's tired, haggard look. The waiters looked at him as if he were an impressive kind of ruin, a man they ought to know but could not quite place. Revere mistook his waiter's solicitousness for something else. "Do they want to hurry us out of here, and we just came in?" he asked Clara.

Swan had no appetite. He had been listening to relatives arguing all day. But he opened his menu and looked at the words, which he tried not to translate into images of food. Clara said, just as he knew she would, "They're having Judd and his wife out to dinner, but not us. I know it." Swan expelled his breath to show how foolish this idea was; he wanted to stop Clara before she aroused Revere's anger. "They knew it was Steven's birthday but what the hell? Anything they can do to hurt me, they do it."

"They're busy, it's a lot of work," Revere said.

He closed his menu. He was over sixty now: a heavy, slack man with sharp bruise-like furrows on either side of his nose. He had a fixed, rather indifferent stare when he did not wear his glasses. Opening his napkin, shaking it out, he glanced down at it as if he had no idea what it was. Then he put it in his lap. They watched him, Swan and Clara, their eyes drawn heavily to him. For a while he said nothing, his face was hard and austere as a mask; then his lips began to tremble. He said, "Don't worry, they'll be sorry. I know how to get back at them."

"Yes, but you won't," Clara said.

He shook his head slowly, gravely. Swan felt cold. All afternoon he had had to sit by his father and hear his father's slowed-down, groping voice, his meandering off onto obscure and foolish problems, and he felt exhausted.

He was exhausted all the time now and never could he locate the core of his trouble. When he had still been seeing Loretta he had had these moments of unaccountable, terrifying exhaustion, as if a pair of great wings were pounding against the walls of his brain and had been pounding for so long that everything was going numb, dying. Unfolding his napkin, moving his silverware nervously needlessly around, he thought of Loretta and wondered what she was doing. What he had last heard about her was nothing surprising— marriage, a baby. Loretta. He kept mixing her up in his mind now with Clark's wife, whom he saw occasionally. But Loretta had been his girl. Narrowing his eyes, he tried to avoid Clara's look and retreated to the secret contemplation of Loretta, who had loved him and had never once been able to talk to him, not once. That last night they had laid together in his car and he had been dizzy with wanting her, a real physical agony he had hardly been able to control, and when she said, "It's all right, Steven," he had prayed in his mind to God, who he understood did not exist and never had, begging: "Let me just be good and kind. I want to be good. I

357

don't want anything else." Loretta had drawn him down to her with her arms and her sweet soft mouth. Never had he said the word "love" to her and he had not said it then—but he had almost thought it—and at the nearness of that thought he recoiled from her, trembling. He was terrified of sinking into that swamp with her. He was not going to drown in her body. Because there was no sweet mild world they shared without consequence: they were Swan and Loretta, two real people, and anything he did to her would not dissolve out and away as if in a dream. It would be real. It would involve them together forever.

"You won't hurt me," she had said.

But it was nothing like what Clara had promised—how strange and simple, how cruel his mother was! You didn't make girls happy in that simple way; they wanted and needed more, and if you couldn't give them anything more?

So he had stayed free of her and he had forced her to become free of him. And Clara had said, hearing it was all over: "Well, I'm just as glad. She was sort of trash anyway, wasn't she?"

Now Clara was shedding the cold haughty look she always wore into stores and restaurants, and as she read the menu a childish, cunning look came onto her face. Swan watched her in fascination. "Oh, this looks good. It isn't too expensive, is it?" she said. She pointed to something and showed it to Revere; he shook his head no, it wasn't too expensive. Swan smiled. He did not know what his smile meant: just the reaction of witnessing rituals, ceremonies that have been repeated many times. Clara always did this. He wondered if she did it with the other men she met here in the city—if she met other men; she was secretive now, in a vague sloppy way—and if they shook their heads, no, in the same way Revere did. When Clara moved her head, slivers of light darted off her diamond earrings. Yes, they were diamond. They weren't rhinestone. But how could most people tell the difference?

That was one of the things that bothered her these days.

"Have anything you want, Clara," Revere said.

They could relax in the shadow of this man and what he had done for them. Swan tried to think of Revere as his father, his *father*, and though the idea of Clara being his mother should have been harder for him to accept, still he could not quite understand what it meant to have a father. What did it mean, exactly? How was he to behave toward this man? He imitated any models he came across—he had

358

been imitating and improving upon Clark's style for years—but at the very heart of their relationship was a sense of dry and forlorn emptiness across which father and son might contemplate each other forever. As Swan was more and more able to understand Revere's problems, his role was becoming simpler in one direction and more complex in another. He was turning into a kind of clerk or secretary. Or a kind of lawyer. Already he had spent time with one of his father's new men—his tax accountant—trying to explain to the man why Revere refused to pay certain things and agreeing yes, yes, it was irrational, but how were they going to get it paid without Revere knowing? The older Revere got, the more crucial it was that the game he played not be violated. He demanded to be fooled, lied to, misled. Swan believed that the people who worked with and for him knew this, but if they didn't, he, Swan, knew it and they would have to listen to him. There were certain things one could tell the old man, certain reports one gave him and others one did not. This was getting simpler because all he had to do was transform himself into a kind of machine to master it. But being Revere's only remaining son was getting more difficult. Robert was never mentioned, Jonathan had vanished out of their lives, and Clark was discussed in the way Revere had always discussed obscure relatives who had failed . . . so that left Swan—Steven—and it wasn't just enough to play chess with the old man and let him win; the old man was getting bored with winning chess. It was becoming necessary to nudge him a little to correct him, before he made a catastrophic blunder and lost everything. Swan thought of how simple everything might be if only his father would die, but the thought was a shameful one.

His father ordered drinks for himself and Clara. Back over Clara's shoulder was a wall mirror framed by a tacky red velvet drape, and Swan tried to avoid seeing himself in it. His mother's hair had been cut the other day, apparently, radically cut so that it hugged her head and crept in alarming bunches of curls up to the crown of her head, urged up there by some kind of trickery. Swan could not decide if she looked good or ludicrous. She could be both at the same time, maybe.

"Steven, you should have ordered a drink too. It's your birthday," Revere said.

"I don't like to drink."

Revere considered this as if he had never heard it before. There were wedges beneath his eyes—dark, tired pouches.

He looked like a man who is thinking constantly, thinking painfully. Swan and his mother were light-skinned, light-haired, and curiously supple and casual beside this impressive old man; to a passer-by the relationship among the three of them would be quite obscure. Swan thought: God knows I don't like to drink. If I got started drinking I might not ever stop. He wished that he could tell this to his father and throw all the blame for it onto that man's lap.

"Bessie looks sort of old," Clara said.

"I didn't notice," said Revere.

"I thought she did. Ronald is in Europe, did you hear that? He's studying in Copenhagen. He's studying neurology."

Clara approached and rode over the words "Copenhagen" and "neurology" lazily, as if she said them every day. Swan could not help but smile. "Ah, Steven," she said, "you should have kept on studying. Why let them get ahead of you? He isn't much older than you are."

"I had enough of studying."

"I never understood that," she said. And it was true: her saddest disappointment had been Swan's refusal to go to college. The principal of his school had even talked with Revere on the telephone about Swan going on to school, and she had begged him, but nothing had come of it. Swan had told Revere that he didn't need any more school to do what he was going to do, and Revere guessed that that was right.

"I just didn't want to do any more reading."

"You always liked to read so. . . ."

"Well, I don't any more."

And that was true too: he did not read any more.

"I just don't understand you, you're so strange," Clara said. She touched her earrings; they were probably too tight. "If I had the chance to learn things, to read all those books and study them. . . ." She grew vague, restless under her son's smile. "I would give anything to be smart," she said. "You think I like the way I am? All my life there were people around me who could see farther than I could and backwards farther too—I mean into the past. History, things that happen and get written down. And they could understand life. But I couldn't, I. . . ." She faltered and Swan felt a soft stab of something like pity, sorrow, wonder: what was she thinking about, whom was she thinking about?

"Well, I don't have time for reading now," he said quietly. "I'm past all that." He was safe forever from the great bulging shelves of libraries everywhere, all those books demanding to be read, known, taken into account—that vast systematic garden of men's minds that seemed to him to have been toiled into its complex existence by a sinister and inhuman spirit.

Revere said, "I never went to college. A lot of manure."

Swan smiled across the table into his mother's mysterious gaze. So, he thought, you see? You see how he feels? You didn't want me to go past him, did you?—Wasn't it enough for me to become equal to him?

That night, lying in the strange hotel room, he cast his mind about for something that would let him sleep. He thought of his cousin Deborah, whom he had last seen at Christmas—a big Christmas party at Clara's. Not a successful party, not quite, but maybe the relatives had eaten more than in other years, stayed later, maybe they had been more friendly, and Clara was obviously willing to wait any number of Christmases to bring them around to the point at which they would embrace both her and Swan—she could wait forever, this Clara Walpole! Deborah had come but probably she had wanted to stay home. He watched her all during the meal, sitting next to her father but not even talking to him, a thin, shy, haughty girl with long brown hair and brown eyes. She looked as if she might be stupid until her eyes moved upon you, then you felt something strange. . . . After the long, loud dinner Swan sat by her and talked. They were alongside the Christmas tree, almost behind it by the window, and outside it had been snowing; he remembered all this. The snow was gentle and peaceful, but inside children were running, shouting—he hated them. Swan told her about going to the city with his father, trying to make her feel some of his confusion, his worry, without exactly telling her.

But she interrupted to say, "I hate your mother, do you know that?"

Swan was stunned. "You what?"

"I hate my own mother too. So it's all right."

She looked up at him and smiled. There was something unreal about her look: she was too young to be looking at him like that.

"Tell me the truth, Steven," she said. "You hate both of them yourself."

"I don't hate them."

"Come on," she said slyly.

"I don't know your mother. And why should I hate my own mother?"

Her face shifted into an expression of disgust, contempt.

361

"You don't tell the truth, so why should I talk to you?" Swan felt embarrassed. They lapsed into silence. She said, after a moment, "You're what they call a bastard. Your parents weren't married when you were born. So why should you tell lies, why should you pretend anything? You're from the outside and everybody knows it."

"I'm not from the outside," Swan said.

"Why should you pretend anything? Anyway, it's what makes you different—being born the way you were."

He had a sudden impulse to seize her, to strangle her. But the feeling came and passed, leaving him just a little dizzy. He felt his lips turning up into a kind of smile, as if she had looked into the very heart of him and had seen what was there but had not been surprised. But even with her he had to pretend: "It isn't true," he said.

So he thought of that girl, about to fall asleep, and he wondered why she was so strange. Even her clothes always looked old, as if they had belonged to someone else years before. In his half-sleep he imagined making love to her but it came to nothing because she wasn't really there.

On his twentieth birthday he was also away from home—in Chicago with his father. And that summer he spent days at a time in Hamilton, arguing with his father's people, and threatening them with things Revere himself had not yet thought of but that sounded crazy enough to be the old man's ideas. They were afraid of the way things were going—didn't he read the newspapers? Didn't he know anything? Of course the back-country Reveres were making a fortune on wheat because of government controls, what did they care if the other interests failed? Swan knew that it was perfectly true that they were making a "fortune" on the farm, but he denied that it was just the government's doing: everything was automated now on the land but not automated in the factories and strike after strike could wear anyone down. He argued with them, he quoted statistics. He brought them magazines he had read and studied and proved points to them, wearily, politely. The farm doesn't matter to the farmer; he had to keep on with other things. Didn't they understand that?

When he was twenty-two he took his father up on the threat of buying out the partners.

"What are you waiting for?" he said.

"They'll change their minds when they hear—"

362

"What are you waiting for?" Swan said, closing his eyes. "You've been talking about this for ten years."

His brain careened past his father's, slipped and skidded around out of boredom with his father's slowness. He had his own ideas. He knew what he wanted to do. In his mind was a map of the countryside from Tintern to Hamilton and he could see it all brought together by a highway four or five lanes wide—why not? Anything was possible, and it was possible to get money from anywhere. He felt a little feverish with the thought of so much power lying latent in the land, waiting for someone to seize it. What had seemed to him at one time impossibly confusing now darted forth spasmodically in a painful clarity—only that much, only that and no more? Why hadn't his father gotten control of more? It was true that they had a fortune, money poured in from the mysterious, fluid world of a soaring economy and buoyed them up on it, a new law passed somewhere to the east shoveled money in to them and they had only to reach out and pick it up—very strange!—but why wasn't there more of it?

As for that lumberyard in town, that should be making more money, why didn't they put someone else in over Clark? The hell with Clark.

"The only one of them I respect is Uncle Judd," Swan said, speaking not loudly but clearly, very clearly, into his father's ear. His father leaned forward greedily to hear what he had to say. "The rest of them I ignore, I can't talk with them. It took me five years to understand that you hate them all but you never got rid of them—why not? Uncle Judd can do it. I won't have to do it. Uncle Judd can do it for us. We'll buy them out and the hell with them."

Revere's stern little line of a mouth smiled slightly.

There were times when Swan was drunk with all he had inherited—he could sit and stare at nothing, not even out the window at the land, and for hours figures and speculations would dance about in his brain. They lived in the midst of a fine factory, this farm, the barns rebuilt and humming with efficiency, cows plugged in and milked out, acres and acres of wheat coaxed into bloom or, better yet, never planted, and he could feel himself as the very center of this big farm, his heart the beating heart of the farm, and the range of his desire, scanning the horizon as far as he could see, was the measure of what they were going to attain someday. "They."

He liked to think that he was dragging them all up with him, all those legendary Reveres, those dead old men and women who had loved and hated one another so fiercely, bound together by a single name and committed forever to living out the drama of that name—

Then he would wake and think, What am I doing?

But he would answer this by flooding his mind again with speculations, rumors, guesses, facts, and if they tried to bluff him out, what he'd do, what he'd say; he'd show them he was his father's son after all. No matter what people had thought when he was younger and shyer, bemused with books. Now he never read and he never bothered with the outdoors. He did not go for walks and he did not look too closely at anything, because he had long ago recognized in himself a strange mystical love for this inherited land that was almost a terror in his blood. The land could lower upon his vision a fine gauze-like screen that jumbled and choked his brain, just as all those books years ago had threatened to splinter his brain and leave him helpless. He would fight it. He felt as if something were growing in his brain the way a baby grows in its mother's belly—a tiny head poking its way through flesh, getting its energy mysteriously and growing, growing. If he knew where this energy came from, he would know the secret to all things.

It was at about this time that he bought a pistol and carried it with him when he drove to the city. When he walked about the city streets alone, he liked to let his hand rest on it, in his pocket, knowing that it possessed a greater power than he did and that this was somehow satisfying. The only time he left it in the car, locked in the glove compartment, was when he picked up a woman somewhere and went with her back to her room: one of those women sitting alone in cocktail lounges, half-pretty or sometimes beautiful, who might have been secretaries or stenographers instead of prostitutes, or who had perhaps a combination of jobs but who knew enough always to keep quiet and to ask him no questions. It was always important to Swan to pay them more money than they asked, because money was the means by which he kept them from him. He wanted no involvement, no emotional involvement even for an instant: it was the only possibility about the women that frightened him. He was afraid that, overcome with passion or anguish, exhausted as if he had run a great distance to their anonymous bodies, he might confess to them that he did not know what he was doing or where he had come from, or why his brain pounded with desires he could not understand. He might confess to them the thought that he had to put out of his mind continuously, that he was a killer who had not finished with his work yet but was waiting for his deed to rise up in him: what if he cried out to one of these women, these strangers who had no idea what his name meant or how heavily it lay upon him, that his brain shifted about desperately to keep away from that thought, that he was a killer? He could list, feverishly, the people he had killed. He could shout into her face those names that would mean nothing to her, his brothers' names, and if this woman to whom he confessed smirked, thinking he was crazy, wouldn't he maybe kill her too?

He was afraid of these women but kept coming back to them, whenever he was in the city. He was afraid of them because they did not know his name or who he was, and they would therefore not know who he was supposed to be—and with them, so free and anonymous himself, might he not forget everything and lash out in a sudden mindless anger he would never be able to stop? For Swan thought that he wanted nothing so much as to destroy everything, and that he did not really want to build it up—he didn't want to step into the place his father had made for himself; instead, he wanted to get rid of it all, destroy it all, everything, the entire world! But, thinking this, he would feel his heart lurch with sorrow, he felt shame rising in him as surely as if Revere had caught him fooling about at the dinner table, years ago. . . .

Once he did say to a girl he met somewhere and with whom he spent several hours: "How do you keep going like this? I mean, how do you keep living?" She had considered the question seriously, knowing that it was a question she might ask herself. Even her considering his question was a kind of professional readiness, an impersonality he admired and feared. "I did something once that made me feel bad, it was something ugly," he said, blundering on nervously while the girl listened. "It was something . . . ugly."

"What was it?"

His mouth jerked into a rigid smile as he remembered Robert, that child he had so long ago overcome, and the vague faces of Jonathan and Clark passed before him . . . but when he replied he said, "I called my mother a name. A certain name."

The girl said nothing, ready to take from him any horror he might say and cancel it out into nothing, just by her blankness. She was like a great silent body of water into which he might throw anything and get rid of it—but what if he had called Clara a bitch? What if he had whispered that name to himself, for certainly she was a bitch and why would that especially bother him?

But then he recalled the afternoon in the library, and that evening in the house, his lying on top of the bed still dressed —still in his shoes—and he remembered Clara talking in her rapid soft dazed voice of how happy she was, and he knew that it was not the name he had called her that frightened him. It was the thought of punishing her. For if he punished her, then that meant she had done something that deserved punishing. He began to tremble, not thinking about her any longer or even about himself, getting to his feet so abruptly that the girl was startled.

"Is something wrong? What's wrong?" she said.

He left her, shaking with an anger he did not understand. He ought to have punished that girl, he thought wildly; she had not been listening to him. She had not cared. Explain to her what he and Clara had done, sum it all up, and she would not have cared. She would not have given a damn.

10

He entered the waiting room. There was an odor of shadow, damp, and linoleum.

"Yes?" said the woman at the desk. She had frizzed gray hair, an untidy look. Swan supposed she was the doctor's wife. Behind her on the wall was an old-fashioned print of an old-fashioned scene—iron-black men grouped proudly around a locomotive. Tiny intricate letters in script proclaimed this scene a historical event.

When Swan looked back at the woman's face she had taken on some of the spidery metallic precision of that print, just as in a painting all things relate to all other things and change them. "Yes? Mr. Revere?"

"Steven Revere," he said.

"Yes, fine," she said. She made a notation in a book. Her pencil was an ordinary kind—yellow, with a clean unused eraser at the end.

Swan sat. There were several others in the waiting room. To one side, on the bench that spanned a little bay window, was a woman with her boy. She had a sad, hardened face; she was Swan's age but that child and the sloppy glamour of her dress and skirt and the two or three petulant lines spanning her forehead marked her for another world altogether. The child fussed and whimpered. The mother made a pretense of bending to him, but she must have known what he would ask. "No," she said. The child wriggled in her arms. "No you don't," she said. When she lit a cigarette, the child broke away and went to the table in the middle of the room. This table was an old cast-off dining room table, of a dark lacquered wood. Its legs bowed outward clumsily and charmingly, as if bending under the weight of years of shabby *National Geographics* and *Reader's Digests* and other magazines. The boy picked up one of the magazines and glanced back at his mother. He made a pretense of ripping the cover off. "No you don't," the mother said. She reached out and yanked him back to her. The boy was unsurprised but he began to whimper. Over his nervous jerking head, Swan's gaze met the young woman's and fell away.

"These kids are so much trouble," she laughed.

No one acknowledged her remark. Across from Swan sat a boy of about nineteen with an older man in a dark suit. The boy's face had that beatific, stunned look of the blind. His eyes were not quite closed but not open either. The child's whimpering made the blind boy nervous, but he could not concentrate upon his nervousness. "Now, how many is this? How many? This is a hard one," the man with him whispered loudly. He was pressing something into the blind boy's hand. He had thin colorless lips that looked fixed in their smile, a professional, ministerial smile that had no mirth in it. Swan stared at this man. The blind boy squirmed nervously in his seat. "Fi-five," he said. His voice was too loud. It was not scaled down to the waiting room. The young mother, smoking her cigarette, flicked away a tiny piece of tobacco from her lip to indicate her dislike of that loud voice. The man in the dark suit smiled more professionally. He tried to entice Swan into smiling with him.

"Now, this is a hard one, a lot harder. I don't think you can do this," he said. He leaned slightly forward as he spoke, drawing everyone in; he even winked toward Swan. He pressed something else in the blind boy's hand. The blind boy's face slipped out of shape with concentration.

"No you don't," the mother said again, mechanically and harshly. The child had ripped a magazine cover off. The mother did not slap him but brought her fist down hard on his back once.

In the chair next to Swan was an old man with white hair

thinly combed across his head. He had not taken his coat off. He was staring past the young mother's head out the window toward the house across the street—this office was in an old brick house not far from downtown Hamilton. The doctor's name was Piggot. Swan had opened the telephone directory to "Physicians and Surgeons" and run his finger along the listings until he had come to that name; in the stark quiet of his hotel room that name had looked just right.

"It's sure trying to get sunny," the younger woman said. She had lifted her chin and her voice came out at a tilt, directed toward Swan. He nodded to show that he had heard. She reminded him of a girl he had known back in high school—not quite Loretta but one of the many girls like her. A full pretty face with a slightly dissatisfied droop to the lips, maybe copied from the movies or maybe sincere. She sighed and flicked ashes from her cigarette toward the ashtray. At the desk the receptionist rose as if to show her disapproval of this; but she was just going back into the other part of the house.

"The doctor will be with you in a minute," she said to Swan.

"Do you have an appointment or something?" the young woman said.

"Yes," said Swan.

"I didn't know you were supposed to make appointments," the young woman said. She frowned. The child was half-lying on the bench on his stomach. "What the hell are you doing? Want to knock your front teeth out?—They're a lot of trouble, kids," the woman said, smiling sourly. "Look, do you all have appointments here? I never made one before. I just came in here and waited my turn."

"We have an appointment for ten-thirty, ma'am," the man in the dark suit said. His blind charge sat erect and nervous, his nose and lips working. He seemed to be smelling the woman as she spoke. "We come every Tuesday."

"She wrote my name down when I came in," the woman said. There was something sharp in her voice. "I should go in next if I have an appointment or not. I got here twenty minutes ago.—Do you have an appointment too?" she said to the old man. He shook his head, no. He looked a little irritated. "Well, I never got one here before. What the hell, are you supposed to sit here all day? It's just to get some pills. I don't like to waste time."

"You can go in ahead of me," Swan said.

She glanced at him and colored slightly. "No, that's okay," she said.

"I called up for ten-thirty too. You can go in ahead of me."

"I don't know," she said, embarrassed. She stroked her child's hair as if it were something that had just captured her attention: fine fawn-colored hair like her own. "I mean, maybe he.... His wife took down my name.... I don't know how she wants to do it."

Swan picked up a magazine and leafed through it. The odor of the little room was intensified in this old magazine, a musty dark scent. Swan saw photographs but did not bother to understand them. He flicked through the pages mechanically. There was this strange confused sense of himself—in a hurry but sitting so still in the wicker-backed chair, calmed down, peaceful. The chair was heavy, like the other pieces of furniture. Its legs also belled out. The furniture, old and scratched as it was, reminded him of his mother's sadly pretentious furniture, the expensive mellow wood of antique reproductions with bowed and clawlike legs, declaring the rigidity of their style of life—French? Eighteenth-century?— out in the vast countryside where the human form itself dwindled under the impact of sun and sky.

The child came over to Swan and touched his arm. He had a remarkably handsome little face; his lips were like the lips of children in old paintings, sweetly shaped as if no sound ever came from them. "Here," he said. He thrust a roll of lifesavers at Swan, opened at one end. The silvery paper hung ripped. Over on the bench his mother was smiling at Swan.

"No thanks," Swan said.

The child look up at him in mild surprise.

"He wants to thank you for letting us go in ahead of you," the mother said. "It's real nice of you. . . ."

"No thanks," Swan said politely, trying to smile at the child. There was something out of focus, something unreal and scattered, in children's gazes, just as there was in the gazes of animals. When Swan bent down to talk to children, he had to pretend, and this pretense tired him. He could not remember ever having been a child. He sat back in the chair as if leaning away from the boy and the mother both; there was something about them that made him nervous.

"Thanks anyway," he said to the woman. He did not like to look at her full, sweet face or into the cozy stupidity of her eyes—what she was seeing in him could make demands

369

upon him he did not want to accept. Had his mother looked at men that way? How many men? And had she, too, used her son? And what had happened afterward?

"For Christ's sake," Swan said. The little boy had been staring up into his face and this got him away.

A patient left the inner door, picked up his coat from a chair, and went out. He moved quietly and apologetically. The grayhaired woman called out another name, and the man in the dark suit rose. "Richard, it's our turn now. There's a table to your right—there—that's it—You know which way it is, don't you? I should let you go in by yourself," he said playfully. He and the blind boy went on back. Swan pretended to read a magazine, nervous because of the woman and the depressing air of this room. Across the way there was a print of something he had looked at when he first came in but had not allowed himself to look at since. He remembered it confusedly: animals painted in a deliberately childlike manner, grotesquely simple. There had been something horrible about that print. Now he tried to read the magazine and tried not to let his eyes rise to the print, and at the same time he thought of himself sitting rigidly in this chair, at peace, for a few minutes at peace, while back at the hotel were the Manila envelopes of papers he had to go through with his lawyer that afternoon, and already in the room, stark and orderly and precise, was the bed he would lie in and the mirror above the bureau that would record indifferently whatever went on in the room that evening.

Deborah was probably getting ready for him, but his thoughts slid away from her and scattered. The floor of the waiting room was covered with old linoleum, worn unevenly. A dark green print with brown stripes, yellow flecks. He tried to remember the floor of the hotel room, but nothing came to him. The floor of his room back on the farm was covered with a rug—one of Clara's precious rugs. Mellow sandy colors with green, blue, yellow. Everything he looked at transformed itself into something else, something connected with her. Clara. He had taken Deborah's hand the last time they'd been together and something had flicked across his mind, and in that instant her hand might have changed into Clara's hand—or it might not have changed—but he had been so shaken he could not remember what he was saying to her.

The doctor's wife came back and leafed through her book. She wore glasses but she brought her face so close to the ledger that Swan could see inside the glasses, a strange intimate glimpse of her eyes. There was nothing much to see. By

370

accident he looked up at the print after all. A reproduction of a painting that must have been famous, it was so awkward and clumsy. To the right, a group of animals in frozen positions, their eyes large and staring—lion, ox, leopard, a bear squatting to eat—attended by children, and to the left, small unintelligible figures in the background. Adults. In disgust Swan looked away. He hated animals and did not like to look at them. He hated even domesticated animals, dogs and cats. He could remember the horse Jonathan had ridden on, taunting him that day Robert had died by accident, and he hated that horse violently, his heart throbbing: Jonathan's old horse and it was still on the farm somewhere, maybe. . . .

Time gaped and he was aware of the waiting room filling with new people. The young mother and her child were gone. He stood, hearing his name, and went through the door the doctor's wife held open. She avoided his eyes as if the doctor inside intended to tell him something fatal. "Yes, come in. Mr. Revere, yes," the doctor said. He sat behind a desk. He wore glasses with metal frames and flesh-colored nose pads. The window behind him glared with light, so that Swan could not see his face clearly. "What did you want to see me about?" the doctor said in a gentle, paternal voice.

"I'm not sure. I have this symptom," Swan said, and wished at once he had not used that particular word; the doctor might distrust him. "I feel sleepy once in a while. I don't mean at night—I mean during the day. Sleepy but not tired."

The doctor made a noise with his lips to indicate he was listening. Swan sat in a heavy, wicker-backed chair by the man's desk. As the doctor examined him superficially—listening to his heart, staring into his eyes and ears, attaching a tight band of rubber around his upper arm—Swan said in a voice that sounded increasingly distant, "Sometimes when I'm driving I get an overwhelming sensation of drowsiness. I feel strange, I only want to close my eyes. I know that if I do I'll have an accident, but somehow this doesn't seem important. . . ."

"How long have you felt like that?"

"I don't know. Off and on, for a few months."

Swan had begun to sweat. He felt that he was a body, a vessel with nothing much in it, delivered over to this man who would check it and decide whether it was worth sending back out into the world again. "How old are you?" the doctor said. He was writing information down. "Twenty-five. No, twenty-six," Swan said. "Occupation?" Swan thought a moment. At the very core of his icy perspiring there was something warm and peaceful. Sleep. He wanted to sleep more than anything else, but if he went back to the hotel and lay down, he wouldn't be able to sleep.

"My father and I run a farm," he said.

The doctor was talking to him. Swan saw the dark pupils of the man's eyes, so real and vivid and kindly. His heart throbbed. "Why are you so nervous?" the doctor said.

"Am I nervous?"

"You are a nervous young man."

When he caught sight of himself in mirrors or store windows he looked lean, rangy, casual—with hair so blond it could only grow on the head on an idiot. Why did this man say he was nervous?

"I think of myself as the opposite of nervous."

"Nevertheless. . . . Your heart is pounding right now."

Swan smiled, as if the doctor had played a trick on him and he must acknowledge it.

"I suppose I'm apprehensive about being here," Swan said.

"Who is your regular physician?"

"I don't have any."

"Where do you go for medical advice? Examinations?"

"Nowhere."

"Surely someone in your family has a doctor?"

Swan did not want to give the name, a "famous" name in Hamilton. He said nothing.

"I'd like a sample of your blood. . . ."

"Fine."

He thought that real pain would distract him. He watched the needle go in, watched in fascination as the blood rose. There were drops of perspiration on his forehead and upper lip.

"Christ," Swan muttered.

The needle withdrew. The doctor's eyes glinted through his thick glasses. "You didn't move," he said, as if to flatter Swan.

"I didn't want to jerk the needle out," Swan said defensively.

The doctor had his back to him. Swan's eyes seized upon something in the opened medicine cabinet above the little sink—instruments of some kinds. He wondered how the doctor would like it if he, Swan, were to jab him with one of those and drain out his blood.

"Have you a history of illness? What childhood illnesses have you had?" He was at his desk again, writing. Swan knew that no one would ever look at that form again but he

372

had to sit still and answer questions; his heart pounding with frustration. "How about your mother? Father? Your grandparents?"

"I don't know about them," he said. "My mother's always been healthy. She's never been in a hospital except to have me. . . ."

"Your father?"

Swan stared at him. Then it occurred to him that the man was asking about Revere. "He's all right. I don't know if anything's wrong with him, he won't go to a doctor." The doctor nodded, his lips shaped "I see." "He's healthy for a man that age," Swan said.

"How old is your father?"

After the visit with the doctor he went to a drugstore to have his prescription filled. He opened the plastic bottle and looked inside: small yellow capsules.

He was hungry so he went to a restaurant, but as soon as he entered the foyer he knew he could not eat. A woman with high-piled red hair approached him with a stack of menus held up against her chest. "No, never mind," he said shakily. He went out. Across the street a statue caught his eye: a general on horseback, man and animal shaped out of some material that had turned bad in the grimy city air. Swan went to a telephone booth and called his lawyer's office but the man was out somewhere: he was picking up something at a dry cleaner's for his wife. Swan left a note with the secretary saying he would see him the next morning at ten. Then he went to a movie.

The movie house was on a side street not very far from the doctor's house. Soot from factories down by the river had discolored everything here—the white background of the marquee, against which the black letters were fastened, had turned a gritty gray. Swan blundered down the aisle, already staring at the screen where two figures argued unintelligibly. The theater was nearly empty. He sat and his foot brushed against crumpled paper. The seat was shabby and comfortable.

At first he made no effort to figure out the story: he watched the man and the woman arguing. He watched their faces, which were handsome but distorted by the black-and-white photography. He supposed that these people, the actors behind these people, were of a breathtaking beauty; but captured on the grainy old screen they were almost ordinary. The scene changed to an airport. Police were awaiting someone. Everyone on camera stared at something off camera. A plane landed, taking some time. A man on board the plane was rifling through a briefcase.... When Swan looked up again the scene had changed to a night club. He wondered if he had fallen asleep, just for a minute. A blonde woman in a low-cut sequined gown was talking earnestly to a man in a tuxedo. Swan rubbed his eyes. The theater was drafty. At the back some children were giggling. There was an odor of spoiled food and dirt in the air. A heavy woman sitting in front of Swan and several seats over was picking her nose and snuffling; she made a loud, self-righteous noise. Swan thought at once of the gun in his pocket. He checked to see if it was there.

"I never loved him. I was just a kid."

"How many times have you told me that?"

"I never loved him...."

"Frankie isn't that type...."

"What about when the police catch up with ... ?"

"Two more of the same, please."

"Not for me ..."

"Yes, two more."

Swan stared at the actors acting out their parts on film. He wondered if those actors were still alive. Their bodies might very well be rotting somewhere, but their spirits were being played out on the screen; there were maybe twelve people in the theater watching. Swan squirmed, listening to them, watching their mouths. Out of those mouths words came involuntarily. They said what they had to say. They did not think and so everything was drawn out of them relentlessly. They had no choice. Someone had written the words for them to say and so they said them, they fulfilled their roles and died on screen or killed others or disappeared. Swan did not understand why watching them made him so uneasy. His back had begun to ache with the rigidity of his posture—he was sitting stiff and straight, he might have been watching himself on the screen and waiting for the terrible moment when he would have to speak his lines.

When he left the theater he was exhausted. It was almost twilight; he had spent an unaccountable amount of time in there. He looked at his watch and saw that it was six o'clock. This was all strange, puzzling. He had supposed he hadn't wasted more than an hour or two in that dirty theater, waiting for time to pass, and evidently about five hours had gone by.

When he came into the hotel lobby, Deborah was waiting for him. She wore a coat of gray tweed and carried a black

374

purse. Her hair was cut short and over her forehead bangs fell in sleek stylish strands; beneath her dark hair her eyes looked enormous. "I was at a movie," Swan said. "I didn't notice the time." He was breathing hard from walking so fast. Deborah let her eyes move coldly around the pretentious little lobby with its worn-out red velvet carpet and fake marble. "Do you want to get something to eat or go upstairs?" he said.

"I'm not hungry."

They took the elevator. It was lined with mirrors on three sides, so that Swan was uncomfortably aware of his profile on both sides of him. Deborah was pulling off her dark leather gloves. He thought she looked in a certain way at her rings—the big jutting diamond and the plain wedding band—and that she had done this precisely for him to notice. When the door opened automatically he pushed her out before him.

"You always stay at ugly places," she said. "You do it intentionally."

He opened the door of the room for her, presenting a final insult: those oyster-white, ventilator-dirtied walls with garish, complicated drapes about a window opening out onto nothing.

"I don't love you, I think I hate you," Deborah said. "There's nothing in you to love. This makes me sick." She threw her gloves down on the dresser top, on his papers. In the mirror her face was olive-pale and shadowed from the unflattering overhead light. "It's strange, I can come up here with you but I couldn't eat with you. I wouldn't have had any appetite."

"What does all that mean?"

"Don't make me angry. Don't you see I'm tired? I don't want to talk."

He turned out the light. She stood for a while in the dimness as if she were alone. Then she turned to him and they embraced, more gentle with each other now that the light was out. Swan was dizzy with the scent of her hair and body; he was so excited that he felt his mind might skip wildly ahead in time, that he might blank out from the tension of the moment. In that cold, unfamiliar bed with the cheap mattress she pressed her face against his throat, hiding her face, and whispered: "You're my only friend. I think about you all the time. I think about how many days it is until I see you again. Why don't you live in town . . . ? You're the only person I can talk to. I don't want to talk to anyone else. I don't trust them, but I trust you. . . . I can say anything to you and you can't do anything with it. You can't make me ashamed. All my life I hated you but I loved you too, I didn't want to love you. . . ."

She had thin, hard little arms and legs. Her body was hardly more than a child's body, but it had a muscular rigidity that was ageless. In the half-light Swan could see her large, eerily fashionable eyes, the eyes he'd been seeing in her for most of his life, and it stunned him to think that she had turned into a striking woman.

"What did your husband say when you told him you were going out?"

"Keep quiet about him."

"Doesn't he wonder?"

"I said keep quiet."

After a while he said, feeling her drowsy and weak, "I went to a doctor this morning." She stirred. "Are you sick?" she said. "No, not really. I don't know," he said. She touched his forehead; it was a gesture Clara might have made. "What is it?" she said. "Nothing. He said I'm too nervous," said Swan. "But you're not nervous at all," she said. "I'm the one who's nervous. You're not nervous at all."

Swan had no idea how quickly time was passing. The room was quite dark. He held her and kept waiting for something to happen, some magical passing-over of his love to her. It had almost happened the last time. He had felt her body coming alive beneath him, straining to be with him so that she was left bathed with perspiration. His mind was dizzied with memories of her, even when they were making love—Deborah as a child, as a girl in high school—the images drifting in and out of his mind as if to make him believe in the reality of this body, this person who was now with him. He was left out of breath, weak, frustrated. Because she could respond to him as violently as she did, she supposed there was something magical about what they did; the hysterical condition he could bring her to left her dull and helpless.

"I'm thinking of going to Europe," she said after a while. "Not this summer, maybe in September. I want to get away from this dirty town."

"Is he going with you?"

She turned away as if he had asked something foolish.

"Well, I'll miss you," he said.

They were silent. Then suddenly it was late and time for her to leave. "Do you remember when we were kids?" Deborah said. "You used to hide in the house, afraid of all those brats? I remember that. . . ." The lamp on the night table was on now; its light was rosy and softened her features. Swan shrugged his shoulders. "Did you have anything to eat today?" she said. "I wasn't hungry," said Swan. He felt heavy and inert. The air was tense between them because she had asked him to take her from her husband, to go away with her, and he had pretended not to understand.

"Christ, everything is so slow," Swan said.

"You must be getting sick. What's wrong with you?"

She lay over him and looked into his face. Her intimacy was a little bossy, a little maternal. "What do you mean, everything is slow? You're crazy."

"Deborah, don't leave yet—"

"Do you know what time it is?"

"Don't leave yet."

"It doesn't mean anything when I come here. I don't know what I'm doing," Deborah said. "I married him to get away from that valley and now I'm here and I have nothing to do, there are books I try to read but I can't read them, I don't know what I want—my house is better than my mother's—I wouldn't want to be anyone else but I'm not happy the way I am. My father always wanted to go to Europe but he never did. I think—if I could get away like that, to Europe—there things would be different. If I could get free and over to another country."

"I used to feel that way too."

"What? But you've never gone anywhere. What do you know?"

"I thought my way through it."

"You think too much! What do you want? Why can't we love each other? There's nobody I care about except you, everybody else bores me, but even you—I don't know— would I give up anything for you? Would I suffer anything?" She made a face. "Look at your mother and my Uncle Curt. They loved each other. For years and years she was his mistress, she lived with him and had his child and took his word for it that he'd marry her. She had faith in him. And he loved her too . . . he loves her. That's obvious. That's why people have always hated them."

Swan pressed his hands against his eyes. "But you're talking about them in front of me," he said.

"I know it, so what?"

He lay still and thought. Then he said, his voice sounding remote to him: "I used to think I could get free to some

377

other country too, but now it's different. I saw a movie this afternoon. . . . I don't know why I'm here, what I'm doing here. I just have to keep going without knowing."

"Steven—"

"I don't know who made me the person I am but I have this strange idea it's someone who's watching me right now. I can feel that person staring at me! And I loathe that person, I hate him with all my insides—he made me come alive and is following it through to the end, and I can never get free—The bastard!"

"What are you talking about? Who?"

"Or maybe it's a woman. I don't want anything else but to be free, but I don't know what that is. I'm sick of the way I am. And this person is watching me—"

"You mean God?"

"God?" Swan said vaguely.

"What are you talking about, are you crazy?"

"I don't want to be a character in a story, in a book. I don't want to be like someone in a movie. I don't want to be born and die and have everyone watching—reading alone. Everything decided ahead of time—"

He was silent. Deborah pressed her cool face against his. He said, "I almost fell asleep walking somewhere today. Did you ever hear of that?"

"Walking where?"

"Oh—on the sidewalk. Nowhere special."

"How could you fall asleep walking?"

He did not answer, but she rejected him with a nervous movement of her hand just as if he had answered.

After a moment he said, "Come back with me. Don't go yet."

"Steven—"

It excited him to be called by that name; it might have been that he was being mistaken for another man. Swan pulled her down to him to hide himself in her body, to get through to her what he knew he had to tell her: that there was great love dammed up in him but it could not get loose. The more rigid that love lay inside him, frozen hard, the more frantic was his body to convince both her and himself that he did really love her. The energy that transformed him came from the very pit of his stomach, bitter and desperate.

She said, "Steven, I love you—I love you. Please. I love you."

At the very end, when he felt his body dissolving outward in a spasm that sucked the breath out of him, he shut his eyes

378

tight upon the flux of lights only to see Clara's face flick in and out of his mind's eye.

Afterward he lay drained and hollow. Deborah was brushing her hair energetically, impatiently, and a strand or two fell loose onto her shoulders. "I don't know what it is. I don't know what I want," she said. The air in the room was hot; it was stifling. Failure lay stagnant about them. He saw that she had brought her own hair brush, decorated with silver flowers and designs, in that big black purse.

After she left, he dressed and went downstairs. He asked for his car. He must have looked strange because the man at the desk stared at him; when Swan returned his stare he looked away. Music was coming from somewhere behind them. Sentimental dance music, love music. Swan waited for the car to come and now it seemed that time was drawn out: there was a gilt clock over the elevator whose minute hand jumped with the passage of each minute, but very slowly, very frigidly did it move so long as Swan watched it. Some people came in, laughing. The telephone rang at the desk. Swan watched the clock. He thought it might be broken, then the minute hand jumped. At this rate it would take him a week to get there, he thought. In his imagination the highway between here and Tintern stretched out for thousands of miles, not marked on any map, a secret distortion more relentless and sterile than the great wide deserts of the Southwest, marked so blankly on the maps he had tacked up in his room at home.

Finally the car was brought around. Swan gave the man a dollar. When he drove off it seemed to him there was a slight shove, as if he were pushing off to sea and someone had given him a helpful shove with his foot. Swan squinted to get his vision clear and saw a policeman rubbing at his nose with a professional look, not three yards away. The city lights were confusing but he knew enough not to think about them. No matter how the night lights shone and wavered before him, he would drive right through them and think nothing of it. He drove slowly. He could not quite believe in the reality of his big automobile, so he had no reason to believe he might crash into someone else. Everyone else was floating by. Then he saw that it had begun to rain: was that why he had thought he was going to sea? At once the rain turned into sleet. The streets would be dangerous. It was late March, struggling into spring. His mother had said just that morning, "It's sure trying to get sunny."

He drove for several hours, straight into the sleet. There was nothing else on the highway except trucks; they flashed and dimmed their lights to greet him. Swan responded mechanically. Outside, shapes and ghostly lights floated by in the night, service stations, roadside restaurants, houses, rising up and falling away in silence. He kept on driving. His foot became numb from the constant pressure; he was afraid to slow up. He felt like one of those actors in the movie he had seen, speeding on into the dark without especially thinking, confident that someone had written out the words and actions for him to fulfill.

He arrived at the farm before morning.

There were no lights on. He jumped out of his car and left the door swinging and ran to the side porch. It had wrought-iron railings, painted white. They were slippery with ice. Swan pounded on the door, panting. Then he thought to take out his key. His fingers trembled so from the cold that he could hardly get the key in the lock. Overhead he heard something. Someone was calling. He swore and jabbed the key in the lock and managed to turn it.

When he got the door open, Clara was coming toward him. She wore a robe that flapped about her. Her hair was wild and astonished; her face was puffy.

"What? Are you drunk? What happened?"

"Is he awake? Tell him to come downstairs," Swan said.

"He thinks it's burglars. He'll get the gun." Clara backed up to yell up the stairs. "It's just Steven!" There was silence up stairs. Then Swan heard Revere's slow, heavy footsteps. "Never mind, it's all right!" Clara said.

"No, let him come down. I want to talk to him."

Clara stared at him. "You what?"

"I want to talk to him. You and him." He could not stop shivering. "We can sit in the kitchen here. Go sit down."

"Are you crazy?"

"Go sit down. Please."

"Your father will—"

"Shut up!"

"Look, who are you talking to?"

"Shut up!"

He pushed her ahead of him. She stared at him, her eyes narrowing like a cat's. She sat down at the table, in the dark. Swan switched on the light. The kitchen was gleaming with new limegreen tile and glass cupboards. Fine polished wood paneling had been put up to hide the old ordinary walls.

"Is he coming down or what?" Swan said. His heart had

begun to pound, hard. He kept listening for Revere's footsteps on the back stairs.

"He's an old man. What the hell do you want with him? Are you in trouble, did the police chase you on the road? Are you in trouble with some girl?" Clara said scornfully. "There's nothing wrong that won't keep till morning."

"Where is he?"

"If you want him, go get him yourself."

They waited. Clara kept looking at him and then away, as if she saw something there she was not yet ready to absorb. He could see her chest rising and falling rapidly, could hear her breath go dry and shallow with fear. His own hands trembled violently. He looked down and saw that he was leaving a small puddle on the tile from his wet feet.

"Yes, look at that, you'll be sick in the morning," Clara said. But her words did not quite convince either of them. Then she said, in an anguished, thin voice, "Swan—"

"Don't call me that!"

"What are you going to do?"

It seemed a long time before they heard Revere's footsteps again. He came downstairs awkwardly; one of his knees had been stiff with arthritis. Swan's eyes burned as he listened to the old man coming.

"Swan—" Clara said.

"Shut up!"

Revere appeared in the doorway. He had put on his overalls—old work pants that were faded and soiled. He stood there and looked at Swan. "What are you doing?" he said.

"Come in here and shut up!" Swan cried.

He took out his pistol and lay it on the counter right by him. His hands were shaking.

"What are you—"

"Shut up, I can't stand you talking!" he shouted at Revere. "Get in here and shut up!"

The old man came in. He stumbled at first but then was all right; he was staring at Swan's gun. Clara sat back limply, looking at Swan. Her face was pale. He had never seen her so old and seeing her like that made something churn in him, something fluttering and mad. He had begun to breathe hard. He stared at them and their faces were harsh from the light, even that gentle light Clara had picked out, which came mysteriously from fluorescent tubing hidden under the cupboards.

"I want. . . ." Swan began. But his words ended in a gasp

for breath. He covered the pistol with his hand. "I want to...." He stared at them helplessly. Some seconds passed: the fluorescent lighting hummed. The clock and the refrigerator hummed. "I want to explain something to you," he said. But as he stood, waiting, no words came to him. His head was stuffed with something warm and inert. His lips seemed swollen, too large to move. Finally he picked up the pistol and raised it; it took a long time coming.

"Swan—" Clara cried.

"Be quiet! I can't stand it!" he said with his swollen lips. "I can't stand it. I—" He tried to straighten up. His spine seemed to stretch longer as he urged it up and back; as he drew in his breath his rib cage expanded magically. "I came back home to explain to him what I was going to do. To us," he said to Clara. His mother's bare toes were curling on the tile floor. "I want him to know why. Then he can explain it, later."

"What did he say?" said Revere.

"Nothing! He's crazy!" Clara said angrily. She got to her feet. Swan pressed back against the counter. He held the gun in front of him, pointed at her. "You, what are you doing? Stupid, crazy! With all your brains, how stupid you are! Look at you standing there! With a face like yours, with brains like yours—standing there like a crazy man! They'll come and lock you up and the hell with you! Swan—" Her face seemed to break. She stared at him as if she were looking for something in him that she did not really want to find. "Swan, everything I did was for you—you know that. Everything I did—"

"I can't stand you talking—"

"But what did I do wrong? All my life was for you—all of it—You crazy fool! Crazy!" she cried. She was about to jump at him. As she spoke, her teeth were bared and he could see flecks of saliva at the corners of her mouth. "No, you're not going to shoot me! You think you can shoot me? Me? You think you can kill your own mother? People can't do things like that, they can't pull the trigger! You can't pull the trigger! You're weak, that's what I know about you, that's my secret about you—you're weak just like he was! You're no better than he was! He thought he knew everything and what did it get him? Nothing! Nothing! You're just like him!"

Swan raised the gun. His mother made a face as if she were about to spit.

"You think you can pull the trigger—well, you can't! You can't!"

At the last instant Swan jerked the gun to one side and when he pulled the trigger it was the old man he hit. Revere was knocked sideways from his chair—he must have fallen but Swan did not see him fall. He had already lifted the gun to his own head.

11

When she was only in her mid-forties she had this strange trouble with her nerves. Sometimes the right side of her body would fall numb, as if asleep, paralyzed. She stayed at the Lakeshore Nursing Home, where she was the youngest patient: at forty-five she looked years younger and the pretty little nurses stared at her with pity. She went on trips "home" —that meant to distant and uninterested relatives in Hamilton—but she was never well there or anywhere, and she could not go back to the farm because that had been sold, so after a while she stayed at the nursing home permanently and in a few years she was not even the youngest patient any longer, though she was still the best looking.

Clark came in to visit her. He drove in every week or so. On Sundays he took her out to dinner at a restaurant in a big white house, with a Negro doorman in coat and tails. Clara would be vague and distracted; she had the air of an invalid nervously waiting to feel pain. If she overturned her water glass, she sat staring at the water running off the table as if it were a catastrophe she might as well see through to the end.

Clark drove her up and down the lakeshore drive. Sometimes he wept, even while driving. Clara sat with her gloved hands in her lap. He talked about his children, about his wife, he talked about the lumberyard and how things were changing. He talked about the past. Clara might have been listening. As the years passed he came a little less frequently, sometimes only once a month. But he always came and he always came alone. He wept easily. He was a big, heavy man with a stomach that hung out over his tight, straining belt. There was something fierce and tender about his flushed face. "Remember," he would say, and off he'd go for a few minutes—Clara would be looking away. "Remember— Remember when Pa— Remember all the trouble they had when—"

He pretended not to notice how irritated she was when he came to visit her during her television programs. She was over fifty now; she had begun to get heavy. On either side of her mouth there were sharp lines. Clark was stunned at how quickly she had aged, but in a while he forgot that she had ever been any different and confused her with his own mother, whom he did not remember now at all. He took her from her television set—she had a very expensive private suite, overlooking a park—and sat with her down in that park, mourning the past, sitting with his fat thighs outspread and his elbows on his knees. When he asked her how she felt, she would answer in a slow, cold voice, a lazy voice that nevertheless insisted upon going through to the end:

"Sometimes I get dizzy. I can't take a bath by myself. It's the food we have to eat, I need better food. I'm afraid to be by myself, at night I think I'll get paralyzed again and they won't come till morning. Everything is so quiet then. I can hear how quiet it is. . . ."

On warm days they walked. The walking was supposed to be good for her; the doctor said so. He told Clark cynically that she would be there the rest of her life, that she had a strong heart and would live a long life yet, long enough to use up whatever money they had. There was a good deal of money, in someone's care, and it was all funneled into this nursing home. On nice days Clark talked to Clara about the nursing home and how lucky they were, this was the best in the state, she would be as good as new and out before she knew it—and so on. One day they were walking somewhere and two girls about thirteen years old, on bicycles, pedaled up suddenly behind them. Both girls had wild, dirty, foreign-looking faces. One of them yelled, "Watch out, you old hag!" because Clara had not moved aside for her.

She was quieter than usual the rest of that day. She sat with her hands in her lap, still and silent and grieved. When Clark tried to talk with her she did not seem to hear him. Looking at her, he felt his throat ache with a grief of his own—his wife did not understand what this grief was, why he drove so far to visit this woman, and he could not explain it to her. He was to keep coming for the rest of Clara's life, for many years, though she would sometimes not bother to look away from her television set when he appeared.

She seemed to like best programs that showed men fighting, swinging from ropes, shooting guns and driving fast cars, killing the enemy again and again until the dying gasps of evil men were only a certain familiar rhythm away from the opening blasts of the commercials, which changed only gradually over the years.